Point Venus

POINT VENUS

by Susanne McConnaughey

WILDSIDE PRESS

I̶T̶ WAS A DAZZLING AFTERNOON; THE SHINING, WIND-TOSSED LEAVES of the coconut palms framed a sky that was immensely clean and blue. On a day like this, Marianna decided, even the veranda was too confining. She filled a woven basket with the things she needed — sewing materials, paste, the white tapa-cloth banners, scraps of calico, the last of the unfinished hats — and carried it out to the shade of the old *tamanu* tree near the river. Across the sunlit sea, Moorea slumbered behind a veil of haze, as if it lay under a spell, she thought idly; an island couchant upon a field of azure.

She sat down on the grass, comfortably cross-legged, her back against the trunk of the tree. Curious how sometimes, for no particular reason, the most familiar scenes took on a pristine newness, as if seen through a stranger's eyes. She glanced about her, savoring the sharpened moment of vision. Nearby was the river, black and clear, which slid down the narrow length of Point Venus and curled into the sea not far beyond where she sat. Westward was the green stretch of Tahiti's coast line, and inland the dark, valley-cleft mountains thrust against the sky. A stranger would find it beautiful, but no stranger could love the place so passionately as she.

In the lavish tropicality of its setting, the mission house, plastered with white coral-lime, and tucked into a square of veranda, looked oddly neat and English. With Calvinistic disdain for the frivolities, there were no flowers planted around the house and outbuildings — trading store, offices and cook house. But the green grass, which spread like a carpet around them, was embellished with clumps of broad, sun-washed banana leaves, with the glossy darkness of *hotu* trees and breadfruit, and scattered with coconut palms, pirouetting across the lawn on their curved, silver-lichened boles. Near the veranda steps was a frangipani tree, each bare, gray branch tipped with a creamy flower; it looked as round and prim as a child's bouquet, Marianna thought.

The mission was virtually deserted this afternoon. Her father was teaching the adult Bible class in the little church down the lane, and the Tahitians who were usually about the place had apparently wandered off to their own houses for an afternoon siesta. The stillness seemed to take on an identity of its own, compounded of the whisper of the coconut fronds and the far rumble of surf, running like a white blaze along the reef beyond the end of the point.

Marianna pulled one of the banners out of the basket, and arranged red calico letters along it. GOD SAVE VICTORIA. Faintly, above the rustling stillness, came the sound of a man whistling, along the lane that led down Point Venus to the mission station. She raised her head, her heart suddenly gathering a small momentum. Jonas Burkham? She shouldn't let him find her sitting here on the ground like a Tahitian woman —

At the same instant, she realized that it didn't matter; Jonas wouldn't care, and neither did she, she thought with sudden defiance. Her father was away, and he wouldn't stay but a moment. Unconsciously, her hand went up to smooth a pin more firmly into the heavy knot of fair hair that looped at the nape of her neck.

He came through the gate in the fence that enclosed the mission property, and swung across the lawn toward her, his seven-year-old son, Tihoti, cantering around and ahead of him like a little colt.

"Hello," Jonas said, smiling. "Don't get up, please. God save Victoria, if you do."

Why did he always look as if he were secretly laughing at her? "Good day, Mr. Burkham," she said. "Hello, Tihoti. My father isn't here, I'm sorry — "

"Doesn't matter," Jonas said. "I found some hinges in town, and brought them over to fix the door to the back veranda."

"That's wonderful! But don't you need them? They're probably the last ones on the island."

"Probably," he said. "Truelove rummaged through every drawer in his stores before he found them."

"You're very kind — " she began.

"I know where the tools are," Jonas said. "If I need any help, I'll shout." He turned away before she could make a reply, whistling as he went.

He didn't mean to be rude; he was merely casual, and perhaps that was what so frequently awakened a faint, unreasonable resentment in her. She picked up her needle again, frowning a little. It was as if she didn't really exist for him, except as her father's daughter, and as schoolmistress for his son. Knowing Jonas Burkham, she thought a little wryly, was at least good practice in humility.

Tihoti, who had trotted after his father, turned back after a few steps and squatted down on the grass beside her. In Tahitian, he said, "Is my hat ready for the procession tomorrow?"

"Speak English, Tihoti," she said gently. "Your father wants you to whenever you can. Yes, it's all done, except for the picture to paste on it. What would you like? A turtle, or a fish?"

"A fish, please, like the one I caught in the lagoon last week."

What an extraordinary resemblance there was between the child and his father, she was thinking. Like Jonas, Tihoti was

5

stockily built; he had the same thick thatch of brown hair growing low on his forehead, his childish nose would someday be as beaked as his father's, and the mouth beneath it as sensual and as curiously vulnerable. One could see his Tahitian mother only in the size and limpidity of his brown eyes, and in the smooth tan of his skin, deeper and warmer in tone than Jonas's olive.

Tihoti was tracing the letters on the banner she had just finished. "God save Vic — Vic — "

"Victoria, Tihoti. She's the Queen in England, my mother and father's country. We hope she'll help Queen Pomare in her troubles with the French."

"Is England your country too, Miss Marianna?"

"Yes, it is. But I've never been there. I was born here in Tahiti, just as you were."

He wasn't really listening, and it was obvious that there was something else on his mind. He shifted to a kneeling position, his small, earnest face close to hers. "Miss Marianna, would you do some help for me?"

"Of course I will, Tihoti."

"Papa won't come to the meeting of the district schools tomorrow, and I want him to so much."

"I'm sorry," she said, distressed, "but if your father can't come, there's nothing I can do — "

"I think he *could* come," Tihoti said judiciously. "He just doesn't want to. He says there'll be too many speeches."

She smiled a little. "I suppose there will be quite a few."

"I don't want him for the speeches," Tihoti said. "Just for the tree-climbing contest, after the feast. I'm in the first one, you know, against Rumi of Punaavia and Toa of Papenoo. I think I can beat Rumi, but Toa's very good. If Papa was only there to watch me — "

Impulsively, she put her arm around him, and pulled his smooth

6

cheek for an instant close to her own. "I'll talk to him, Tihoti, I promise."

He jumped up, his face alight. "Oh, now he'll have to come! Is that big eel still living by the stone in the river?"

She nodded, watching him as he ran to the riverbank, her eyes thoughtful. Tihoti couldn't possibly understand the reluctance she felt to do what he had asked her; she didn't entirely understand it herself. Jonas adored Tihoti; he would do anything for the child, and if sometimes he seemed thoughtless, it was only because he had a rather highhanded way of ignoring things that seemed unimportant to him. Probably Tihoti would be sent to the meeting tomorrow in the same faded *pareu* and ragged shirt he was wearing today, in bitter contrast to the carefully made garments — no matter how ludicrous they might turn out to be — that most of the other children would be wearing. Certainly his mother would never make the effort to outfit him properly, and it would simply not occur to Jonas.

She pulled the other banner onto her lap, spelling out LONG LIVE QUEEN POMARE down its length. How long was it since Jonas Burkham came to Tahiti? Nine or ten years, perhaps; she had been less than twenty at the time. There was nothing remarkable about his arrival. He had deserted from an American whaler, and at first had been identified only with the other renegade sailors who plagued the missionaries by their idle, wenching, brawling way of life. She remembered her astonishment, one day about six months after Jonas's arrival, to find that such a man was actually working.

She had gone into Papeete to buy supplies from Mr. Truelove's warehouse for her father's missionary store in Matavai, and was waiting in his shop while the goods were piled aboard Mr. Truelove's small boat, in which she would return to Point Venus. Mr. Truelove, his round face somewhat agitated, had drawn her behind a pile of packing cases in the rear of his store.

7

"Marianna, I'm sorry, I can't go out to Matavai with ye today. There's a cargo just in from Valparaiso that I must check over. But I've a good lad working for me now — a Yankee — and I'll send him along to see that everything gets there shipshape." He hesitated for a moment, and then went on: "I may as well tell ye, Marianna, that he's a runaway sailor, but believe me, my dear, he's different from the riffraff that usually skips off here in the island. He's — well, he's *eddicated*. Damme — I beg your pardon, Marianna," Mr. Truelove waved his hands helplessly, "damme, Marianna, the lad's a gentleman!"

She could still remember her impression of Jonas as Mr. Truelove introduced them: his thick hair, his bold nose, and the bright, sardonic eyes. His stiff bow had fitted incongruously with his sailor's blouse and trousers, and with the elaborate tattooings that ornamented his bare forearms.

He had been silent as they walked to the waterfront together, and had handed her aboard the boat with exaggeratedly formal politeness. There was no breeze in the bay, and as the four natives who manned the oars rowed them around the point toward Taunoa, Jonas had sat opposite her in the small stern, their knees nearly touching, his eyes fixed on her face in an unwavering stare.

Around Coconut Point a little wind sprang up, the small sail bellied out, and the Tahitians drew in their oars. For a while they coasted in silence along the clear, blue water between the reef and the shore, and then Jonas spoke.

"A girl," he said, as if to himself. "A veritable young lady, in fact." His voice, low and curiously soft, minimized the roll of his American *r*'s. "A maiden young lady in a white dress and white skin. I had — happily — nearly forgotten that there were such creatures."

Marianna's cheeks reddened, and she kept her eyes averted from the bright, persistent inquiry of his gaze.

8

"Tell me, Miss Moore — Miss Marianna Moore," he went on, "how long have you lived in Tahiti?"

"All my life," she said. "My father has been a missionary here for more than thirty years."

"Born a Tahitian — and raised a Calvinist! What an unholy copulation of circumstances."

It was only then that Marianna realized that he was drunk — solemnly, politely, but indubitably drunk. Her face stiffened.

Jonas was sweeping off the wide straw hat he wore, had risen to his feet, and was making an unsteady bow. "I beg your pardon, ma'am. I should have said *combination.*"

One of the native oarsmen shouted facetiously at Marianna, and at her reply, in the Tahitian language, the four men burst into laughter. Jonas had looked at her in liquorish astonishment, as if she had performed a miracle. She turned her head to gaze shoreward, away from him, but she could still feel his stare burning along her cheek. Could she not joke in Tahitian if she chose? It was almost insulting, his obvious surprise at her familiarity with what was, after all, her native tongue.

Neither of them had spoken for the next hour, and they were approaching Point Venus when Jonas pulled a bottle from his pocket and raised it to his lips.

Marianna turned around to him. "I must ask you not to drink any more."

"And why not, my dear young lady?"

"Because you are quite drunk enough already."

"Drunk enough for what?" he asked with ironic innocence.

"I neither know nor care," she said irritatedly. "But I must tell you that I cannot approve."

Jonas looked at her a moment. "We have here the missionary credo — see no pleasure, hear no pleasure, have no pleasure." He corked the bottle carefully, raised it in his hand, and flung it into the water. "Thou still unravished bride of bigotry!" he said.

9

They had not seen each other for many months after the remainder of that uncomfortable day, but, inevitably, Marianna had heard about him from time to time. Surprisingly, he had continued a favorite with Mr. Truelove, and only stopped working for him when his long-awaited funds arrived from America. Mr. Truelove was less astonished than disappointed by this affirmation of Jonas's gentle background. "A good lad. I'm sorry to lose him. Always knew he was no ordinary sailor."

Jonas had bought a small schooner, and in the intervals between his trips to the other islands to trade for pearl shell had settled into a fairly regular life in Tahiti. His liaison with Tihoti's Tahitian mother, Turia, was remarkable on the island only because it had endured longer than most relationships of its kind; the fact that he had never married her was of no concern to anyone, outside of mission circles.

It was her father's friendship with him that had brought Marianna once more in touch with Jonas, and that had started two or three years before, when Jonas and Turia, Tihoti's mother, moved to Matavai, not far from the mission station. There was an honesty in Nathaniel Moore that appealed to Jonas; and Nathaniel, deeply lonely sometimes for intellectual companionship, had become very attached to young Burkham. When Jonas's book of essays on Tahiti, warm, humorous, a trifle bitter, had reached the island, most of the other missionaries were coldly resentful of his comments on their influence, but Nathaniel, benignly going his own way, had continued to see Jonas as before.

Marianna could admit now that, armored in the bright confidence of her youth, she had been stupidly priggish on that day so long ago. She had learned a good bit about people in the last few years, she thought, and a little about Jonas Burkham — at least, that it could do no good to try to change him, and could only hurt her. Even so small a thing as Tihoti's request involved an interference with his settled prejudices that she dreaded. She liked Jonas well enough, but there would always be, she thought, a vestige of that old discomfort in her relationship with him. ". . . unravished bride of bigotry." It was curious how the memory of that first encounter still had the power to make her wince.

She raised her eyes from her sewing, and saw Tihoti still playing by the river, poking in the water with a long stick. How long it was taking his father to repair the door . . .

Jonas carried Nathaniel Moore's tools back to the shed, and came around the corner of the house. There was Tihoti, playing by the river, and Marianna was still sitting on the grass, her blue dress pleasantly dappled by the shade of the *tamanu* leaves.

He slowed his approach, regarding her lazily. He could never think Marianna Moore pretty, certainly — she was entirely too thin for his taste — but there was something appealing in her face. Perhaps it lay in her direct gray eyes, perhaps it was the arresting incongruity of her mouth, curved and full, decidedly not the mouth for a spinster schoolmarm. The rest was suitable enough, God knows — the way she pulled her fair hair severely back from her face, and the overemphatic modesty of her dress. How old was she, he wondered idly. Twenty-seven? Twenty-eight? Only a few years younger than he, but how little real living had come her way during those years.

He was standing almost directly over her before she looked up and saw him, and he was mildly startled to see a sudden flush run up through the tropical sallowness of her lifted face. Her gray eyes seemed to darken in color, as a cloud shadow darkens the sea.

"Oh! You've finished?"

"All done," he said. "It wasn't much of a job."

"It's very good of you. My father will be immensely grateful."

11

He dropped down on the ground beside her, and gestured at one of the objects scattered on the grass. "What *are* those things?"

"Hats. For the children to wear in the procession tomorrow. It's the annual meeting of the district schools — "

"The great day," he said. "I know. Tihoti hasn't allowed me to forget."

"The children are rather excited about it," she said tentatively.

He had picked up one of the hats and was turning it in his hands, whistling softly under his breath. It was a cocked shape, made of bullock hide, with a fish, cut out of red calico, pasted on the front. A pungent smell of imperfectly cured leather floated from it.

"Very fetching," he said. "Did you make them all?"

"Oh, no, the children helped a lot. We — they've been working on them for weeks."

"You spoil them," he said teasingly. "No wonder Tihoti loves his teacher."

She didn't answer, but in the swift glance she gave him before she bent over her work again, he thought he saw something almost like reproach. Why was she always so wary of him, he asked himself impatiently.

He leaned back on one elbow, watching her paste a turtle on the crown of a hat, and answered his own question with wry amusement. To Marianna Moore he must seem an unregenerate sinner. He drank, he swore, he didn't go to church — and if his life with Turia seemed almost tiresomely respectable to him by now, he'd bet his bottom dollar it didn't to Miss Marianna. She was the perfect daughter for a missionary, he thought; and yet, at times he had seen her — with the children, with the natives — when she wasn't at all prim and stiff, as she was with him. *Aita peapea,* it didn't matter. She was a good teacher, and Tihoti adored her.

"Where is the meeting tomorrow?" he asked idly.

"In the field, at Papaoa. You're — not going?"

"I don't have to," he said, "I can imagine it too well. The children's procession, with the smallest ones stumbling over their wooden swords. The meeting in the chapel. The speeches. The prayers — the long, long admonitory prayers. Then the feast, with more speeches, and Pomare Tane pulling on the bottle of rum he has sneaked in, and the Queen watching him with that look of resignation on her good brown face. And the band from the *Vindictive*, playing 'God Save the Queen' and 'Rule, Britannia' in the intervals, while Mr. Moerenhout and his French protectorate cohorts look on and glower helplessly."

"You've forgotten the contests," she said. "The children's contests, after the feast. Tihoti's going to be in one, and he's tremendously eager to have you there."

"Did he tell you that?"

She nodded, her gray eyes fixed on his face.

"Does it really mean a great deal to him?"

"It really does."

"Is that all there'll be in the afternoon? Only the contests? No more speeches?"

She gave him a sudden, almost conspiratorial grin. "We-ell, perhaps just a few closing remarks."

The quality of that smile was surprisingly appealing. "Maybe I could go for a little while — "

"That's wonderful!" she said. "Tihoti will be so happy! Tell me, Mr. Burkham, what is the news from town?"

"Not much," he said. "Pomare Tane got drunk again, and gave three of the Queen's silk dresses to one of her maids of honor — "

"I meant about the French," she said hastily. "Has the protectorate government been stirring up any more trouble?"

"How can they, with the *Vindictive* in the harbor, bristling with British guns? Everyone's acting as if the protectorate didn't exist."

"It shouldn't!"

"Yes. Still I wonder sometimes if your Mr. Pritchard is doing the wise thing in encouraging Queen Pomare's defiance."

"*Our* Mr. Pritchard? He isn't a missionary any more!"

"No, but the reforming spirit dies hard. I'm not sure Pritchard is doing Queen Pomare a favor in holding out hopes of British intervention against the French."

"Perhaps Mr. Pritchard, as British Consul, has access to fuller information than we have."

"Perhaps Mr. Pritchard, as a former missionary, can get his guidance directly from heaven," he said ironically.

" 'The will of the Almighty, as revealed to the missionaries on Tahiti, admits of no misinterpretation.' "

By God, it was a direct quote from his own book! Her tone was very bland, but he had caught a spark of something like amusement in the quick, sidelong glance she gave him. Talking to Marianna was more stimulating than he had expected. The green shade of the *tamanu* was cool and pleasant, and along the riverbank the golden flowers of the *purau* trees were dropping softly to the grass. He stretched out his legs more comfortably. "You're a well-read young lady, I see."

Before she could answer, their attention was caught by the creak of the gate. In front of the house a lanky, black-clad figure was tying up an equally bony horse. Heigh-ho, it was Richard Johnson, the young missionary at Tiarei, a few miles beyond Point Venus. Jonas got to his feet.

"Here comes your godly friend from Tiarei," he said. "I'll be off. No use to risk an exhortation on a pretty day like this."

He whistled for Tihoti, nodded to Johnson, and started for the lane, oblivious of the sudden look of hurt that passed across Marianna's face.

14

Jonas had timed his arrival to a nicety. The prayers and the speeches were over, the interminable mess of the feast was over, and it looked as if the contests might begin at any moment. Marianna would know. He tethered his horse to a tree near the edge of the sun-dappled grove and set off through the crowd to look for her.

Everyone on the island must be here today, he thought. There was Queen Pomare sitting in state, surrounded by a bevy of her maids of honor, dressed in white, with prim chip bonnets incongruously shading their handsome, tawny features. Behind the Queen was a standard-bearer, holding the red and white Tahitian flag, a crown in a chaplet of coconut leaves embroidered in the center of it. Commodore Toup Nicolas of the *Vindictive* sat next to Pomare, magnificent with gold braid and an aura of British invincibility. It was at Commodore Nicolas's suggestion that the Queen's symbol had been added to her flag; the French protectorate government, in the person of Monsieur Moerenhout and his two colleagues, had objected waspishly, but Pomare had said that she intended to wear the crown and keep its symbol in her flag. She was, in spite of the French, still sovereign of Tahiti — at least so long as the *Vindictive* was there.

The Queen's husband, Pomare Tane, stood nearby, looking hot and bored, and near him was a group of the principal chiefs of the island, in a motley array of military uniforms, which were, in most cases, far too small for their massive frames. Children darted everywhere, looking excited and important, and their parents, dressed in their starchy Sunday best, laughed and chatted beneath the trees. The black-clad English missionaries were like so

15

many crows, Jonas thought, scattered through this crowd of bright-plumaged birds.

There was Mr. Truelove, waving at him amiably, and there, by God, was Lily Nicholls, talking to one of the officers from the *Vindictive*. Young Mrs. Nicholls, who lived with her husband on their sugar-cane plantation not far from Jonas's little house in Matavai, was childless; and he had a sudden glimpse into the loneliness and boredom of a life that could have sent her forth to such an occasion as this. A green riding habit clung coquettishly to her rounded figure, and her small, vivacious face, turned up to her companion's, seemed to say that perhaps this encounter had repaid the tedium of the morning.

He moved on, his eyes searching the crowd. There was Marianna, talking to Richard Johnson. He waited a moment, until Johnson, summoned by one of the other missionaries, turned away.

Jonas touched her lightly on the arm. "Good day, Miss Marianna."

"Mr. Burkham!" she said. "Good day." Why did that guarded look come so suddenly into her eyes, he wondered a little resentfully. As if to cover it up, she was saying rapidly, "You got here just in time; Tihoti will be so pleased."

"Good. Has the great day gone off well?"

She smiled. "About as you described it."

"In such matters I am a prophet — without honor."

"Tihoti did beautifully in the spelling tests," she said.

"Did he! He has accomplishments at seven I haven't yet mastered at thirty-five. The other day he astonished me by spelling 'Nebuchadnezzar' — correctly, too, I surmised."

"Oh," she said, "he was fascinated by the sound of the word. Tihoti's so eager to learn new things! Please don't think I force Nebuchadnezzar on all my helpless pupils."

What a pleasant voice she had, Jonas was thinking; warm and a little husky, not like an English voice at all. Softened and

16

transmuted by the years in Tahiti, it gave a curious music to the precise neatness of her British accent and the primness of her words.

"Of course you do," he said teasingly, "and Shadrach, Meshach and Abednego, too. School with Miss Marianna is undoubtedly a fiery furnace of learning."

"From which most of the pupils emerge untouched."

"You're much too modest. Hello, there's Tihoti now."

The little boy ran up to them, his face eager. "Oh, Papa, I'm so glad you came! Are you going to watch the contests?"

"What else?" Jonas asked, smiling.

"First prize is a suckling pig," Tihoti said. "I want to win it so badly!"

"You will. Your mother's getting the oven ready right now. We'll have a feast tonight."

Tihoti's face fell. "Papa, if you don't mind, I'd rather keep it — as a pet."

Jonas touched him fleetingly on the cheek. "It'll be your pig, son. Do as you like."

"Oh, thanks! But Toa of Papenoo says he's going to win it and eat it. I don't want it et, Papa."

"Try hard then, Tihoti."

"I will. Look, they're ready to start now!" He pulled excitedly at his father's arm. "Over here, Papa!" As they turned away, he called back over his shoulder. "You come too, Miss Marianna."

Smiling a little, she followed them. A few yards away a hollow square of spectators was already forming around three large coconut trees, and Mr. Pritchard was waiting, a large red handkerchief in his hand, to give the starting signal.

She found a place near the tree where Tihoti stood tensely watching the handkerchief, his small face set and determined. A few feet away she saw Jonas, smiling at Tihoti and giving him an elaborate wink of encouragement, but as the handkerchief

17

dropped from Mr. Pritchard's hand, and the three boys jumped toward the tree trunks, an odd look of anxiety erased his smile.

The trees were well chosen for a contest, each about thirty feet high and somewhat slanted, with a cluster of nuts clinging just below the scalloped tufts of fronds at the top. The boys clasped the ringed trunks with their hands and feet, jerking upward as swiftly as monkeys on a pole. Marianna, who all her life had seen such feats of climbing, and in her childhood — prudently far from the parental eye — had even tried it herself, watched them with detached interest. The boy from Papenoo was a better climber than Tihoti, but he had got off to a slow start, and the question was whether his superior skill could prevail over Tihoti's determined energy. She glanced briefly at Jonas, and saw that his jaw was set as if he had clenched his teeth. How badly he wanted Tihoti to win!

She lifted her eyes again to the climbing boys. Tihoti was at the top now, just ahead of the other boys. He reached out to pick a nut, turned his head to look over at Toa, then suddenly clutched convulsively at the tree.

Her own gasp of horror as the child slipped was lost in the concerted, animal hiss of all those who watched. Across from her, Jonas lunged forward. For an instant that would be forever frozen on her mind, Tihoti's small body hurtled through the air, and thudded against the ground just beyond reach of Jonas's arms.

Marianna got to him nearly as soon as Jonas. The child was unconscious, but still breathing; his head lay twisted against one shoulder like the head of a flower on a broken stem. Together she and Jonas touched him, lightly, fearful of moving him, searching the faint fluttering of his pulse.

"Water!" Marianna said. "Someone get water."

Half-consciously she heard Mr. Pritchard's authoritative voice behind her commanding the crowd to fall back and give the child air. Someone set up a shout for Dr. Ferguson, and another

18

voice, in Tahitian, said disgustedly, "No use. He's still at the table, drunk as a pig."

Jonas said sharply, "Let no one else touch him, Marianna," and then someone thrust a calabash of water toward her.

The terrible tremor of her hands steadied as she took it, dipped her handkerchief into the water, and began tenderly bathing Tihoti's forehead. A gruff Scotch voice at her elbow said, "I'm all right, Burkham. I'll not hurt your bairn."

Dr. Ferguson knelt down beside her and laid his ear gently against Tihoti's chest, his red face sober with concentration, his eyes closed, listening. Jonas was staring at him as if he would tear out with his eyes the knowledge that registered in the doctor's brain. After an interminable time, Dr. Ferguson straightened again. "I'm sorry, Burkham. The boy is gone."

"Do something!" Jonas said fiercely. "Do something!"

"It's no use, lad. I'm sorry."

Jonas stared down at Tihoti, then carefully he laid the small wrist he was holding across the boy's chest. After a moment he raised his eyes and Marianna saw that they were dazed with an intolerable comprehension. She reached across Tihoti and touched Jonas on the shoulder, urgently flooded with the necessity to give him what comfort she could. "It's the Lord's will, Jonas. His wisdom is greater than ours — "

He flung her hand away so abruptly that she almost fell backwards. "Don't give me that cant!"

He leaned forward, gathered up the small limp body, and got to his feet. Marianna, shaken with sudden sobs, stared up at him, her face distorted with tears. For a moment Jonas stood there, holding Tihoti in his arms, his eyes blank with grief; then, as the crowd parted silently, he turned and carried the boy away.

"A DREADFUL MISHAP," RICHARD JOHNSON SAID. "DO YOU NOT THINK, Miss Marianna, that such contests should be prohibited?"

Marianna moved the teaspoon restlessly in her empty cup. If only he would stop talking about it, she thought! "Tahitian children must learn to climb, in order to pick the nuts. I never before heard of one falling." She looked down into her cup. "But Tihoti was half *popaa* — half white — you know. His white blood counted against him."

"Ah, of course," said Johnson. "His white blood and his unchristian heritage." His eyes shone with earnestness behind his neat spectacles, and his prominent Adam's apple quivered with the words. "The wages of sin is death!" An apt quotation always seemed to bring him a glow of satisfaction, as if he found reassurance in wrapping up the all-too-frequently untidy problems of life into neat little bundles tagged with the Scriptures.

Marianna was spared the necessity of replying by Teaui, coming to clear away the tea things, her feet bare, her vast body billowing mundanely under the chaste folds of her Mother Hubbard. Teaui had worked faithfully for the Moores for some twenty-five years; she was one of Nathaniel's first and most dutiful converts, but the years of evangelism had in no way altered her inborn raciness of speech and viewpoint.

She addressed Marianna in Tahitian, contemptuously secure in the knowledge that if she spoke rapidly enough Johnson would be unable to understand her.

"Has Fallen-Chin had enough to eat by now?"

Marianna nodded helplessly.

"Good. Where is your father?"

"He went to Tona's, to make arrangements for Tihoti's burial."

Teaui's face softened. "Poor little piglet. May he rest in Jesus." She rattled the dishes onto a tray. "I hope your father returns before dark. He'll have a chill on his bowels if he doesn't. Tell him I'll have something hot for him in the cook house when he gets back."

She padded heavily away, and for a time Marianna and Johnson sat in silence. The sun had already set, but the brief light of evening was still nacreous across the darkening waters of Matavai Bay, still trickled roseately through the trees. As they watched, the color faded, extinguished by gray, swiftly rising shadows. Death of a day, Marianna thought. She got up and lighted a coconut-oil lamp on the table by the wall.

Nathaniel Moore, his shoulders drooping, came around the corner of the house, riding a tired and sway-backed nag. He dismounted, threw the reins to one of Teaui's grandchildren who waited on the lawn, and sank into the chair Johnson pulled forward for him.

"A distressing visit, I expect, sir?"

Nathaniel nodded. "Turia is hysterical with grief, and Jonas a shade too composed. Tihoti was their only child, you know."

"Tragic," Johnson said. "Tragic!"

Marianna's fingers twisted together. "Isn't there something we can do for them, Father? *Something?*"

"I don't think so, my dear. Mrs. Nicholls was there, and offered her carpenter from the sugar plantation to make the coffin. She was of great help to Jonas — considerate and kind, most kind."

Lily Nicholls, Marianna thought miserably, had not failed Jonas when he needed help. Lily, vain and self-centered, but nonetheless kind, had been able to give comfort, while she, with her years of mission training, had only aggravated his grief with her attempt at solace. For an intolerable moment she hated Lily, hated Jonas, and, most abjectly, hated herself.

21

"Mrs. Nicholls!" Johnson was saying. "But I have heard shocking things of her and her husband. They drink excessively, they give ungodly parties, with dancing. I myself have seen her in Papeete with her face painted like a Jezebel!"

"She was no Jezebel today," Nathaniel said gently. "In Tahiti one hears a great many evil reports of people. Sometimes it is not wise to put too much credence in them."

"Are all the arrangements made for the burial?"

"Yes. Tomorrow morning, at ten."

"You're planning to give the boy a Christian burial, sir? The child of sin! Why, his parents are not even —"

"A Christian burial?" Nathaniel Moore interrupted him firmly. "Yes, truly Christian." He pushed his chair back and got up. "Marianna, my child, is there supper for me in the cook house? I see a light still there. If you will forgive me, Brother Johnson, I think I will retire. I am rather fatigued. Good night. Good night, my dear."

As he moved away, slowly, a little stooped, his silver hair vaguely shining in the dim light of the lamp, Marianna hoped that Johnson would not notice that her father had again forgotten the household evening prayers. She was well aware that the group of new, younger missionaries to Tahiti were critical of the older, regarding them as lax and overtolerant, even worldly, made so by their years of association with the easygoing people they had come to convert. How could they understand, those newcomers, the years of patience and toil, hope and discouragement, that had molded such a man as her father? Small wonder that Nathaniel, more than forty years in Tahiti, was mellowed to a ripe faith that sometimes overlooked the pettier precepts of its hard, dogmatic core. For twenty years he had been widowed, his children, all save herself, were gone from him; and the enduring loneliness of those years, active as they were, had left its mark upon him. The early rigidity of his beliefs had softened almost imperceptibly; now he seemed cloaked in gentleness.

22

Johnson's voice brought her back to her sense of duties as a hostess. "Could we talk for a little in Tahitian, Miss Marianna?"

"Of course." With an effort she pushed away her weariness, and kept it from her voice. His Tahitian was too limited to speak of any but the most trivial things, and her thoughts could wander at will, but as she responded, correcting his mistakes with patient tact, supplying him with new words and topics, she felt a smothering sense of despair.

Such moods did not come to her often; she was too buoyant by nature for that, and the ordered activity of her days left her little time for doubts and introspections. She had the serenity that comes from constant service to others, and a love of gaiety as deeply rooted as any Tahitian's; yet sometimes, as tonight, these things slipped hopelessly away from her, leaving her only with a sense of futility and loneliness. At such times all things seemed to mock her: the soft sensuality of the night, lighted with nearby stars, the scent of flowers and vanilla that hung in the air, muted laughter from one of the native houses along the point.

She realized that Johnson had had to ask her the same question twice over, and with the long habit of self-discipline she turned her thoughts to him. Poor creature! How lonely he must be, out there in Tiarei, barred from any real communication with his Tahitian neighbors by his inability to speak their language. Yet even if he knew it he would only be shocked and wounded by its incessant earthiness.

"Enough Tahitian," she said gently. "Let us take a rest in our own tongue for a while."

"I'd like to," he said. "You've been very patient, Miss Marianna. I'm afraid I'm not a very apt pupil."

"Of course you are. You mustn't be discouraged. My father said he was in Tahiti ten years before he felt that he had mastered the language."

"Ten years! It's a long time." He pulled his chair around next to hers, so that he faced out over the star-streaked waters of the bay. "If it weren't for my visits to Point Venus, I don't know how I could face that prospect."

"It's good to feel that you enjoy coming."

"There's something I would like to ask of you," he said tentatively.

"Do ask me, then."

"In all of Tahiti there's not one soul to call me by my Christian name. Could you do that for me, Miss Marianna? Marianna?"

How childishly wistful he sounded! "Of course I can," she said.

"Say it, please!"

"Yes, Richard," she said, smiling.

He leaned toward her impulsively, taking her hand in his. "You don't know how good that sounds to me!"

His touch was firm and astonishingly pleasant. There was warmth in it, and comfort, and something else that evoked a faint, unspinsterish tingle in her blood. She drew her own hand hurriedly away, and said as lightly as she could, "I hope it makes you feel a little more at home. I know how sorely you miss England."

"England!" he said. "My England! How extraordinary it seems, Marianna, that you, a young English lady, have never been there."

"It just happened that way," she said. "My two sisters were educated there, and my brother. But my mother died when I was very young, and Father needed me here."

"Poor child," he said softly. "Forgive me, Marianna. But it must be very lonely for you, so much away from your own kind."

The sympathy of his tone and words stirred in her like a yeast. "I have not regretted it — often."

"I don't want you ever to regret anything again," he said fervently.

Still oddly stirred, and a little embarrassed, Marianna pushed back her chair. "I should regret depriving you of your sleep, Richard. It is getting rather late, you know."

24

He was on his feet instantly, and again his hand clasped hers. "Of course," he said, "how thoughtless I have been. You must be very tired, after this tragic day."

At his words the agonizing and ineradicable picture of Tihoti's fall flashed into her mind, shattering in an instant the momentary illusion of comfort she had felt. She drew her hand away from Johnson's touch, suddenly unable to speak, overwhelmed by the remembrance of Jonas's blank, grief-stricken face, and his rebuff of her clumsy attempt to ease his pain. "Don't give me that cant!" Jonas would never remember his words, but she would; in humiliated and impotent regret, she always would. Jonas, Jonas, she thought bleakly, I loved Tihoti too.

She raised her eyes to Johnson's, steadying herself against the effort of speaking. "I am — a little tired," she said. "Please forgive me. I hope you rest well, Richard."

THERE HAD BEEN A SUBTLE CHANGE IN JONAS BURKHAM IN THE two months since Tihoti's death, Lily Nicholls was thinking. In the strong morning light she could see a tracery of gray in his thick brown hair; his face was thinner, and his nose seemed more bold than ever above the surprising tenderness of his mouth.

She stood beside him on the steps, chattering gaily, desperately searching for a ruse that might postpone the inevitable moment when she would be left alone. As he turned to go, she bent down and pulled a flower from one of the low plants beside the steps. "Look at this, Mr. Burkham."

Out on the roadway Anthony Nicholls, already mounted, waited impatiently, his heavy legs clasping the horse's flanks, his face red above his white stock.

25

"Come on, Burkham," he called. "You can't kill cattle here. Lily, let the feller go!"

Lily held out the flower to Jonas. "It's a *tiare Tahiti* with a red mark on it. I've never before seen one that was not pure white."

He took it from her outstretched hand. "Nor I. It's like a drop of blood." He tucked it into his shirt, smiling down at her. "I'll keep it, Mrs. Nicholls. Perhaps it'll bring me luck on the hunt."

He had bowed, turned away, and mounted his horse before she could make a protest. Lily watched the two men canter away, her lips petulant; then she moved listlessly up the steps to the veranda, the lacy ruffles of her thin morning gown trailing behind her.

The veranda, comfortable with cushioned chairs, was over-bright in the morning sun and the reflection from Matavai Bay sparkling in the distance. Lily grimaced, and wandered into the cool dimness of the drawing room. There were bowls of fresh flowers on every table; branching corals and primitive carvings struck an exotic contrast to the polished grace of the Chippendale and Sheraton they had brought from England. But today the ordered perfection of the room was oddly irritating to her. It was too complete; there was nothing left to do.

Nothing to do, nothing to do. Anthony and Jonas would not be back from their cattle hunt in the mountains until dusk, and the two young officers from the *Vindictive* whom she had expected to lunch with her had sent word that they would be kept by their duties from coming. The day lay endlessly before her, like an interminable desert that she must somehow cross.

For a moment she thought of having her horse saddled for a ride, but her head was still pounding from last night's wine; the mere idea of joggling about in the sun was intolerable.

She turned to the gilt-framed mirror and regarded herself moodily — the small, rounded figure in a trailing white gown, the artfully careless tendrils of black hair that curled about her face, the childish red mouth, the faint blue smudges that lay beneath her dark eyes. Six years in the tropics at least had not ruined her complexion; it was as white as the day she left England. She turned away, still seeing herself as clearly as she had in the mirror, and watched her own languid progress across the room with the detached eye of an observer.

Even when she was alone, Lily did not fail to strike a graceful attitude. Tiredly, she drooped down upon a sofa, the folds of her gown swirling about her feet. On the table beside her were Lord Byron's *Poems*, a worn copy of *The Mysteries of Udolpho*, and a novel by Lady Caroline Lamb. On it too was a brandy decanter, half full, and two small glasses. Lily looked at the decanter speculatively. The day was still young, but surely it would be ridiculous to suffer through the hours till evening when just one little drop would make her feel herself again. For an instant she forgot to pose. She straightened, poured out a glass of brandy and drank it off hurriedly, almost furtively; then, more slowly, she filled the glass again, put it within reach on the table, and lay back on the sofa.

Objectively, but with the objectiveness of a sympathetic onlooker, Lily regarded herself as she lay there. Here she was still young, still beautiful, still eminently desirable, caged like a prisoner on a small and savage island thousands of miles from the world where she belonged. In six years she had not been to a concert or to the theater, to a ball or rout; in six years her only society, save for the officers of visiting warships, had been that of missionaries and merchants. Her mouth trembled with the pity of her own plight, and inevitably her thoughts turned back over the chain of circumstances that had brought her to this place.

Miss Lily Villiers had been a person of some importance in London society when, at seventeen, she had first been presented to it. Her mother had seen to that, shrewdly and systematically using her own fortune, her husband's aristocratic connections, and Lily's beauty so successfully that many people were prone to overlook the background of trade with which that fortune was undeniably tainted. There was only one flaw in the strategy, and that was Lily herself. Romantic, rebellious, spoiled, she lived in a world of heady dreams. When Anthony Nicholls appeared to dazzle her with tales of an adventurous life, her heart and her imagination were so captured that the threats and pleadings of her mother were futile.

Nicholls was a dashing figure, an admitted soldier of fortune, of obscure origins, who lived, he said, for adventure. The pictures he drew for her of the life that they might share together were perhaps as fascinating to her as Anthony himself. When he got hold of a sum of money (just how she now sometimes wondered) they ran away and were married, and shortly afterwards sailed for the South Seas, she with her maid, Anthony with his valet. Even the rigors of that long voyage, even the word she had received from her mother that she no longer considered her a member of the family, could in no way quench the excitement she felt. With the vision of pearl shells and savages and adventure to lure her on; with, best of all, the vision of herself as the heroine of a great romance, nothing could daunt her.

But they had, after all, encountered few adventures. Anthony had settled in Tahiti, had established a plantation and sugar mill, and surprisingly enough had prospered. After a year or so it had become prosaic. The things that had at first so stimulated her imagination became the matter-of-course fare of everyday life. Once the plantation was started and the house finished, there was little to do. They might as well be farmers, she thought bitterly. Even her maid and the valet had left them — had gone to Papeete and set up a thriving grogshop for sailors.

And Anthony, fattened and secure for the first time in his life, had lost a good deal of his former dash. He could indulge in sodden bouts of drinking and still oversee the plantation conscientiously enough to maintain its prosperity. Anthony, thought Lily, had become impossible, adventure a chimera, romance a flickering illusion. Occasionally she had surrendered to the delicious flurry of an affair with an officer from a visiting ship, and each time she was convinced that life was once more within her grasp. But these affairs had ended inevitably with the ship's sailing. Men were free, men could rove the world and mold their lives to their own sweet taste, but she was helplessly trapped.

If *she* were a man, if only she were not penniless, totally dependent upon Anthony . . . Angrily, she drained off her second glass of brandy, and was about to pour a third when she heard the sound of voices outside on the veranda.

Jonas Burkham — back so soon? Hastily, she jumped up, rearranged her gown and hair, and went to the doorway.

Jonas was standing on the veranda, leaning on the arm of one of the native servants, his face rather drawn, his lips twisted in a smile.

"Forgive me, Mrs. Nicholls. I had a little accident. Anthony insisted on sending me here, and your man would not be dissuaded."

"Of course," she said, "but what is it?"

He grimaced. "My horse slipped and fell going up the mountain trail, and caught my foot beneath him. It's nothing, really — just a twisted ankle."

"I am so sorry! Come in at once and sit down. I'll bring some bandages for you."

When she returned to the drawing room with some white cloths and a bowl of cold water, Jonas was sitting on the sofa unloosening his shoe.

"This is unforgivable — "

"Don't be absurd," Lily said. "Take off your boot and I'll bandage your ankle. It may be sprained."

He said no more, absorbed in the pain of getting the shoe off

29

his foot. Underneath the stocking the skin was beginning to discolor; the ankle was badly swollen.

"It must be bandaged at once," Lily said. She dipped a cloth into the water, wrung it out, and began to wind it about his ankle. "No use to protest, Mr. Burkham. You are quite at my mercy, you see."

Her fingers, slender and white, with pink pointed nails, were tender, almost caressing, but childishly inept.

"I'm afraid I am not a very experienced surgeon, Mr. Burkham. Perhaps I should have sent a servant for Marianna Moore. She would do this perfectly."

"No doubt," Jonas said dryly. "And when she had finished she would hand me a Sunday-school tract."

"How wicked you are!" Lily said. She straightened up, laughing. "I, on the other hand, shall give you a drink."

"How wise *you* are. And how kind." Gratefully, he took the glass she offered him. After a moment's hesitation, she poured out another for herself, and sat down beside him.

"How is the ankle now?"

"Much better. Thanks to you, Mrs. Nicholls."

She leaned toward him, her ruffles brushing his sleeve. "I can't say that I am glad you hurt your ankle, Mr. Burkham. But I am glad, selfishly, that something brought you here today. I was very — lonely."

The wistfulness of her tone, the little droop of her lips, were fully as effective as she could have desired.

"Lonely!" Jonas said. "It's a sin against nature for someone as — for someone like you to be lonely."

"Are you never lonely, Mr. Burkham?"

"I suppose most people are," he said carefully. "You, I, your husband, everyone — sometimes even when we are together."

"But you needn't be."

"Why not?"

30

"You are a man," she cried. "You can go where you wish, see whom you choose — you are free!"

"As free as most men are free," he said noncommittally.

In the little moment of silence Lily looked at him sidelong. Jonas Burkham was unlike any man she had ever known, but he was undeniably attractive. Today his hard imperviousness, which for so long had both attracted and annoyed her, seemed softened. He was less mocking than usual, more human, and more vulnerable. She shivered suddenly, and got up to pour him another glass of brandy.

When she came back with it, she sat very near him on the sofa.

"You chose to come to Tahiti," she said. "And you chose to stay. There is nothing to keep you here if you wish to go."

"No," he said, "there is nothing to keep me here — now."

Instantly she saw her mistake; she had reminded him of Tihoti. "I only meant," she said, "that you have been strong. You have made your own life, after your own pattern."

"And you," he said, "did you not choose to come here?"

"Yes," she said wistfully. "I thought it would be an adventure."

He smiled a little. "And adventure was what you wanted most?"

"Don't laugh at me!" she said. "I was very young — and foolish, I know."

Her hand had been lying near his on the sofa, palm upturned, helpless as an abandoned flower; now she moved it forward until it brushed lightly against his. After a moment he opened his fingers and folded them around hers.

"You are still very young," he said.

"And very foolish?"

"And very beautiful, I was about to say."

Their glances caught, Lily's wide and appealing, his a little quizzical.

"No one has told me that for a long time," she said softly.

"Haven't they? Perhaps they didn't dare."

"Perhaps the trees can't talk!" she said with sudden passion. "What else is there in this beastly country?"

"Is that the way you feel about it?"

"It's like a prison!" she said. "Nothing to do — no one to talk to." She leaned toward him, her eyes limpid with tears. "Is it wrong to want to live?"

"You're marvelously alive," he said.

"Am I? Perhaps I am now, with you." Impulsively, she bowed her head, her voice muffled against his chest. "Help me to live, Jonas!"

For an instant she felt him stiffen, then slowly his arm moved up to hold her. Gently, he lifted her face and looked down at her. "Lily," he murmured. "Poor, beautiful Lily."

She let her head fall back against his shoulder, her lips trembling. For a moment he stared down at her, then he bent his head and pressed his mouth against hers.

Gradually she relaxed in his arms; little by little she let her own ardor respond to his — carefully, slowly, so that he was always in the lead and she could offer him the sweet servility of her surrender. And gradually the real despair that she had felt gave way to a rising tide of elation. He would not leave her now — not now, not now!

After a time she pulled away from him, leaning back against the sofa, looking up at him beneath languid lids. Now she could picture herself as he must see her — soft, disheveled, with crushed red lips; her breast white under the lacy ruffles, and his brown hand searching, searching. Then even that image faded, and she was swept away at last by the only emotion she knew that was strong enough to make her forget herself.

It was dusk when Anthony Nicholls came back from the hunt. He found Lily in bed, propped against a heap of pillows, dreamily polishing her nails.

32

"What's the matter, Lily? Are you feeling ill?"

"Only a little tired," she said. "How was the hunt?"

Anthony sat down on the edge of the bed, relieved. There were to be no complaints, then. His hand fell against something lying on the bedclothes — a white, faded flower with a red mark upon it, like a little drop of blood. He brushed it carelessly to the floor.

"Quite sporting," he said. "We got two young bulls. The men can salt them down tomorrow and we'll give one to Commodore Nicolas for the *Vindictive*."

"Good. He'll be out here to dine tomorrow night, you know, with a party of the officers."

"I remember." He hesitated a moment, his heavy fingers patting at his mustache. "It'll be the last party, I'm afraid, my dear. I saw Moore on the road and he tells me he heard in town that the *Vindictive* will leave next week."

To his surprise she merely widened her eyes and caught her lower lip with her teeth. "The *Vindictive* leaving? So soon? What a pity!"

"It is a pity. They were good fellows. But there'll be other ships along."

"I suppose there will," she said, almost indifferently.

Amazing how well she had taken the news. He got up, stretching. "I must tell you about that second bull, Lily. There was a close thing. I was standing behind a rock and . . ."

He could not have guessed from the polite attentiveness of Lily's expression that she heard scarcely a word he said.

᭝᭝᭝

QUEEN POMARE, SITTING BY PARAITA, HER CORPULENT PRIME MINISter, surreptitiously pried off her shoes and rubbed her bare toes together. Across the narrow table the French Consul, Monsieur

Moerenhout, was still talking. The glazed windows of the state chamber made the room warm and stuffy, her stomach told her it was time to eat, and besides, she had heard all this before.

She fixed her brown, impassive gaze on the contortions of Monsieur Moerenhout's left eyebrow, which jerked convulsively as he talked. Why couldn't he go back to the land of small, pale men where he came from, she thought, and leave Tahiti alone? When he first came to the island, ten years or more ago, she had found him very agreeable; he was so ready with a joke or a compliment, or a sly and flattering pinch. Foolish woman; she hadn't seen then that his friendliness had been merely a means of getting what he wanted from her, concessions for pearl fishing, property, trees to cut for lumber so that he could make himself rich. Morehu was all for Morehu, she reflected dourly; if it hadn't been for him and his greedy ambitions there would never have been all this trouble with the French.

Her thoughts slid away from him to her husband, Pomare Tane, who had ridden off that morning with several of the court followers for a picnic in the Fautaua valley. They would have had their swim by now, the ovens of food would be nearly ready to open, and Tane would already be guzzling from one of the two bottles of rum she had spied in his pockets as he went out the palace door. It wouldn't be long before he'd be making jokes with one of the girls — Terito this time, probably, the sly little piece!

Would Morehu never run out of words? She straightened up, interrupting him in mid-phrase.

"Did you give that rum to my Tane?"

"Rum, Madam? What rum?"

"You know what rum," she said impatiently.

"Really, Madam," Monsieur Moerenhout said. "Does it matter? What I was saying to you is of real importance. I must ask you to listen — "

"Did you give him the rum?" she persisted.

34

He shrugged. "Your husband came over and begged for it, as always. What could I do?"

"You know his weakness!" she said. "Pritarde will be very angry when he hears of this."

"Pritchard is always angry at something," he said. "In the old days you weren't so concerned with what Mr. Pritchard and the missionaries would think."

"In the old days I wasn't very clever about choosing my friends!"

He glared at her a moment, then he said smoothly, "It is because I am your friend that I have come here to warn you now. When you and the chiefs asked the protection of France—"

"I did *not* ask the protection of France!"

"You signed the treaty."

She leaned forward, the look of anger in her eyes suddenly kindled to a blaze. "I signed because I was forced to! Because you demanded 10,000 dollars if I didn't—and where did Pomare have 10,000 dollars? I signed because the French Admiral said he would fire upon my people if I did not! Because I was torn with the pains of labor, bringing forth another son whose birthright you would take away!"

"Let us return to the point, Madam," Moerenhout said icily. "The treaty is signed, the protectorate set up, and I, as one of the three officials who administer it, must demand again that you stop flouting it by flying your personal flag, as you have been doing."

Helplessly, she glanced at the huge bulk of Paraita, who sat stolidly beside her, his fat fingers toying with the carved handle of a palm-leaf fan. Paraita had been a useful and intelligent Prime Minister, who ordinarily took most of the burden of government from her shoulders. But in the matter of the French and their protectorate he had always been singularly lackadaisical . . . She glanced away again, a new suspicion sidling into her mind. Paraita would do anything for money. Could Morehu have bribed him?

35

The noon cannon shot from the *Vindictive*, bold and authoritative, boomed across Moerenhout's voice. The sound gave her assurance. Pomare was not without friends! Morehu and his two associates were merely noisy nuisances, and when her sister Victoria, in Beretane, heard of the annoyance they were causing her, she would send warships to banish them from the island.

"I have a right to my royal flag," she said, "and I shall keep it. Why do you always make such a fuss?"

"Look here, Madam!" Monsieur Moerenhout said. "When the protectorate was established, nearly a year ago, Admiral Dupetit-Thouars could have hoisted the French flag above Tahiti, had he chosen. Instead, out of regard to Your Majesty, he preferred to leave your old flag, merely putting the French colors in one corner as a sign of alliance, and as a safeguard to you if it should be attacked by another power. That flag has already been recognized —"

"You talk too much, Morehu," the Queen said wearily.

Interrupted again, he stared at her angrily, and some of the hardness that lurked not far beneath the polish of his manner stiffened his voice. "You would do well to listen to me, Madam! Remember, you can't break a treaty without provoking war, and you can't play with the honor of a powerful nation like France with impunity."

"I don't want to play with France," she said. "I just want them to leave me alone. I'm still Queen in Tahiti, and I shall still fly my flag. Go away now."

His face reddened. "You may be Queen, but you're acting like a foolish child! You don't know what you are doing!"

"I know that you are a bad, troublesome man," she said. "Go away!"

Moerenhout reached across the table, and shook his fist under the Queen's nose. "You're an ignorant savage, Pomare! Remember, I warned you!"

36

The Queen pushed back her chair and got up, signaling Paraita to follow her. "He reminds me," she said to Paraita, gesturing disdainfully at Moerenhout, "of a nagging husband too impotent to mount his wife and be done with it." Still barefooted, her head held high, she swept regally out of the room.

A SLOW STEADY BREEZE FROM THE SOUTHEAST RIFFLED THE WATERS of Papeete Bay and swelled the sails of the *Vindictive* as she stood out for the pass in the reef. Commodore Nicolas was in luck, Jonas thought; it was a perfect day. Too perfect in the opinion of those who were left behind; the faces of the hundreds of watchers who lined the waterfront were slack with melancholy, as if they said farewell to a beloved friend. He had been a fool, Jonas decided, to come into town to watch this — funeral.

A little ahead of him he saw Mr. Truelove, staring bleakly out at the bay, and had started forward to speak to him when he glimpsed Anthony and Lily Nicholls standing just beyond. It had been a week since that day with Lily, and he had not seen her in that time. Now he observed that she was crying; like the Tahitian *vahines* he had passed along the beach crying their brief and facile tears for the sailors who had left them, Lily mourned for the *Vindictive*, for the lost parties and flatteries and flirtations. Abruptly, he turned away.

It had not been easy to stay away from her during the past week. The sweet forgetfulness that she could give him drew his thoughts insistently through the empty days. It had been a hellish week. Turia, put off by his sullen despondency since Tihoti's death, had spent more and more time away from their little house — just where he did not know, nor did he inquire. He had tried to forget himself in writing, but when he had found that it was impossible to fix his thoughts on his work he had given up even the attempt at it. Once, driven by his loneliness, he had gone to see the Moores, but the savagery of his mood was only deepened by the unchanged benignity of Nathaniel's gentle welcome, and Marianna's astringent friendliness. If his schooner had not been in dry dock he would have set out for the Tuamotus or Manga Reva — it didn't matter where, so long as he could get away for a time. But the schooner was riddled with dry rot, and it would be a long time before she was fit for the water again.

From the *Vindictive* came the first boom of the royal salute. Jonas turned his head, and saw Queen Pomare, sitting in the carriage that Commodore Nicolas had brought her as a gift from Queen Victoria, her back straight and firm, her head lifted, and the tears coursing down her brown cheeks. Here was a woman with real reason to weep, Jonas thought; that long, measured farewell must sound like a death knell to her hopes for British aid and protection against the French. At the side of her carriage stood the Reverend Mr. Pritchard, the Queen's closest adviser. It was a bad day for Mr. Pritchard too, no doubt of that.

It had been seven years now that Pritchard, first as a missionary, and then as British Consul, had fought against Monsieur Moerenhout and his flagrant ruses to incite the anger of France against the Tahitian government. For the past six months, since his return from England on the *Vindictive*, Pritchard and the Queen, backed up by Commodore Nicolas and the *Vindictive's* sixty guns, had conducted the affairs of the island as if the protectorate and the French provisional government — Monsieur Moerenhout, the French Consul, now styled "Royal Commissioner of France," and his two satellites — did not exist. To Mr. Pritchard, today must seem perilously like a day of reckoning.

The final shot of the *Vindictive's* twenty-one-gun salute died away, and the ship coasted silently toward the pass in the reef.

38

Jonas turned away from the empty glitter of the bay and glanced back at Pomare's carriage. One could scarcely recognize in this matronly, care-ravaged woman the gay, imprudent wanton who had queened it over the island when he first arrived ten years before. In the past she and her unruly court, with their light-hearted disregard of Calvinist moralities, had been the despair of Mr. Pritchard and all the other missionaries; now she clung desperately to Pritchard as the one person who could save her country from the French.

He watched him speculatively as Pritchard raised his hat, bowed to the Queen, and turned away. Apparently the British Consul had seen Jonas too, but instead of nodding stiffly, as he usually did, he came directly up to him.

"Good day, Mr. Pritchard."

"Mr. Burkham, good day. Could you spare the time to step over to the Consulate? I'd like a word with you."

"Of course," Jonas said.

Already the crowds were dispersing as they walked along the waterfront to the lower end of the bay. Pritchard's house, set in a shady lawn between the mission church and school, was the only one in Tahiti, with the exception of the Nichollses' and the Queen's palace, that boasted glazed windows. Jonas, following Pritchard's spare, alert figure up the steps of the veranda, reflected that this was the first time he had been inside the Consulate. Pritchard had not, until now, sought out a man whose published writings included a chapter of stringent criticism of missionary methods in Tahiti.

Pritchard led him past a comfortable sitting room into a book-lined office at the rear of the house, motioned Jonas to a chair and seated himself behind a littered desk. He picked up a pen and twirled it in his fingers. "Mr. Burkham, Tahiti needs your help," he said abruptly.

"My help?"

39

Pritchard jabbed the pen dramatically toward Jonas's midriff. "The pen is mightier than the sword," he said. "You are a writer, Mr. Burkham. Your book has had a wide success in England and in America — a deserved success." A momentary smile illuminated the intent seriousness of his features. "I don't always agree with your opinions, but I cannot help but admire the writing. Your pen could be a powerful weapon, Mr. Burkham."

Diplomatic cuss, Jonas thought. "Thank you," he said dryly. "But just how do you wish me to use this — weapon?"

"For Tahiti. To inform the people of England of the true facts of the protectorate — that it was imposed by trickery and force, that Pomare, far from soliciting it of her own free will, as the French have blandly declared, was driven to sign the treaty by threats and chicanery." He leaned back in his chair. "I believe that the word of an American, a disinterested observer like yourself, would carry much weight. There are those, you know, who consider *my* word somewhat suspect."

It was impossible to resist that smile, Jonas thought. Small wonder that George Pritchard, whose fiery zeal and patient energy were augmented by a charming persuasiveness, had become the most influential of the foreign residents of Tahiti.

"I'd do anything I could to help," Jonas said. "You can count on that. But France is a powerful nation, Tahiti small and helpless. If Tahiti is included in France's plans for colonial expansion, what can you or I or all Tahiti do to prevent it? Only Britain can do that. It seems to me that Tahiti's fate will be settled between Whitehall and the Quai d'Orsay."

Pritchard leaned forward in his chair. "Quite so. But governments, thank God, are still influenced by their people, and if the people of England are aroused to a real awareness of this outrage, their leaders could not ignore it."

"It's hard for me to understand Britain's intentions in the matter," Jonas said. "And yours, as British Consul. You're in rather a delicate position, aren't you, until you have received definite instructions from your government?"

A sudden flush ruddied Pritchard's cheeks. "I have been trying to act in accordance with the promises of aid and protection made by the British government to Queen Pomare."

"Promises?" Jonas asked incredulously.

"Mr. Burkham," Pritchard said stiffly, "since Captain Wallis discovered these islands, seventy-odd years ago, there has always existed the closest accord between Tahiti and England. Our missionaries have been here for nearly fifty years. You yourself observed the friendly interest Commodore Nicolas took in the Queen's plight. I cannot believe our government will be less interested."

"Perhaps not."

"Both Pomare and I have written the strongest sort of appeals for British assistance, and I await an answer at any time."

"France has shown her intentions plainly enough," Jonas said thoughtfully. "If Britain opposes her, it will mean war. Are you prepared to see Britain and France at war, Mr. Pritchard?"

"I'm not prepared to see helpless and innocent people suffer! Can we be justified in ignoring tyranny and injustice because of a fear of war?"

Unanswerable question, Jonas thought drearily. When all alternatives are evil, how does a man choose? His own instincts, like Pritchard's, ranged themselves on the side of battle, but for many months he had suppressed them, trying to look beyond the small, sea-washed boundaries of Tahiti to the world that would suffer in a bloody struggle for her cause. Yet now he could feel his heart leap at the challenge; for the first time since Tihoti's death his mind quickened to a problem with joyous decisiveness. Perhaps this was how men chose; to give meaning to their own lives, and purpose to their convictions. He got to his feet.

41

"If you will give me the facts," he said, "I'll do anything I can."

Pritchard pushed together a pile of papers and handed them across his desk. "They're right here," he said, smiling. "You can see I counted on your help." He followed Jonas to the door. "Give my compliments to the Moores when you go back to Matavai," he said. "As a matter of fact, it was Miss Marianna who suggested that you might be willing to undertake this task."

So it had been Marianna's idea, not Pritchard's at all. As he walked out into the sunshine, Jonas felt an odd sense of deflation. His interview with Pritchard had awakened in him a surprised admiration for the man; he had felt a pleasant satisfaction that Pritchard had chosen him to help in the cause closest to his heart. Now it appeared he had a meddling spinster to thank, who schemed to get his thoughts off Tihoti and into channels which she herself would approve. To hell with redemption; what he needed was a drink.

A few hundred yards beyond Pritchard's house, the sign of the Boar's Head, incongruously English, hung from a mango tree in front of the little shack where the Nichollses' ex-valet and maid had set up their business. Today the place, without a noisy crowd of sailors from the *Vindictive* gathered at the bar, seemed strangely empty. Simpkins, the proprietor, poured Jonas a tot of rum.

"I think me old woman's got something for ye, Mr. Burkham. I'll just step back and see."

When he reappeared from the back room he held an envelope in his hand. "Mrs. Nicholls left it 'ere. Said to give it to ye, if ye was in."

Jonas ripped it open and stared down at Lily's childish scrawl:

Why have you not come? Why have you not anserred my notes? It is neither freindly nor just of you. Anthony goes Tuesday to the plantation in Moorea for a week or two. Please come then. I must see you — I *must*. I die of despare unless you save me.

42

Slowly he folded the note, and thrust it into his pocket. "Pour me another rum — a double. And have one yourself, Simpkins."

"Thank ye, sir." Jonas avoided the man's eye as they raised their drinks, but he thought he could detect a leer in the barkeeper's words. "To the ladies, Gord bless 'em," Simpkins said blandly.

Silently, Jonas drank off his rum. To the ladies — to Marianna's frosty virginity; to Lily Nicholls's itch for excitement; to Turia, his lovely brown wench, wherever in God's name she was. He threw some coins on the bar and pushed back his stool with sudden resolution. After all, Tihoti had been Turia's son, too. It was high time he tried to make amends to her for his churlish behavior of the past few weeks . . .

Outside, as he turned along the waterfront toward the mooring of his little boat, he glanced out at sea. The *Vindictive*, now far beyond the reef, was only a white speck against the horizon; but the Queen's carriage waited where he had last seen it, and Pomare still sat there, staring out at the vanishing ship.

⁕⁕⁕⁕⁕⁕⁕⁕

LILY FLIPPED OVER THE PAGE. "HERE'S THE PICTURE I WAS LOOKING for, Marianna. You can see that skirts are fuller than they were, and the waistlines very high — right up under the bust, like this." She got up from the bed pulling her silk negligee tight under her breasts.

Marianna looked up, her eyes preoccupied. "The styles are lovely," she said, "but they hardly seem suitable for me. Those little puffed sleeves, and the low necklines. Can you imagine what Papa would think?"

Lily shrugged. "But, my dear, they are the latest fashion." She laughed a little shortly, and threw the journal on the bed. "At

43

least they were the fashion a year and a half ago when they were sent to me."

Marianna pulled the book toward her and began leafing through the pages. "Here's one that might do," she said. "I could make the sleeves longer, and draw the ribbon higher at the neck."

Lily bent over the page. "Um-m," she said. "Very simple, of course. What material did you say you had? White muslin? A pity it isn't lawn; it would fall so much more gracefully." She studied the picture, her dark head tilted to one side.

She was like an exotic bird, Marianna thought. She and Lily must seem a curious combination! But although their friendship started with the fact that they were the only white women in the district, and much the same age, it had deepened into an affection that overlooked the disparity between their lives and temperaments. She had always resented the missionary ladies' disapproval of Lily — there could be no real evil in anyone so openhearted, so generous and so kind. For a distasteful moment she remembered the latest gossip of Lily. Lily and Jonas Burkham . . . It wasn't true; she couldn't, she wouldn't, believe it!

"This dress might be pretty, Marianna, with a wide ribbon at the waist, and the ends of it falling clear to the hem," Lily said. She looked up, her face suddenly alight. "D'you know, I've the very thing! It's the end of a piece I used some months ago, but there's enough left."

She jumped up and rummaged through a drawer. "Here it is," she said triumphantly. "Pale green — charming, with your fair hair and gray eyes." She pushed the spool of shining ribbon into Marianna's lap. "No use to protest. I'd never use it, and it's just the thing for you."

Marianna touched it lightly. "You mustn't give me this, Lily! It's much too handsome — "

"Nonsense — I insist! And here's the picture, too." She tore it out, folded the page, and thrust it into Marianna's hand. "There!

44

Now see that you don't change it too much. It's no sin to be prettily dressed."

"If that were the only sin I'd be a saint," Marianna said. "It's been two years since I've had a new gown. But the ribbon makes up for that, Lily. The children are going to love my finery!"

"The children? And what about your beau?"

"My beau?"

"You put on a very poor show of innocence, Marianna. I hear by the grapevine that young Mr. Johnson rides to Matavai at least once a week."

Marianna laughed. "Don't put too much credence in the grapevine. You know how it exaggerates."

"Does it?" Lily said. She got up, trailed restlessly around the room, peered out the window that opened on the road, and turned back to Marianna. "What's he like, this young missionary? D'you like him?"

"He's — I feel sorry for him."

"I suppose that's answer enough." She had seated herself at the dressing table and was staring moodily at her reflection in the glass.

"When will your husband be back from Moorea, Lily?"

"Next week, sometime. I got word from him this morning." She picked up a comb, and began abstractedly to rearrange the careful disorder of her black curls.

"That's good. It must be lonely for you without him."

The vivid face in the mirror darkened. "Lonely? Isn't it always lonely here?" Lily's high, languid voice was charged with sudden intensity. "One can't talk all day to the land crabs! Tell me, Marianna, what do *you* do? What have you done today, for instance?"

"Today? I'm afraid you'd find it very dull, Lily."

"Tell me," Lily insisted.

To describe her day to someone like Lily would sound as if she were complaining. What had she done? Made bread, and helped

45

Teaui roast meats for tomorrow, which was the Sabbath, when no cook fires were lighted. Prepared the Sunday-school lessons. Made a poultice for one of the neighbors' children, who was sick. Rapidly she discarded any intention of telling her these things. Lily had a well-meant but disconcerting habit of pitying her for things that did not need sympathy.

Lightly, she said, "I clerked in the trading store while Papa made a sick call. Old Mama Ruau came in — you know her, don't you?"

"The old woman who lives by the stream?"

"Yes. She had a basket of arrowroot that she wanted to trade for a bottle of cough elixir. I gave it to her, and then I remembered it was the third bottle she had bought in a month. Naturally, I was concerned, so I asked her how her cough was. 'Cough?' she said. 'What cough?' So I explained what the elixir was for, and asked her why she needed it. 'As sauce for the mango *poe*,' she said. Her grandchildren love it!"

"I must try it," Lily said. "Raitua's cooking is so monotonous."

"We've some liniment that might be good with a savory," Marianna said. "Who knows? I must get back, Lily. It's nearly time for Papa's supper." She got up, holding the ribbon and the picture in her hand. "Thank you for these, and for your help. I'm quite giddy with the idea of my new dress. I can't start it until Monday, but I'm afraid I'll dream of it all day tomorrow."

"And that will be a mortal sin, I suppose?"

"Not mortal, I hope — "

The sound of footsteps and a man's voice, calling from the next room, cut across her words. "Lily, are you hiding from me? Where are you?" Before Lily could answer he had come to the door of the bedroom, saw that Marianna was there, and stopped abruptly.

Jonas Burkham. For a moment Marianna felt paralyzed, unable to move or speak. As from a distance, she heard her own voice saying confusedly, "I was just leaving . . . good-by, Lily. Good day, Mr. Burkham."

She could never remember whether they replied or no, but she could remember the curious look on their faces. What was it — guilt? Annoyance? A shade of condescending amusement? She found herself on the path by the river, with no very clear recollection of how she had got there, and halted her steps, Teaui's words buzzing like flies against her mind . . . "Turia's off lying with half the district, but Tona doesn't care. He's got a new woman — the rich *popaa* at the plantation. Maui says he's up there most of the time."

So it was true, after all. She couldn't deceive herself any longer. She leaned against the trunk of a tree, closing her eyes against the vision of the cool and shadowed river. Why should she be so shaken? She had always overlooked Lily's faults, and even her father had accepted Jonas as a friend. Life in Tahiti engendered tolerance; relationships such as Jonas's with Turia were so commonplace that they had come to be, if not condoned, almost taken for granted. But she was rocked now with a feeling of passionate condemnation. This was different, this was different!

She opened her eyes, and in a moment of bitter honesty knew that it was not different. It wasn't just moral judgment that influenced her feeling; there was something more personal in it than that. She straightened away from the tree trunk and discovered that she still carried a folded paper and a spool of ribbon in her hand. She unfolded the paper and stared down at the printed, doll-like face that simpered up at her, at the coy display of white shoulders and bosom, at the wide skirts sweeping gracefully to the ground. Slowly, she crumpled it in her hand, and then with two quick movements flung the paper and the spool of ribbon into the quiet water.

47

Mᴀʀɪᴀɴɴᴀ ꜱᴛᴇᴘᴘᴇᴅ ᴏᴜᴛ ᴏꜰ ᴛʜᴇ ɴᴏɪꜱʏ, ʀᴇᴅ-ꜱᴘᴀʀᴋᴇᴅ ᴅɪᴍɴᴇꜱꜱ ᴏꜰ the blacksmith's shop, and stood irresolutely for a moment in the sunshine. Her hair was damp beneath the wide brim of her woven hat, and the folds of her riding habit clung limply to her body. It had seemed a pleasant break in the monotony of her days to start off to town this morning, but now she felt only exasperation at the delay that would prevent her from getting back to the country that night.

Obviously there was nothing for it save to go to the Pritchards', which meant that Georgie and the baby would have to sleep in William's room, and that there would be an endless remaking of beds, all done to the accompaniment of Mrs. Pritchard's birdlike chirps of reassurance that it was no trouble, no trouble at all. Marianna shrugged resignedly, and set off down the lane toward the hot, blue glitter of the bay.

Along the water a breeze was stirring, carrying with it the familiar odors of Papeete; jasmine and vanilla, a reek of whale blubber, and the faint, decayed sweetness of copra, delicately seasoned with the fresh scent of the sea. Out in the bay H.M.S. *Dublin,* recently arrived, rested at anchor, and there were scores of her seamen strolling along the wide waterfront road, each with a flower-decked *vahine* clinging to his arm.

Marianna glanced at them as she walked along. Englishmen, men from her own land, yet there was something about the intent look of purpose in their eyes, an urgent, animal air of concentration, that made them seem more alien to her than the dark faces of the natives who passed her with a smiling, casual greeting. She drew over to the comparative quiet of the shaded side of the road and paused beneath a giant mango tree to adjust the trail of her

48

riding skirt which had pulled loose from the loop that held it up out of the dust. An opening door just beyond her let out a momentary gust of brawling voices, and she looked up to see that she was in front of the Boar's Head grogshop. A drunken sailor, coming out of the door, lurched toward her, and as she started on he lunged forward and grasped her by the arm.

" 'Ello, sweet'eart."

She looked at him in astonishment. "Let go of me!"

"Wot's your 'urry, sweet'eart? I 'aven't seen a little piece of w'ite-meat in a long time."

Helplessly, she tried to tug away from him. "Let me go!"

The man only tightened his grip, and his grin revealed two rows of stumpy, blackened teeth. "Now then, dearie. That's no way to treat a gent!"

The door to the grogshop swung open again and Jonas Burk-ham stepped out onto the path. "What the devil!"

"Mr. Burkham!"

Advancing, Jonas said, "Get out of here, sailor!"

" 'Oo says so?"

"I do," Jonas said.

The sailor dropped Marianna's arm, staggered toward him and swung wildly. Jonas shifted slightly, and raised his fist in a short arc. The sailor fell to the ground and lay there, a surprised hand fingering his jaw.

"You barstard! I'll get me shipmates — "

Jonas took Marianna by the arm. "Let's move along," he said. "I don't like the neighborhood."

Still shaken, Marianna walked beside him, her arm trembling a little in his friendly grasp. "Thank you," she said huskily. "Thank you so much."

"Don't thank me," Jonas said amiably. "I rather enjoyed it. Are you all right?"

She looked up, caught the amused solicitude in his glance, and

49

instantly remembered that this was their first meeting since the encounter, two weeks ago, in Lily Nicholls's bedroom. She had supposed that he had been purposely avoiding her, but if he felt any embarrassment now, he certainly didn't show it. She drew her arm away from his hand. "Perfectly all right," she said.

"Good. Where are you going? I'll take you there."

"It's not necessary, thank you."

He continued walking beside her, humming softly under his breath. When Marianna stopped, he stopped too.

"Mr. Burkham."

"Yes?"

"Are you going back to Matavai this afternoon?"

"Yes. I was just about to leave."

"Would you be good enough to give a message to my father?"

"Gladly."

"Tell him that my mare went lame on the way in, and Poti says she shouldn't be ridden for a day or two. It's not serious, only a pebble in her hoof, but I shall have to stay in town tonight with the Pritchards."

"I'll tell him, of course. But why don't you sail out with me? It will be much cooler and more pleasant than a morning ride — and I should like you to very much."

Too quickly, she said, "I couldn't."

"Why not?"

"Because — how would I get the mare to Matavai?"

"Poti's boy can ride her out," he said patiently. "I'll tell him now, and meet you at the boat in a few minutes." A crowd of noisy sailors and their *vahines* bore down the road toward them, and Jonas drew Marianna out of their way. "Perhaps you prefer the company in town?"

Marianna caught sight of Jonas's woman, Turia, walking with a petty officer from the *Dublin*, their arms tight around one another's waists. There were white flowers in Turia's black hair, and

50

the vigorous lines of her tall, proud body showed plainly even beneath her Mother Hubbard and the bright *pareu* which was twisted about her hips. If she saw Jonas, she gave no sign.

Oddly embarrassed, Marianna turned back to him, her lips framing the first words of an inconsequential remark, but his wry smile stopped her.

"I never did have good luck with women," he said.

Impulsively she asked, "Where is your boat?"

The slight lift of his heavy brows was his only betrayal of surprise. "In front of the French Consulate."

"I'll meet you there, if that is agreeable," she said, in her most schoolmarmish voice.

"Perfectly." He bowed. "My luck improves."

He turned and swung away before she could reply, and her caught breath expelled itself in a little gasp of anger. There had been no mockery in his voice, but the words had flicked across her like a lash. Slowly, she started along the road. It would never do to betray to Jonas that her pride smarted under his casual phrase. After all, she was merely taking advantage of a convenience that he had offered her, and her indifference to him was demonstrated by the fact that she could put up with his company for a couple of hours as well as not. Her role, she decided, was bland, impersonal friendliness. Unconsciously her steps quickened toward the boat.

They set off with a fresh, steady breeze behind them, and by the time Jonas had trimmed the sheets to his liking, they were well out into the bay. He sat down beside her, and took the tiller from her grasp. "We'll be home before sundown at this pace."

"Yes."

To her annoyance she could think of nothing more to add, and Jonas, settling back comfortably against the sternboard, made no further attempt to speak. His easy acceptance of the silence that lay between them only increased her own discomfiture with it;

she felt as if it were dilating with the pressure of her thoughts, like a monstrous bubble. Determinedly, she stuck a pin into it.

"It's good to see an English ship in the bay again."

Jonas's glance followed the direction of her gesture toward the *Dublin*.

"For what it's worth."

"You don't sound pleased."

"I saw Mr. Pritchard this morning," Jonas said, "and I don't think he's pleased either."

"No? Why not?"

"The *Dublin* brought him a letter, from the Foreign Secretary. He didn't favor me with a reading of it, but I gathered that Lord Aberdeen warned him against offending the French. Apparently Britain doesn't regard Tahiti as important enough to risk a dispute with France on her behalf."

Marianna caught her breath. "If Britain won't come to our aid, who will?"

"Who indeed? It looks to me as if we're in for a rather sorry time."

"But the French have no right to be here! They're stealing the land from helpless people. Britain can't let them do that!"

"Britain hasn't been entirely guiltless in that respect herself," Jonas said dryly.

"You condone it, then?"

His smile was a little too broad. "I come from a country where liberty is rather widely commended," he said. "I don't condone anything that interferes with a people's freedom."

"If it weren't for the Papists the French wouldn't be here," Marianna said. "They're not content to convert mere pagans on an untouched island, they want to impose their creed on heretics."

"And there isn't room here for two ways to worship God. Is that it?"

"It isn't that," she said defensively.

52

"In America we believe in religious freedom, too."

She was suddenly reminded of that other time they had sailed along this shore to Matavai. *Thou still unravished bride of bigotry* . . . "When your country was first settled it belonged to the red Indians, didn't it?"

Jonas let out a little whistle. "*Touché!*" he said.

Marianna's eyes were on the bright fan of drops spraying back from the fingers she trailed in the water. "The Tahitians have a saying that one day foreigners will take over their island, just as the guava trees have overrun the land."

"That's a dire prediction," he said. "The guavas are a pest. Didn't the missionaries first bring them here?"

"I'm afraid they did," she said ruefully. "You can add that to your list of our errors."

"Oh," he said. "You mean my book. I gathered some time ago that you had read it."

"I have indeed. With great interest — and some discomfort."

"You mean that you agree with it?"

She looked at him, smiling a little. "Did I imply that?"

"I couldn't tell. Do you?"

"With some of it," she said. "But I thought you were unfair to blame so many of Tahiti's ills on the missionaries. After all, there have been many influences here. Someone had to offset the evils that whalers and trading ships and escaped convicts from New South Wales have brought here."

"You're quite right. But it never seemed necessary to me that the Tahitians should be forced to become hypocrites about the things that seemed most natural to them — dancing, wearing flowers, ornamenting their bodies with tattooing, even certain innocent sports."

"Perhaps if you'd been here forty years ago you might have thought differently."

"I probably would have been dancing right along with them,"

53

he said. "But even if I hadn't, I don't see why their *maraes* should have been destroyed, and their pride in their old legends and tales. Why couldn't the missionaries allow the natives some compromise with the past, instead of doggedly trying to turn them into full-blown Puritans?"

"We should never have started this topic, Mr. Burkham," she said lightly. "It's still half an hour's run to Point Venus, and we shall quarrel the whole way."

"On the contrary," he said. "I'm glad you read the book, because that means you read about yourself, too."

"Myself?"

"Do you remember that I wrote of the extraordinary devotion and self-sacrifice of some of the missionaries and their families? Of their attention to the minds and bodies of the Tahitians as well as to their souls? I was thinking of you when I wrote that, and of your father and Mr. Nott and one or two others. But mostly I thought of you — your patience in teaching them, your kindness and skill when they are ill or in trouble."

"They are my — people," she said. "Neighbors and friends. Anyone would do the same."

"Perhaps. But the fact remains that you have done it."

The warm surprise she had felt at his words flooded through her, and for a moment she could say nothing. How kind he could be when he chose — and how friendly! It took an effort of will to remind herself that this was the man whose small, barbed ironies had so often provoked her — the man who was Lily Nicholls's lover . . .

"I've been wanting to tell you," he said, "how much I appreciate all that you did for Tihoti. You gave him things neither his mother nor I ever could have, and he loved your school."

The bitter humiliation that she had felt ever since his words to her on the day of Tihoti's death suddenly melted away. "Tihoti was my favorite pupil," she said softly. "I miss him every day."

54

"I know you do," he said.

His glance was direct and honest; for a moment it held hers like a friendly touch. Ahead of them the green stretch of Point Venus reached languidly into the sunny sea. How quickly they had got this far, Marianna thought; it seemed as if they had left town only a few minutes ago.

His mind, momentarily sharpened by the brandy he had drunk, seemed quite apart from the drowsy satisfaction of his senses, like a critical, somewhat malevolent observer of his body. He finished buttoning the cuffs of his shirt, and pulled on his coat. Behind him he could hear Lily's voice. "You aren't going to leave me now?"

Oh God, Jonas thought, what a lot these white women could learn from the Tahitians, if only they would.

"I must," he said shortly.

She straightened up against the pillows, pushing her disheveled curls back from her face. "But it can't be more than three o'clock! And Anthony won't be back until six, at least."

He was reminded suddenly of a time he had been swimming in the bay and a piece of seaweed had become entangled about him, soft and limp, yet clinging stubbornly against his efforts to kick free of it. "I must go," he said again; and then more gently, "You shouldn't take such chances, Lily."

"I haven't a great deal to lose," she said moodily. She stood up, pulling her robe about her, and poured two stiff drinks of brandy into the glasses on the table. She held one out to him. "At least you'll have a drink with me, before you go."

He took it and sat down, holding back his words of protest. She would have it even if he were not there; it was common knowledge in the district that Nicoli *Vahine* was drinking, if not as spectacularly as her husband, at least more steadily. He looked at her with sudden compassion.

"You're very beautiful, Lily," he said.

The lift of her lips, the bright pleasure in her eyes, gave him a feeling of guilt; it was so pitifully easy to please her. She came closer to him as if she calculated an advantage and wanted to press it home.

"When will you be back, Jonas?"

His eyes slid away from her face. "How can I say, my dear? You know how careful we must be."

"We could ride together in the mornings," she said eagerly. "Couldn't we, Jonas? No one could talk about that, could they?"

"You know they could," he said.

"You choose to think so," Lily said bitterly. "If you really cared about being with me you would find opportunities enough — *make* opportunities."

"Lily, please don't," he said.

For a moment she said nothing, studying the glass that she held in her hands. He could not see her expression, but he was uneasily aware of the ungracious echo of his own words hanging in the silence between them. It was a relief when she raised her head, speaking lightly as if she had forgotten what had gone before. "While I think of it, Jonas, you must tell me about your fight with the sailors. It sounds wonderfully dramatic."

"My fight with the sailors?"

"Yes. Your gallant rescue of Miss Marianna in Papeete. I hear you battled three of them, great stalwart brutes, and left them lying bruised and unconscious in the road."

"The grapevine gets more inventive every day," Jonas said. "There was only one sailor, rather small, and very unsteady on his feet. I gave him a little shove, and that was all."

"You're much too modest," she said. "And besides, you spoil a good story. But even this way it's easy to see how exciting it must have been — for Marianna."

"I can't see why."

"Oh, yes," she said archly. "Imagine her feelings at this chilavrous — chivalrous — battle on her behalf. I've seen her look at you, and I think she's more than half in love with you."

"Good God, Lily, what an insane idea!" He stood up abruptly, and she saw his irritation.

"I didn't mean it," she said placatingly. "I was only trying to tease you." She jumped up and put her arms around him, standing close against him.

Unwillingly, he held her. The clarity of his mind had been clouded over by the last glass of brandy, and now it held only one idea — to get away, to get away as quickly as possible.

"Jonas, don't be angry with me. You do love me a little, don't you?"

"How could I not?"

He felt her body stiffen away from him. "You make an art of evasiveness, Jonas."

"I did not mean to be evasive," he said.

"Ah, no, you mean nothing," she said bitterly. "Nothing, nothing, nothing." In sudden fury, her small fists beat against his chest. "You treat me like a woman of the streets," she cried, "like casual dirt!"

He wrapped his fingers about her wrists, holding them firmly. What was there to say? It was always like this; always she wanted more of him than he could give her, sentimental analysis of emotions he did not feel, romantic ardor that he could not or would not simulate. "Don't talk like that."

Her hands quieted in his grasp. "You're rude and selfish," she said. "You don't care for me at all."

It was hard to keep the impatience from his voice. "You know how I feel about you, Lily."

"That's just the trouble," she said. "I do know." There was sudden animosity in the glance she directed at him, and then she swayed against him once more.

"Stay with me, Jonas. Have one more drink."

"No more," he said. "I must go."

"But you'll be back? Promise you'll come next time I can see you —I'll let you know."

"I'll come," he said shortly.

Outside, in the searching brilliancy of the sunlight, he recognized that he was drunk; at this hour, with nowhere to go, nothing to do, there was a stupid and burdensome futility to it. He stood for a moment, purposeless and indecisive, and then, head down, he turned away from the road, up the river path that led to the wild solitude of the valley. He had to be alone, away from the wise curiosity of the natives, away from anyone who might see him stripped to this naked self-disgust.

He opened his eyes against the golden afternoon light and lay for a moment staring up at the delicate, dimensional pattern of green leaves above him. Already there were shadows crawling up the floor of the valley, but the sun was still bright and lavish against the higher slopes. Apparently he had slept for less than an hour, but so profoundly that it took an effort to reorient himself.

His back ached where he had lain against the root of a tree, and the taste of his mouth was thick and bitter. He rolled over on his stomach and dropped his forehead against his folded arms. He could remember his walk, two or three miles up through the narrow valley, and he remembered sprawling down on this shaded ledge above the river. But the things he had been thinking along the way, which at the time had seemed of such significance to him, were lost. All that remained was the gradually shaping recollection of the hours he had spent with Lily. His dry lips sketched a grimace against the rough cotton of his shirt sleeves.

The dissatisfaction with his life and with himself that had been mounting within him since Tihoti's death overwhelmed him now; there was no aspect of his present existence to which he could turn with pleasure or with pride. All of the activities which had once sustained and enlivened him seemed to have lost their charm. Once he had found a calm, engrossing joy in his work, but now he could not concentrate on it; the simple, everyday occupations that used to seem so satisfying — fishing with his neighbors, working in his garden, building improvements for his house and boat — had become pointless to him. He had been fond of Turia in an amused, emotionless sort of way, and since she had left him, he found himself missing her, not because of any real need or desire for her, but because of the long habit of their association together.

He remembered how Lily, hopelessly pinioned by circumstances, had once cried out to him that he was free. Perhaps he was, but for what? Where should he go, now that the life he had so carefully built up for himself in Tahiti had been shattered by a small body hurtling from a treetop? Not back, certainly; he could never go back to the narrow New England town of his youth, to his father, critical and forbidding . . .

It would be months before the schooner would be in repair again, so that even the prospect of the temporary escape of a pearling voyage was too far in the future to satisfy him now. He wouldn't have to wait for the schooner, of course, he could always sign on a ship and roam the world again, but the idea of returning to the routine hardships of a stinking whaler no longer appealed to him. I'm getting soft — soft and lazy, he thought wearily; like those spineless creatures who, never knowing what it is they want, appear only to seek their own disaster.

The one thing left to him was his love for Tahiti and its people, but recent events had made him feel like an unwilling spectator of its dissolution. From the first advent of white men on their island the Tahitians had been marked for death, and now, perhaps, they were doomed to die in ignominy.

He remembered an ancient prophecy that the old men still murmured: The palm shall grow, the coral spread, but man will die. This very valley was full of desolate reminders of how that had already come to pass; it was scattered with stone *paepaes* which fifty years ago had supported flourishing houses, now abandoned and in ruins, torn apart by the green fingers of the jungle.

For a long time he lay still, his head bowed against his arms, and little by little the weary treadmill of his thoughts gave way to an awareness of his physical discomfort. The brandy he had drunk throbbed behind his forehead, his mouth was dry and his muscles stiff and cramped. The cool laughter of water falling into the stillness of the river just below him gradually edged into his mind, and with it the idea of a swim as solace for the physical and mental malaise he felt.

He raised his head, his fingers already fumbling with the fastening of his shirt, and glanced down at the dark clarity of the pool below the waterfall. At once he saw that someone was already swimming there — someone whose white limbs moved languidly beneath the surface of the water, whose long, fair hair undulated lazily with the movements of her head. Like a mermaid, Jonas thought dazedly; and then he noticed a little pile of clothes laid neatly on the bank, with a poke bonnet set beside them. Marianna, by God! — and naked as Eve. His throat stiffened with silent laughter. Deliberately, he pushed aside a leaf that was in his way, and peered down at her.

After a moment he forgot the sly meanness of what he was doing, and watched her with growing curiosity. There was a graceful sensuousness in the way she swam that revealed a deep, relaxed contentment in what she was doing. She moved across the pool to the waterfall, pulled herself up on the rocks behind it, stood for a moment veiled in its flashing white foam, then

60

dived deeply, sliding like a silver fish beneath the surface. Marianna, he realized with astonishment, was as much at home in the water as any Tahitian.

He saw that he had stumbled across a clue to a certain incongruity in her nature that had long puzzled and eluded him. For years he had regarded her simply as Miss Marianna Moore, missionary's daughter and capable schoolmarm, whose natural intelligence was limited by the narrowness of her training. Occasionally he had pondered the curved mobility of her lips, which seemed to suit a more worldly or passionate woman; and sometimes he had caught a gleam of amusement in her eyes when he least expected it, but these momentary signs of another Marianna were at once erased by his habitual acceptance of her as she appeared to be. Her serene forehead, the candor of her gaze, the cool dignity of her bearing, had so far outweighed these other glimpses of her personality that he sometimes doubted he had seen them.

He had been blind, he thought; he had forgotten that Marianna, whose mother had died when she was very young, whose father was dreamy and impractical, had no doubt been allowed to run wild with her Tahitian playmates. How much she must have learned from them that no English young lady would ever know! From childhood she would have accepted as natural the talk of those around her. The broad humor of the Tahitians, their earthy cynicism, their constant preoccupation with the senses, their bland and devastating avoidance of euphemism, had been as familiar to her as catechisms and prayer meetings.

He saw that she was swimming toward the bank just below him. Now, surely, was the time to look away, but he made no move to do so. There was good Biblical precedent for his behavior, he reflected sardonically — Susanna and the Elders, David and Bathsheba . . . Marianna pulled herself out onto the grassy bank of the stream, stood up, and raised her hands to

61

twist the water from the long, wet-gold pennant of her hair, and on that instant Jonas's laughter died within him. So this was the drab and angular Marianna! — this sylvan creature with small bones, delicately fleshed, whose taut, uplifted breasts were firm as a young girl's, whose tender curve of belly and thigh straightened into the long, graceful taper of her legs. Barely breathing, he watched her as she dried her hair and brushed the drops of water from her body, her tanned forearms in curious contrast to the smooth, white pallor of her flesh.

The low branch of a *purau* tree, studded with yellow blossoms, hung above the stream beside her, and as he watched, she broke off one of the flowers, tucked it Tahitian fashion behind her ear and bent over the water to catch her reflection. After a moment she pulled the flower away, and with a gentle gesture of resignation let it drop to the quiet surface of the pool.

Shaken by an unexpected compassion, Jonas dropped his head against his arms. I shall have to avoid her after this, he thought confusedly; I shall never be able to think of her in quite the same way again, but always see her as she is now, naked and defenseless and oddly moving. He had seen more than he intended; spied upon not only her body but something far more personal and vulnerable than that.

For several minutes he waited without moving, then cautiously he raised his head and looked down at her again. She had dressed, in a severe black gown that completely masked the slender grace of her body, and she was pinning her still-damp hair into a prim knot at the back of her neck. As he watched her she stooped, picked up her bonnet, and stood for a moment looking at the smooth slide of the river; then, with a barely perceptible straightening of her shoulders, she turned and started off along the path that led down the valley.

Jonas watched her go, outwardly indomitable, and yet, it seemed to him, profoundly pathetic. What was her life, beyond mere duty? Only a waste, warmth that must be repressed, yearnings and instincts that must not even be acknowledged. It was shameful and unfair that he should know these things about her, and yet just now he felt a curious gratitude to her. It was the first time since Tihoti's death that he had fixed his thoughts on anyone besides himself.

♪♪♪♪♪♪♪♪♪♪

Halfway to the top of one tree hill jonas dismounted, leading his tired horse up the steep, gullied road. The sun was hot, and the stones slipped and rolled under his feet, but even so it was good to walk for a little. There was a certain relief from futility in physical action.

God knows the trip to town had accomplished nothing except to increase his own anger and sense of frustration, but in a way he was glad he had gone. At a time like this the Queen needed friends, for what they were worth, and at least he could carry her message out to Nathaniel Moore at Matavai. Poor woman, how she had wept; her dark face had seemed indelibly marked with the pattern of her tears. Automatically his hand went to his pocket to feel again the stiff edges of the envelope she had given him.

A few days before, *La Reine Blanche*, French frigate of sixty guns, under the command of Admiral Dupetit-Thouars, had sailed into Papeete Bay. It was the same man, in the same ship, who had forcibly imposed the French protectorate more than a year ago, and his return seemed like the recurrence of a bad dream. On his last visit Dupetit-Thouars had been only a captain; now, rewarded with the title of Admiral, he brought word that King Louis Philippe had officially accepted the protectorate of Tahiti.

Impatient of the thousand rumors that flew before the news,

63

Jonas had gone to town to see for himself what the situation was. He had arrived in time to see three more French men-of-war drop their anchors in the harbor, and to note that they were loaded not only with troops and guns and ammunition, but also with laborers and craftsmen and artificers of all kinds. That afternoon Monsieur Bruat, one of the numerous officials who headed up this colony of interlopers, was formally installed as "commissioner" of the island. The farce of Monsieur Moerenhout and his dummy protectorate was ended; it was obvious that the French meant business.

At the top of One Tree Hill Jonas flung the horse's reins over the branch of a *purau* tree, and dropped down in the shady grass. Far below him was the wide blue sweep of Matavai Bay, and to his left the lagoons, edged by the frothing reef, clung like a necklace to the land. Fifteen miles across the channel the dark spires of Moorea notched the sunny sky . . . Damn the French, he thought, why must they come here? The land was not his by birthright, but his love for it had made him a part of it, and he knew, as well as the natives, the angry grief of the helpless against the aggressors.

Why had they come here, he asked himself again. There were no gold or minerals or other wealth to tempt them, only a pitifully small output of copra and vanilla and arrowroot and sandalwood. The only things here of human value were peace and beauty and a way of life, and these they had come not to enjoy, but to change. They had come, he thought, because someone was whoring after power, because the idea of an expanded, far-flung French Colonial Empire was an impressive political red herring, and might serve for a while to divert the people from their grievances at home. And they had come, too, because they doubtless knew full well that the only thing that might stop them — the British Navy — would not be directed to do so.

There was nothing here for the British either, he thought bitterly; and however sentimentally the English people might feel toward Tahiti, their government was something less than sentimental. In Jonas's opinion, Pritchard, whose word was supreme with Queen Pomare, was making a tragic mistake in urging the Queen to shape her policies on the hope of intervention by the British.

Reluctantly, he got to his feet. It was no pleasure to be the bearer of bad news. He mounted his horse and rode slowly down the other side of the hill, around the foot of the bay, past the Nichollses' white, verandaed house, and along the shady road that led beyond the church to the Moores' house, near the end of Point Venus.

As he had half expected, the Moores' broad, flowerless front yard was full of people; it was the focal point of the district, where, in any crisis, a few came to seek advice and everyone came to give opinions. It looked almost like a picnic ground, he thought, with children frolicking in the shallows at the edge of the river and fat brown babies sleeping contentedly on shaded mats, but there was no air of picnic gaiety. The voices that greeted him with the usual friendly *"Ia ora na,* Tona," were unnaturally low-pitched and grave, and he felt at once that they were waiting for the news that he had brought from town, although they would ask no questions until he had talked to Mora and Marianna.

He tossed the horse's reins to one of the boys, and went up the steps of the veranda. Nathaniel Moore rose and gave him a welcoming handshake. Beyond him he saw Marianna, and was pricked again by that odd sense of embarrassment he had felt in her presence ever since the day, two weeks ago, that he had seen her bathing in the river. Her greeting was as courteous as usual, but lately, for some undefined reason, its habitual coolness had begun to nettle him.

That pompous ass of a Johnson was standing beside her, Jonas saw, unreasonably annoyed; he nodded to him, and then turned to greet Taua, the chief of the district, and Tetua, his wife. When

65

they had all seated themselves again, Nathaniel turned to him inquiringly.

"Well, Jonas. What news do you bring us?" He spoke in Tahitian, so that Taua and Tetua would understand.

"First of all, sir, a message from the Queen." Jonas took the envelope from his pocket and handed it over to Nathaniel.

"This was written today?"

"Just before I left town."

The old man ripped open the envelope and pulled out a brief note. He stared down at it a moment, and then handed it over to Marianna, his hand shaking a little. "You read it, my dear."

To my dear brother in Christ, Mora, greetings. The Farani have come and they demand that I take down my flag. There will be word of this tomorrow morning, and I would like for you, my good friend, to be with me then. Please say to my people in Matavai that I wish them to be quiet and to make no disturbance. The Beretane will help us when they hear of this thing that is done. Peace be with you,

POMARE

Marianna put the letter down and looked questioningly at Jonas.

"Mr. Pritchard got a notice from Admiral Dupetit-Thouars," Jonas said, "saying that 'in consequence of actions alike hostile and offensive to the dignity of the King of France' he would no longer recognize Queen Pomare as sovereign, and if the flag is not down by noon tomorrow he would take official possession of the islands."

Taua was the first to break the heavy silence. "This was his very word?"

"As nearly as I can say it in your tongue, Taua. It's simply a pretext, of course — whether the flag is down or not, he'll find some excuse to seize the land."

The chief rose to his full six feet three, his chest swelling, his

66

great head thrown back. "The pigs! They think to steal our land and our birthright. Well, those puny Farani, they will find that Tahitians can fight!"

Nathaniel Moore's face was drawn and old. "We must keep peace, Taua — peace at any cost."

"They have many men, Taua," Jonas said, "and many guns. And there are thousands more where those came from. France is a huge and powerful nation."

The chief looked directly at Jonas. "You are my friend, Tona. And you will help us, will you not?"

"You know I will," Jonas said, "if I can." He turned to Nathaniel Moore. "Would you like me to go with you to town?"

"Thank you, Jonas, I would — "

"Let me go with you, Brother Moore," Johnson said eagerly.

"That's kind of you, Brother Johnson, but Mr. Burkham knows the French tongue. I believe we shall need his help."

Johnson pursed his lips. "Just as you say, Brother. I shall make it my duty to stay here and protect Miss Marianna."

What absurdity, Jonas thought. Can Marianna possibly respect that egregious idiot? He glanced at her, and discovered that her look was upon him, Jonas, direct and full, naked with a warmth that he had never seen in her eyes before. Before he could recover from his little shock of surprise, she passed by him on her way to the door. Incredibly, she reached out and touched his arm for an instant. "Thank you for going with my father, Mr. Burkham," she said softly. "I am immensely grateful."

So it was only gratitude that he had glimpsed in her look! With exaggerated formality, he made her a little bow. "Anything to please a lady," he said.

Taua had stepped to the railing of the veranda and was looking down at his neighbors. His deep voice, heavy with grief, tolled out into the silence. "My friends, I have sorrowful news for you . . ."

THE MEETING BETWEEN THE QUEEN AND ADMIRAL DUPETIT-THOUARS accomplished nothing. The Queen, although threatened, cajoled, and urged with sweet French logic, resolutely refused to take down her private flag; and the Admiral, equally adamant, declared with finality that if it were not lowered by noon he would take possession of the island in the name of France. The meeting had not lasted long, and at its finish the Queen had retired to her palace, issuing an order to her subjects to remain quiet and make no disturbance.

The five men who had gathered on the veranda of the British Consulate had merely been marking time since then, waiting until noon. There had been little conversation among them. Jonas sat in a corner of the veranda, smoking a cigar and watching the others. Mr. Darling, the missionary from Burder's Point in Punaavia, had sat for the last half hour with his head buried in his hands; behind his fingers his lips moved silently in prayer. Mr. Pritchard stood by the railing, his face granite calm, watching the groups of natives who clustered in the yard below and out along the waterfront. Nathaniel Moore sat with his reflective gaze turned to the ceiling, apparently engrossed in the activities of the lizards, stolidly stalking their insect prey. Behind him marched the steady footsteps of Captain Tucker, in command of H.M.S. *Dublin*. In full uniform, glittering with gold braid, he strode back and forth, as if he were pacing the quarter-deck of his ship, and managing to look, Jonas thought, like a full parade of naval strength. Occasionally he would stop his pacing and glare out at the bay, which bristled with the masts of French warships, his long chin set in anger, his eyes bleak with frustration.

68

He stopped now, and before he spoke Jonas knew what he would say. "Look at 'em," Tucker said fiercely. "Just look at 'em! The whole ruddy French Navy to take an island that can't claim two muskets for its defense!" He turned, facing the others. "Here I am, with a fifty-gun frigate, and what can I do? Even if I had the orders — which I haven't — what could I do against that damned flotilla?"

Nobody answered him, and Mr. Darling did not even look up from his devotions. "Look at 'em," Tucker said again. "*La Reine Blanche*, frigate of sixty guns. *L'Ambuscade*, frigate of fifty guns, *L'Uranie*, fifty guns, *La Danae*, fifty guns, *La Meurthe*, corvette of thirty guns, that ridiculous steamship, *Phaeton*." It was the fourth time he had counted them over, spitting out the names in his atrocious French accent as if they were so many unmentionable epithets. "It's enough to make a dog sick!"

Jonas turned his head away as the Captain began his pacing again. Out in the bay there were small boats clustered like water beetles against the side of each ship; and as he watched he saw that the soldiers lined along the decks were beginning to climb down over the sides and take their places in them. Mr. Pritchard looked down at the watch he had been holding in his hand, and for the first time in two hours snapped shut the case.

"Gentlemen, it is half after eleven. I suggest that we walk over to the Queen's palace. We can at least stand by her while this — deed is done."

They got to their feet at once, and the Captain picked up his dazzling hat. "I shall go along with you," he said, "like any civilian. Damme, I'm as helpless as one, now."

The Queen's palace, a white frame house, larger than any other on the island, and surrounded by a spacious lawn, was a block back from the waterfront. In front of it was a tall flagpole, with the Queen's flag — the red, white and red stripe of the Tahitian flag, marked with Pomare's insignia, a crown surrounded by a chaplet of coconut leaves — flying defiantly from its top. Out on the roadway was the Queen's carriage, with her coachman seated on the box — a tall young Tahitian dressed in a tattered, too-small uniform coat and a calico *pareu* twined briefly above his bare legs.

The five Englishmen found a place beneath one of the trees that shaded the lawn, and waited there, watching the crowds of people who were gathering, sullen-faced and quiet, around the front of the palace. Tucker gestured toward them.

"Will they make trouble, d'you think?"

Mr. Pritchard answered him. "No. Not today, at least. How can they? But it's impossible to foresee what may happen in the future if the French impose their yoke too harshly." He set his mouth in a thin line. "We shall counsel peace, of course — peace until Britain can be notified of this heinous crime, and can take the steps to undo it."

"You sound pretty confident that they will do that, Reverend."

"I must have confidence in my country's good faith, Captain Tucker."

Tucker's shrug set his gold braid winking in the sun. "To be sure. But I've spent a good part of my life in dealing with Admiralty Boards and government powers-that-be, and I know how mule-headed they can be sometimes."

"England will scarcely betray a helpless country that she has befriended for nearly half a century," Pritchard said heatedly.

"I am afraid Pomare will be betrayed by some who are closer to home," Nathaniel Moore said. He nodded toward a small group of men, taller and more imposingly dressed than the others, who stood at the foot of the steps to the palace veranda.

Tucker followed his look. "Who are they, sir? I've been wondering."

"Those are some of the greatest chiefs of the island — large landholders, proud of their ancient lineage, whose families in

70

earlier times considered themselves far superior to the Pomares. Some of them still do, I expect. Their allegiance is not to the Queen, but to themselves."

"Who is the tall, fine-looking one in the black coat?"

"That's Tati, chief of Papara. He —"

Mr. Darling held up his hand for silence. "Listen!" he said.

The breeze from the bay carried sound with it now — the sounds of drums rolling, and then of band music in martial rhythm. Unconsciously, they raised their heads, listening quietly, and all the others gathered there fell silent too, so that the only sounds were the gentle scraping of the palm leaves and the gradually increasing *poum-poum* of the music.

A low wail went up from the crowd, the sound of many throats uttering the grief-laden Tahitian exclamation, "*Aué!*" Jonas turned his head and saw that the Queen had come out of the palace and was standing on the veranda steps with her family. She wore a black silk gown with a white collar, clasped at the waist with a golden girdle, and her dusky face was shaded by a white poke bonnet. One hand rested on the shoulder of her eldest son, Ariiaue, whose sturdy, six-year-old figure was dressed in a crimson velvet coat, white satin trousers, and on his head a cap trimmed with gold lace and gold buttons. Behind the Queen stood Pomare Tane in an elaborate uniform, with another little boy and a small girl clinging to his hands. Behind him was a nurse, with a baby in her arms.

The Queen stood quietly, her head held high, her eyes fixed on her flag, gay in the brilliant sunshine. She did not look down even when the first troops marched around the corner into the roadway in front of the palace.

Jonas watched them come, ten abreast, marching smartly to the music. How small these Farani looked, in comparison to the Tahitians, but they were trained and they were well armed. He tried to count them as they marched by and formed a hollow square around the flagpole. There must be five hundred in all, not counting officers, nor the innumerable French civilian workers they had brought, who lurked, puny and gray-faced, among the fringes of the crowd.

Pritchard held his watch open in his hand again, and Jonas saw that it pointed to one minute to twelve. A slight, fair-haired French officer stepped forward, raised his sword, and said a few sentences in French in a loud, shrill voice. Pritchard leaned toward Jonas. "That's d'Aubigny, captain of the corvette. What does he say?"

Jonas kept his eyes fixed on the officer. "He says that they will lower the flag — and that they take possession of this island in the name of Louis Philippe, King of France."

The soldiers had raised their muskets and as d'Aubigny's sword dropped, a volley sounded to the skies. Three times they fired, and as the smoke cleared away, they saw that the Queen's flag was being lowered down the mast. The tense silence after the roar of the muskets was broken only by the frightened cry of one of Pomare's children; then, as the flag fluttered to the ground, d'Aubigny, his face blackened with smoke, stepped forward, put his foot on it and screamed out, in broken English, " 'Ere goes the crown of England, once more in the dirt!"

The French soldiers cheered. Jonas saw the crystal of Pritchard's watch crack sharply under the involuntary pressure of his thumb. Captain Tucker's face was grim under his elaborate hat, his eyes turned to the French tricolor that now waved from the top of the mast, his arms stiff at his side.

D'Aubigny was shouting more orders and some of the troops were marching off, behind the band, while others lined up along the edge of the roadway. Pritchard took Jonas by the arm. "Come, Burkham. We must take the Queen to her carriage and bring her at once to my house. I may need you to translate if any of these Frenchmen try to stop us."

72

The Queen had not moved. Pomare Tane was holding the sobbing little girl in his arms, trying to comfort her. Pritchard bowed to the Queen, and spoke to her in Tahitian. "Allow me to take you to your carriage, Madam."

She looked down at him, her eyes refocusing as if they had been looking into a great distance, and nodded. She took his arm and they started slowly down the walk, with her husband and children following behind her.

Three French priests in long black gowns and tricornered hats were standing near the walk, and just beyond them Admiral Dupetit-Thouars was shaking hands with Monsieur Moerenhout. The French Consul was dressed like a dandy in new finery; his smile was broad, and his eyes triumphant. With them was another uniformed Frenchman and a smart-looking Frenchwoman, dressed in a style that was drawing unwilling glances of envy from the Tahitian *vahines* who saw her. That must be Commissioner Bruat and his wife, Jonas thought . . . Like Pritchard and the Queen, he looked straight ahead as he passed the group.

It was then he saw that Captain d'Aubigny was standing beside the Queen's carriage, waiting there with a small detachment of soldiers. Jonas stepped up beside Pritchard just as he and the Queen came to a halt in front of the carriage steps. When Pritchard made a move to hand the Queen up the step, d'Aubigny held out his arm across the carriage door.

"*Je regrette*, Madame," he said stiffly, "it is not permitted for you to go in the carriage. This vehicle is now the property of France."

The Queen was looking at him in uncomprehending bewilderment, and Jonas felt an angry wave of blood mount to his face. In rapid French, he said, "What right have you to take the Queen's carriage? Does French thievery extend to small things as well as great?"

D'Aubigny's eyes snapped around toward Jonas. "And who may you be, sir?"

73

"My name is Burkham. The Queen has asked me to interpret for her. It is scarcely an agreeable task, under the circumstances."

"You are an Englishman, I suppose?"

"No, I am American."

"So." D'Aubigny looked at him, appraisingly. "Do your duty, then, and translate for me, but watch your words, and don't meddle into things that don't concern you. Ask the Queen to be so kind as to give me the keys to the palace. It is to be taken over for the use of Governor Bruat and his lady."

"*Governor* Bruat?"

"Monsieur Bruat has that honor. There is a proclamation being issued now that will make his position clear." He spoke impatiently. "Tell the Queen that she will be expected to take nothing from the palace except clothing and small personal possessions. All furniture and fittings are to be left just as they are."

"You cannot be serious!"

D'Aubigny's small blue eyes sparked dangerously. "If you do not at once translate my words, I shall have to use force to show you how seriously they are meant!"

Jonas gave him a long stare, and then turned to Pomare, explaining in Tahitian as gently as he could what d'Aubigny had said. She looks like a child that has been struck, he thought, and for a moment he feared that she would break, but as he continued speaking he saw a kind of stiffness come into her face. Behind her, Pomare Tane said violently, "Why, the filthy, thieving swine — "

She held up her hand. "Be quiet, Tane!" To Jonas she said, "You are quite sure that they mean to take all of my things?"

"I am quite sure, Madam."

"The drawing-room furniture that was sent to me by my sister, Victoria? The set of dishes brought by Commodore Nicolas? All of the fine gifts that my father and I received throughout these years?"

He nodded.

74

Pomare turned to Pritchard. "Pritarde, what must I do?"

Pritchard looked at her despairingly. "I am afraid there is nothing you can do, Madam," he said heavily, "except to give them up."

For a moment or two Pomare stared down at the ground, and then she raised her eyes to Jonas. "Tell the Captain," she said steadily, "that one of my servants will bring him the keys to the palace. And tell him too, that among my possessions he will find the barrel organ that was given me by Admiral Dupetit-Thouars, five years ago. Tell him I regret that it is now broken, and no longer makes music, but that perhaps it wasn't a very good one in the first place."

Jonas looked at her — at the overplump face and figure that had once been beautiful, at the direct, courageous clarity of her brown eyes, and at the sensual, laughter-loving mouth that was set now into a firmer mold — and he made her a sweeping bow.

"Your servant, Madam," he said. "It will give me much pleasure to tell him your very words."

In midafternoon jonas and nathaniel moore started back to Matavai. Near Papaoa Point, about midway between Papeete and Point Venus, they stopped at the house of Henry Nott, the oldest missionary, in years and service, on the island.

Nott was the only one remaining of the original group of missionaries who had come to Tahiti forty-seven years before in the ship *Duff*. He had been a young man then, a bricklayer by trade, but his stanch spirit and native intelligence so far outweighed his lack of educational training that he became the foremost among them in the battle for souls. It was he who stayed behind when all the other missionaries fled to Port Jackson during

75

the troubled years of war between Pomare, father of the present Queen, and the other chiefs; he who had persuaded Pomare of the wisdom of accepting salvation; and he who had inspired the final battle, in 1817, which had, with the aid of British guns, established Christianity — and the Pomare family — supreme in the islands. But perhaps Nott's most remarkable achievement was his translation of the entire Bible into Tahitian, setting the orthography of the words as he went along.

He had made only two visits to England in all that time, and after the last, old and sick, he had come back to his Tahitian home to wait for death. He sat quietly now, his feet wrapped in a blanket, listening intently while Jonas and Nathaniel recounted the events of the day. Only his eyes moved as he watched them, and his hands, which rattled like dry leaves against the arms of his chair.

"Pomare walked back to the Consulate with us," Nathaniel Moore was saying, "and the people began to gather outside, calling for her, and begging her to let them attack the French."

"Ah," Nott said softly, "with their bare bodies against the French guns?"

"Just so," Nathaniel said. "She told them that they must keep quiet, and do nothing, and then Mr. Pritchard spoke to them and told them he had written England and that they must be patient and wait for the answer to his letter. They were more docile then, and soon people began to come bringing gifts for their Queen, who is now destitute, and some of the chiefs came to see her, weeping, and she wept too."

"Where will she go now?" Nott asked. "Out here, to Papaoa?"

"No. She cannot. They have taken all her lands and properties."

"But her father is buried here — and her grandfather, too." Nott raised a shaking hand to brush back the lock of white hair that had fallen across his forehead, and Jonas found himself longing to jump up and help him to do it.

"It doesn't matter to them. They have taken everything. To-night she is going to stay aboard the *Dublin*, and tomorrow Captain Tucker has promised to send some of his artificers to fix up the little courthouse near Pritchard's as a residence for her. Apparently he talked to Dupetit-Thouars, and got him to agree to that."

"And what is Mr. Pritchard going to do?"

"He struck his Consular flag this afternoon, and wrote a note to Bruat, protesting the action taken by the French and saying that he must resign his duties, since he was accredited as Consul not to a French possession but to a French protectorate."

"I scarcely imagine they'll be grieved to hear that," Jonas said.

"I think not," Nathaniel Moore said. "But a man of Mr. Pritchard's mettle is going to be a thorn in their side even if he has no official position."

Henry Nott turned his sharp, turtle-lidded glance to Jonas. "What are you going to do about all this, young man?"

"Whatever I can," Jonas said.

"Hmm. It would be good to be young again," Nott said. "The Lord's word is peace, but the Lord ever sided with the weak against the oppressor, and the least we can do is follow His example."

For a moment they were silent, then Nathaniel Moore said:

"The new Governor, Bruat, has already posted a proclamation referring to the 'ex-Queen of Tahiti.'" He turned his gentle gaze on Nott. "In it he promises 'full religious toleration.' What do you make of that, Henry?"

"Vastly gracious of him," the old man said ironically.

"He also promises banishment from the island," Jonas said, "to anyone, native or foreigner, who shall either in word or deed prejudice the Tahitian people against the French government."

"It strikes me, young man, that you studied that proclamation pretty carefully," Nott said.

77

Jonas smiled. "I may have cause to remember it, sir."

The door to the house pushed open and an old Tahitian woman came out on the veranda. She greeted Nathaniel Moore deferentially, and nodded to Jonas. Her face was incredibly wrinkled, but her slender body was still as upright as a young girl's, and she spoke firmly. "I am sorry, Mora, but I think Noti has made enough talk now. It is time for him to rest."

The old man made a gesture of protest, but the other two got at once to their feet. "You treat me like a child, Pua," Nott said fretfully.

"Your wife is gone, Noti," Pua said. "And her last words to me were that I should look after you. Don't act like a child, and I won't treat you like one."

Grumbling, Nott pushed at the blanket with his palsied hands. "Help me up, then. I will at least walk out to say farewell to my guests."

Jonas gave him an arm, and they went slowly down the steps onto the lawn. Pua leaned across Nott to speak to Jonas. "I hear your woman has left you, Tona."

"Pua, watch your words," Nott said, but in the tone of a man who has made this reprimand a thousand futile times before.

Pua gave Jonas a toothless, malicious grin. "What was the matter? Weren't you man enough for her?"

Jonas laughed softly. "Maybe I wasn't enough men for her," he said.

They stopped for a moment in the dazzling sunshine near the trees where the horses were tethered. Nott raised his shaking hand to gesture toward the green, tree-covered point beyond, silvered at the water's edge with feathery casuarina trees. "Do you remember, Nathaniel," he said, "when we saw a human sacrifice on that very point?"

"I shall never forget it."

78

"And Pua here — good, faithful old Pua. She hasn't missed a prayer meeting in twenty years, but when she was a young woman she was an Arioi, and killed three of her own infants after their barbarous custom." He shook his head. "We've seen great changes, Nathaniel, great changes. But today something has happened to this island that we could never have foreseen." He paused, and on his next words his voice shook a little. "I never thought to die on French soil, Nathaniel."

A LETTER FROM QUEEN POMARE TO QUEEN VICTORIA OF ENGLAND:

November, 1843

MY DEAR FRIEND AND SISTER QUEEN:

My government is taken from me. Think of me, have compassion on me in my affliction and helplessness. Be quick to help me for I am nearly dead. I run to you for refuge, to be covered under your great shadow. I am like a captive pursued by a warrior, and nearly overtaken, whose spear is close to me.

May you be blest.

POMARE, Queen of Tahiti.

A letter from Pomare Tane to Tapoa, King of Bora Bora:

December 12, 1843

TO TAPOA AND HIS FAMILY:

Peace be to you and to your little child also.

The land is not well. The letter has not yet arrived from England for which we are waiting; we are living in fear and trouble. If anything is heard that is displeasing to France, the person is fastened in irons and sent away. Were it not for the English ship of war, we should have long since scattered to

79

the mountains. The English ship of war is our only place of refuge.

The French are erecting fortifications, for which purpose they are cutting down coconut and breadfruit trees. One French ship of war has gone to the Marquesas for the purpose of bringing French soldiers to Tahiti. The desire of the people is to fall upon the French and utterly destroy them; but this is not agreed to, although it is the general wish of the people entirely to annihilate these Frenchmen; and if but a word had escaped from us, imparting "Come!" a disturbance would have long since ensued. But we are waiting with patience for the letter from England; for should we begin now ourselves we understand that no assistance will be granted us from England hereafter.

Peace be to you and to the child.

POMARE, TANE.

⁂

THE LAMP FLARED UP FOR AN INSTANT WITH A PROTESTING HISS, then settled again to a gentle, steady glow. In contrast to that momentary brightness the light seemed more dim than ever. Marianna wove her needle into the seam, put her sewing on the table, and sat for a moment rubbing her finger tips across her eyes. Teaui had gone to her house, Nathaniel Moore was spending a day or two at Papaoa with Mr. Nott, and the profound quiet of the point, broken only by the far-off mutter of surf, underlined the restlessness that knotted within her.

Jonas wouldn't come now, she told herself again; it was after eight o'clock. Perhaps he didn't know that her father was away, but he knew that the old man was in the habit of going to bed very early each evening. Naturally, he would not come this late.

But the unacknowledged sense of waiting, the cumulative disappointment at his absence that had been the background of all her thoughts for the last two days could not be dispelled by such reasoning, and her nerves still tautened with a furtive hope.

With a momentary flash of understanding she thought of Lily Nicholls — of Lily as she had seen her the evening before, when she went over to the Nichollses' plantation to return a book she had borrowed. Anthony Nicholls had gone to town, and Lily, disappointed in her expectation of seeing Jonas Burkham, and recklessly indiscreet from the brandy she had been drinking, had poured out to Marianna the whole flood of her feelings about Jonas and his treatment of her. Ignoring Marianna's protests, she had railed against his selfishness, his stolidity, his cruelty, only to confess the next moment that she could not endure her life without him. Her outburst had produced in Marianna a feeling of sick distaste, but the memory of it was not nearly so disturbing to her as the sudden sympathy, born of insight, that stirred in her now.

She got up abruptly, as if to shake off her thoughts, and moved over to the railing of the veranda. Beyond the prosaic confines of the house the night beckoned with a thousand stars. After a moment she turned back, took a roll of woven matting and a cushion from the shelf against the wall, and carried them out to a grassy patch of darkness near the water's edge.

She spread the mat on the ground and sat down, clasping her hands around her knees. To the south the mountains of Tahiti blacked out the lower stars, and across the bay she could see the gold flare of torches held up by invisible fishermen in invisible canoes to attract flying fish within reach of their hand nets. The familiar sight all at once seemed strange to her; strange that people must go on fishing and gathering fruits and repairing nets, regardless of the circumstances that tightened like a noose about their necks.

81

For the past week the district had hummed with rumors that fighting men were assembling in the mountains of Hitiaa, to the east. It was said that they were building a camp there, gathering supplies and ammunition; preparing, in spite of their Queen's pleas that they be patient, for an open rebellion against the French. The fear of war had changed by degrees to expectation of it; and Marianna knew the Tahitians well enough to be sure that they would prefer the useless gallantry of a bloody and unequal protest to saving their own skins. In the more than two months since the French had seized the island, she and her father, weighing the news that Jonas Burkham brought them nearly every day, had come to realize the inevitability of conflict, but her father, sustained by the unquenchable optimism of his faith, could view it with less distress than she.

If only Jonas would come, and she could talk to him . . . Impatiently, she brushed aside the wish, and stretched out on the mat, staring up at the stars. What in the world was the matter with her, she asked herself in childish bewilderment; what was the ferment at work within her that seemed to threaten the long-practiced serenity of her life? One could not blame everything on the French! She probed through the pattern of her days searching for the source of her malcontent. School to teach in the mornings, afternoon sewing classes with the girls, lessons to prepare, Sunday-school classes, catechisms to hear, prayer meetings and church services with her father, the daily round of household duties with Teaui . . . all this was as it always had been. Yet gradually it was becoming clear to her that this was not enough.

She was conscious of an insistent longing, deep within her, for a life and experience of her own. For twenty-seven years she had been only a spectator of the vivid scene around her. She had accepted her role gladly, without a thought of protest, but now the long habit of self-abnegation was becoming irksome. Too often lately she became bored and impatient, flicking at the hours

82

as one might riffle the pages of a book, eager to see the ending.

It was as if the whole of her life were now spent in waiting — but what was it that she waited for? For Jonas's visits? No, no, she told herself quickly; or if that were so, it was only for the pleasure they gave her father, and her own interest in the news he brought . . . Dear God, please have Jonas come here, now.

Instantly shamed, she shut her eyes against the stars, and turned over, burying her face in her arms. Incredibly, in that bleak moment, she heard Jonas's voice calling across the darkness.

"Hello," he said, "is anyone at home?"

She sat up quickly. "Just I — Marianna," she answered, and it seemed to her that her voice shook a little. "I'll be right there." Hurriedly she smoothed back her hair and brushed at her skirt. She had not had time to rise when she saw him standing in the darkness beside her.

"My father isn't here," she said. "He has gone to Papaoa."

"No matter," Jonas said. Before she could get up he dropped down on the matting beside her. "I'd like to talk to you, if I may."

She sat up a little straighter, pulling her skirts around her ankles. Could he hear the ridiculous tattoo of her heart? "Of course," she said.

"I've been in Hitiaa the past two days," Jonas said. "Just got back this afternoon."

If only she had known he had been out of the district all the while she waited for his visits . . . She pushed the admission quickly out of her mind, and said, "How was it there? Are the rumors true?"

"Quite true," he said. "They're making a camp in the mountains, under the leadership of Paofai, and literally hundreds of men are flocking in to join forces."

She caught her breath. "There will be war, then?"

"Sometime, certainly; I don't know when. They're itching for

open rebellion. In Papenoo it's the same way. The people are talking of building a fort in the upper valley. And here in Matavai — "
He hesitated.

"Go on," Marianna said.

"I talked to Taua this afternoon," he said reluctantly. "He's already making plans to fortify the plain at Mahina. That would be the logical place for a battle if there should be fighting here in the district."

"A battle — at Mahina!" she said. "It's practically in the school-yard."

"I know," he said somberly.

"But they'd be mad to fight against the French!" she cried.

"Perhaps," he said. "But that's what they will do." He twisted around so that he faced her, and she could feel his eyes searching out her expression in the darkness. "Nothing's going to stop them, y'know, no reasoning, no pleas, no description of the odds against them. There's only one thing to do, and that's to help them."

"If there's no way to stop them, of course we must. They're so defenseless — so pitifully unready."

"Yes," he said. "It's going to be pretty bad. I've been thinking about it a good deal, and I have to tell you now that I believe you and your father would be much better off to move to town, where at least there are friendly ships standing by."

"We can't do that!" she said. "Father wouldn't think of leaving the mission — and neither would I."

For a moment she glimpsed his brief and unexpected smile. "I rather thought you'd say that," he said. "And since you refuse to be sensible, will you be even more foolish and give me your help?"

"In any way I can," she said. "Of course I will."

"Good. The most important thing, then, is the question of arms and ammunition. I've checked in the district, and it seems that most of the families own at least one musket of some sort —

84

Taua even has an old fowling piece that was given his grandfather by Captain Cook. But many of them are in bad shape — rusted, or out of repair. Farenui and I — he's good at that sort of work — want to gather them together and put them into proper condition."

"I see," she said. "But how can I — "

"Wait," he said. "Here's how you can help. We'll need a place to work, and a place to store the guns. What we need," he said, and his voice was tinged with some of its old irony, "is a cloak of respectability and the protection of a woman's skirts."

"It doesn't sound like a very dashing role," she said. "But if it's what you need — "

"It is, and there's more to it than that. You keep the keys to the outbuildings here at the mission, don't you?"

"Yes."

"What's in the wooden shed in the grove behind the schoolhouse?"

"An old printing press. It hasn't been used in years."

"Good," he said. "Would you be willing to let us use that building?"

"Certainly."

He went on rapidly, scarcely waiting for her answer. "It would be the perfect place — secluded and forgotten. We can build a false floor beneath the present one, with enough space between for storage. When we weren't working in the shed we could leave it looking as it always has, so that no prowler would suspect anything out of the ordinary." He leaned a little toward her, looking at her sharply. "I'd prefer that your father knew nothing of this, Miss Marianna. After all, the missionaries have had to promise submission to the French Governor, and your father might, in all conscience, have to object."

"I won't tell him," she said.

"It's settled, then," he said. "Our second problem is this: I have

85

a small forge, good enough for melting up odd bits of metal into musket balls. But I can't do it openly — I must find some spot sufficiently hidden from the noses of French spies. Do you know of such a place?"

She reflected for a moment, warm with the awareness of the accord that had flowered between them. She had never seen Jonas so direct before, so open and approachable. If only he were always like this . . .

"Up in the valley there's a waterfall with a pool below it — I've sometimes gone bathing there — "

"Have you?" he said, with an odd inflection.

She went on, not noticing it. "There's a rocky ledge above the waterfall with some dry caves opening onto it. Not even many of the natives know how to get there. I think you'd find it a safe place to work."

"It sounds good," he said. "Someday soon will you show me how to reach it?"

"Yes." For a moment she was silent, her mind circling around the things that he had suggested. "I remember my father telling me," she said slowly, "that many years ago, when Pomare's father was at war with the Atehurans, the natives melted up type from the mission printing press into musket balls, and tore out leaves from their books to make cartridge papers. That printing press in the shed would never be missed, and there are a lot of old schoolbooks around somewhere — "

She was interrupted by Jonas's joyous shout of laughter.

"What's the matter?" she asked.

"Nothing," he said, still chuckling, "except that Miss Moore, missionary's daughter and guiding light of the church, proposes to destroy mission property in the interests of illicit warfare."

"My father paid for the press with his own money," she said defensively, "and the books are worn beyond any other use."

"Don't explain," he said. "I think you're wonderful."

86

She sat quite still, staring out across the bay. A large and tardy moon had lurched above the mountains to the east, touching the ripples with gold. There had been no mockery in his voice this time, she thought.

Jonas turned toward her averted face, a little concerned at her silence. "Marianna," he said softly, "can't you and I be friends?"

His use of her name without its formal prefix, the intimacy of his tone, stirred her like a caress. Slowly, she turned her head toward him. "Why not?" she asked simply.

For a moment he stared at the pale oval of her face, and at the full curve of her lips. A few tendrils of her fair hair had escaped from the severity of her coiffure, and the moonlight, shining through them, transformed them into a nimbus about her head. He raised his hand to touch them. "Are you a saint, Marianna?" he asked quizzically.

She looked at him, wonderingly. Impulsively, he drew her to him, and kissed her on the lips.

For a few blind, explosive seconds she yielded to him completely, lost to everything except the warmth and sweetness of his lips against hers, the dizzying closeness of his embrace. Then, through the confusion of her senses, she became aware that there was brandy on his breath and the unmistakable scent of Lily Nicholls's perfume on his cheek. Abruptly, she pulled away from him and sat for an instant in frozen silence. "I think you should go now," she said.

For a sharp and scarcely endurable moment she could feel his look searching her face, then he got to his feet. When he had gone, she dropped her face between her hands, still shaken with the sweet, insidious response he had surprised in her. After a long time she raised her head, and was confronted by the cool validity of the stars. The *hupé*, the breeze that flowed down from the mountains every night, cool as glass and scented with flowers, touched against her arms and face, and she shivered suddenly. She got to her feet, picked up the matting and the cushion, and started toward the secure and comforting glow of the lamplight shining from the house.

She would have to see him soon again; there was no way to avoid it. She could not let her own emotions stand in the way of the plans they had made. She would have to meet with him and work with him on a cool and friendly basis, as if nothing had happened. There was no time to waste. Why had he not come today? Did he dread the encounter as much as she did?

Not Jonas! she thought. Jonas, whose kisses were as indiscriminate and meaningless as the touch of the wind, would attach no importance whatever to that — incident — of the night before. And neither did she, neither did she . . .

"A penny for your thoughts, Marianna," Richard Johnson said.

She flushed. "They're not worth nearly that." What a fortune I'd have laid by today if they were, she thought bitterly.

"I'm afraid I've come at a bad time," he said. "You've been so quiet. Perhaps you're feeling tired — "

"Not at all, Richard." With an effort, she injected some life into her voice. "Tell me your news! How are things in Tiarei?"

"All right, I suppose," he said. "If it weren't for the language. I'm afraid I make dreadful mistakes, Marianna. Sometimes when I preach, the people start to giggle and nudge one another."

It was easy to imagine how humorous the people of Tiarei would find him, solemnly blundering into the most shocking of solecisms. Even his appearance would tickle their fancy — his meek chin, his prominent Adam's apple, the awkwardness with which he moved his lanky frame. She looked at him, stirred by a feeling of contrite pity.

"It's a wicked language, Richard. The whole meaning of a word can be changed by one small wrong emphasis on a vowel. There are lots of pitfalls for a beginner."

88

"And I probably drop into them all," he said ruefully.

"Of course you don't! You've made tremendous improvement in the last few months."

"Thanks to you."

"You're much too modest, Richard. Let's speak Tahitian now, so that I can flatter *you*."

"Not now," he said. "Will you take a stroll with me, Marianna? Along the bay? The sunset promises to be very fine."

Someone had just opened the gate that led in from the lane, and she leaned forward quickly. Only Poriri, bringing a string of fish around to the cook house. Jonas wouldn't come! How stupid of her to start at every creak of the gate.

"You're not too tired, Marianna?"

"No, no, I'd love a stroll." In her effort to make up to him for her wandering attention, she had put too much enthusiasm into her voice, but he did not seem to notice. He followed her down the veranda steps and across the lawn to the water's edge, humming softly under his breath.

"You cannot imagine how much I look forward to these visits every week, Marianna."

She had forgotten until his arrival, an hour ago, that this was his day to come to Matavai. "Father and I look forward to them too, Richard."

"It's wonderful to be here," he said happily. "Wonderful to be with you!" They had come to the edge of the river, and he took her arm. "Shall we walk along this way?"

Along there lay the spot where she and Jonas had sat together the evening before. "Let's go the other way," she said hurriedly, "out toward the end of the point. We can see the sunset better there."

As they turned along the edge of the river she was suddenly overwhelmed by the memory she had been trying to avoid; so vividly that she could feel again the unthinking, dreamlike ecstasy that had possessed her with Jonas's lips against her own, and the

89

sharp, jealous hurt of her realization of where he had been before. I was easy, she told herself contemptuously, easy as Lily Nicholls must have been. Sisters under the skin . . .

"Perhaps you can guess, Marianna, why I wanted to come out here, where we wouldn't be interrupted."

She looked at him blankly, then suddenly, with an almost physical sensation that her heart was dropping in her ribs, she knew what he would say. While she had been preoccupied with the thought of Jonas, to whom she meant nothing, Richard had had his own preoccupation, and one that should have been her own. "To — see the sunset," she murmured foolishly.

"No, my dear. Not that. Don't put me off again, Marianna. You know wha I've been hoping for — longing for."

"I know," she said humbly.

"I dream of it all the time, Marianna. The things we could do together. With you as my wife, there is nothing we couldn't accomplish. Give me your answer this time — please do!"

"Oh, Richard, I did! I've told you — there's Father to think of — I can't leave him alone."

"Your father would be the first one to want you happily settled, Marianna. He's not as young as he once was, my dear, you must realize that. I know he worries about your future, doesn't he? Be honest, Marianna."

She looked down at the ground. "I suppose he does."

"And if we were married, you could still see him every week! We could come here, as I do now, and he could visit us out there, in the house I'd build for you. Perhaps he'll retire some day, and then he could come and live with us."

If she lived in Tiarei there could never be another time like today, this nightmarish day of watching and listening for Jonas's approach, of waiting, waiting — for nothing! With sudden honesty she saw that it was not dread of that encounter that had tormented her throughout the day, but hope — hope of seeing him. The admission shook her more than anything else had done.

She looked up and met Richard's eyes, desperately earnest and sincere behind his glasses. She had been unfair to him all along, she must make some amends. "You're wonderfully kind, Richard —"

"I'm not kind, Marianna," he said seriously. "I want you for my wife. Oh, my dear, I need you so much!"

Something melted within her at his words. To be wanted — to be needed — that could be more important than anything else. Love wasn't everything, she told herself defiantly. Her father had married a woman who had been one of four sent out by the London Missionary Society to Port Jackson, shortly after the turn of the century, for the express purpose of mating with the lonely missionaries on Tahiti. Henry Nott's wife had been among them, and her own mother had been the last of the four to be chosen. Surely it would have been wholly fortuitous under the circumstances if Nathaniel Moore had fallen romantically in love with his future wife; and although she knew that her father *had* loved her mother, that love must have come as a result of their shared life and hardships rather than as a wild and sentimental passion. It could be the same with her and Richard — Richard, whose flattering sympathy and interest in her filled a desperate need; Richard, who was offering her the steady security of his whole future . . .

"I don't want to hurry you, Marianna. I've told you that before. But it's hard to wait, with nothing to look forward to."

Oh, yes, she could understand that! "You needn't wait any longer, Richard," she said slowly.

He dropped her arm and stopped short, facing her. "D'you mean that? Do you know what you're saying, Marianna?"

"I think I do."

They had come to the end of the point, where the river flowed silently across the black sand into the whispering sea. Across the rosy, silvered water she could see the rim of the setting sun impaled for an instant on one of the dark peaks of Moorea.

"Look at me, Marianna."

The eager happiness of his expression struck at her heart. He was a good man, and he deserved to be happy. If she could make him feel like that, it would be cruel to deny him.

"Will you give me your answer now, Marianna? Will you be my wife?"

"Yes, Richard, I will."

Someone else seemed to have spoken the words, some disembodied voice, frighteningly like her own. With a sense of panic, she seemed to hear them repeating themselves about her in the quiet air, clamorous and irrevocable. "I will, I will, I *will* . . ."

Richard reached out and took both of her hands in his, holding them tightly. After a moment he pulled her toward him, and she felt his lips against her cheek, searching clumsily for her mouth. It shouldn't be like this! Instinctively, she drew away. "I'm sorry, Richard," she said in confusion, "it's just so soon, you know. I haven't — quite got used to the idea yet."

Behind his glasses his blue eyes were regarding her with gentle approval. "I understand, my dear," he said quietly. He dropped her hands and went on, his voice regaining its customary ringing confidence, "Believe me, I admire and respect you all the more for your attitude."

⁂

M R. PRITCHARD, WAITING IN THE ANTEROOM BEFORE THE CLOSED doors to Governor Bruat's reception room, pulled his watch from his pocket and for the second time cast a look of angry incredulity upon the hands beneath the broken crystal. He had been summoned — summoned, hah! — to meet the Governor at ten o'clock, and it was now twenty-five minutes past the hour. It was an outrage; the Governor was not so busy a man as that. No doubt he was sitting in there on one of Pomare's chairs, drinking wine with his officers.

He came to a halt by the window. Two French soldiers, in red coats, were parading rather languidly back and forth between the sentry boxes at each corner of the lawn. It must be good and hot for them in that sun, Mr. Pritchard thought with satisfaction.

Five minutes passed, and Mr. Pritchard's fingers began to drum against the sill. The Governor was wasting no time in displaying an augmented insolence now that the *Dublin* had left. Three days before, the *Basilisk*, British government ketch of two guns, had sailed into the harbor, bringing orders for the *Dublin* to go to Hawaii, pick up the admiral of the station, and proceed to Mexico to watch over what Mr. Pritchard regarded as some very negligible disturbances there. As if this were not bad enough, the *Basilisk* had been instructed by the admiral to salute the protectorate flag; but, since the protectorate no longer existed, no salute had been given. Commander Hunt of the *Basilisk* seemed a sensible fellow, Mr. Pritchard reflected; and once the dispatches he had sent in the *Dublin* with Captain Tucker reached England, there would be British ships of war aplenty at Tahiti — and not to salute the French flag, but to shoot holes through it!

An aide came to the door and beckoned Mr. Pritchard into the next room. He noted that the Governor did not rise to greet him, but motioned him to a chair at the opposite side of his desk.

"I prefer to stand, thank you," said Mr. Pritchard stiffly.

Governor Bruat shrugged. "Joost as you please," he said mildly. "Meestair Preetshard, perhaps you know for why I have ask you to come 'ere."

"I do not, sir," Mr. Pritchard said. "Captain Tucker told me before he left that you had refused my temporary reappointment as British Consul. I have no official position on the island."

"I was forced to refuse the appointment," the Governor said, "because it was well known that you were 'ostile to the protectorate, and to the French government. 'owever — " he held up his hand for silence as Pritchard started to speak. " 'owever we know that, position or no, you have more influence with the Queen and the nateeves than anyone else on the land." He smiled at Mr. Pritchard's angry face, and put the tips of his fingers together. "We are not fools altogether, you know."

Mr. Pritchard made him a slight, ironic bow.

"So," the Governor continued, "it has come to our ears that the nateeves are much discouraged since the *Dublin* leaves, and that they are determined to rise up against our aut'ority and throw it over." He stared sharply at Pritchard, and the smile had left his face. "For this, Meestair Preetshard, we hold you personally responsible."

"I protest, sir!" Pritchard said angrily. "In all fairness you must admit that I have done everything in my power to persuade the Queen and her people to submit to your laws, and to make no disturbance against them."

"Ah, yes," Bruat said, "and 'ow have you done this? By telling them to 'ave patience and wait until Britain can come to their aid. It is not so that we 'ope to keep the peace!"

"I have done what I can," Pritchard said, "and so have the English missionaries. It was they who sent warning of the threatened uprising, was it not?"

"Per'aps. But this is not enough. There are still t'ousands of men in the mountain camps, and there is much discontent everywhere. This you will take steps to change."

"Your belief that I can is very flattering," Pritchard said icily.

"I do not believe, I know it," the Governor said. "And I 'ave sent for you today to warn you that unless you cease to encourage this rebellion, and persuade to them submission, we will be forced to deport you from Tahiti."

"Deport me!" Pritchard cried. "That would mean war!"

"You think?" Bruat said. He got to his feet, and Pritchard saw that the interview was at an end. "As you know, I am a man of the military, and this business of the *diplomatique* does not go so well with me. When there is a *crise* of this kind, I must act. Good day, Meestair Preetshard."

The Queen sat at her writing desk, her head bowed, the quill pen waiting in her hand. Behind her Mr. Pritchard paced the length of the small room, going over in his mind what he had dictated. Greetings from Pomare to her chiefs and people . . . pray that you be orderly . . . obey the laws . . .

That should be meek and wishy-washy enough to satisfy them, he thought. When he spoke again his voice regained some of its old forcefulness. It took all of Pomare's concentration to keep her pen abreast of his words.

". . . Do not believe that Britain has cast us off; we still have one little ship left to watch over us, and two large vessels of war are expected here shortly. Wait patiently for the letter from England." Mr. Pritchard paused, and then went on more mildly. "Do these French people no wrong, neither enter into any quarrel with them. Be kind to them, and bear all with great patience; take me for your guide; wait patiently, and pray fervently, that we may be delivered from the great afflictions that have fallen upon us, the same as fell upon Hezekiah whom the Lord delivered . . ."

Pomare looked up at Mr. Pritchard as his voice stopped. "That's all," he said, rubbing his hands together. "I believe that will take care of everything."

꧁꧂

JONAS BENT OVER TO HELP MARIANNA UP THE LAST STEEP ROCK that led to the ledge above the waterfall, but she did not appear to see his outstretched hand. She pulled herself up to the shelf of rock beside him, and sat still for a moment to catch her breath. Below them, in the dark ravine, there was the white flash of an *itatae*'s wings. The mournful wail of its cry shrilled diminishingly across the silence.

Jonas looked about. "It's just as you described it — perfectly hidden." He glanced down at the pool, thirty feet below. "I've been down there before, but I never suspected this ledge existed. How did you find it?"

"Teaui showed it to me years ago, when I was just a child." She gestured toward the low caves that bored into the cliff of rock behind them. "It's an ancient burial place. The bones of some of her ancestors are hidden in those caves."

Jonas was wandering about, inspecting the ledge. "The only difficulty will be to get the forge up here. It's a stiff climb. I don't wonder that you wanted to send Teaui's boy to show me the way." He stopped for a moment, looking down at her. "I must apologize for insisting that you come yourself. I wanted to make sure that no one else would be in on our plans, but if I'd known how steep the climb was — "

"I didn't mind the climb," she said in a low voice.

"We can get the forge to the pool easily enough," he said, "and arrange some sort of block and tackle to hoist it up here. Fortunately, there's plenty of dead wood about for the fires."

"Yes." She picked up a stone and carried it over to a small cairn that stood in front of the cave. Jonas watched her as she placed it carefully on top of the pile.

"I think you have done that before," he said curiously.

She reached down and touched the warm stone with her fingers. "My brother and I used to come here sometimes to play when we were children. We always added a rock to the cairn."

He moved over to where she stood. "Did you? And what did you play? When I was a boy in America we used to play at being Indians."

She looked up with a little smile, and he realized, with a sudden shock of pleasure, that it was the first time she had looked at him directly in the two weeks since that night beside the bay when he had kissed her.

"Perhaps our games were rather alike," she said. "Henry and I used to pretend that we were Tahitians. We'd try to make bark cloth, and carve out wooden bowls, and kindle a fire without a lucifer."

"You must have had a good time."

"We did. But we were always regretting that we hadn't been born Tahitian instead of English, so that we could run wild and free like the other children."

When he saw that she intended saying no more it seemed important to him to try to keep this mood of simple friendliness, to break through the wall of reserve that she seemed determined to maintain between them. He found himself wanting to hear her speak, in that oddly blunted voice of hers. It was a tropical voice, he thought; warm and colorful, more suited to the native tongue than to English. But how chary she was of it lately — as if it gave her away too much, and must be kept strictly within the bounds of polite conventionalities.

"It's been more than a year since I've seen your brother," he said. "Where is he now?"

"The last word we had was from the Fiji Islands," she said. "He went there in the schooner, trading for pearl shell, and from there he intended to go west. We are always hoping, on every ship that comes in from Port Jackson, to get a letter from him."

Henry Moore probably doesn't waste his valuable time in writing to his father, Jonas thought. It was curious about the missionary children who had grown up in Tahiti: they might almost be divided into two distinct groups. There were the sanctimonious ones, like the Darling girls, in Punaavia; prim, narrow, ultra-English, sheltered from the Tahitians and raised to believe in their own superiority to the natives; and there were the wastrels, or the villains, like Captain Henry Moore, whose hypocritical piety did not mask his ruthless cupidity from even his own father. His most probable business in the Fijis was blackbirding or stealing from the natives at the point of a gun. Marianna was the single exception he could think of: she did not fall into either category, and yet what a delicate balance she had to maintain between the two worlds into which she had been born.

"You must miss your brother," he said tentatively.

"We played together a great deal when we were children," she said.

"I've often wondered about your childhood in Tahiti," he said. "It's a curious place in which to raise a young English lady."

"Perhaps. But I'd nothing to compare it with; it seemed perfectly natural to me."

"Which did you learn to speak first? English or Tahitian?"

"Both at once I suppose, since I don't even remember."

Anything more noncommittal than her replies would have amounted to positive rudeness. Baffled, he said, "I envy you your native land. But sometimes I wonder if you can really know how much beauty you were born to, since you can't compare it with any place else."

"I think I know," she said. She turned away. "Have you seen all that you wish to, Mr. Burkham? I must be getting back now."

It was only too obvious, as they scrambled down the steep rocks, that she was deliberate in refusing his proffered help, and his chagrin at her coolness mounted unreasonably. The impersonality between them on which she tacitly insisted was becoming absurd. Damn it all, he thought, I'm not going to eat her! He had been conciliatory, he had done everything in his power to please her. What more did she want?

In the past weeks they'd worked and planned together like two men, linked by circumstances in a daily intimacy. He knew her qualities by now — her courage and her common sense, her profound love for Tahiti and its people. He also knew that beneath her quiet and matter-of-fact exterior she was a woman first and a missionary's daughter second. In spite of her reserve her eyes betrayed her, and her mobile mouth . . .

When they reached the path beside the pool he put out his hand and caught her for a moment by the arm. "Let's rest a minute," he said. "It's so cool and pleasant here."

"As you like," she said.

His look strayed to the smooth, transparent water. "The pool is as dark and clear as a glass of wine," he said. "One day when I was here — a little the worse for brandy — I thought I saw a mermaid in it."

She glanced at him quickly, and he saw a look of startled surprise in her expressive eyes. The memory of her as he had seen her that day quickened in him, and with it the pity he had felt for her defenselessness. "I was mistaken of course," he said. "It was only an illusion, Miss Marianna."

"Brandy must foster illusions," she said constrainedly. "Shall we go, Mr. Burkham?"

All the rest of the way down the valley they did not exchange another word. Jonas found himself noting the grace of her walk; if she were dressed in a *pareu* and shawl, instead of those abominably ugly clothes, with her fair hair hanging down her back, one might take her for a blonde Tahitian. . . .

From the deep shadows of the woods they stepped abruptly onto the sandy dazzle of the Broom road, and almost bumped into the lanky, black-clad figure of Richard Johnson. He stared at them in astonishment.

"Marianna! Where have you been? I've been looking for you everywhere."

Before she could answer, Jonas said amiably, "Just taking a little stroll in the woods, Johnson. Very refreshing on a day like this."

"I had promised to show Mr. Burkham an old burial cave up

in the hills, Richard. He's writing a book on the ancient customs of the island, you know."

Damme, thought Jonas admiringly, how well the lady lies!

Johnson took Marianna's arm. "I am afraid you are fatigued, my dear. You should not walk so far in the heat of the afternoon."

"I'm not at all tired," she protested.

"Oh, but you are; I can see it," he said. The glint of his eyeglasses turned on Jonas. "You must take better care of my fiancée, Mr. Burkham."

"Your fiancée!" Jonas said incredulously. "You're going to be married?"

"I have the honor of telling you Miss Moore has promised me her hand."

Marianna and this stilted prig! It was impossible! With an effort, he erased the amazement from his voice. "I see. May I offer my congratulations?"

Marianna was gazing down at the ground, but Johnson smiled at him proudly. "Thank you, sir. I am a very fortunate man."

"You are indeed." He looked directly at Marianna, forcing up her gaze. "And when is the wedding?"

She raised her eyes, and he thought he saw a sort of appeal in them. "It's not — settled just yet," she said. "We have made no plans — I cannot leave my father at this time."

"I see," he said again. "I hope you will be very happy, Marianna."

"Thank you," she said, almost inaudibly.

"I've always thought marriage an enviable state," he said, "for other people." This time he was certain of it; under the light flick of his words, the appeal that he thought he had seen in her eyes turned to unmistakable misery. "Well," he said brightly, "I've heard it said that in circumstances like this, three is one too many. My regards." He grinned, made a sweeping bow, and swung off down the road.

Johnson's hand tightened on Marianna's arm. "Do not tell me you aren't tired, my dear. I can see it in your face."

100

It was a moment before she spoke. "Perhaps you are right," she said.

⣎⣎⣎⣎⣎⣎⣎⣎⣎

MR. TRUELOVE, HIS ROUND BODY NIMBLY BALANCED ON HIS SMALL feet, bustled down the ladderway from the warehouse above his store, and picked his way past barrels and boxes to the small packing-case-enclosed space at the rear that served him as an office. Horoi, chief of Tautira, was waiting for him there, magnificently swathed in scarlet tapa cloth which all but hid the faded pantaloons he wore beneath it.

He crushed Mr. Truelove's hand in his, and said, "Greetings, Terutove."

Mr. Truelove, genuinely pleased to see the old chief, suppressed his involuntary grimace of pain. "Welcome, Horoi! What brings you to town?"

Horoi's dark, regal features, faintly traced with the blue imprint of ancient tattoo marks, were set and somber.

"I have come to judge for myself whether the words I have heard are true. The Queen imprisoned on a ship, and the puny Farani kicking our people about like dogs!"

"The Queen is not imprisoned, Horoi," Mr. Truelove said. "The *Basilisk* is a British ship, and she went there of her own free will, to claim British protection."

"I know, I know," Horoi said, "but she dare not come ashore for fear the Farani will capture her, as they have some of her chiefs, and she cannot talk to her people. Is not that imprisonment, Terutove?"

"I suppose so," Mr. Truelove said wearily. "Things are very bad, Horoi. You are running a risk to be here yourself."

"I have done nothing — yet," Horoi said. He gave Mr. Truelove

101

a sly smile. "I came to town to get some tobacco and some candles. Write that down, Terutove."

Mr. Truelove reached for a piece of paper, and Horoi drew nearer, dropping his voice. "Can anyone hear our words, Terutove?"

"No."

"Good. This, then, is why I came. My people are already preparing for war, but they lack muskets and the money to buy them."

Mr. Truelove looked up quickly. "Yes?"

"Terutove," Horoi said, "do you remember the grove of *tamanu* trees that shades the *marae* of my ancestors in the valley behind my house?"

Did he remember that grove! There were trees in it that were six feet in diameter, with trunks that went up without a branch for forty feet. It was dizzying to think of the price timber like that would fetch in Valparaiso.

"You have asked me many times to sell those trees," Horoi was saying, "and I would not. I worshiped the old gods there for many years, and my ancestors before me. Those trees have seen the ancient ceremonies, and the bodies of sacrificed men have hung from their branches." His deep voice, trained to oratory, took on a note of awe. "Years ago, when Tati of Papara sold the trees of his *marae* to Morehu, it was seen that their cut trunks gushed with blood, and the waters of the river were reddened with it. But those trees were sold to the enemy of our people, Terutove, and mine shall be sold to save our people."

"You will sell me the trees, Horoi?"

"Yes. If you will promise me one thing. I must have muskets and powder in exchange. Nothing else will do."

Mr. Truelove's round face creased in anguish. "But I cannot promise, Horoi! The last firearms I had were sold — to Paofai, to equip his people in the mountain camp. And if the French knew that, they would arrest me."

102

"Then send your ship for more, Terutove."

"The French are searching our cargoes," Mr. Truelove said thoughtfully. "But it might be possible, I suppose, to hide the guns under the other cargo. I have long been wanting to go to Valparaiso, but these three months since the French seizure have been too unsettled. I can't leave my family if there is a chance of actual fighting . . ." He looked at Horoi, his eyes alight with sudden decision. "Here's what I'll do, Horoi. I'll go to the *Basilisk* and wait on Commander Hunt. If he thinks the prospects fair enough, I'll go to Valparaiso for your guns. But not a word of this to anyone."

Horoi held out his hand, and Mr. Truelove clasped it unflinchingly.

"Good, Terutove! And God go with you."

The *Basilisk,* anchored about a stone's throw from the beach opposite Mr. Pritchard's house, swayed gently against the almost imperceptible swell of the lagoon. On the quarter-deck Commander Hunt, his hands clasped thoughtfully behind his back, paced slowly up and down, considering Mr. Truelove's questions.

"How long would the voyage take you, Truelove?"

"I'd likely be home in five months or under. But there's been so much feeling since the French imprisoned the four chiefs that I was afraid to leave my family."

"I don't believe there'll be any uprising," Commander Hunt said. "I talked to Governor Bruat yesterday, and he has agreed to release the chiefs as soon as the people's excitement cools down."

"Why did they arrest them in the first place, then?"

"For creating unrest. For showing Pomare's letter to the people."

"But that letter urged them to obey the French!"

"They objected to the part about the British ships. I was afraid when I heard of it that Mr. Pritchard had gone too far."

103

"Poor Pritchard," Mr. Truelove said. "He gets the blame for everything."

Commander Hunt only shrugged.

"You think there'll be no fighting, then?"

"No."

"What about Pomare? Will the Governor let her come ashore?"

"Not unless she comes as a private individual, amenable to the laws of France. She won't do that, of course."

"She'd be a fool if she did," Mr. Truelove said hotly. "They'd capture her sure as you're standing there."

"I'm afraid so. We're still keeping a strict watch here on the ketch in case they should try to attack us."

"It makes me blood boil," Mr. Truelove said. "When I think of the state things are in I think I should get away from the island before I lose me temper and get clapped into irons meself."

"We should try to remember, Mr. Truelove," Commander Hunt said, "that for the time being we are in a French colony, and that none of the things Governor Bruat has done are at variance with the French code. I think that it will be best if you and Mr. Pritchard and the others who have interests here in Tahiti consider yourselves English subjects resident in France, and act accordingly."

"Hrrumph," said Mr. Truelove. "I'll go to Valparaiso, Commander, and save meself that trouble for a while. Could I pay me respects to the Queen before I go ashore?"

The neat, nautical severity of the *Basilisk's* main cabin was strangely overlaid with a motley confusion of domestic effects. When Mr. Truelove presented himself at the door he found the Queen seated cross-legged on a mat on the deck, with one of her maids beside her, sewing on what looked like a dress for the baby. Pomare Tane was sprawled on the couch, snoring loudly, and two of the children were playing with a spyglass at one of the portholes. From the deck above could be heard the voice of Ariiaue, the Prince Royal, shouting to the seamen.

The Queen greeted Mr. Truelove with pitiful eagerness, and motioned him to a seat beside her.

"It's good to see you, Terutove. And how are things ashore?"

"Not so good without you, Pomare. How is it for you? Are you tired of living aboard a ship?"

She made a little face. "Our feet ache for the land, Terutove, although the Commander and the others are very good to us. It is better than being imprisoned by the Farani. But the children get so restless!"

"I used to see them swimming about the ship. Don't they do that any more?"

"We dare not let them," she said sorrowfully. "The French have threatened to capture them."

"Oh, no!"

"Yes." She glanced over at the two beside the porthole, and lowered her voice. "Bruat has already asked the Commander if he would put Ariiaue ashore so that the child might reign in my place. And when the Commander refused, Bruat said, 'Pomare would still have three children with her — enough to keep any mother happy!'"

Mr. Truelove delivered a juicy Tahitian oath, and the Queen nodded approvingly. "Only yesterday," she went on, "Paraita, my fine Prime Minister, and the great Tati, of Papara, came to see me to try to persuade me to give up Ariiaue to Bruat. They quoted the Scriptures to persuade me that it was my Christian duty." She pointed dramatically. "There they stood, with their pockets full of French money, and talked to me of honor and duty!"

"Not all your chiefs are faithless, Pomare."

"No," she said. "Paraita, Tati, Hitoti — these are the worst. And Hitoti's own brother, Paofai, is one of the greatest of my defenders. Brother against brother — it is for that that my heart grieves the most."

"They are the ones whose fathers fought your father in the old days, Pomare," Mr. Truelove said gently. "You must not grieve over men who have kept alive a vengeance so long."

"Perhaps not," she said. "I have many friends. Your country will help me, Terutove — that is all I wait and pray for."

Mr. Truelove, who had his private opinions on that score, merely nodded, and got to his feet. Over on the couch, Pomare Tane awakened, cocked an eye at him, and said lazily, "Greetings, Terutove. Do you go ashore now?"

"Yes."

"Send me a case of rum, then, like a good fellow. This salty air produces a great thirst."

Mr. Truelove, with pursed lips, nodded his acquiescence, and turned back to the Queen. "Is there something I can send for your comfort, Madam?"

"Oh, yes," she said eagerly. "If I might have some *mahie*, and a bunch of *fei*, and some nuts from the *mape* trees. *Aué*, this British food is full of wind!"

WHEN MRS. PRITCHARD HEARD THE DOOR TO THE COAT CLOSET PULL open, she put down her sewing and went out into the hall. As she had feared, her husband was there, putting on an old black coat.

"George," she said reproachfully, "you're not going out in weather like this?"

Mr. Pritchard reached for his hat. "I must, Eliza," he said.

"But it's raining torrents! And you've already got a cold."

106

"It's nothing," he said, repressing a sneeze.

She sighed helplessly, and then asked, "Where are you going?"

"Aboard the *Cormorant*, to see Captain Gordon. The boat will be at the beach to fetch me at noon."

"Well, it's only quarter to twelve," she said. "There's no use in your standing for ten minutes in the rain waiting for it."

"I suppose not," he said lifelessly.

Mrs. Pritchard, regarding him sharply, felt a larger worry cut through the cloud of smaller ones that hung in a perpetual haze around her thoughts. "George, what is the matter? What's troubling you?"

He gave her a look of patient despair. What *wasn't* troubling him?

It was two weeks now since H.M. Steamship *Cormorant* had puffed into the bay, and the first wildly hopeful excitement of the natives had had plenty of time to be replaced by disappointment. Mr. Pritchard's own hopes had suffered a sad disillusionment. The British government had sent out the *Cormorant* only to appraise the situation in Tahiti, and Captain Gordon had neither the power nor the authority to do more.

The net result of this letdown had been to increase the murmurs of revolt among the Tahitians. Three days ago, Governor Bruat, alarmed by fresh rumors that the men in the mountain camps — now some 5000 strong — were about to attack the town, had proclaimed all to be rebels who did not immediately lay down their arms, and had sailed off in the French steamship *Phaeton* to Taravao Bay, to try to persuade or compel them to disperse.

He had left Captain d'Aubigny as Commandant Particular to govern in his absence, and d'Aubigny, wasting no time, had yesterday declared the port of Papeete to be in a state of siege, and under the rule of martial law. Bruat was bad enough, Mr. Pritchard thought, but d'Aubigny was far more dangerous — a fanatic

107

and a scoundrel. Some day he would go too far, and that, perhaps, was just what was needed to jostle the home government from their pusillanimous apathy . . .

His wife's voice, plaintively repeating her question, cut across Mr. Pritchard's unhappy reflections. "George, what *is* the matter?"

"You know as well as I do, Eliza," he said. "Under this martial law we're no better than prisoners in our own homes."

"Then how can you go out now?" she asked triumphantly.

"It's permitted until evening gunfire," he said. "Eliza, you'd better read that proclamation again. It's important to all of us."

He had turned, and was rummaging in the closet for his umbrella, but the long habit of didacticism kept his words going through his search. "All Europeans and natives must be in their houses at evening gunfire, and stay there until morning gunfire. They must not receive anyone during that time, and the police patrols can demand entrance or openly force and search any house if they suspect someone is there."

He emerged from the closet empty-handed, and regarded her balefully. "If they find anyone there, they can arrest the visitor and the entire household, destroy the house itself, and use the materials to make guardhouses for the French. Eliza, where in the world is my umbrella?"

She looked into the closet, found it instantly, and handed it to him. "We shall have to be more careful than ever," she said. "George, I do wish you wouldn't go out today."

"I must talk this over with Captain Gordon. Some of the new laws refer to the boats and crews of foreign ships."

"But you know how the French hate you, George. They watch your every move. It makes me dreadfully uneasy."

"I've done nothing that they can object to," he said irritably. "I cannot cower and hide from them; I must be firm and put my trust in the Lord." Struck with sudden pity for the distress that showed in her face, he pulled her toward him and kissed her

108

awkwardly on the forehead. "Good-by, my dear. I'll be back by teatime."

When the door closed behind him, she went into the sitting room and watched from the window as he crossed the road through the driving rain to the waterfront. As usual, there was a French sentry on guard near the front of the house, and another one on the beach, watching the *Basilisk*. Today a small group of soldiers, led by an officer, was patrolling the waterfront, but this was not unusual; in the past few days there had been sentries and patrols everywhere, and drums beating to quarters at the slightest rustle in the leaves.

Mr. Pritchard had reached the makeshift jetty, and she saw with dismay that his umbrella had blown inside out. Then, with a shock that sent her hand to her heart, she saw the French patrol confront him, and two of the soldiers, obeying the gesture of their officer, seizing him by the arms. Scarcely aware of what she was doing, she ran to the door, across the veranda, and down the steps into the rain. Abruptly her way was barred by the sentry.

"*Pardon, madame,*" he said, extending his arm.

Frantically, she screamed across his shoulder. "George! George! Where are they taking you?"

She could see her husband's face turned toward her as the soldiers started to march him away, and the sound of his voice came to her faintly, but the words were lost in the wind and the rain.

Mr. Pritchard, awakening from a brief, uncomfortable doze, saw gray and sodden daylight filtering through the musket loopholes, the only windows his prison afforded. He sat up a little straighter against the wooden wall, and with stiff fingers pulled his watch from the pocket of his sopping trousers, and held it to his ear. Still running, thank God! He peered intently at the hands, and saw that they stood at twenty-six minutes after five. That

109

meant that he had been in this hell-hole for something over sixteen hours, without food or water or dry clothing; and he wondered bleakly if the French were intending to starve him to death.

Now that he was fully awake his mind began dully to retrace the nightmarish details of his imprisonment. They had brought him through the rain directly here, to the blockhouse the French had built on the brow of the mountain above the town. He peered around through the gloom, painfully reorientating himself to his surroundings.

The room, which comprised the whole of the blockhouse, was about fifteen feet long by ten feet wide. A wooden ladder in one corner led to the trapdoor in the ceiling, ten feet above, through which he had been thrust so many hours before. Overhead was a roofed platform where the guards were stationed; he could hear them shuffling about, talking, rapping the butts of their muskets on the floor, and hawking and spitting so continually that some of the cracks in the ceiling were beginning to drip with their saliva.

The walls and ceiling of the room were of wood, adamantly solid; he had investigated them carefully the day before. There was only the bare ground for a floor, and the heavy rain, draining down the hill behind the blockhouse, had washed in under the walls so that it was ankle deep in mud. There was no furniture in the room, just a soggy mattress on the ground, and a damp and muddy blanket and bolster, which he had propped behind him as he rested, half sitting up, throughout the night.

One thought had sustained Mr. Pritchard throughout the hours of his imprisonment: If the French chose to make a martyr of him, well and good; they were doing a thoroughly fine business of it. But they must have forgotten that Britain would not stand by and see her representatives treated thus! To be sure, technically he was no longer British Consul to Tahiti, but when the people at home were informed of this outrage against one of their citizens,

110

their anger would scarcely be diverted by so picayune a point. Perhaps he would not survive to enjoy the sight of the British Navy sailing vengefully into Papeete Bay, but that possibility, aside from the consideration of what it would mean to Eliza and the children, scarcely troubled him. Justice, justice, justice, whatever the cost!

He got painfully to his feet, shivering uncontrollably, and was racked by a sudden spasm of coughing. All at once the fact of his physical misery overwhelmed him, and he forgot his resolute martyrdom. Briefly, he bowed his head for an incoherent prayer, and then climbed determinedly up the ladder in the corner and rapped against the trapdoor.

He could tell by the instant silencing of their movements that the guards had heard him. "I demand that you take me to see Captain d'Aubigny," he said loudly.

There was silence, then someone giggled and a voice said, "No speek Angleesh."

Desperately, Mr. Pritchard raised his voice. "I go — see Governor! You tell my wife where I am!"

Someone said, "*Ah, taisez-vous!*" and again there was silence.

Frantically, Mr. Pritchard turned over in his mind the French phrases that he knew — *Bon jour, Parlez-vous anglais?* — these would scarcely do. Perhaps they had picked up a little Tahitian in their months on the island. . . .

"I must have something to eat and drink," he said.

A voice, pitched to falsetto, answered him in deplorable Tahitian. "Will you sleep with me?"

Outraged, Mr. Pritchard started down the ladder, and was nearly at the bottom when he heard the trapdoor cautiously opened. He looked up and saw the barrel of a musket pointed down at him, and then a man's head appeared in the opening. "*Regardez*," the soldier said, "*quelque chose à manger.*" He beckoned Mr. Pritchard up the ladder, and cautiously handed him a small tray on

111

which were two slices of bread, a couple of bananas, and a thick porcelain mug of water. Mr. Pritchard grasped it, and the trapdoor snapped shut above his head.

Gingerly, he carried the tray down the ladder and over to one of the loopholes for light. On top of the bread there was an envelope, sealed with the official insignia. With trembling hands he put the tray on the driest part of the mattress and tore open the envelope.

The document it held was printed in the form of a proclamation, with Tahitian and English translations appended. Mr. Pritchard, shaking with rage, read it through twice.

French Establishments in the Ocean.

A French sentinel was attacked in the night of the 2nd to 3rd March. In reprisal, I have caused to be seized one Pritchard, the only daily mover and instigator of the disturbances of the natives.

His property shall be answerable for all damages occasioned to our establishments by the insurgents; and, if French blood is spilt, every drop shall fall back upon his head.

The Commandant-particular of the Society Islands,

(*Signed*)   d'Aubigny.

Papeete, 3rd March, 1844.

Angrily, Mr. Pritchard balled up the paper in his hand, and threw it with all his force across the room. A tissue of lies! If a French sentinel had been attacked, this was the first he had heard of it; and as for his being the instigator of disturbances among the natives, it was the baldest trumpery. He had known all along how hopeless resistance would be without British support, and he had spent his days in urging them to keep the peace. He hurried across the room, retrieved the paper from the mud, and carried it back to the light. March 3rd, it was dated. That was yesterday, the day of his arrest, and it seemed most improbable that a document of this sort could be prepared and printed be-

112

tween noontime and night of the same day. He narrowed his lips, considering. So far as he knew, there was no proof that there had been any attack on a sentinel at all, only d'Aubigny's word. He was capable of anything, that man!

And since that was the case, only God in His wisdom could say how long he might be kept imprisoned here in this filthy dungeon. Mr. Pritchard went over to the mattress and sat down heavily against the wall. He picked up a piece of the bread and began to munch on it, his unseeing eyes fixed on the gray vista of the hours that stretched before him.

"It's WONDERFUL OF YOU TO COME AND STAY WITH ME, MARIANNA," Mrs. Pritchard said again. "I don't know what I'd do without you. This waiting — "

"I know," Marianna said. "Waiting is the worst of all."

"Four days," Mrs. Pritchard said. "Four days! And George so ill with the fever and dysentery in that awful place! Where *is* the doctor?"

"He'll be here soon," Marianna said soothingly.

"They won't let the doctor see him alone, you know, and they won't even allow him to go down into the room where he stays." Her faded blue eyes filled with the tears that never seemed far below their surface. "Poor Mr. Pritchard has to climb a ladder to let the doctor feel his pulse, and even that exertion induces a tremor and excitement."

"And Dr. Ferguson," Marianna said hesitantly, "has he been — all right?"

"Bless you, my dear, he hasn't taken any spirits these last three days! Isn't it wonderful? The Lord's will! People are very kind, aren't they?" Her hands fluttered in a helpless gesture. "Some people, that is. To think of their taking George away like this! Isn't it unbelievable, Marianna, that such a thing could happen in our day and age?"

"Preposterous!"

"Captain Gordon, of the *Cormorant*, has written twice to Captain d'Aubigny, demanding my husband's release. Both times he replied that he is being held legally, under the code of France. Captain Gordon says that if Mr. Pritchard were still British Consul they wouldn't dare to imprison him, but since he resigned his official position, there's nothing to be done."

"They'll find some way, I know they will."

"Oh, yes, my dear. The Lord will watch over us. But I'm frightened, Marianna! The natives are so aroused!" Her birdlike voice dropped to a piteous whisper. "They've threatened to burn the town if he isn't released. And if they commit a single act of violence, it will all fall back on Mr. Pritchard's head!"

Poor woman, how many times had she said it before? Marianna put an arm around her and pulled her close. "Don't worry about it, you mustn't worry about it. The people understand that now; their chiefs have told them. No one would think of doing anything that could hurt Mr. Pritchard."

A gruff voice at the door said, "Presume I can come in out of the r-rrain!"

Mrs. Pritchard jumped up. "Oh, Dr. Ferguson, you're here at last!"

The doctor, a short, solid man, stumped heavily across the room, leaving a footprint of mud at every step, and sank into the chair Marianna pulled forward for him. "Beastly weather," he said. "Beastly!" His face, ordinarily flushed and ruddy, had a sallow, liverish look today; there were lines around his mouth, and his hand shook violently as he raised a handkerchief to mop his forehead.

114

"How is he, Doctor?" Mrs. Pritchard asked breathlessly.

He turned his baleful stare full upon her. "Not well, ma'am."

Marianna moved closer to Mrs. Pritchard, and took one of the agitated hands in her own firm clasp.

"His fever is high, and his pulse unstable." He cleared his throat loudly, and spat into his handkerchief. "On the way into town I encountered d'Aubigny, and told him if your husband were not released very soon he could not survive."

Mrs. Pritchard's fingers clutched like a vise around Marianna's hand. "What did he say?"

"As nearly as I could make out his abominable English," the doctor said, puffing, "he refused. But he will grraciously permit me to take medicines tomorrow, and to go down the ladder to examine him." His Scotch *r*'s rolled with the heavy sarcasm of his voice.

"Was Mr. Pritchard able to talk to you at all, Doctor?" Marianna asked.

"With the guards there, he could only answer my questions about his condition. However, he started to tell me one thing, in Tahitian, which seemed to be important to him. They wouldn't let him finish the sentence."

Mrs. Pritchard leaned forward. "Doctor, what was it?"

"Something about the third drawer in his desk. That was all they let him say."

"Oh!" She ran out of the room, and in a moment was back, carrying a drawer full of papers. "Here it is!" With trembling fingers, she began to sort through the papers. "Here are some bills of lading . . . some letters from Lord Aberdeen . . . this is his certificate of ordination . . . some letters from his mother (she's dead now) . . . his appointment as British Consul — "

"Let me see that," Dr. Ferguson said.

"Certainly, sir."

She went on with her rummaging while he was reading it, and

115

only stopped at his exclamation of surprise. "Look here! This document appoints Pritchard Consul to the Friendly Islands as well as to Tahiti! Did you know about this, ma'am?"

"Why, yes," Mrs. Pritchard said vaguely. "I had forgot — it was several years ago, and it was only some sort of legal formality. Some of our people were down there trading for sandalwood, and they wanted advice — "

"Was this appointment ever recalled or canceled?"

"No, sir, I'm sure it wasn't."

"And Mr. Pritchard did not resign it?"

"No, he didn't. He only resigned in Tahiti because it was no longer a French protectorate — "

Dr. Ferguson slapped his heavy hand against the arm of his chair. "We may be able to scare a little sense into those Frrenchmen with this! When Bruat finds out that Pritchard is still an official representative of the British government, he won't dare hold him any longer. Let me take this paper, ma'am."

"Of course," Mrs. Pritchard said tremulously. She looked at Marianna, her pale face suddenly aglow. "The Lord's hand is in this."

The doctor heaved himself to his feet. "And the hand — none too steady, ma'am — of one Bruce Ferguson, M.D."

THE PRINCE OF PEACE, NATHANIEL MOORE THOUGHT TIREDLY. HOW would He counsel now? What would He tell these hapless people, struggling against a force too big for them to understand? Three days ago, the first shot had been fired — fired by the Tahitians on some French soldiers, out in Taravaó. Now there was bound to be retaliation. What should they do? Meekly accept their punishment? Meekly give up their land?

You could scarcely blame the Tahitians for that incident in Taravao. French soldiers, sent out in the corvette *L'Ambuscade*,

116

to build a fort across the narrow isthmus, had tried to force some women back to the ship with them. Hearing their cries, their men had gone to the rescue, and in the fighting that followed, three or four Frenchmen had been killed. Should they have done nothing, those Tahitians; should they have let their wives and sweethearts be debauched without a protest? Surely that would have been asking too much, and yet those shots in Taravao would reap a deadly harvest.

"Papa," Marianna said, "do have another cup of tea."

"No more, thank you, my dear."

"You look so tired," she said. "It worries me. Have you been doing too much?"

"No," he said ruefully. "Not enough. I've just been — thinking."

"I know. I can't think of anything else. It's the real beginning, isn't it?"

"The beginning of the end," he said.

"Don't say that, Papa! It sounds so — hopeless."

"Where is there hope, when men are killing men?" he said. "I'm too old to find a source of hope in that. I've seen it happen before, and it was always useless."

"I wish we knew what they were going to do now," she said restlessly. "It seems so ominously quiet."

"I saw Farenui by the church," he said. "He tells me that young Burkham rode to town today. Perhaps he'll be back with some news before long. He was very good about keeping me abreast of things while you were away."

"Oh. Was he?" Her fingers traced an absent pattern across the surface of the table.

"It's good to have you home again, my dear," her father said.

She looked up. "It's good to be back. I didn't want to stay nearly so long, but Mrs. Pritchard seemed to want me. It was hard to get away."

"Poor woman," he said. "Left all alone, with nine children to look after."

117

Curious, he thought, that the actual outbreak of hostilities should come after Pritchard had left the island. At least no one could say that George Pritchard had been the instigator in this particular affair. After five days in prison, the French had secretly transferred Pritchard to one of their ships, and then, after she was safely outside the reef, they had put him aboard the British ship *Cormorant*, bound for England. No one had been allowed to see him; even Mrs. Pritchard had been permitted only a brief farewell, after he was safely aboard the *Cormorant*.

"She's like a mother hen," Marianna was saying, "clucking and worrying over her brood. I wanted to bring Georgie back to Point Venus with me, but she couldn't bear to part with even one chick."

"I don't suppose your young man could come to town while you were there?"

"My young man?"

"Richard Johnson," he said patiently.

"Oh," she said, flushing. "No. I — it was too far. I haven't seen him."

"Have you sent word to him that you're back home?"

"Well, no. Not yet. There's been so much to do." Her voice trailed vaguely away on the words, and he looked at her sharply.

"Marianna, are you sure you are quite happy about — "

"Listen, Papa," she said hastily, "I think Mr. Burkham is coming now. Don't you hear a horse coming along the lane?"

"You have very sharp ears, my dear," he said dryly.

She must have been listening very intently to have heard that sound so soon. It was another minute or two before horse and rider appeared at the clearing, beyond the tangled riot of guava trees that overran the land on either side of the lane. Nathaniel went to the top of the steps as Jonas dismounted, tied his horse to the fence, and came toward them across the lawn.

"Good of you to come over, Jonas."

"I can't stay but a moment," Jonas said. He came up onto the

118

veranda and stood leaning against the railing, his tanned face framed darkly against the fading light of the sky. "Miss Marianna. Glad to see you back."

"Thank you," she said, almost inaudibly.

"You look as if you brought us bad news, boy."

"I have, sir. Very bad. The *Phaeton* went out at dawn this morning, on a punitive excursion around the island. Apparently she's been instructed to fire on every hut along the way."

"To fire! But why?"

"In revenge for the death of those French soldiers out in Taravao. Sporting little idea, isn't it?"

"But it's the innocent who'll suffer!" Nathaniel Moore said.

Jonas nodded. "They've bagged a few already. One old woman in Faaa was killed, and two children in Punaavia. Quite a few others have been maimed. Reports have been trickling back from the districts all day."

"It's butchery!"

"Yes. But it needn't be so bad from now on. Word has spread ahead of the ship, and the people are fleeing up into the valleys until she passes by."

"Where is she now, d'you think?"

"About Tautira, I imagine. She'll probably be paying her call on Matavai about eleven or twelve tomorrow morning."

"What's to be done?"

"I've talked to Taua," Jonas said, "and he'll see that everyone in the district is notified to go up into the Ahonu valley tomorrow morning. Doubtless it'll be quite a picnic. Will you get word to your people here on the point, and come up in the morning?"

"Of course."

"Good. I'll be going along, then."

"Mr. Burkham," Marianna said, "you must be tired from your ride. Won't you take a cup of tea?"

"Your national panacea? No; thanks very much." He pushed himself away from the railing. "I've still got to go and warn the Nichollses. Sort of a latter-day Paul Revere, y'know. As a matter of fact, I guess you wouldn't know."

"One if by land and two if by sea," she said unexpectedly. "I make it a rule to keep informed of enemy exploits."

He gave her a wry smile. "It isn't the British who are coming this time, worse luck. And it doesn't look as if they will."

Nathaniel Moore was regarding them, a troubled look in his gentle eyes. "My boy, do you realize that the people on the ship are going to see the fort Taua's been building at Mahina? That raw earth around the breastworks and entrenchments will be plainly visible from the sea."

Jonas shrugged. "They're bound to know about it sometime, sir. And why not? No use pretending this isn't war."

"I suppose not," Nathaniel Moore said slowly. "I suppose not."

After Jonas had gone, Marianna went into the house, and he sat for a long time, watching the silver colors of twilight spread across the waters of the bay. The warm air was quiet; the only sounds were the lazy mumble of surf along the reef, and nearby the gentle swish of a palm-leaf broom as Poriri swept *purau* blossoms from the grass. Even the tall, frail shiver of the banana leaves was stilled in the evening calm. God creates tranquillity, Nathaniel thought; but man devises guns.

⁂

ANTHONY NICHOLLS LAY SPRAWLED IN THE BIG CHAIR, HIS HEAD cocked drunkenly forward on his chest, his feet stretched out before him. Lily, dressed in a riding habit, stood over him, kicking furiously at his legs.

"Wake up, Anthony! For the love of God, wake *up!*"

120

She seized him by the shoulders and shook him with all her strength. His head lolled back and forth on his neck, and his red jowls shuddered flabbily, but still he did not open his eyes. Lily let go of him, and his head fell forward on his chest again.

"You drunken fool!" she said contemptuously. "Stay here and be killed, then!"

She went over to the door and stood there for a moment, listening. Above the restless clash of the palm fronds in the wind, she heard the sound again, a dull, heavy boom to the east. The *Phaeton* must be nearing Mahina by now, and once it did, escape from its guns up into the valley of Ahonu would be completely cut off. Jonas Burkham had told them, the evening before, that there would be plenty of time in the morning to make their way up to the valley, but now, it appeared, it was too late. Disturbed and frightened, Lily had taken a heavy sleeping draught before she went to bed, and Anthony, obviously, had spent the night bolstering his courage with brandy. Angrily, she kicked aside the empty bottle beside his chair. The servants had already fled, and there had been no one to awaken her in time. . . .

She clenched her small fists, glaring down at Anthony, then went into her bedroom, came back with a pitcher, and flung the water into his face. He coughed once, stirred, and resumed his snoring. Lily smashed the pitcher against the floor, and began slapping at his face. Anthony grunted and threw out his arm in an unconscious gesture of defense. She stood back from him, sobbing.

If only she knew where to go, she'd leave him to his fate! Where was Jonas? Why did he leave her alone here to die? He had forgotten her, no doubt, in helping his precious natives. She could go to the devil as far as he was concerned!

Through her sobs she heard another *boom* of the guns, louder this time, and nearer. In a panic she turned, started for the door, and almost collided with Jonas. She threw her arms around him and buried her face against his throat.

121

"Oh, Jonas, you came!"

He pushed her away rudely, and she looked up to see Marianna Moore just behind him, her fair hair disheveled by the wind, her gray eyes dark as a patch of stormy sky in the pallor of her face.

"Lily, for Christ's sake," Jonas said, "why didn't you come to Ahonu? Where's Anthony?"

She gestured toward the chair. "There," she said, "too drunk to move." Jonas stepped forward to look at him, and Lily moved over beside him. "I couldn't leave him to die alone," she said plaintively, and unconsciously her hands strayed to her hair.

Bending down, Jonas tried to lift Anthony from the chair, then straightened. "I can't budge him," he said. "He must weigh fifteen stone."

"What are we going to do?" Lily asked fearfully.

Jonas ignored her, looking over at Marianna. "I told you not to come, Marianna! Now look at the fix you're in."

"There was nothing else to do," she said.

Jonas stared down at Anthony. "I'll stay here with Nicholls," he said, "and you take Lily back with you."

"There isn't time," Marianna said. "You know there isn't time."

"No," he said. "Well then, go along the road and up One Tree Hill. You'll be all right up there."

"You forget the soldiers."

Lily started. "Soldiers! What soldiers?"

"French soldiers," Jonas said impatiently. "Marching along the shore, under the protection of the steamer's guns. They're firing some of the houses and plantations along the way."

"They'll burn us out of the house!" Lily cried.

"I don't think so," Jonas said. "It's the natives they're after, not you Britishers." .

"They've spared the mission stations along the way," Marianna said. "It's probably a matter of policy with them." She looked at Jonas thoughtfully. "I think perhaps we're best off here, Mr. Burk-

122

ham. They'll probably not fire across the point because of the mission, and I doubt if the ship will come into the bay for fear of running aground on the Dolphin Shoal. We'd be out of range of the guns here in that case, wouldn't we?"

He considered it a moment. "Yes, we would, I suppose. It's as good a plan as any." What a woman, he thought irritatedly; she'd probably preserve that glacial formality if we were meeting the end of the world together.

"Since we're here," he said, "we may as well consider it a morning call, and make ourselves more comfortable. You're a shocking bad hostess, Lily. You haven't even offered us a chair."

Lily sank down on the sofa and began to cry, mopping at her eyes with a small lace handkerchief. When Marianna came over to take her hand, she pushed her petulantly away, and turned to Jonas. "Don't talk of courtesy," she cried. "What do you know of it, you — you beachcomber! You can be hateful even when I may be about to die!"

"If you are going to die, Lily," Jonas said, "it is through your own bad management. And I, like an ass, came over to die with you — and so did Marianna. Can courtesy go much further?"

"I hate you!" she said, sobbing. "I hate you, I hate you!"

Marianna turned away from them and went over to the window, her lips compressed, her eyes darker than before. There was something in their bickering that showed more nakedly than any caress the extent of their intimacy.

"Your nerves are shattered, Lily," Jonas said. He went over to a cupboard in the wall, poured out a glass of brandy and handed it to her. "Drink it," he said. "But only this one, mind you."

He helped her to steady the glass at her lips. After a few moments she stopped crying, and began furtively to try to restore her appearance. "You used to yearn for adventure, Lily," Jonas said. "Now that you have it, shouldn't you give it a better welcome?"

Two reports from the *Phaeton's* guns cracked through the air

123

so loudly that the china figurines in Lily's secretary rattled on their shelves. Lily clutched her glass.

"They must be at Mahina," Jonas said. "Opposite the fort. I suppose they've seen it by now."

Marianna turned her head toward him. "Was it your idea to plant Pomare's colors and the British flag above the fort where the French could see them?"

"No, it was Taua's." He grinned. "I only brought the banners back to him from town."

"How very helpful!" she said.

"Damn it all, Marianna, there's bound to be fighting! And it might as well be at Mahina, where we are at least prepared for a battle."

"They'll be back for it," she said. "Your invitation was too cordial to resist."

Lily drank off the rest of her brandy and sat up a little straighter. "How soon will the ship be around the point?"

"In just a few minutes, I should think."

"Oh," she said. She twirled the empty glass in her fingers, and then, seeing that Jonas had taken the bottle out of her reach, put it down on the table. "Is Anthony — awake?"

"No," Jonas said.

Lily looked over at Marianna. "Don't stay by that window, Marianna. It's too dangerous!"

"Grapeshot would hardly respect these walls, Lily," Jonas said.

Lily's hands fluttered. "I'm sorry I behaved the way I did just now, Marianna," she said. "I'm grateful for your coming."

"Charming," Jonas said. "Let's all kiss and be friends."

For a few minutes no one spoke. The bursts of firing had died away, and the only sound in the room was an occasional muffled snore from Anthony Nicholls.

"There's the ship!" Marianna said. "Just coming around the point."

124

Jonas went over to the window and stood beside her. "It looks as if you were right. They're holding their fire."

Marianna moved to the other window. Behind them, Lily said tremulously, "How can you watch it so coolly? They might start firing any second!"

"They're staying outside the shoals, Lily. You needn't worry any more."

"Here come the troops," Jonas said.

Lily ran to look. "Jonas! There must be hundreds of them! They'll come here, I know they will, and ransack the house — "

"Don't be silly!" Jonas said sharply. He stared out at them, his fingers drumming against the sill, his heavy eyebrows drawn together in a scowl.

"They march as if they were exhausted," Marianna said.

"Probably are." He leaned forward, his eyes narrowing. "In the name of God, what do they think they're doing!"

The soldiers had stopped to gather up some dried coconut fronds, and were kindling them into a torch.

"They're going to burn us out of here," Lily cried. "Like rats!" She began to sob, resting her forehead like a child against the windowpane.

Marianna went over to her, putting her arm around Lily's shoulder. "Don't be frightened, Lily. Look! It's the cane field they're burning."

The soldiers had put their torches to the jungle of sugar cane that grew down to the road, and, as she spoke, the flames leaped up, fanned by the heavy wind, and dug into its thick ranks.

"They've figured the wind exactly," Jonas said. "Thank God Anthony left that strip of lawn between here and the field! At least the house is safe."

Above the wind they could hear the sharp crackling of the flames, and the acrid smoke began to twist through the cracks around the door and windows. Dimly, beyond the white cloud of

125

smoke, they could see that the soldiers had formed ranks again and were marching away in the direction of One Tree Hill.

Anthony Nicholls stirred in his chair, grunting a cough. "Bring me a drink, Lily," he said thickly.

Nathaniel Moore walked slowly, for he was very tired. Near the river, and about three hundred yards short of the end of Point Venus, he halted. It took a few minutes' search in the tall grasses to find what he was looking for, but at last he discovered it — a squared piece of basaltic stone. He sat down upon it with a little sigh. The stone had formed the entrance step to the first church built on Tahiti by the missionaries, and it held for him a thousand reminders of the old days.

He had come not to bring those memories back; rather he had been drawn here because they gathered so thickly about him that he could think of little else. This morning at Papaoa he had officiated at the funeral of his old friend Henry Nott, and now that that undaunted spirit lay in its final rest, there was time for him to retreat into the beckoning past. Henry still lived, here; he could almost imagine that he saw the reflection of his sturdy, again-youthful figure in the polished stillness of the river.

Henry Nott, with his childlike trust in Jesus Christ, his unquenchable belief in the Gospel as the only remedy for the sins and sorrows of men, his common sense, his tenacity, his tireless endeavor in the work that he had chosen, had been the soul and spirit of those early days. If Henry had ever suffered a moment's doubt, no one had known of it. Nathaniel laid the palms of his hands against the sun-warmed stone, and remembered a morning, forty years ago or more, that he had sat just here, homesick

126

and discouraged, and had told Henry of his feeling of defeat. Henry had quoted to him gently, "How shall they believe in him of whom they have not heard? And how shall they hear without a preacher? And how shall they preach, except they be sent?"

He had lived his life in answer to that question. And near its close, Henry, the bricklayer, with his inspired (there was no other word for it) understanding of the Tahitian language, had stood before his Queen, Victoria, and presented to her the enduring monument to his life and work, the Bible in Tahitian. He had permitted nothing to deter him in that work, not his own sickness in the later years, not any circumstance however distasteful. Nathaniel remembered how Henry used to work with King Pomare, father of the present Queen, while the King reclined on a couch across the room with his male favorite. Henry would bend his eyes to his book to avoid seeing what passed between them, but he could not shut out the sound of their words from his ears, and he would emerge from those sessions exhausted with spiritual shock, but with a few more pages of the Gospel clutched triumphantly in his hands.

Nathaniel sat so quietly that a small lizard ran up on the stone beside him, chattered for a moment, and was gone with a flick of its tail, insouciant and unafraid. With Henry's death there was none left of the missionaries who had come to Tahiti in the *Duff;* and of the group who had arrived four years later, on the *Royal Admiral,* there were only himself and John Davies, whose mission was in Papara, on the other side of the island. He scarcely saw John Davies any more; the old man had become too feeble to travel very often, and stayed in Papara, buried in his books and scholarly pursuits.

They had all lived here together, in a house that had been built by Brother Bicknell and Henry Nott. He remembered the anxiety and the uncertainty of those early days, when they were totally dependent on the bounty of the natives for their daily food; and

127

the times of greatest stress, when chief fought chief in battles that sometimes raged around their very door. The church they had built, on whose doorstep he now sat, had been torn down by the missionaries themselves when they feared that it might make an ambush for the rebel natives who were fighting King Pomare. And the huge garden just beyond, which they had planted with seeds brought from Port Jackson and tended with such loving care, had been plundered and burned in one of the wars.

Anthony Nicholls's burned field of sugar cane came to his mind. That meant a financial loss to Nicholls, no doubt, but not the loss of all that gave him subsistence. The thought reminded him of the visit he and David Darling had made to Governor Bruat a week ago to protest the useless cruelty of the *Phaeton's* punitive trip around the island. The Governor had told them that it was done merely to intimidate the natives; they were like dogs, he had said; give them a beating and they will lie down at your feet. How little the Governor knew of the people he had come to subjugate! But he would learn — he would learn.

He should have known them in the early days, when all aspects of their living, ruled by tradition and custom, took on a dignity and beauty that had impressed him even as he tried to substitute Christian tenets for their pagan ones. It wasn't Christianization that had destroyed the timeless pattern of their lives, he thought; it was the greedy fingers of Western civilization reaching in to tamper with all the things that they had held good. They were a nation of individuals, the Tahitians, yet Bruat would learn how well they could unite in a common hatred. . . .

It seemed to him that it had not taken long for this island to fill in all his horizons, so that it became his only world. And yet he could remember still the daily anguish of waiting, during the first five years, for the word from home that never came. For five years they had no letters, no supplies from the outside; their only contact with civilization had been an occasional whaler or trading schooner that put in to pick up fresh foods. And when, at the

128

end of five years, someone sent out a chartered schooner from Port Jackson with the supplies and mail that had accumulated for them there, the news had seemed old and remote as history, and the supplies were nearly all ruined with time and sea water.

There had been years when he had possessed only one pair of shoes, which were carefully preserved to wear on the occasion of a ship's arrival. He and Henry Nott had made a preaching tour of the island, walking barefoot all the way, and he could hear Henry's voice now, as they splashed through the streams that crossed their path, pointing out cheerfully to him the convenience of this circumstance. He remembered the hospitality of the people they had stayed with along the way, and their heartbreaking indifference to the Word that he and Henry brought them.

That was at a time when the diseases introduced by foreign ships were ravaging them most terribly. The people, dying in bitterness, said that the British and their foreign God had sent them the venereal diseases, the intermittent fever, the crooked backs and consumption; and sometimes when he and Henry had invited them to hear their word, they had replied derisively, "Let us go and listen, we shall be cured of all our diseases today."

Nathaniel bent his head, and the heavy gold of the afternoon sunlight splashed across his silver hair. The memory of Teina, the beautiful, slender Tahitian girl whom he had loved, returned to him, and with it the sharp pang that all the years had not succeeded in dulling. The missionaries forbade any marriage to a heathen, and when, sick with longing and anguish, he had refused to live with her, she had cried and clung to him like a child. Six months later she gave herself to a sailor from a passing whaler, and within a year she was dead of the venereal disease.

He had been torn then with a terrible doubt, and at times it still tormented him. His faith had never been so firm and dauntless as Henry's. Sometimes it had seemed to deteriorate merely into a blind and pagan thankfulness to a God who had created so much that was marvelous and beautiful. Still, it had sustained him all

129

these years, and he had done the best with it that he knew how.

His had been an arduous and difficult life, yet a good one, and in many ways rewarding. He felt now as if he held it all in his hands, to look back upon, as he might look back through a book he had been reading when he neared the end of the story. Well, the final page was not far away, and if it weren't for Marianna, he would turn it without regret. He shouldn't worry about her, he supposed; Johnson was a good and pious young man, and with him she would share the work that she was best fitted to do. Still, he could not help but wish that Johnson had more of the qualities of Jonas Burkham — Jonas whom he loved as a son, in spite of his heretical philosophy and his mode of life.

He raised his head and saw that the lengthening shadows were black across the river, although through the trees he could still see the blue sparkle of the sea. He drew in his breath sharply. Tahiti! To him the island, and all that surrounded it, was pervaded by some quality that was stronger than the mere fact of its physical perfection. It was impossible to define that quality, but it was there, lying deep in the valleys that creased the mountains; in the cool, flat shine of the streams; in the haze that veiled the peaks of Moorea across the channel. It was something that gave the land a strange and fugitive meaning, as if each place had been beautiful so many times, under so many shifts of sun and rain and stars, that it was suffused with the essence of all its past.

He laid his hands together in the attitude of prayer; then, slowly, he got to his feet and started home.

JONAS WENT BACK TO HIS POSITION AT THE REARMOST OF THE TWO trenches that cut across the plain at Mahina, and climbed up on the sand breastwork. From where he stood the flat land, cleared of its trees, sloped almost imperceptibly to the black sand beach. Just beyond the pass in the reef the French steamship *Phaeton*, towing the big sixty-gun frigate *Uranie*, was working cautiously in to shore. In the clear dazzle of midday he could plainly see the frigate's heavy guns, run out for action. In a few more minutes she and the *Phaeton* would be broadside to the land, and close enough to begin their fire.

It seemed incredible that this peaceful scene, the curved green land and shiny, sea-tongued beach, would soon be shaken with battle. Around him he could hear the low voices of the Tahitians talking together, even an occasional laugh. Their handsome, curiously sophisticated faces showed a look of fiercely expectant joy, as if they yearned for what was to come.

Thank God, all was in readiness! The *Uranie* and the *Phaeton*, with about six hundred troops and Governor Bruat on board, had set out for Mahina five days before, but a heavy southeast gale had sprung up, forcing the *Phaeton* to cast off her tow. In the time it had taken the two ships to work up they had had ample warning to prepare for the attack. Taua had nearly three hundred men in the field, two hundred and thirty-odd equipped with muskets; the rest with spears and clubs. The supply of ammunition was not large, but adequate; the greatest deficiency was powder. The trenches were well made, and sufficiently far back from the sea to be out of range of the ships' guns.

Behind the plain to the south was a heavily wooded valley, thrusting to the mountains; if the Tahitians were forced into a retreat the French would never dare to follow them there. To the west were the conical hills, smothered in bush, that lay between Mahina and Matavai. That was the greatest weakness of their position, Jonas thought; if the French could escalade those hills they could command the whole length of the trenches with their fire. He had begged Taua to prepare against this, but Taua had insisted that no one but a Tahitian, well acquainted with the

131

land, could possibly find the path up through the hills, and had concentrated his forces at the fort.

Even with the immediacy of battle just before him, Jonas knew again a cold doubt. Suppose the Tahitians were victorious? Suppose they could hold this fort, and kill enough Frenchmen to discourage further attacks for a while? What then? They could not go on forever pitting a handful of muskets against cannons, their small resources against the power of France. Their only hope was that, against a stout enough resistance, the French would tire of the struggle, and abandon a project not important enough to them to warrant so great a cost.

Slim as it was, that hope was enough. The Tahitians were committed to it by now — to that and their fervent belief in aid from Britain — and he would help them in any way he could. It was all that had given meaning to his life since Tihoti's death.

But he loathed the role Taua had commanded him to play. The French must not know that a *popaa* was helping them, Taua had said; as an American and a neutral, if he were unsuspected by the French he could be of great value to the Tahitians. He must stay far enough back to be safe at all times, Taua insisted, and he must not be recognized. Well, there was small chance of that, Jonas thought; his face and arms were burned nearly as brown as a native's, and his clothes were as nondescript.

He took up the spyglass that hung around his neck, and fixed it on the ships. Tenders were being lowered and troops were scrambling over the sides to embark in them. As he watched, one of the pinnaces capsized in the surf and he could see the men struggling in the water. His heart began to pound. This was it!

He saw Taua in the center of the trench in front of him, dropped the glass, and ran toward him. "Tell your men to attack now!" he shouted. "Get down there before the firing starts, and catch them in the surf! The French won't fire so close to their own men."

Taua didn't turn his gaze from the beach. "We can't take them when they are helpless," he said. "Wait until they are equal with ourselves."

"Good Christ, man!" Jonas cried. "This is war! Take them while you can!"

"It would be unfair," Taua said imperturbably. He looked briefly at Jonas. "You know your orders, Tona. Get back to your position, and stay there!"

His authority could not be challenged. Jonas shook his head helplessly, and turned back. He had just reached the rear trench when the broadside began, an incredible, pounding concussion of sound that shattered the air and roared back in echo from the hills. Instinctively, he flattened out behind the parapet of sand. After a moment he cautiously raised his head. Thank God, the barrage did not quite reach to the first of the trenches. If Taua would wait now until the French advanced beyond the protection of their guns, there would be a good chance of throwing them back.

He raised the glass with fingers that trembled slightly and saw the dirt spurt up in patches across the plain from the impact of grapeshot, and the delayed explosions of shells. Behind the smoke and dust he could dimly see the first party of French troops scrambling into position on the beach. In the trenches on either side and in front of him the Tahitians waited tensely, their weapons in their hands. And then, incredibly, he heard the sharp report of a nearby musket shot, and saw Taua wave them forward. With guttural shouts they leaped over the breastworks and streamed down the plain, dodging through the curtain of fire, toward the French troops. Jonas grabbed up his own musket and started down behind them, screaming senselessly in English, "No, no, you fools, not now!"

On the breastwork of the first trench a powerful brown arm reached out against his chest and forced him back into shelter. "Go back, *popaa*, before I throw you back!" Jonas nodded help-

133

lessly and watched the Tahitians run through the barrage toward the French troops. Three fell and a fourth was hit directly by an exploding shell. Someone just behind him snatched up the bloody musket from the ground.

The Tahitians had come up to the French by now, and the French were falling back toward the beach. For a few hope-filled minutes he watched the distant struggle, then more guns began to roar from the ships, and he saw the Tahitians retreat toward the safety of the trenches. Now and then one would stop and pick up something quickly from the ground. He narrowed his smoke-filled eyes incredulously. The crazy, gallant bastards were reaching for the shells as they fell, and cutting off the fusees before they could explode!

He fell back in the trench out of their way as the first of the retreating men scrambled over the parapet. One of them, white teeth flashing in a brown face, thrust an unexploded shell into his hands, and said, "Now we'll have powder! Keep these for us!"

Jones laid it aside, and went along the trench. One of the men was carrying a bloodied French bayonet, and another was puzzling over the mechanics of a French musket. The wounded were brought back and laid side by side in a widened hollow of the trench.

Jonas found a calabash of water and took it to them, and was binding up a gushing arm wound when he heard Taua's voice in his ear. "Only about eight lost so far, Tona, and I'd swear we got at least twenty of those pigs!"

Jonas nodded without turning.

"We'll attack again as soon as the guns let up," Taua said. "Tona, my musket is jammed!"

"Take mine," Jonas said. "And leave me a man to help carry the wounded farther back."

As the ship's firing slacked off, the men left the trenches again and charged down the plain. There was no time to watch them

134

now; with the help of Tavi, the native whom Taua detailed to stay behind, he began carrying the wounded back to the rear trench.

He had no idea how long they worked there together, toiling back and forth between the trenches, bearing the torn and heavy bodies of their comrades; time seemed to stand still under the blazing impact of the sun and the roar of the guns. After a while he became aware of a kind of rhythm in the battle that raged below them on the plain. Ordinarily, the frigate's guns spoke steadily in units of five; but whenever the Tahitians got too close to the French troops the battery would be doubled or trebled, and they would be forced to retreat again. Each time they came back they brought with them a few more wounded, and on the field of battle the number of lifeless bodies, both French and native, was gradually increasing.

From the position of the sun Jonas guessed that perhaps an hour had passed, an hour that in some curious way took on the quality of eternity, and yet was fleeting as a moment. He knelt in the trench beside a man with a great hole gaping in his torn belly, but whose hand gripped Jonas's arm with the strength of a vise, and who gasped out words that he must say while there was still time. "I hit — Bruat!" he said.

Jonas bent closer to the tortured face. "Bruat! Did you kill him?"

"No," the man said, "but — he fell." He clenched his teeth against his pain, and then said, "After I was — hit. I still had — slingshot. Threw rock . . ." His hand pulled away from Jonas's arm, came back in the abortive gesture of a throw, and then fell limply at his side. For a moment Jonas looked at him, and then, gently, he laid a piece of *pareu* cloth across the lifeless face.

At the sound of a woman's voice behind him, he jumped to his feet. Marianna, by God! — in a faded blue dress, with her face and bare arms streaked with scratches. "Great Christ, what are you doing here!" he said.

135

"Mamu!" she said curtly. "Listen to me! Teaui's son and the other boys were scouting in the woods. They found that Hitoti came here with the French, and showed them the path up to the hills." She swept her hand toward the rounded hills to the west. "They're already moving up there with their guns! Four field-pieces, the boys said. Big ones."

"Oh, God!" he said. His eyes had followed the direction of her gesture. "How long ago did they start up?"

"About twenty minutes. I came as quickly as I could, around through the woods."

"All right, then get back just as quickly."

She didn't move. "I can help you with these wounded."

He turned on her with a sudden fury. "Get *out* of here, I say! When they start firing there won't be a chance for anyone in these trenches."

She reached out and caught his wrist in her fingers. "Jonas! What will you do?"

"We'll have to go back into the bush. They won't follow us there."

Her fingers tightened around his wrist. "Please take care. Please!"

For a moment they looked directly at one another. "I will," he said. "Watch the lantana going back. Your skin is torn to ribbons."

"Jonas," she said, "bring the wounded to the schoolhouse when you can. We're ready for them."

"We will. Now, for Christ's sake, *go,* Marianna!"

She dropped his wrist. "Take care," she said again. She turned, starting back along the trench, and Jonas jumped over the parapet. The hell with Taua's orders! He ran down to the forward trench, found Tavi, and told him quickly what Marianna had said. Together they climbed over the sand embankment, and raced down through the bursting shells to warn their men.

136

Not more than two hours later the *Phaeton* and the frigate were outside the pass, well beyond firing range of shore, and making to the west for Papeete. There was no longer any need for caution. The French had prudently declined the natives' invitation to follow them into the woods and continue the battle there, and although the victory had been clearly the invaders', it seemed a rather useless one, since they could not follow it up.

Emerging from the bush, Jonas and Taua made a tour of the battlefield, picked up the abandoned guns and carried them back to the trench. They stopped abruptly. The four wounded Tahitians they had been obliged to leave behind now lay grotesquely dead in the trench, each with a bayonet hole in his chest.

"The filthy pigs!" Taua said fiercely. "They left some of their own dead on the field in their hurry but they still took time to come back here for *this*." His dark face twisted in a grimace, momentarily like the violent expressions that were forever frozen on the faces of the dead men below him. "Four more. That makes seventy we lost, the way I counted, Tona."

"Sixty-nine, I think," Jonas said tonelessly. "And there are about twenty Frenchmen lying out there on the field. How many more did they lose, Taua?"

"At least a hundred more! Not counting their wounded. Their losses were double ours, I know it!"

Jonas, after a moment, turned wearily away. The dead could wait; but he could not. He had to know, now, if Marianna had got safely back home. She might have been killed . . . His pace lengthened almost to a run.

She should never have taken a chance like that! And yet, if she had not come when she did, the consequences of Hitoti's treachery would have been even more disastrous. When the fieldpieces on the hill opened up, enfilading the trenches, only those who were evacuating the wounded were caught in the fire. The losses had been severe, but had Taua's forces been trapped between the trenches and the shore not a man would have been left alive. Bless you, Marianna, and your arrogant, reckless soul . . .

From the doorway of the schoolhouse he saw her, bending over one of the wounded. There were a score of them, lying on pallets in ordered rows. For a moment he stood watching her.

The face she raised to him as he spoke her name was deathly white, except where scratches marked her cheeks and forehead. But when she saw him color rushed to her cheeks, and her eyes grew dark and enormous. She's almost beautiful, Jonas thought wonderingly.

"Jonas!" she said. "Jonas."

"Yes," he said. "Are you all right?"

She didn't answer, her eyes searching over him, over his blood-stained clothes. "Jonas, you're hurt!"

"No," he said, "that's the blood of braver men." His wry smile twisted under the grime that coated his face. "Unlike you, I am not even scratched."

"Thank God!" she said, and her voice was very low. In the moment before she turned back to the man she had been tending he stared at her incredulously, startled at the profound relief that shone in her eyes and rested on her expressive mouth.

※※※※※※

MARIANNA WAITED ON THE PATH WHILE HER FATHER CLOSED THE door of the church with his unfailing air of ceremony. He put on his hat and took her arm with a little sigh.

"Only eight souls for the service this morning," he said.

"I hardly expected more," Marianna said. "They wouldn't dare come down from the hills, Papa, with the French troops marching out this way."

Her words seemed to have made no impression on him. "It made

138

me think of the old days," he said, "when we would go about the island preaching, and sometimes there would be only two or three to listen."

A land crab scuttled out of their way into his hole at the side of the road. It was almost the only sign of life to be seen any more, Marianna thought. In the weeks since the battle at Mahina the district had become virtually deserted except for a few old people and children; all of the men who were of fighting age had moved, with their families, up to the encampment in the valley of Papenoo, a few miles to the east. With no one to work the cane fields, Lily and Anthony Nicholls had moved to the Inn in Papeete a week ago; the Moores and Jonas Burkham were the only white people left in Matavai.

Nathaniel Moore was looking contemplatively at the thickets of guava trees that spread beneath the tall coconut palms on either side of the road. "I can remember when this was one of the most beautiful groves on the island, Marianna. There were just the palms and breadfruits then, and soft, shadowy grass underneath. It was like Arcady. Now you have to cut your way through from here to the river."

"I'd like to have seen it then," Marianna said.

"It was a time to remember," he said in his gentle voice. "But when I see the guava trees I am always reminded of our errors. Mistakes, once sown, that spread and scattered like these little trees. We planted them with the best of intentions, but sometimes ignorance is as great a sin as any."

"When I see them," Marianna said, "I think of the French taking over the land."

"Ah," he said. "You are young. You can still put blame more easily on another than on yourself."

"You can't be serious, Papa!"

He made no reply, walking along with a remote look in his faded, kindly eyes.

139

"How," she persisted, "can you compare the missionaries' self-lessness in coming here with what the French are doing?"

"I've learned not to make comparisons," he said. "And I'm trying to learn the uselessness of brooding over past mistakes. But there is no one of us from the outside, Marianna, who hasn't brought some bad thing to this island. And yet we brought them salvation. I try to remember only that. We brought them the eternal life."

"You have brought nothing but good, Papa," she said stoutly.

He turned his head toward her, smiling a little. "It's nice to be defended," he said. "Don't worry about an old man's mood, my dear. It cannot trouble you. After all, you're no outsider. This is your native land."

They had come to the clearing in front of the mission, and stepped inside the wooden fence. Marianna glanced out toward the bay.

"Look, Father, there's the *Phaeton!* Out there, at anchor."

He shaded his eyes against the sun, and looked across the water. The steamship lay quietly, the French flag hanging limp at its masthead. One of its boats, filled with men, was being rowed across the water to the black beach at the foot of the bay.

"They've come to join forces with the troops that are marching here," Marianna said. "But why? Why? There's nothing to bring them here now!"

"They're chasing the tail of some rumor, I imagine," Nathaniel said. "We needn't worry, my dear. This is the Sabbath. No one will break the peace."

They watched them for a few moments, then moved up onto the veranda. Marianna stood at the railing, staring out across the bay; her father had taken a chair behind her, his Bible open on his knees. Taut with uneasy speculations, she found herself envying his settled Sabbatical calm. After a little he said, "Do sit down, child. You generate restlessness like a thunderstorm."

She turned toward him. "I'm sorry, Papa. I can't help wondering what they're up to. Would you like something to eat?"

"No thank you, not now." He looked up at her suddenly. "Marianna."

"Yes?"

"Is it only the invasion that troubles you? That has made you so restless these past few months?"

"Why Papa! Am I so bad as all that?"

"No, of course not, my dear. But you haven't seemed quite as — serene as usual, lately, and it worries me."

"It's just my natural bad temper, then. You mustn't worry."

"Don't evade me," he said. He was silent a moment, staring down at the book in his lap. "Are you quite sure, Marianna? About marrying Richard Johnson, I mean?"

When he looked up she turned her head a little so that her face was averted. "Of course I am, Papa."

"Then why do you refuse to settle on a date? Why do you keep postponing it?"

She leaned down and kissed him lightly on his silvery hair. "I'm in no hurry to leave you, you know."

As he started to reply the sharp, distant sound of musketry fire cut across his words.

"Listen!" Marianna said. "It's the French!"

Nathaniel Moore got up, and caught at her arm as she started for the veranda steps.

"Where are you going, Marianna?"

"To find out what they think they're doing!"

"Stay here! You mustn't go!"

"But I've got to know. They must be stopped."

He shook his head. "We can't stop them. Stay here. We'll know soon enough what they're about."

They waited together at the railing of the veranda, and gradually the sound of the shots came nearer. After a few minutes a col-

141

umn of French troops appeared, firing methodically every few moments into the guava thickets on either side of the road. Behind them were men on horseback, and then more troops.

Just inside the mission clearing they halted, and one of the officers rode forward to the foot of the veranda steps. He reined in his horse and raised his hat, and they saw that it was Governor Bruat.

"Good day, Monsieur Moore," he said. "Mademoiselle. I regret to disturb you."

"What is it you wish, Governor Bruat?" Nathaniel Moore asked.

"We 'ave come 'ere because it was said that the men of Matavai were plotting to attack us. What do you know of this?"

"Nothing, sir," Nathaniel said. "There have been no fighting men in Matavai since the battle, a month and a half ago. I think you have been misled."

"Perhaps. I 'ope it is so."

"Did your men have to fire into the trees along the road?" Marianna asked sharply.

Governor Bruat regarded her gravely. "It was their orders, mademoiselle. It would be most easy for the nateeves to make an ambuscade in there." He turned again to her father. "Since we are 'ere, I must ask your favor, m'sieu. Unhappily, one of my men 'as become drunk. He cannot walk or ride a 'orse, he is quite 'elpless. I wish your permission to leave him 'ere while we march on. In any other case I 'ave fear he might be attacked by the nateeves."

"Leave him, then," Nathaniel said. "He will be quite safe here."

"Thank you," the Governor said. "It is most regrettable. We will return for him later."

He raised his hat to each of them, bade them good day, and turned his horse about. Marianna and her father stepped back out of the sun into the shade of the veranda, and then, as he heard the Governor call out his name, Nathaniel moved forward to the railing again.

142

"He is just 'ere, inside your fence," the Governor called. "He will not waken soon."

Nathaniel waved his hand in acknowledgment, and turned back to Marianna. The sharp report of a musket shot rang out, and Nathaniel, an expression of shocked surprise on his face, fell forward to the floor.

For an instant Marianna was too stunned to move, then she dropped to her knees beside her father. There was a jagged hole in the back of his head, and as the blood began to seep from it she tore the kerchief from her neck and pressed it senselessly against the wound. After a moment she turned his face up from the floor, and saw by his glazed eyes that he was no longer conscious.

"Father!" she said. "Dear God, my father!"

For a few eternal seconds she knelt over him, his head supported in her hands, deaf to everything but the stertorous gasp of his breathing. On a sudden instant it died away; his struggling mouth slackened and was still. With desperate gentleness, she rested his head against the floor, and felt for his heart, but she did not need further proof to tell her he was dead. "Father," she whispered. "Oh, Papa, no!"

A lock of his soft, silver hair had fallen forward across his brow. She touched it gently for a moment, smoothing it back into place. He would feel better so . . .

Around the corner of the veranda Teaui came running, her bare feet pounding the boards with the weight of her huge body. "*Auê!*" she cried. "Marianna, what is it?"

She bent down beside them, and like Marianna put her hand against Nathaniel's chest. "*Mora* is gone!" she said. "He's gone!" She began to sob wildly, rocking back and forth on her heels.

After a few seconds Marianna reached out and took her by the arm. "*Mamu*, Teaui. Be quiet, and let him rest."

Teaui's sobs grew softer and Marianna became aware that the sounds of firing still persisted, quick and erratic, as in battle.

143

"What are they doing?" she asked tonelessly. "Now that they have killed him, cannot they leave us in peace?"

Teaui drew in a sobbing breath. "It wasn't the French who shot him. It was one of our people." Her voice ascended to a kind of wail. "The boys and old men were waiting there for the French. That shot was meant for Bruat." She raised her head to Marianna. "Two of my grandsons are out there fighting now, and there must be seventy or eighty others."

"It doesn't matter who fired the shot," Marianna said stolidly. "It was the French who killed him." She bent over her father, her face locked in a mask of grief. "I think we'd better carry him inside. He looks — uncomfortable." Her voice broke a little on the word.

As she straightened up she saw Teaui's youngest grandson peering around the corner of the veranda, his black eyes wide with fear. "Tioni," she said, "when the fighting is finished go and find Tona. Tell him that Mora is dead. But take care. Don't go until it is safe."

He nodded, and dodged back out of sight. Together, she and Teaui lifted Nathaniel's frail body and carried it inside to his bed. Marianna stood beside him, his cool hand clasped in her shaking fingers. He is gone, she told herself; he is gone.

The words were meaningless sounds in her mind. She had no idea of the passage of time, but after a while she noted dully that the sharp rattle of musketry fire had ceased. When Teaui came back into the room sometime later, she was sitting stiffly on a chair at the side of her father's bed.

"Marianna," Teaui said, "Bruat is outside. He wants to see you."

"I won't see him. Tell him so."

"I did," Teaui said fiercely, "but he insists. He says he will come and find you if you will not go out."

Marianna set her lips together, and got up. "I'll stay here with Mora," Teaui said.

144

Governor Bruat had dismounted and stood at the foot of the veranda steps, his hat in his hand. As she came out Marianna saw that Teaui had been scrubbing the veranda, and had pulled a table over the dark stain on the boards where her father had fallen.

She went to the top of the steps and stopped there, her body straight and stiff, her white dress still streaked with her father's blood. "Well?" she said.

"Mademoiselle," he said, "I cannot tell you how deeply I regret this unhappy — "

She cut him short with a curt gesture. "Did you have some business with me?"

He bit his lip, and looked at her appraisingly. "Yes. Of an importance, or I would not deesturb you at this time." When she made no reply, he went on, "I 'ope you understand it was not my men who fired the shot that hit your father. *Au contraire*, we were taken by surprise, unhappily, and four of my men are dead, in result. Several others are wounded."

"And the Tahitians?"

He shrugged. "I cannot say, mademoiselle. They 'ave all fled away. It is said that they stopped fighting when they knew that your father — was gone."

"What is it you want with me?"

"Mademoiselle is clever," he said. "There is a necessity that I must ask. My troops must stay 'ere a day or two to make sure there is not a nateeve left in the district to make further trouble. They must 'ave shelter and a place to cook. In short, mademoiselle, I need the mission and its buildings as barracks for my men."

"And where are we to go?" she asked stonily. "I — and my father?"

He drew his hand across his forehead. "There is no place for you to go?"

"No." She hesitated, and then went on, painfully. "He would wish to — lie in Papaoa. There is a friend who will take us there

145

in his boat, but as you see, there is no wind this afternoon."

"I see." He looked up at her compassionately. "Stay then, mademoiselle, if you will keep inside the house. I will instruct my officers to keep the men to the veranda and outbuildings. But who will stay with you?"

"Our old servant, Teaui."

He shook his head. "This is hard, mademoiselle, but it is of a necessity. I cannot allow any nateeve to remain in thees district after sundown tonight. No one — man, woman, or child."

She caught her breath. "Just Teaui — "

"No, mademoiselle," he said gently. "It is very hard, but thees is a war, and war is never easy. Surely you have some white neighbor nearby?"

"There is only one white person left in the district," she said. "I have already sent for him."

"And will he stay, you think?"

She bowed her head.

"*Bon,*" he said. "It is arranged." He took a step forward, and unwillingly she recognized the sympathy in his face. "If I can be of service, mademoiselle, or 'elp with the arrangements in any way, believe me I will be most 'appy."

"You cannot help me," she said. "I do not want your help."

Jonas drew his watch from his pocket and tilted it toward the light that burned dimly from the two coconut-oil lamps on either side of Nathaniel Moore's bed. Nearly midnight. He glanced over at Marianna and saw that she had not changed her rigid position in the chair, and that she still stared fixedly in front of her. In the last hour she had not moved, except when occasionally her fingers, laced together in her lap, twisted and tightened together.

If only she would weep, he thought, or lose herself in an outward show of grief, it might relieve some of the strain. But in all

146

the hours that he had been there she had been cool and matter-of-fact, cutting off all his attempts at sympathy as if she did not dare to accept them.

He got up and went over to the window. The night was still redly illumined by the big bonfire on the lawn. Two French sentries paced sleepily up and down in its light. All around them there was quiet. Earlier in the evening there had been many sounds — the tramp of footsteps, men calling out commands, the startled squawk of chickens as their necks were wrung. The soldiers had killed one of the Moores' cows, and roasted its meat over the fires; there had been laughter then, and snatches of song. But now all except the sentries were asleep, some were lined along the veranda, or huddled in blankets on the ground near the fire.

The deathly stillness pressed against him like a weight. He turned back to his chair again and sat down, determined to force Marianna out of her silence.

"The breeze will be best around eight in the morning," he said. "Will you be ready to go by then?"

Her wide, dark eyes swung around to him and focused on his face. "Quite ready," she said.

"We'll sail directly to town," he said. "You can stay with Mrs. Pritchard, and make your arrangements there."

"Yes," she said.

"What about your — what about Johnson?" Jonas asked.

Her gaze dropped away from his. "Teaui said she would get a message through to him somehow. I imagine he'll be here in the morning, before we leave."

"It's a pity he couldn't be with you sooner," Jonas said tentatively.

Her answer was oblique. "It's hard on you," she said, "you've had to do everything." She gestured at the unpainted wooden coffin that waited on the floor beside the bed where her father lay. "You made a good job of — I appreciate it."

147

"It was very simple," Jonas said. "I found the lumber in the Nichollses' old tool shed. It was good to have something to do."

"I — haven't been able to tell you how grateful I am for all your kindness," Marianna said painfully. "But this — waiting — is too much to ask of you. Won't you go into the other room now? Perhaps you could sleep."

"And leave you here alone?" he asked impatiently. "Don't be absurd!" He looked at her, his heart suddenly wrenched by the quiver of her lips. The effort of her composure had stretched her taut as a steel wire. "Marianna," he said gently, "wouldn't it help if you could talk some of your father? Or tell me how it happened exactly, and all the little things that went before?"

She shook her head. "I can't," she said. "I can't. Not yet." Her fingers twisted apart, and she grasped at her arms above the elbows. Jonas saw that she was shivering uncontrollably. He got up at once, went over to her, and put his hand lightly on her shoulder.

"Marianna," he said, "you mustn't stay here any longer. Go into your own room, and go to bed."

"No," she said.

"But you must. Even if you can't sleep, you must try to rest. Tomorrow will be a long and difficult day, and you must be in condition to meet it."

"I mustn't leave him," she said stubbornly.

He could feel the inward shaking of her body, and his hand tightened on her shoulder. "That's a barbaric idea," he said angrily. "It's not worthy of you. Think what your father would want you to do! He would only be grieved if he knew you were destroying yourself for a mistaken sense of duty."

Moved by sudden impatience he stooped down and picked her up in his arms. Too surprised to resist, she let him carry her into the prim, seldom-used front parlor. There was a lamp burning on the round table in the center of the room, and the Venetian blinds were pulled closed against the windows. He put her down on the

148

old mohair sofa that stood against the wall, settling her snugly into a corner of it. For a moment he stood looking at her.

"You're cold," he said. "You ought to go to bed, Marianna."

She dropped her head against the back of the sofa and stared up at him. "Please, no," she said. "I couldn't sleep — I couldn't bear it." Her voice was almost a whisper.

"All right. Is there a blanket on your bed?"

She nodded. Jonas brought back the blanket and wrapped it about her knees. "Did your father keep any spirits in the house?"

"There's a bottle of brandy in the cabinet over there. He had it — for emergencies."

"I consider this an emergency," he said, a touch of irony in his voice. He poured two glasses of brandy and handed one of them to her. "Drink this," he said. "You need it."

Steadying the glass with both hands, she drank it off, meekly as an obedient child. He filled it again, and put it on the table. "More of this a little later," he said authoritatively. "Are you comfortable?"

She nodded dumbly. He sat down beside her, taking her cold hands into his own and rubbing them gently. How slender her bones were under the soft flesh; the look of capability in her long fingers was like a glove over their essential frailty.

"Marianna," he said quietly, "have you thought about what you will do, after — it's all over?"

"Not much," she said. "I couldn't — there hasn't been time."

"I know," he said. Gradually, the taut fingers were beginning to relax under his own. "Do you think you'll stay out here in the country?"

"I don't know. Perhaps. It's the only home I've ever known."

"With all your neighbors gone, it won't be quite the same, you know. Still, you were planning to make a new home, in any case. I suppose, under the circumstances, that you won't postpone your marriage much longer, will you?"

Her hands tightened in his, and she pulled them away from his

149

touch. "I suppose not," she said in a stifled tone. She leaned forward, picked up the glass of brandy and swallowed part of it.

"Not too fast," he said. "You're not used to it."

To his astonishment, she drained off the rest of the brandy, and reached for the bottle to pour out more. Gently, he took the glass from her hand.

"You told me it would help," she cried. "You told me!" For a moment she stared at him, seeing the look of amused understanding in his eyes, and the shape of tenderness on his lips, and then she bent her head against her hands, shivering violently. Jonas put his arm around her and drew her close against him, holding her head against his shoulder.

"Can't you cry, Marianna?" he asked softly. "It would help you more if you could cry."

"I want to," she said in a muffled voice. She turned her head so that she could look up at him. "I want to — so much!"

Her eyes were blank with the uncomprehending despair of a hurt child, and the mobile lips, so close to his own, were trembling. Moved by compassion, he bent his head and kissed that piteous mouth. For a moment her body tautened in his arms, then, as he drew her closer to him, he felt the tension leave her, as on a long sigh; her body relaxed and yielded to his encircling arms as if their warmth and strength were a haven from her unendurable loneliness.

Poor child, poor child! With a feeling of confused surprise he recognized in himself a welling of protective tenderness that he had never known before with any woman, and something more, something that drew him back again and again to her lips, to her soft cheeks, to the closed white mystery of her eyelids. Unbidden and unwanted, the familiar hunger swelled along his veins; and through his caresses, through the confusion of his senses he breathed her name, softly and wonderingly. The light pressure of her arm behind his shoulders tightened convulsively in response,

150

her lips parted beneath his, pressing against him in a breathless and ardent demand, and then, abruptly, she pulled away from him, hiding her face between her hands.

He sensed the agony of her spirit, the desperate bewilderment and the self-contempt. Why must she fight so bitterly against her own humanity? He pulled her stiff and resisting body into his arms again, pushing her head against the hollow of his shoulder, and began gently stroking her soft, disheveled hair. After a little the resistance slacked out of her muscles, and she began to cry.

For a long time she wept, soundlessly, wiping away her tears with the handkerchief he had given her. Gradually the tremors that shook her became more widely spaced, lessened, and gave way finally to a gentle, steady breathing. He lifted his hand from her hair, and knew that she was asleep.

Carefully, so as not to disturb her, he drew her closer against his chest, lifted her feet and his own along the length of the sofa, and drew the blanket over them both. He stared thoughtfully at the shadows that flickered along the ceiling from the guttering lamp. After a time the light went out completely, and for a long while Jonas waited in the darkness, with Marianna cradled in his arms; then his cheek settled gradually against the scratchy coolness of the mohair, and he too slept.

〰〰〰

Jonas pulled the dinghy up onto the black sand beach, and put out his hand to help Marianna, but Johnson was already giving an awkward and unnecessary push to her arm as she stepped from the boat.

"D'you think Teaui will be at the mission, Marianna?" Jonas asked.

151

"I'm sure she will," Marianna said. "I saw smoke coming from the cook house as we crossed the bay."

"It was good of you to bring us out here, Burkham," Richard Johnson said. "And now we mustn't take any more of your time. I think you will understand that Miss Moore and I have many things we wish to discuss." His resonant voice was pitched to a hearty, man-to-man tone.

"Perhaps Mr. Burkham would like to have something to eat with us before he goes home, Richard."

"Thanks, no," Jonas said. "I'm anxious to see if there's anything left of my shack." He turned a purposely wolfish grin on Johnson. "I'll be back later if I'm hungry."

Johnson picked up Marianna's *pareu* cloth bundle, and they started through the trees toward the mission. Around a curve in the path Marianna stopped short, and gave a little cry.

Her hand was resting on the silvery trunk of a great breadfruit tree. Above it was a deep, neat gash in the bark, completely encircling the tree.

"It's been girdled!" he said, astonished. "Why, that means the tree will die!"

She made no answer, touching the wounded bark with her fingers as gently as if it were a hurt child.

"Look at that coconut over there," Johnson said. "It's had the same treatment!"

He crashed off through the grove, examining each tree trunk as he went. When he came back she was still standing by the breadfruit tree, motionless, her face bleak.

"They've girdled every coconut and breadfruit tree in the grove, so far as I can see," he said. "The French must have done it, Marianna, before they left."

"Who else?" she said stonily.

"Why do you suppose they did this?"

"To cut off the food supply. To starve the people."

152

"Were these your trees?"

"They were Taua's, but their fruit was for anyone who needed it."

They had come to the edge of the mission clearing, and saw that Teaui was standing in front of the cook-house door. Marianna ran to her, throwing her arms about her, and rubbing her face like a child against the smooth coolness of Teaui's brown cheek. "You're all right, Teaui! You're back — I knew you would come back."

"Of course I'm back," Teaui said soothingly. "As soon as the Farani left we came down from the hills, I and a few others." She held Marianna at arm's length and looked at her searchingly. "Poor little one, come home to sorrow! You look like a *tupapau,* my child."

"No matter. Is everyone all right?"

"*Maitai,*" Teaui said. "Only two were hurt in Sunday's fighting, and they will get well. But the land, Marianna! You've seen what they did to the trees?"

"Yes. Oh, yes!"

"And your own things, too. They have stolen or dirtied everything!" Her broad, humorous old face twisted in disgust. "There's not a chicken left, nor a cow nor a calf. They took Mora's good shirts and most of the blankets and nearly everything from the trading store — cloth, and nails and thread and tools! They've even been here in my cook house," she went on heatedly. "There's scarcely a plate left, and *aué,* Marianna, they took my big frying pan!"

"How about the horses?" Johnson asked.

"They took the colt and Mora's gelding, but the old mare is still in the field, and that broken-down beast of yours." Her look showed only too plainly the scorn he always aroused in her. "Even the Farani didn't want that nag."

"Teaui," Marianna said hastily, "we've had nothing to eat since

153

dawn. Is there enough food to prepare us a little lunch?"

"There is, my child. I brought down *fei* and oranges from the hills, and one of the boys caught some *otavo* along the reef."

"We'll go to the house then, until it is ready."

The veranda was not much changed, she saw, although some of the cushions were missing from the chairs. Teaui apparently had done her best to put it in order, for the table was drawn again over the spot where her father had fallen. She looked away from it, and reached for the bundle that Johnson was carrying. "Won't you sit down, Richard, while I take these things into the house? I'll not be gone long."

She went into her own room first, pulled off her hat and bent forward to see her reflection in the small, cracked mirror above her chest of drawers. How pale her face was — like a ghost, as Teaui had said. She picked up a comb to tidy her hair, but her fingers were shaking uselessly, and she laid it down again. After a moment she turned away, and went to the door of her father's room, across the hall. Teaui had made it neat and clean, but the blankets and linen were gone from the bed, and the bare, exposed mattress gave a look of poignant desertion to the room.

He is gone, she thought dully, he will never return; and the aching loneliness for him that had been mounting within her for the past three days knotted like a fist in her throat. She turned into the hall that led to the veranda, but at the door to the parlor she paused, then slowly, as if drawn against her will, she opened it and went in.

Only a gray and shadowy dimness filtered through the closed Venetian shades, and in its light she could see that the room was unaltered, except that the fringed cover from the table in the center of the floor was gone, and the small globe map that her father had brought from England. As if to a magnet, her gaze swung around to the mohair sofa where she had slept in Jonas's arms throughout the night after her father's death.

154

She pressed the back of her hand against her mouth, remembering the flood of despairing realization that had poured over her when she awakened to the first light that next morning. Carefully, she had gotten up, rearranged the blanket over him, and crept out of the room, but not before she had seen by his momentarily opened eyes that he too was awake. Tactfully, he had feigned sleep for another hour, and when at last he joined her in her father's room she had gained sufficient mastery over herself to greet him with careful composure. Richard had come to the mission within an hour or so, and since then she had not had to be alone with Jonas. . . .

The impact of the emotions that had worked in her for the past three days shook her now. Even her grief for her father could not run clear and single-minded and uncomplicated; mixed into it, like a scarlet thread in a black skein, was her remembrance of Jonas, and her shocked horror at her body's shameless response to him. That very night — the night her father died! Yet even her recoil from the thought acknowledged that Jonas, in his own way, had known best how to comfort her. The intimacy of his kisses, fleeting as it had been, had established a curious feeling of kinship with him, and demonstrated an understanding sympathy that went far deeper than any words. But now it was over, and must be forgotten. Her hand dropped away from her mouth, and she straightened her shoulders.

Richard jumped to his feet as she came onto the veranda, and settled her into a chair beside his, taking her hand tenderly. "Poor Marianna," he said. "I know how lonely you must feel."

She leaned toward him, moved by the kindness of his tone. "Thank you, Richard. I know you do."

"But it won't be for long, will it, Marianna? We can be married now, can't we?"

If she could not find happiness soon again, at least she could try to give it to Richard. "Yes," she said. "I wanted to talk to you about that. About the future — "

"And I to you. I've got good news for you, my dear. Just the news you need, I hope."

At her questioning look he went on eagerly: "You know that the missionaries had a meeting last night, in the schoolhouse in Papeete, but I haven't had a chance until now to tell you of the decision we came to. It was agreed that under the present circumstances it would be unwise to maintain the mission in Tahiti as before, and that as soon as the *Camden* comes into port again we would sail for England or other stations."

She looked at him in astonishment. "Richard! You can't mean it! *All* the missionaries are going to leave Tahiti?"

"Well, not all," he said a little uncomfortably. "Some of the older men who have made their homes here for so many years decided to stay, but the rest of us are leaving. Howe and Jesson and Joseph and I will go to England, Buchanan to the Harvey group, and Mr. and Mrs. Wilson to Samoa. It's the only thing to do, Marianna. You must see that."

She had pulled her hand from his grasp, and sat squarely facing him, her eyes intent on his. "And whom does that leave here? Mr. Davies, old and sick, out in Papara, and Mr. Darling at Punaavia. Will Mr. Barff stay in Huahine and Mr. Simpson in Moorea?"

"Yes. And Thomson has decided to move to Papeete, and take over the station there."

For a moment she was silent, and then she said as calmly as she could, "Richard, I can't believe that you have made the best decision. It seems to me that Tahiti never needed our help more than it does right now. The people up in the mountain camps are already holding their own services, with no one to guide them. The consolation they can get from their religion is all they have to hold to — they're hungry and sick and besieged, and they're turning to God as they never have before."

"They will still have guidance," he said, "but it would be impossible for all of us to stay here. The French are making it hard

156

for us to travel from district to district, and you have seen what they have done out here to cut off the food supply. There's bound to be more fighting. It would be like living on a battleground."

She shook her head. "That's not important," she said.

"Not important! The danger? You can say that after what happened to your father?"

Steadily, she said, "My father's death was an unhappy accident. In his early years here he lived constantly in far greater danger than any we know now. If the mission is abandoned it will mean the desertion of everything he worked and suffered for all these years."

"It would be foolhardy to stay," Johnson said stubbornly. "I can be of more use as a live missionary in some other part of the world than I could be dead in Tahiti. What's more, I was thinking of you, Marianna. As my wife, you must be protected. There's nothing left here for you." He leaned forward. "You need England, Marianna — home, and security, people — your own kind."

"Tahiti is my home," she said. "And these are my people."

He looked at her incredulously. "You mean that you will not leave?"

For a moment she hesitated. "Will nothing change your decision to go?"

"Nothing," he said sharply. "Anything else is out of the question."

"Then I must release you from our engagement, Richard. I cannot go with you."

"Think what you are saying, Marianna!"

"I have," she said sadly. "And I can't change it. I'm truly sorry, Richard, but it would be impossible for me to leave Tahiti in a time of trouble. Can't you understand? England isn't home to me — it's an alien land. I can't desert my own people just when I might be of some use to them."

"You're very tender of the natives," he said, and his Adam's

157

apple worked convulsively with his emotion, "but you seem to have little regard for *my* feelings. I do not lightly ask someone to be my wife."

"I'm sorry, Richard," she said wearily. "It seems to be a deadlock, doesn't it?"

"Everyone knew that we were engaged," he said. "This is a great hurt to me, Marianna."

She looked over at him, suddenly noting the stubborn set of his mouth above the weak chin, and the pallid anxiety of his eyes cloaked by the sparkle of his glasses. There was something petulant in his tone that angered her unreasonably.

"I cannot suppose your hurt to be so great," she said carefully, "since you prefer to seek your own comfort and safety in England to staying here with me."

Before he could answer Teaui came waddling up the steps with a tray of food which she put on the table. Richard drew up two chairs, handed her into one with exaggerated politeness, and they ate their lunch in silence. At least his appetite hasn't suffered, Marianna thought dully.

When they had finished, he pushed back his chair and got up. "Do you need me here for anything?"

She shook her head.

"Very well, then, I must get back to Tiarei." He hesitated. "You will not reconsider, Marianna?"

"No."

"So be it," he said heavily "If you ever need my assistance I will be glad to help you — as a friend." He bade her a stiff and formal farewell, and went down the steps without looking back.

A few minutes later she heard the sound of his horse's hoofs along the road, and as it gradually faded away she felt a strange and surprising sense of freedom, as if she were released from a narrow prison into the open air. She put her hand against the railing of the veranda and stared out over the bright sheen of the bay. She was free, yes — but for what? She turned away from the bay, and faced toward the empty house.

"But what are you going to do, Marianna?" Sara Darling persisted.

It was hard to disguise the weariness of her voice as she answered. "How can I say, Sara? I don't know — I must have more time."

"It's been nearly two weeks since your father went to his reward. You can't go on like this much longer."

"No," Marianna said shortly. She let her gaze slide past Sara, sitting opposite her at the dining table on the veranda, to the twilight beyond. The bay, clasped by the darkening land, was silken calm, placidly mirroring the flagrant rose and gold and azure of the sky. Near the shore the trees stood out in sharp perspective, still momentarily glowing with vanished sunshine; the arched grace of the palms, the broad, glossy-dark breadfruit leaves, and the paler tangles of *purau* tree and guava were intensely still beneath a cloak of green, unnatural light. Against that background Sara's thin, tight-lipped face, with its careful framework of curls, looked oddly out of place.

She looks pinched and wintry, as England must, Marianna thought . . . Impatiently, she pushed her chair back and started to pile their supper dishes together. Sara took the tray out of her hands.

"I'll carry these out to Teaui," she said. "You rest a bit."

Sara Darling, daughter of the missionary at Punaavia, had come to Matavai with her father and mother shortly after Marianna's return ten days before, and had insisted that they leave her there,

159

despite Marianna's protests. "You must not be alone with your grief," she had said, as if there were something faintly indecent in the idea of it. Doggedly, she had seen to it that Marianna's sorrow should be well chaperoned at all times; her presence was as persistent as the ticking of a clock.

The past three days had been the worst, for until a few hours earlier, when the sun finally broke through, it had rained steadily, a chilly, pervasive, inexorable rain that kept them closely confined to the house and one another's company. It might be unchristian, Marianna thought, but she had never liked Sara Darling, even when they were schoolgirls together in the South Sea Academy, over in Moorea. Sara had never learned to speak Tahitian, and had taunted her for playing with the native children, calling her a little black savage. . . .

By means of her insistent probing, Sara had elicited the fact that Marianna no longer intended to marry Richard Johnson, and her shocked remonstrances at this state of affairs had alternated undeviatingly with her queries as to what Marianna's plans would be. Nor had she been behindhand with suggestions. Marianna must move to Punaavia and live with the Darlings; well, then, she must go to England and stay with her sisters; at the very least she must move to town and leave this lonely and deserted district.

If only Sara would leave her alone, so that she might think things out for herself! — but the long nights when she lay sleepless in her bed and stared into the darkness had produced merely a deep and hopeless bewilderment. Her father's death, apart from the grievous sense of loss she felt, seemed to have deprived her life of all stability and direction. There was simply no meaning to it any more, nor any purpose. And with the virtual desertion of the district, there was nothing left of the old, ordered routine to sustain her.

There had been enough to keep her busy, to be sure — all of the small chores that follow so prosaically upon the heels of

160

death. But her work had lacked the continuity that it used to have, and the frightening part of it was that its end could be so quickly achieved. A day must soon dawn in which she would have nothing to do at all. . . .

She shivered suddenly in the warm, clear air, and her gaze, as it had so many times before, sought out the darkening road. Jonas had gone to Papeete five days before to put his schooner in the water; apparently he had not yet returned. After Sara Darling came she had seen him but once, and she suspected that he had deliberately stayed away because of his dislike of Sara. He had been kind, she thought with a touch of bitterness, but his charity would cease as soon as it became irksome to him.

Sara came up the veranda steps with a lighted lamp, and put it on the table beside her. "It isn't healthy to sit in the dark," she said reprovingly. She sat down, drawing her chair close to the lamp. "I had to take Teaui to her house. She was afraid of meeting a *tupapau* on the path. Shocking how superstitious these natives are."

"Poor soul," Marianna said. "It's dreadfully lonely for her here, with all of her people up in the hills."

"She wouldn't have to stay if you would be sensible about leaving."

"I know," Marianna said. "Let's not talk about it tonight, if you don't mind, Sara."

"Suppose I read to you then," Sara said. "I was glancing through a volume of sermons this afternoon and found one called 'God, Our Comfort in Bereavement.' It should be helpful."

Listening to Sara read entailed no obligation to answer at intervals. Marianna got to her feet. "I'll fetch a better lamp from the parlor."

The lamp needed more oil, and when she had filled it Marianna decided that a thorough trimming would do it no harm. When she could no longer legitimately postpone her return, she came out on

161

the veranda, carrying the lamp before her. With her eyes fixed on its light, she did not see Jonas Burkham standing in the shadows at the foot of the steps until she heard his voice.

"Good evening. May I come up?"

The lamp jerked in her hands, and she put it hastily on a table. "Of course! Good evening, Mr. Burkham."

He came up the steps, greeted Sara briefly, and took the chair Marianna indicated, his eyes fixed on her face. The lamplight found no reflection in her pallor; the heavy knot of hair at the back of her neck seemed to drag the skin tight against her cheek-bones, and her eyes, enormous in her thin, pale face, looked tired and haunted with unshed tears. "You're not well, Marianna," he said roughly.

"I'm perfectly well," she said. She stepped away from the light and took a chair in the furthest periphery of its glow. Sara laid aside the book she was holding, and gazed curiously at Jonas, her face set in lines of prim forbearance.

"What is the news in town, Mr. Burkham?"

He shrugged. "Considerable excitement," he said, "and small accomplishment. The Tahitians are playing a game with the French — harrying them off their legs with rumors of attack from every quarter. The drums beat to arms every half hour, and the French troops are marched and countermarched to every point of the compass." He laughed shortly. "It's almost possible to feel sorry for the poor devils. They're so exhausted they don't know what they're doing. I saw a group of them on the road given orders to 'fall in' and they were knocking their own heads with their muskets trying to shoulder arms."

"But there's been no actual fighting?"

"No. The Queen's still begging her people to keep peace, but most of the men are in the encampments by now — at Papenoo and Fautaua and Punaavia. I saw your father in town one day," he said to Sara, "and he told me that when things are quiet the

162

men come down from the camp to chapel on Sundays, and leave their muskets stacked outside the door."

"How dreadful!" she said. "I feel that I should be with him and poor Mama in this hour of trial."

"You should, Sara," Marianna said urgently. "I've been telling you just that."

"My duty is here with you," Sara said primly.

Nearby the hollow boom of a coconut dropping to the ground broke into their momentary silence. "Have things been quiet here in the district, Marianna?" Jonas asked.

"Dull as a week of Sabbaths," she said. She saw the look of shock on Sara's face, and went on hastily. "How about your schooner? Are the repairs finished?"

"The old lady's finally recovered," he said. "We put her in the water yesterday." He swung around in his chair, facing her directly. "I hear that you — I understand that your plans are somewhat changed."

"If you mean that I'm not going to marry Richard Johnson and go to England," she said coolly, "you are right."

"Then what do you intend to do? You can't stay on out here."

"That's just what I've been telling her," Sara said triumphantly.

Jonas ignored her. "The French are planning to build a fort here. Right on the point, Marianna. You can't possibly stay."

She made a small, futile gesture of despair. "So they will take my home too."

He went on, as if she had not spoken. "I talked to Mr. Thomson in town about it. He wants you there very much, to teach school for him. There's a little cottage at the Inn you could rent, and Mrs. Buelle said you could take your meals at the Inn."

"You have already spoken to her?" Marianna said. "How very — kind." How very officious, her voice had indicated.

Some of the concern in Jonas's eyes was replaced by a look of wary amusement. "As a matter of fact, I have. I also took the

163

liberty of engaging Poti's wagon and horses to come out for your things a week from today."

"Perhaps you'd be good enough to pack up for me, too," she said icily. "You seem to have taken all the other arrangements out of my hands."

"It would give me great pleasure," he said. "Helpless women have always appealed to me."

Sara was staring in amazement at them — at the flush that had suddenly flooded through Marianna's pallor, at her hands, taut on the arms of her chair, and at Jonas, who had pulled a cigar from his pocket and was regarding it with amused speculation.

"When I go," Marianna was saying in a carefully controlled tone, "you won't be troubled with any women at all in the district — helpless or otherwise. There just won't be any here."

"I was afraid of that," he said regretfully. "And for that reason, among others, I too am moving to town."

Marianna's eyes were wide and intent upon his face. "You, too?"

"Yes," he said. "There's nothing left here. I'll live aboard the schooner when I'm not on a voyage." He pushed back his chair. "Good night, Miss Darling. Good night, Marianna. I'll be back to see about that packing."

She got to her feet as he went down the veranda steps, and for a moment stood indecisively by the table. Suddenly she caught up a lantern and lighted it from the lamp. "He has no lantern," she said, not facing Sara's astonished eyes. "I'd best take him one."

At her call he stopped by the gate. Quickly, she came to him across the dark grass. "Here," she said, "you'll need a light tonight — there's no moon."

"Thanks," he said. He took the lantern from her, watching her face in its light.

"Mr. Burkham," she said rapidly, "I do appreciate what you have done. I'm sorry I was rude."

He laughed. "Don't be sorry," he said. "I quite enjoyed it. But

I'd prefer it if you got angry directly with me, instead of using me as whipping boy for Miss Sara Darling."

"You understood that too?" Her lips curved suddenly in an unexpected smile. "You did sound most awfully like her, you know."

"I'll try not to again," he said. He looked down at the lantern for a moment. "I wasn't being altogether altruistic in planning your future, Marianna. As it happens, there are a few things I can do for the natives, now that I've got the schooner again. I can run supplies around to Papenoo, and carry information to them, and I'll need your help."

"My help?"

"Someone I can trust," he said, "someone to cover up for me, and find things out, and be my liaison with respectability. Don't worry about it now."

He said good night to her then, and went off down the road. For a few minutes Marianna stood there in the cool starlight. To be needed once more, to be needed for something, however small . . .

She turned back toward the house, her hands tranquil at her sides. I shall sleep tonight, she thought.

The day she left Matavai to move to town was bright and windy; boisterous with the rattle of palm fronds and the clash of swaying leaves. White clouds rode swiftly across the sky, and beneath the gusts of sunlight and shadow the landscape was dazzlingly vivid in the clean, clear rush of air.

The carter's wagon, loaded with her goods, had started on its way an hour before, and Jonas, who had ridden out from town that morning, stood waiting at the foot of the veranda steps. At the top of the steps Teaui, shaking with sobs, was holding Marianna in her huge embrace, and as Marianna kissed her brown cheeks and finally drew away, he saw that her face was tight with the effort of her composure.

She held her shoulders very straight as she came down the steps; in her long, trim riding skirt and soft, native-woven straw hat, weighted down with a band of sea shells, she had a look of fine distinction. Jonas helped her into her saddle. "You look like a great lady," he said, "about to go for a canter in the Mall."

"In this hat?" she asked. She turned back to Teaui as the horse started slowly to walk away, and there was a break in the careful lightness of her voice. "Good-by, little mother! Let me know always how you are."

He saw that she could not trust herself to speak for a few moments, and they rode silently along the shady lane, past the deserted church, past the schoolhouse, out onto the road at the foot of the bay. A sudden spate of sunshine, running before the wind, flooded across them, and all the muted colors — green of the leaves, jewel blue of the bay, and the shiny black sand of the beach, scalloped with white surf — leaped into startled life. Marianna reined in her horse, looking back at the long arm of Point Venus reaching along the flank of the bay.

"I've lived here all my life," she said, "yet I feel as if I'd never really seen it until today."

"And it looks different to you?"

"Not different," she said, "but strange. Nothing has changed — except my own point of view. I can never take it for granted again."

"You will come back," he said.

"Come back? You know better than that, Jonas. As a visitor, perhaps. But I can never — come back."

He looked at her quickly, warmed and surprised at her use of his given name. "I do know," he said. "I felt the same way when I left America. I suppose most people have to make a break like that sometime. It isn't easy to cut away from an old, familiar life — but there are always new lives ahead." How insufferably sententious, he thought disgustedly. There was no valid comfort that he could give her, and perhaps it was foolish to try.

166

She leaned forward, patting the neck of her horse, her face momentarily hidden from him by the wide brim of her hat. "And now I'm going to look for mine," she said. "Thanks to you, Jonas. I can never tell you how grateful I am for all you've done. Sending the wagon — bringing the horse out — "

"Nonsense," he said, grinning. "I was only being officious. By the way, when did your visitor leave?"

"Sara? A couple of days ago. Her father came out for her and took her back to Punaavia."

Before he could reply they heard the sound of horses' hoofs behind them, and voices calling their names. They turned and saw that a group of natives were riding toward them, splashing through the shallows of the river where it flowed across the road.

"It's Poriri," Marianna said, astonished, "and Tane, and his sister, and Manu, and Taua's daughter — "

"Our old neighbors, down from the hills! I hope there hasn't been trouble with the French!"

In a moment the riders came up to them, five men, each with a musket slung across his back, and three girls, riding astride, with gay *pareus* twisted above their slender legs and their long wavy black hair streaming behind them in the wind. Their arms were laden with wreaths of flowers, and there were woven bundles hanging across the bare backs of their horses. They drew rein beside Marianna and Jonas, laughing and calling out greetings. Teaui's son, Poriri, leaped from his horse.

"*Ia ora na*, Marianna! *Ia ora na*, Tona! We heard you were leaving the district today, and we came to say farewell."

He held up his hand to Marianna and she jumped lightly down from the saddle. "Poriri! All of you! You shouldn't have come — you know the danger — "

"We have our guns," he said boastfully. "If the Farani come, we'll shoot them in their skinny behinds."

The others were crowding about her, the men shaking her hand, the girls kissing her on the cheeks. "We had to give you our farewells, Marianna. We couldn't let you go away without that."

The girls took the soft, fragrant wreaths of flowers from their arms and threw them over her head, settling them about her neck, and one of them pulled a *tiare* blossom from her hair and tucked it behind Jonas's ear. "We'll miss you too, Tona."

Tane came forward with a length of white tapa cloth in his hands. "Mama Ruau made this for you. Said to tell you we worthless young things wouldn't even know how."

"Dear old Mama," Marianna said softly. The bark cloth was as soft and fine as a piece of Irish linen. "How is she?"

"*Aué*, her bones ache with the dampness of the hills, but her tongue is as lively as ever."

Manu held out a piece of woven matting. "Naria sent you this. She was sorry she could not come herself."

"She's not ill?"

"No," he said, smiling proudly. "I've made a child in her again — she's swelling like a melon."

"It'll be another man to fight the French," Marianna said. "You wait and see."

The other men were transferring the bundles to Jonas's and Marianna's saddles. There was a suckling pig, squealing and twisting in a pandanus halter, a long plaited sack of oranges, a bunch of mountain plantains. "It is too much," Marianna said. "You shouldn't have brought me all these things."

Poriri looked at her very seriously. "It could never be too much for you, Marianna. The things that you and Mora did for us we can never give back to you."

She blinked rapidly, and her eyes were very bright as she answered. "Hear my word, Poriri. There is still some flour and sugar and tea in the mission storeroom. I left it there for all of you — Teaui will show you where. Take everything — leave nothing for the French. If you can carry it, take up my father's mattress to Mama Ruau, to keep her old bones from the damp. Take something to everyone, if you can, as a gift of love from me."

"We will," he said. "We'll leave nothing for those robbers. And we'll keep your fine things safe for you, Marianna, so that when we are rid of the Farani you can come back and live among us again."

"I'll pray for that day," she said.

"How are things in the camp?" Jonas asked.

Poriri shrugged. "We live," he said, "and we are free men there. But the sun doesn't linger long between the walls of the mountains, and there has been much sickness."

"Is there enough to eat?"

"Plenty of *fei* and oranges and *mape* nuts, and our pigs and chickens find enough to eat. We could live there forever without going hungry, but we miss the fish and coconuts and all the fat foods of the lowlands. We've started gardens, though, and when things are quiet we go down to the shore and bring back as much as we can carry. You should see the fort we're building," he said proudly, "and the entrenchment, clean across the narrows of the valley."

"I want to see it," Jonas said. "When I come I'll try to bring you some powder and ammunition."

"*Auê!*" Poriri said. "That will be better than food for our bellies!"

Marianna was talking with the three girls; her face and voice were animated, and her laughter sounded out in clear joyousness. How easy she was with these people, Jonas thought, how released from whatever it was that held her when she was her cool, English self. In Tahitian she could chaff, talk freely, speak her emotions with unembarrassed openness. These were her old playmates, he realized suddenly, her real friends. Reluctantly, he reached out and touched her arm. "I'm sorry, Marianna, but we must be on our way if we're to reach Papeete before dark."

He helped her into her saddle, and she leaned down, shaking hands with each of them again, her face vivid with tenderness.

169

Hina looked up at her mischievously. "With all those flowers and gifts you look like a bridal couple, you and Tona. When is the wedding, Marianna?"

Jonas turned to mount his horse, as if he had not heard. "I'd be an old woman if I waited for Tona," Marianna said lightly. "Wish me better luck than that, Hina."

Good girl, he thought, relaxing; you deserve better luck — someone who's neither a prig like Johnson, nor a bloody fool for freedom, like myself . . .

As they rode slowly away one of the girls started to sing, a *himene* that Marianna had taught them. "Rock of a — ges, cleft for me . . ." The Tahitian words, the shrill, plaintive wail of the women's voices, high above the joining bass of the men's, the strange twists of emphasis and melody that they gave the familiar tune made it barely recognizable to him, and soon, as they went along the road, it was lost in the rush of the wind.

At the top of One Tree Hill he and Marianna stopped to rest their horses, looking back down on the broad sweep of the bay. On the road by the beach they saw that the others were still singing; although they could not hear the melody they could see that the rhythm had changed, and that Hina and the other two girls were dancing, the wild and tantalizing dance of ancient times, while one of the men pounded out the provocative beat with a stick against the trunk of a tree.

Marianna looked at them thoughtfully. "Father worked here for forty years, preaching against dancing and tattooing and all the old heathen customs — and now we haven't even left the district before they are openly dancing again."

"They always danced," he said, "back in the hills or at night, when there was no missionary *popaa* to interfere."

Her look met his, a little derisively. "D'you think I didn't know that?"

"I wasn't sure," he said. "And what about those flowers they

170

gave you? I thought the missionaries taught that wearing flowers was a badge of harlotry."

"Presumably my friends forgot," she said gently. "I won't dare wear them into town." She raised a strand of creamy white flowers to her lips, shutting her eyes for a moment at their fragrance. "But aren't they beautiful — aren't they beautiful?"

"Sometimes I wonder, Marianna," Jonas said, "if you are not more Tahitian than puritan."

She took a last look at the land below them, and turned her horse about. Her words came back to him faintly on the wind. "Sometimes I wonder myself," she said.

THE INN, A MODEST WOODEN BUNGALOW NEAR THE BEACH ON THE eastern curve of Papeete Bay, was almost hidden from the road by the great trees that surrounded it. From its veranda, where meals were served on fine days, there was a vista of sunny water bounded by the surf-washed reef, and the dark, dreamlike fantasy of Moorea's mountains rising from the sea far beyond. The proprietors of the Inn, Mr. and Mrs. Buelle, were a quiet, respectable couple who would have seemed far more at home at a village tavern in their native England than in this tropical setting.

Mrs. Buelle, busy in the kitchen from morning till night instructing an ever-changing procession of native serving girls and helpers, never quite achieved the bland, English meals for which she strove; always there was some alien fruit or fish or vegetable which refused to lend itself to her ideas of what was suitable to eat. And Mr. Buelle, who enjoyed, as he said, puttering about a bit with flowers, was in a state of chronic amazement at the gaudy

171

exuberance his efforts produced. Scarlet and purple bougainvillea blazed from the pillars of the veranda; hibiscus bushes were showered with rosy blooms; banked fires of red and orange sparked from the neat croton hedges; and the round beds of cannas which punctuated the lawn were a shrieking cacophony of color. On windless nights, when the moon toned every flower to sober silver and black, the blooms still made themselves known, and the air was indecorously heady with the scent of jasmine.

Outside of Marianna, the only permanent guests at the Inn were the Nichollses, who occupied one wing of the bungalow. Her own little house, shrouded in flowering vines, was about a hundred paces nearer the beach. It had only one room, which served as bed- and sitting room, and a tiny veranda, big enough for three chairs and a table, but it was neat and attractive. With the books and personal things she had brought in from Matavai, it already seemed quite homelike.

After two weeks her days had settled into a quiet pattern. The mornings were the best, when for four hours she taught in the frame schoolhouse next to Mr. Pritchard's old church, where Mr. Thomson was now the pastor. She felt almost at home then, in the same comfortable routine she had known for so long, and had it not been for Mr. Thomson's strict insistence on more catechisms than she or her father had ever thought necessary, and his frequent, unexpected visitations of the schoolroom, when he stood soberly observant, watching her from the doorway, she might have been back in Matavai again. So far he had always nodded approvingly and slipped away again, but there was something about his silent appearances there that made her a little uneasy. Still, he was a good man, she told herself, and his strict conscience, his rigid concepts of duty, were after all what had held him from deserting to England as Richard Johnson and the others were doing.

After lunch at the Inn, there were the long, quiescent hours of

172

the afternoon to be got through. Sometimes she went to see Mrs. Pritchard, to help her in her packing up for England; sometimes she called on Mrs. Truelove or Mrs. Thomson, to sew and chat with them. More frequently Lily Nicholls came over to her cottage, still sleepy from her after-lunch siesta, bored and nearly always restless, and settled down on the veranda beside her to gossip, to complain or, when she was in a better humor, to talk of her life in London, until it was time to go and change her dress for dinner.

Lily had been touchingly glad to see her. Without resentment, Marianna realized that the warmth of her welcome was in direct ratio to the measure of Lily's unhappiness; Lily was clutching at anything that would help her through the pointless and terrible ennui of her days. It was impossible to approve of Lily, who made so little attempt to improve her own life, who slept through most of the mornings and part of the afternoons, who brightened into animation only at dinnertime when her breath was heavy with brandy; but it was impossible not to feel sorry for her, too. It was apparent from the frequent noontime ravage of Lily's pert and still nubile beauty that she wore the evening through with drinking in her rooms, even when Anthony was away in Moorea, as he often was.

And Anthony away was scarcely less dreadful than Anthony at one's side. Sober, he took refuge in a grumpy and pompous silence; drunk, with his heavy red face more scarlet than ever, he would launch into long and muddled anecdotes of his own adventurous career, and punctuate anyone else's remarks with his booming and meaningless laughter. It was hard to imagine what he and Lily were living on now, since the plantation in Matavai had been destroyed, and all the young men in Moorea had left for Tahiti to join the encampments in the hills. It was known to everyone in Papeete that his trips to oversee the plantation in Moorea were merely pretexts to visit the native mistress he had there, and presumably Lily's profound indifference to him was deep enough to encompass that knowledge too.

Marianna had scarcely seen Jonas since coming to town, although his schooner was moored little more than a stone's throw from the beach in front of her cottage and she frequently glimpsed him working about the deck, or rowing to shore in his dinghy. Occasionally he took his dinner at the Inn, sitting at one of the two long tables on the veranda with her and the Nichollses. He was always friendly when they met, inquiring solicitously about her welfare, but he had not troubled to come to see her; and she told herself, a little bitterly, that now he had got her safely settled, and considered his duty to her discharged, she was no longer of interest to him.

This afternoon, as she brushed out her hair and twisted it again into a neat, shining knot, she found herself wondering, as she always did at this hour, whether he would be on the veranda when she went over for her evening meal. She leaned toward her small mirror, settling the lace collar into place at the base of her throat, her smooth forehead creased in a frown. Dinner, which was at five-thirty at the Inn, so that everyone could be in his quarters by evening gunfire at seven — a mandate of the French martial law — was always rather a difficult time for her. And having Jonas join them invariably made things worse instead of better. Lily would be electrically tense in Jonas's presence, either arch with him, or chidingly sulky at some fancied slight. And Anthony, when he had failed several times to rivet their attention, would turn to Marianna and force her polite response to one of his long and boring stories. Why, then, should her wayward heart make such a clatter at the mere possibility that Jonas would be there?

She was the first to take her place at their table this evening. At the next long table down the veranda five or six French officers and officials, who dined there nearly every night, were already seated. Captain d'Aubigny, Monsieur Moerenhout, Monsieur Reine — they had all jumped politely to their feet at her appearance, and made her their customary bows, to which she replied with a cool, "Good evening."

Beyond their quick and animated chatter she could hear Jonas's low voice talking to Mr. Buelle in the room behind the veranda that served as bar and parlor. Marianna sat rigidly at the table, staring across the sea at the shadowy pinnacles of Moorea, her nerves alert for the sound of his footsteps.

She was still alone at the table when he came out and took the chair beside her. "Hello, it's good to find you here."

"I'm always here," she said. "A fixture, like the napkin rings."

"How's life in town by now? Is it bearable?"

"I'm bearing it," she said, "but I'm afraid I'm a rustic at heart."

"I too." He leaned toward her, lowering his voice. "I know how you've been feeling, Marianna. Damn it all, I miss your father constantly. He was the wisest man I ever knew."

The sympathy in his voice, the sincerity of his words, moved her more than she dared to show. She looked at him a moment wordlessly, and nodded her head.

"I've been wanting to talk to you," he went on, "but the *Moana* has kept me drudging like a slave. Is your cottage all right? Is Thomson giving you enough freedom to teach school the way you want to?"

"Everything is fine," she said. "I'm sorry the schooner is so demanding."

"There's no tyrant like a small boat. A wife could be no worse. Have you noticed the new foresail? I'm going to try it out some day, outside the reef. Perhaps you'd like to come along."

"I'd love to." His hand, brown and strong, was resting on the white cloth by his plate. A little breathlessly, she said, "I haven't sailed along the reef for a year or more. Are there still rainbows in the spray when it blows back from the breakers?"

175

Before he could reply Lily Nicholls came rustling along the veranda, dressed in crimson silk, her dark curls piled coquettishly atop her small head. As Jonas helped her into a chair, Marianna saw that Lily's eyes were very bright, and that there was a trace of rouge on her smooth cheeks.

"I'm sorry to interrupt this charming tête-à-tête," Lily said, "but after all, I cannot starve."

So she was going to be arch this evening. "We wouldn't think of letting you starve," Marianna said.

"You're rather late for one so hungry, Lily."

"I've been hunting for my comb," Lily said peevishly. "Anthony's off to Moorea again, and doubtless has it in his pocket. It was my favorite one, too. I hope the Moorean beauty he gives it to will properly appreciate it."

It was the first time she had ever spoken so openly of Anthony's peccadilloes.

"Lily," Jonas said lightly, "you show a touching confidence in your husband's behavior. Are you always so harsh in your judgment of men?"

Lily gave him a long look across the table. "I've had few reasons not to be," she said.

Miatu, the Inn's newest maidservant, came out with a tray of soup bowls, splashing one down at each place, and giggling as she brushed against Jonas's sleeve.

"Speaking of men," Jonas said, "have you heard the latest of Pomare Tane's escapades?" His dark, beaked face held a look of intentional blandness.

"No," Marianna said quickly. "What was it?"

"He found the keys to Commander Hunt's wine cabinet on the *Basilisk*, and managed to polish off a bottle of brandy during the morning. It was only discovered when he decided to walk ashore and stepped airily off the deck right into the bay — "

"I know all about it," Lily said rudely. "And so does Marianna.

Miatu told us, this noon. It took three sailors with boathooks to fish him out again."

"Five sailors, in my version," Jonas said. "I wish you wouldn't spoil my story, Lily. After all, exaggeration is a fine art."

"Akin to lying," she said, "at which you've had some practice. Jonas, your hair wants cutting."

Jonas touched the thick crisp hair at the back of his neck. "I was thinking of growing a pigtail," he said mildly, "like sailors used to wear. Don't you think it would be becoming?"

"Charming," Lily said. "With a little bowknot to fasten it off."

"I can't believe you're right," he said. "Marianna, help me out. Do you think I need my hair cut?"

Marianna didn't look up from her soup. "I hadn't noticed," she said.

How churlish her voice had sounded! She reached for her water glass, her cheeks reddening, and found herself wishing that Anthony Nicholls were back again. Anything was better than this role of middleman between Lily's coquettish rudenesses and Jonas's amusedly tolerant efforts to sidestep them.

For the rest of the meal she said little, except when they addressed her directly, and when at last Miatu came out to gather up the dishes, she felt as if it were an escape to bid them good night, and cross over the lawn to the lonely sanctuary of her little house.

After evening gunfire, at seven, an unnatural stillness descended upon the village, broken occasionally by the sharp barking of a dog as the sentries passed by in their patrol, or by the sound of singing, borne across the water from one of the ships in the harbor. Only the French were free to come and go as they pleased. Everyone else, native or foreigner, had to remain in his own house, and receive no visitors; the officers and crews of

177

foreign ships had to be back aboard their vessels. If their ship's boats were found on the beach after seven they would be destroyed.

For Marianna it was the hardest time of all. It was no use to try to read or sew for very long; the coconut-oil lamps gave out too feeble a light for that. In desperation, she had formed the habit of going to bed very early each evening and waking with the dawn, but there was always a black hour or two to be faced every night after dinner, when sleep was still beyond her reach.

During those hours she came to realize the empty futility of her life; during those hours her daytime mask of serenity slipped hopelessly away, leaving her faced with an aching and unbearable loneliness. As the twilight deepened, she put down her book and sat staring before her. Shortly before seven, Jonas passed by and waved good night to her; from the shadows of her veranda she watched him row out to the *Moana,* climb aboard, and hang a lantern from the mainmast.

There was a small and selfish comfort in that light; the shining lamp against the dark mast of his schooner told her that he, too, was alone. Perhaps even Jonas, behind his swagger, behind the amused, sardonic face he turned upon the world, knew his own lonelinesses, his own moments of panic and despair.

For a long time she sat there, watching the stars emerge from the blackening sky and seek their watery reflections between the ships that were strewn across the bay. Here, in the quiet dark, there was no escape from the knowledge that had been haunting her so long. I love him, she thought tiredly; of course I love him, I've always loved him.

When she went inside, her last look was for the lantern, glowing in mute salute across the water.

She awoke at cockcrow the next morning, got up, threw her dressing gown across her shoulders and went out to the veranda to sniff the early morning air. A few stars still glittered, close to the horizon, but a cold gray light was fingering through the darkness. The lantern on Jonas's schooner had burned out during the night, and the spars were barely distinguishable against the sky. The sound of a soft and cautious splashing in the water at the side of the boat attracted her attention, and she moved forward to the railing of the veranda, staring surprisedly through the murky dimness.

Presently she could discern that a small outrigger canoe had pushed away from the *Moana*, and that someone was paddling quietly to the beach. There was no one else about; the only sounds were the far and nearby discordant crowing of the cocks. The last stroke of the paddle sent the bow of the canoe up on the sand, and its occupant stepped out into the shallows, pulling the little craft clear of the water. Marianna moved back into the shadows and watched the small figure cross the beach to the lawn in front of the Inn. She could see now that it was a woman — a girl with a *pareu* wrapped tightly about her body, in the native style, and with long dark hair hanging below the shawl she had thrown about her head. Miatu, she thought, with a sick feeling of revulsion; stupid, giggling Miatu, with her flat round face and her slim, animal body . . .

But as the woman came closer she saw that it was not Miatu; that the face half hidden by the shawl was pale and that beneath the *pareu* small white feet whispered swiftly across the grayness of the dewy grass. Lily Nicholls, of course! Lily, disguised as a native girl, slipping furtively across the lawn and opening, with practiced quietness, the door to her rooms. So this was the lost and pathetic Lily whom she had pitied — this was how Jonas passed the long hours when she had felt so close to him in loneliness!

Marianna turned toward her doorway, sick and trembling. Clumsily, she groped her way across the room to the bed and lay down, her face against the pillow. Fool, fool, jealous, miserable,

179

ludicrous fool that she was! Impotently, she pounded her fists against the mattress, and then at last lay still, tasting the bitter salt of tears on her lips.

ᗰᑎᖘᑎᖘᑎᖘᑎ

THE LITTLE *Basilisk* SHOOK DOWN THE SAILS OVER HER NAKED spars and edged forward slowly with the gentle breeze, as if reluctant to leave the spot where she had been anchored for six long months. On her quarter-deck Commander Hunt picked up his spyglass and directed it to the masts of H.M.S. *Carysfort*, waiting just outside the pass through the foaming reef. The late afternoon calm held well; the *Carysfort* scarcely swayed against the horizon. Commander Hunt, who had had time to do some reading in Tahiti, decided that she was as idle as a painted ship upon a painted ocean. A jolly good thing, too. It would be no small task to transfer the Queen, in her present condition, to another ship if there were even the suggestion of a sea running.

The *Carysfort* had arrived two days before, on July 11, and her captain, Lord George Paulet, had kept her standing on and off the reef outside the harbor while he conferred with Governor Bruat. The news that Lord Paulet brought from Europe — that King Louis Philippe did not recognize the seizure of Tahiti and wished merely to preserve the protectorate — had not gone down well with the Governor, who protested that he had received no official intelligence to this effect. But after several interviews with the persuasive English Lord, he had at last agreed to grant Queen Pomare permission to go to one of the Leeward Islands — Bora Bora, perhaps, or Raiatea — and remain there unmolested until definite word came from France.

Commander Hunt glanced down at the deck below, where

Pomare, surrounded by her children, stood waving a tearful fare-well to the hundreds of her people who crowded along the beach. Why was it that one referred to her condition as delicate, he wondered fleetingly. She must be eight months gone, at least, and she looked as hugely ponderous as a four-rigger under full canvas. It was surprising how much they were going to miss the old girl, he thought, but it was a lucky thing she could at last get on shore again, among her own people. For the past six months he had done a pretty good job as nursemaid and royal guardian, but damned if he could play midwife too. The Royal Navy couldn't expect *that* of her officers.

For the next half hour he was too occupied with maneuvering the ship through the pass and coming up alongside the *Carysfort* to think of Pomare again, but when the buffers were all in place and the two ships safely grappled together, he turned the command over to his mate and went down to the deck to make her his formal farewell. Her face was marked with tears, and it was obvious that she was struggling still to suppress them, but he could see that there was something that she wanted to say to him and his men. He gestured them to silence, and Georgie Pritchard, who had volunteered to come aboard as interpreter — the *Basilisk* was returning to Papeete harbor that same evening — stepped proudly to her side.

Georgie's childish voice following the Queen's pauses was firm and clear, a credit to his father. "The Queen says that her heart is filled with sorrow to say good-by to Commander Hunt and all the officers and men who have guarded her so well. She wants to thank each one of you for your goodness to her and her children and Pomare Tane. She says better forever to stay aboard the *Basilisk* than to trust herself to those dirty French. She says she takes their word no farther than a dog could spit. She says if it wasn't for her children and the rumble in her stomach for native food again, she would not leave you now. But for the sake

181

of the little one in her belly she must be free again to walk the land."

Commander Hunt made what he hoped was a suitable response in halting Tahitian. When he finished he was surprised to see the Queen hold up her hand for their further attention. Georgie Pritchard listened to her rapid instructions, and nodded intelligently. "Her Majesty says," he said importantly, "that she has been listening to the speech of all on board, and that she has learned enough English to say a farewell herself."

The Queen stepped forward, her brown, beautiful eyes turning from one face to another, like a mild and maternal benediction. She drew a deep breath. "I am fill," she said, and her voice was charged with tenderness, "I am fill with love to every barstard on dis boat."

She broke into tears then, and turned away. On the *Carysfort* Lord George Paulet, his uniform glittering with gold braid, came forward to help her aboard. The shrill sound of his boatswain's piping was lost in the roar of cheers that went up, full-throated, from every man aboard the *Basilisk*.

W‌HEN MR. TRUELOVE STEPPED ASHORE ON THE SHADED BEACH AT Hitiaa, on the eastern side of the island, Navi, chief of the district, and ten or twelve of his followers were waiting there to greet him. He saw that their glances kept sidling toward the *Nelly T.*, anchored in the lagoon midway between reef and shore, but they asked him no question until he had been supplied with fruit and drinking nuts, and was seated on the grass-strewn floor of Navi's house, with his host beside him and the others squatting in a respectful semicircle just behind.

"Where do you come from, Terutove?" Navi asked finally.

"From Tautira," Mr. Truelove said, "on the same errand that brings me here. The Governor gave me a passport" — he grimaced involuntarily — "so that I could go around to the stations and fetch the property the missionaries left behind them."

"*Aué!* Then the missionaries are really going to fly to Beretane!"

Mr. Truelove swallowed a mouthful of banana. "Did you love them so dearly?" he asked.

"The young one in Tiarei was a chickenhearted fool," Navi said candidly. "He cringed if the wind was rough in the palms. But it's an evil omen if they leave. It means they have no hope the Farani will stop attacking us."

"Things have been more quiet lately," Mr. Truelove said. "Perhaps the Farani will give up before long." There was no conviction in his tone.

"They may as well," Navi said ominously, "because we Tahitians never will." He gestured up at the ceiling above them. Two or three muskets were stuck into the woven thatch, with packed bundles slung from them. "The guns are loaded," Navi said, "and if the French return to Hitiaa we'll take a farewell shot at them, burn down our houses, and go up again to the mountains."

"You're well prepared, I see."

"For one shot," Navi said. "But we need more ammunition and more guns." He pushed a wooden platter of fruit closer to Mr. Truelove, leaning toward him earnestly. "We've gathered hundreds of coconuts to trade, Terutove, and a great quantity of arrowroot. Did you bring supplies for us on your boat? We know you've been across the sea."

"Some flour," Mr. Truelove said, "and some cornmeal and rice. And a few bolts of cloth."

Navi's eyes were intent on his face. "I didn't mean that. You know what I meant."

"The French forbade me to bring back any firearms," Mr.

183

Truelove said virtuously, "and you wouldn't expect me to break their laws." He took a meditative swig of coconut water. "However, I must warn you that this shipment of goods has some peculiarities. The cloth is strangely heavy to carry, and the rice and flour must be eaten carefully because there are hard grains in it that might break your teeth. And the cornmeal —" he shook his head, sadly — "the cornmeal is not edible at all, I'm afraid. I wouldn't recommend striking a fire near it, either."

Navi's dark face was suddenly illumined with exultant intelligence, and one of the men behind him raised an imaginary musket in the air, saying "*Pau, pau!*" very softly.

"When can we bring these goods to shore, Terutove?"

"Any time," Mr. Truelove said. He wiped his mouth on the back of his hand, and turned a look of innocent diffidence on Navi. "But please don't open them until after I have gone," he said. "It would embarrass me greatly to know that there were any defects in my goods."

Whenever a ship sailed away from the island, those left behind were forcefully and rather unpleasantly reminded of the insular character of their lives. In an hour of farewells to friends who in all likelihood would never return, Tahiti had a dismaying way of shrinking from a complete and absorbing world to a mere pin point of unimportant land surrounded by vast seas. Its daily concerns, ordinarily so magnified by the minuteness with which they were examined, dwindled briefly to insignificance, and no one felt quite comfortable again until the ship had dropped below the horizon and could be forgotten.

The sense of being apart from the rest of the world, of being left behind, had never been stronger in Marianna than when she watched the brig *Feejee,* chartered from Port Jackson to take the departing missionaries to Valparaiso, draw up its anchor. The knowledge that she herself could have been among those leaving only intensified its sharpness. There was no one aboard, save Mrs. Pritchard and her children, whose absence she would regret, but her mind went straining after the things that they would see: the great continents, the changing weathers; above all, England. To Marianna, who had never been farther than the island of Raiatea, 120 miles to the northwest, England was as familiar as the words and pictures in her favorite books, and as hard to visualize accurately as the kingdom of heaven.

Well, she had rejected England, and had clung, with what might be more fright than bravery, to all that was familiar. But the dull and arid bitterness of the past month, since the morning she had seen Lily steal back from Jonas's schooner, mocked at her choice. She had begun to feel curiously abnormal, as if she were the only human being in the world who walked alone, the only one who had no whole relationship to bind her to another soul.

Georgie Pritchard, leaning precariously across the *Feejee's* taffrail, had spotted her, and waved his arm in a huge salute. She waved back to him, and let her gaze slide along the faces of the others who were lined at the railing. Mr. Howe, Mr. Jesson, Mr. Buchanan, Richard Johnson . . . Richard was looking the other way. Sara Darling came up beside him, and he turned to take her arm. Sara's decision to leave had been made only a week ago, and it was rumored that when they reached England, she and Richard would be married. For a moment her eyes were wistful as she watched them. It would be good to have someone who would take your arm . . .

At a light touch on her elbow, she turned her head. Jonas was standing there, looking at her gravely, and he kept his hand on her arm until she withdrew it.

"Are you sorry you're not aboard?"

"Should I be?" she asked defensively.

He looked down at her, his heavy eyebrows arching a trifle. "I hope not," he said. "We need you here."

She looked out at the ship. "So you have said. But I don't know why." Her voice was very low.

"You've given me small chance to tell you why," he said. "It's quite obvious you've been avoiding me for the past few weeks. And when we do meet, you're cool and distant as the Andes. What's the matter? What have I done?"

A dull flush crept into her cheeks. He had done nothing that she had any right to criticize; she could in no way make demands on him or try to regulate his behavior. "Nothing, of course." She turned toward him, making an effort to speak lightly. "It must be my pedagogic manner."

"Ah," he said roughly, "I know you better than that." He took her arm, felt it stiffen at his touch, and let it go abruptly. "I was going to suggest that we walk back to the Inn together, if you've nothing better to do."

Unexpectedly, she murmured, "Nothing could be better."

He glanced at her sharply, and then laughed. "That's handsome enough — for the moment. But I expect enormous docility from now on to make up for your past rudenesses."

To be with him, to watch the gestures of his brown-skinned hands, the play of expression across his beaked face, was like coming into the sunshine. "I didn't intend to be rude," she said. "You must be imagining it."

"You were churlish," he said. "No one could have been ruder — not even I. What's more, I was forced to try out the new foresail with only Farenui to admire it."

"I admired it too," she said, "from a distance. I saw you that day, skimming along the reef like an *itatae*."

They turned their backs to the *Feejee*, and started toward the green shade of the trees on the other side of the road.

186

"I prefer my audience closer at hand," he said. "Never mind. By way of punishing you, I've appointed you chief agent in the newly organized Truelove-Burkham espionage service. You haven't even given me a chance to tell you, Marianna, that you are now a spy."

"What *are* you talking about?"

"You may well ask," he said portentously, "because your life is in my hands. Unless you're kind to me I'll turn you over to the French authorities. You're completely at my mercy."

An unfamiliar feeling suddenly flowed through Marianna, a curious sensation that her bones were turning to fluid. A little breathlessly, she said, "What are my duties? Only to be kind?"

"That's the most important one," he said, smiling. "Let's wait till we're back at the Inn to discuss the others."

When he had seated himself beside her on her little veranda, he told her of the arrangement he had made with Mr. Truelove. "Ostensibly, I'll be working for him again — using my schooner to take his goods to the other islands, and helping him in the warehouse. Actually, we'll be doing all we can to get supplies to the people in the mountain camps and establish some sort of communication between them and the Queen."

Sometimes, as she knew, natives from the camps managed to slip by the French outposts and come into town, carrying messages and gathering information to take back to their leaders. Since the lull in the fighting, there had been quite a number of them — ordinary people, who would not be suspect even if they were observed. "That's where we need you, Marianna — you know so many of them well, and if someone like Teaui came to town, for instance, nothing would be more natural than for her to see you. If they all came to Truelove or me, the game would be up before it got started. But you can be a liaison between us, and if we're careful, I don't think it will look suspicious."

"Oh, no."

"There will be a certain risk," he said gravely, "and I hate to think of exposing you to it. Think it over before you decide."

"I have decided," she said. "The risk is nothing. I'd welcome the chance to see my old friends now and again, and if I can be of use to them, nothing would make me happier."

"If it would make you happy," he said teasingly, "Truelove and I can only bow to your wishes."

"What shall I tell them when they come?"

"Everything," he said. "The latest movement of the French, what fortifications are being built, which natives have turned traitor to the Queen. Sometimes there'll be more specific information. Next week, for instance, I'm taking a cargo to Raiatea in the *Moana* — the French have granted me a passport — and on the way back, without their knowledge, I'll run in at Papenoo with some supplies. You must tell them to keep a watch for me, and to start a signal fire in the mountains if there are any French about."

"When will that be?"

"In about three weeks, probably. I'll let you know all the details in a day or two."

He leaned back in his chair, stretching his arms above his head, looking across at the cool symmetry of Marianna's features. Too bad she always pulled her pale hair so severely back from her face; if it were softened a bit she might be almost pretty. There was a faint flush in her cheeks just now, a lilt to the curve of her lips, and her dark gray eyes were clear and shining. Her eyes, he decided idly, were really beautiful. "You look as if being a spy agreed with you," he said.

"It's the most pleasant assignment I've had in months," she said warmly.

He brought his hands down to the arm of his chair, and pushed himself to his feet. "Good. Did I tell you I was moving?"

"Moving?"

"This afternoon, to the spare room in Dr. Ferguson's house.

188

That way I'll be able to get about the village at night, if it should be necessary. Sleeping aboard the schooner was like being a prisoner in solitary confinement."

"It must have been unbearably solitary," Marianna said.

The unexpected irony of her tone pulled his glance sharply to her face. The happiness he had seen in it before was quite erased, her chin was high, and there was a set look to her lips. Heigh-ho, so she knew about Lily, and her missionary blood was roused! "It was not unbearable," he said, "but I think I can be more useful if I have some freedom."

"And freedom is what you're working for, isn't it?"

She had risen too, and her eyes, which had been averted, suddenly swung up to meet his. For an instant their glances locked, direct, unveiled, and oddly antagonistic. The soft glitter of the air between them seemed to quiver with the words that neither of them spoke.

"'It's more important to me than anything else," he said. "Goodby. Thanks for your help."

*️⃣

Lɪʟʏ ɴɪᴄʜᴏʟʟs sᴀᴛ ᴀʟᴏɴᴇ ᴀᴛ ᴛʜᴇ ᴅɪɴɪɴɢ ᴛᴀʙʟᴇ ᴏɴ ᴛʜᴇ ᴠᴇʀᴀɴᴅᴀ, automatically taking food from the dishes that Miatu passed to her, and scarcely tasting it after she had put it on her plate. At the next table four or five Frenchmen, Captain d'Aubigny and Monsieur Moerenhout among them, were animatedly chattering; the sound of their voices and laughter filled her with a furious envy. Anthony was in Moorea, Marianna was dining with the Trueloves, Jonas had been away in Raiatea for more than a week, and there was no one, no one, to rescue her from the stifling loneliness that faced her.

She stared out morosely across the quiet shimmer of the bay. If only Jonas were back, they might have had an evening alone together. Yet even if he were there, as things stood between them now, they would no doubt end by quarreling. Her lips tightened, and she picked up her fork. Jonas was becoming impossible. His calm assumption that their affair was merely a convenience to them both, his habit of being jocose when he should have been tender, matter-of-fact when he should have been ardent, bluntly sensual when her soul cried out for protestations of undying love, had brought them to a point almost of enmity. But with Jonas one could not even be enemies; his maddening indifference turned every quarrel into a one-sided affair that left her feeling frustrate and foolish.

Still, anything would be better than this empty isolation. . . . She pushed a piece of mango about her plate, drearily reviewing the day that had just passed, and the evening that stretched before her. In the morning she had washed and dressed her hair, at noon she had talked briefly with Marianna, and then through the hot and endless hours of the afternoon there had been nothing; sleep had evaded her, her novels had been read to shreds, all that was left were the endless games of patience at her desk in the room that she was growing to hate. And tonight, what was there? A chat with Mrs. Buelle in her parlor, listening to her inevitable review of the shortcomings of the Inn's maidservants; or more games of patience in the flickering lamplight, and a few glasses of brandy to put her finally to sleep.

The easy tears welled into her eyes, and she brushed them hurriedly away with her napkin. At the next table the Frenchmen were getting to their feet; they made her their quick, stiff bows, and all of them, except Captain d'Aubigny, turned down the veranda steps toward the road. D'Aubigny remained, still standing beside the table. As she glanced toward him, he bowed again.

190

"I beg not to be impolite, madame," he said, stepping toward her, "but would you favor to join me in a glass of wine?"

There was something in his eyes as he looked down at her that made her suddenly alertly aware of the artless perfection of her black curls and of the soft folds of her sprigged muslin gown clinging against the white swell of her breast. She hesitated only for a moment. "If you like," she said faintly.

As he turned away to fetch a bottle of wine and glasses from the other table she hurriedly brushed the last sparkle of her tears up into the black sweep of her lashes. When he came back and pulled out the chair beside her she could see again in his eyes the warm and exhilarating reflection of how she looked to him. "Is it permitted to pour you of wine, madame?"

"*S'il vous plaît*," Lily murmured.

His neat, sharp face glowed with pleasure. "You speak of French a leetle?"

"A leetle," Lily said, smiling.

"Ah, now you mock of me," he said. "*Maintenant il faut parler en français pour me faire au niveau de vous.*"

At her look of bewilderment a wise little gleam came into his eyes. "We will speak Angleesh," he said, "if madame will be so kind as to help my errors."

"I would be delighted to," Lily said, "but you make so few."

"You deceive me weeth charm," he said. "*Vraiment*, it loses one's language to live in this savage island. A try for the barbaric Taïtian; a leetle Angleesh for purpose to quarrel in; and in my own tongue, only men to talk it. I 'ave lost the know of 'ow to talk to a beautiful lady."

"I don't think you need worry on that score," Lily said.

"So, you are kind, as good as beautiful," he said triumphantly. "Now I am 'appy for the first time in thees barbarism!"

Miatu had come out on the veranda to clear the tables. She stopped short when she saw Lily with d'Aubigny, and cast a

191

dour, resentful glance at the back of Lily's head. D'Aubigny was leaning toward her.

"Tell me you will be kind enough to let me geeve you a leetle glass of cognac," he said eagerly.

Lily's wide, upswept glance was a masterpiece of diffident acquiescence. "It would be very nice," she said.

As he turned away to explain in sweeping gestures to Miatu what he wanted, she studied him obliquely. He was a Frenchman, of course, and naturally she hated the French. He wasn't even a very handsome Frenchman. He was rather small, and his waxed mustache was absurdly precise, but his attempts at English were amusing, and he was trying hard to be agreeable. Surely it could do no harm to spend a few minutes chatting with him. Anything was better than returning to that lonely room. . . .

Miatu came back with a bottle of brandy and two glasses, slamming them sullenly down on the table. D'Aubigny uncorked the bottle, filled the glasses, and handed her one with a little bow. "A votre santé, madame."

Lily took a meditative sip, and then another. "Don't you like being here in Tahiti, monsieur?"

"Like it?" he said. "Madame, it is the ends of the world! My home was always Paris — I cannot be 'appy in the society of sauvages."

He went on to tell her in detail what he thought of life in Tahiti, and to contrast it with the pleasures of Paris. It was not long before he had found out how she felt about it too. Lily, gazing innocently in the other direction while he filled her glass again, found herself thinking how easy and sympathetic he was to talk to. Poor man, it wasn't his fault that he was assigned to such an unpleasant mission, so far away from home. . . .

It was nearly dark when she saw Dr. Ferguson mounting the veranda steps with his ponderously unsteady gait. D'Aubigny, talking confidentially, his sharp, neat nose close to her ear, was saying, ". . . and the women! No man of good taste can be amuse' by a dark, eegnorant *sauvage*. I tell you, madame, now ees the first hour of civilize I 'ave spent on thees island."

He looked up then and saw Dr. Ferguson, leaning against the pillar at the top of the steps, gazing at them owlishly through the gathering gloom.

"Mrs. Nicholls," the doctor said thickly, "is this — Frrenchman — annoying you?"

"Not at all," Lily said uneasily.

"If he is," Dr. Ferguson said, raising one arm unsteadily, "I'll knock his blasted head off!"

"It's quite all right, Dr. Ferguson."

"All right, is it! You can stomach the company of poor Pr-ritchard's persecutor?" His Scotch r's rolled like thunder.

D'Aubigny jumped to his feet, his sharp face pointing toward the doctor. "I must remind you, monsieur," he said harshly, "that it is past the hour of curfew. Eef you do not go 'ome at once I must oblige to put you in the 'and of the police."

The doctor grunted. "Sit down, Frenchman, and let me get my bottle of rum. I'll take it home rright enough. The society here is hardly to my liking."

He went inside, where he could be heard talking to Mr. Buelle, and soon came out, a bottle tucked under each arm. He didn't speak as he passed them and went down the veranda steps. Lily, nervously aware of his righteous disapproval, was trembling a little. She straightened in her chair.

"It's curfew time for me, too," she said.

"But no!" d'Aubigny said. "The laws of France apply never to so beautiful a lady." He leaned toward her, and his hand brushed fleetingly against her bare arm. "You 'ave cold, madame! You must take a glass of cognac for your chill."

Lily hesitated, and he lowered his voice pleadingly. "Please, madame! Do not deny me thees small 'appiness."

193

Dr. Ferguson had disappeared among the shadows of the road, and in the sky above the bay enormous white stars were bursting into view. Lily's hand stole out for her empty glass. "Just one more, then," she said.

ﬡﬡﬡﬡﬡ

On a hot and drowsy afternoon in late September as she was coming away from a Bible class at Mr. Thomson's, Marianna saw the small, trig shape of the *Moana* making bare headway through the pass in the reef. She stopped abruptly in the road, staring out at it, her heart lifting with sudden thankfulness. It had been more than four weeks since Jonas had left in the *Moana;* by his own calculations he should have returned to Papeete several days since, and she knew, now that it was relieved, how great her anxiety for him had grown.

Within an hour the *Moana* was swinging to anchor at its old mooring in front of the Inn. Marianna, waiting on the veranda of her cottage, in her coolest and most becoming white dress, could see Jonas and Farenui, his native sailor, working about the deck; after a while he disappeared below for what seemed an endless stretch of time. Twice she put aside the book that she was pretending to read and went inside the house, to peer searchingly at her reflection in the mirror and smooth with impatient hands the pale, heavy knot of her hair. And twenty times she told herself not to be a fool, that it might be a day or two before he would stop by to see her.

At last Jonas reappeared, and the native boy rowed him to the beach. His face and hands were very tanned, she saw, and his shoulders, buttoned into a starched white jacket that was too small for him, looked even more bulky than she had remembered.

194

Her heart racing, she watched him cross the road directly to her cottage, and when he came up the veranda steps she was waiting at the top to greet him.

"Welcome home!" she said warmly.

He took her hands, smiling at her. "That's the greeting I was hoping for."

A moment of sheer happiness burst open within her like a flower. "It's good to see you. I've been worrying about you."

Her hands were still clasped in his, his gaze, a trifle quizzical, was searching the frank radiance of her face. "Have you? I don't deserve it in the least."

She pulled her hands away, and indicated a chair for him, suddenly shy. "I've been uneasy ever since the *Phaeton* left for Raiatea a couple of weeks ago. I was afraid you might run into trouble."

He sat down in the chair beside her, and pulled a cigar from his pocket. "I took care to avoid it," he said. "D'you mind if I smoke?"

"Of course not. What happened? Tell me all about it, please."

"First about you," he said. "Have you been all right?"

"I've been fine," she said. "Now tell me. Did you see the Queen? Did you go to Papenoo?"

"We were in Papenoo last night," he said. "Left there at dawn this morning. Everything went off perfectly, and with luck the French should never know that I was there. I'd rather not go into details, Marianna. It's safer for you not to know."

"Oh. All right. Now back to Raiatea. Is that where you went first?"

It was; and he found the Queen and several chiefs at Uturoa, on the north side of the island. The Queen's baby, a daughter, born a few weeks earlier, had been christened Victoria, and Pomare was in hopes that her royal sister in England might return the compliment by naming some future daughter Pomare.

195

But in spite of her joy in her new child, she still lived in constant fear of seizure by the French, and came daily to the schooner begging for more weapons to use in her defense.

The Raiateans had started to build a fort at the entrance to Uturoa harbor, on flat, unprotected land. When Jonas had pointed out to them that any frigate could shell out its defenders and blow it to bits in the course of an hour, they left off work on it and begged him to find them a better spot. With Tamatoa, chief of Raiatea, he had spent days of searching, and had at last fixed on the valley of Vaiaao, in the southwest part of the island. Vaiaao, shut in by inaccessible mountains on every side except that facing the sea, could only be approached by a long and tortuous passage through the shallows of the lagoon, and was out of range of any firing from the sea.

It was the most beautiful spot imaginable, Jonas told Marianna, a mountain gorge lush with great shade trees and watered by a good stream. In the valleys beyond were plenty of fruits and *fei* and other food plants that could sustain the Queen's party for an indefinite time. Properly fortified, it would be virtually impregnable.

There had been great anxiety when the French steamer *Phaeton* was sighted outside of Uturoa harbor, and the Queen and her followers had fled to Vaiaao. The French had sent a boat in pursuit of her, but had given up at last, baffled by the intricate passage through the reefs. When they tried to get letters to her, no one would deliver them. A boat sent ashore to survey the harbor at Uturoa had been met by Tamatoa on the beach. "Don't come ashore," he told them, "or you'll cut your feet on the oyster shells." It was figurative warning, for there had never been oysters in Raiatea, and when the French disregarded it, Tamatoa's followers had seized the boat and forced them to return to the steamer. After a few fruitless days the steamer had left, headed for Bora Bora and Huahine and the other islands in the Leeward group.

"What did you do while the steamer was there?" Marianna asked.

"I went fishing," Jonas said, grinning. "I fished as if my living depended on it. Afterwards, when the coast was clear again, Tamatoa asked me to go back to Vaiaao and help plan the fortifications. They were even building houses there by the time I left."

The smoke from his cigar curled into the still air outside the veranda like a silver plume. Marianna, watching it, watching his face as he talked, listening to the lazy and casual cadences of his voice, low and curiously foreign with its American accent, found herself thinking more of Jonas himself than of his words; of the friendliness that now and again flowered so spontaneously between them, and of the joyous sense of being alive that washed over her when she was with him. And occasionally she permitted herself a warm and secret look into the knowledge she held so carefully at the back of her mind — that he had come to see her first of all, before Mr. Truelove, or Dr. Ferguson; before Lily Nicholls. . . .

"Tell me about yourself," he said.

She shrugged. "There isn't much to tell. Things have been pretty quiet. The only real excitement was a couple of weeks ago, when the French seized a boat that was on its way to Raiatea and put everyone aboard in prison. The camp in Punaavia was getting ready to attack the town in revenge, but the captain of an English ship that was here intervened with Governor Bruat, and he released the prisoners in time to prevent it."

"I can hear that sort of news from anyone," Jonas said. "I want to hear about you. How is your teaching job?"

"All right, I suppose. At least, the children are. Mr. Thomson — " She hesitated.

"What about Thomson?"

"He's rather a — difficult man. His ideas are so rigid."

197

"A fanatic, isn't he?"

"I suppose so. I'm afraid he doesn't understand Tahiti very well. He wants me to teach a school for fallen girls," she said diffidently.

Jonas let out a shout of laughter. "Teach them how to fall? Or how to rise again?"

For an instant he glimpsed that quick, mischievous quirk of her lips. "I imagine they know both better than I."

"Has he considered how big his enrollment would be?"

"Don't laugh," she said. "What can I do about it?"

"What did you tell him?"

Her tone was more demure than the brief sidelong glance of her gray eyes toward his. "I said I thought perhaps it was too great an undertaking."

"But he persists?"

"He does," she said sadly.

The dinner bell from the Inn cut across the late afternoon quiet. "Shall you dine here?" Marianna asked.

"Yes. May I go over with you?"

Crossing the lawn he asked her about the Nichollses.

"Anthony's been away," she said. "In Moorea. And Lily's been — here."

It was an oddly incomplete answer, and he thought he knew why, a few moments later, when they had seated themselves at the table on the veranda. Lily herself, dressed in scarlet silk, holding a glass of wine in her hand and laughing tipsily, appeared in the doorway from the inner room. Just behind her shoulder they saw the smooth, foxlike face of Captain d'Aubigny.

Lily stopped short at the sight of Jonas, and some of the wine splashed from her glass to the sweeping ruffle of her dress. "So the sailor is home from his peri-lous voyage," she said, in a high, mocking voice.

Jonas, who had risen, made her a brief bow. "So it would seem," he said.

198

"And how were the girls in Raiatea?"

"Very beautiful," Jonas said blandly.

D'Aubigny, his small, neat figure elegant in his dress uniform, stepped forward and made his bows to Marianna and Jonas. In his hand was an open bottle of wine, which he put down on the table, in front of Lily's place.

"Madame," he said to Lily, "I regret it ees time I must go to the dinner of the Governor." He hesitated a moment, said something to her quickly, in a low and urgent tone, and they heard the words "Au revoir." He bowed again, and was gone, and Lily sat down, a little unsteadily, at the table.

"They must have been beautiful," she said, "or you wouldn't have stayed there so long."

"I'm flattered," Jonas said, "that it seemed long to you."

"A censhury," she said. "Simply a censhury." She finished off her glass of wine and filled it again from the bottle. "Have some wine, Marianna. And Jonas. Miatu, bring two more glasses!"

"What fine new friends you seem to have made in my absence," Jonas said distastefully.

Lily lifted her glass. "Rrravissants," she said deliberately. She put her lips to the glass, and raised her dark eyes to Jonas in a hard and scornful stare. "At least they are more attentive than my old ones."

Marianna felt her stomach knot like a fist against her ribs. When Miatu brought in the glasses, Jonas filled one for himself and one for Marianna, giving her a warning glance that said "Take it!" as he handed it across to her.

Marianna and Jonas scarcely touched their food, and Lily made no pretense of eating at all, drinking her wine, and staring moodily out at the road.

"How is Anthony?" Jonas asked.

"Away," she said thickly. "Moorean girls — beautiful too." She pushed her chair back, and a curious, glazed expression of concentration came into her eyes. "I don't — feel very well."

199

Jonas was at her side before she finished speaking. "Let's get her to her room! Take her other arm, Marianna."

Lily was a limp, almost lifeless weight between them, but when they reached her room she lurched suddenly out of their hands, to lean over the washstand, retching violently.

Marianna caught her as she crumpled to the floor, and Jonas lifted Lily from her arms, putting her in a chair beside the bed. "She's not ill," he said, seeing Marianna's stricken face. "Only drunk. Fix the bed for her, Marianna."

He bent over Lily, unfastening the row of tiny buttons that closed the front of her dress. When Marianna turned back from the bed, Lily was in her shift, her head lolling against the back of the chair, her dress and stays in a careless pile on the floor where Jonas had thrown them. He had taken one of her shoes off, and was kneeling on the floor, rolling down her stocking with swift, impersonal fingers. Marianna, bending over to help him with the other one, found herself thinking that it was like undressing a corpse.

Jonas carried Lily to the bed, matter-of-factly pulled her shift down below her knees and tucked the coverlet about her shoulders. Marianna poured some water onto a cloth and brought it back to bathe Lily's flushed, unhappy face.

"Should I — should one of us stay here with her tonight?"

He shook his head. "She'll be all right — as good as ever in the morning." There was no scorn in his voice; it was completely dispassionate.

Marianna smoothed back the tangled curls above Lily's forehead. Lily turned her face to one side, breathing stertorously. "Poor Lily," she said softly. "Poor Lily!"

She took the cloth back to the washstand, picked up Lily's clothes, and hung them neatly across the chair. Jonas was waiting for her by the door, and they went out together into the soft, warm twilight, stopping in the shadows of the tree before her cottage.

"Poor Lily," Marianna said again. "What will happen to her?"

"She's lost," Jonas said, in that same dispassionate tone. "There's nothing we can do to help her."

For a moment he stared at Marianna as if he would like to say something more, then he shook his head almost imperceptibly.

"It's nearly curfew time," he said. "Good night, Marianna."

Frowning a little, she watched him walk away, then she went up the steps to her cottage. Her thoughts went back to Lily, and she was filled with a profound and helpless pity. And all at once she knew that she would never be jealous of Lily Nicholls again.

A LETTER FROM QUEEN POMARE TO QUEEN VICTORIA:

ENCAMPMENT AT VAIAAO, RAIATEA
September 27, 1844

O GREAT QUEEN OF BRITAIN:
MY ELDER SISTER:

I am wandering in this place and that place, on mountains and in valleys with fear. This is my word to you: do not regard with strictness my errors and ignorance, shelter me with your great and royal compassion that I may not faint in the day of heat.

POMARE

AT EXACTLY TEN O'CLOCK IN THE MORNING, THE HOUR OF HIS SUMmons, Mr. Truelove stood in the bare unpainted courtroom of the new frame building the French had built across from the Queen's palace, facing Monsieur Reine, Judge of the Peace, who sat behind a desk on a raised dais in front of him. The morning was warm, and Mr. Truelove was dressed in a black worsted suit, with his best heavy silk stock wrapped twice about the high collar that reached to his chin, but these facts could not altogether account for the icy sweat that moistened Mr. Truelove's palms and prickled coldly along the middle of his back.

Monsieur Moerenhout, now director of native police, a few gendarmes, and a secretary sat at a table just below the judge. There was no one else in the room. The judge picked up a gavel, rapped it sharply on the desk, and Mr. Truelove asked himself, for the hundredth time since the summons had reached him the day before, what these demned Froggies had on their minds. The weapons he had smuggled to Horoi to pay for his grove of *tamanu?* The muskets and powder he had taken to Hitiaa a couple of months ago? Or maybe his part in sending young Burkham to Raiatea with supplies for the Queen, and that extra shipment to Papenoo . . . He pulled his plump body more erect and decided doggedly to bluff.

The judge began to speak, translating into English the paper from which he read. Mr. Truelove had been sent for, by instruction of the Governor, to be censured and reproved. It was well known that he was hostile to the French government, and had aided and abetted the natives in opposing it. Specifically, he was accused of having sold powder to the natives of Tiarei when he had gone there to collect the missionaries' effects in August of this year, 1844. A *procès verbal* had been issued against him, but the Governor, in his clemency, although convinced of Mr. Truelove's guilt, had ordered it to be quashed in the hopes that his mercy would have the good effect of deterring him and others from committing similar offenses . . .

Mr. Truelove, surreptitiously wiping the palms of his hands against his trousers, was seized by hilarious relief. They were barking up the wrong tree altogether — he hadn't sold a thing in Tiarei that time. Automatically, his face assumed an expression of outraged innocence. It wouldn't even be necessary to bluff.

The proceedings against him were stayed, the judge said, but

202

he was warned to avoid misconduct in the future. In the case of renewed offense he would be subject to trial by military and naval officials, and if considered guilty, might be conducted from court to military execution . . .

Military execution! A wonderful indignation surged up in Mr. Truelove. When the judge finally signaled that he might speak, he was sputtering with unfeigned rage.

"Be demned to the Governor's mercy," Mr. Truelove said magnificently. "I'm not guilty of the charge! Put me on trial, if ye dare, and I'll abide by the consequences even if they lead to me death." He leaned forward, shaking a plump finger at Monsieur Reine's nose. "Ye can tell the Governor for me, young man, that my country won't allow one of its children to be murdered in cold blood without exacting a rigorous account for the same!"

A look of astonishment crossed Monsieur Reine's face. "It is not according to my instructions to return any answer to Monsieur le Gouverneur," he said with dignity. He leaned forward, his voice almost paternal. "I want only to advise you to be more careful in the future . . ."

"Good day to you, sir," Mr. Truelove said. "I'm not looking for your advice."

Outside, in the warm sunshine, he paused to pull a kerchief from his pocket. I expect that'll show those demned Froggies, he thought. But when he lifted the kerchief to mop his forehead, his hands were shaking uncontrollably.

꧁꧂

SINCE CURFEW, TWO HOURS EARLIER, THERE HAD BEEN SCARCELY A sound to disturb the quiet of the soft November night; only the far obbligato of surf and the nearby whisper of leaves. Marianna, sitting on her veranda, could endure it no longer. The pointed stars, pushing through the darkness, pricked like goads against her flesh, and the *hupé,* sidling down from the mountains laden with the scent of flowering trees, brushed coolly by her cheeks, fresh as youth and as mockingly evanescent. She pushed back her chair and went inside the house.

By lamplight she undressed and put on the white nightdress, with a ribbon drawn tight beneath the bosom, that she had copied from one of Lily Nicholls's. She was standing in front of the mirror about to take the pins from her hair when she heard a faint scratching at the door, and Jonas's low, urgent whisper.

"Marianna!"

Swiftly she pulled on her dressing gown and opened the door. Jonas stepped inside, shut the door quietly behind him, and went over to the lamp, turning it down until only the faintest glimmer of light flickered through the room.

"The sentries," he said briefly. "Pull down the blinds."

She crossed the room, dropping the rolled rattan shades against the two small windows. "Did they see you?"

"No chance. But they'll be back on their rounds again shortly. I don't want them peering in the windows."

"What's happened?"

"Farenui's not on the schooner." Farenui was the native who had worked for Jonas in Matavai, and who shipped with him as sailor on the *Moana.*

"How do you know?"

"I swam out to see him. He wasn't there."

For the first time she noticed that there were dark, wet patches on his shirt, as if he had put on his clothes immediately on coming out of the water. "Where is the dinghy?"

"Tied up by the schooner. He could have swum in, of course."

"He sleeps ashore sometimes, doesn't he?"

"Sometimes. But he usually tells me first."

204

"Is it so important to see him tonight?"

"It might be. I found out that we may have been spied on when we went in to Papenoo. If the French get to him before I can warn him he might give the whole show away."

Marianna sank down to the edge of the bed, and motioned Jonas to the only chair in the room. "What did you hear?"

"Vahine told me tonight" — Vahine was Dr. Ferguson's woman — "that one of the natives at Papenoo is a cousin of the eminent and double-dealing Paraita. Name of Momoe. She thinks he too may be in French pay."

"Momoe!"

"D'you know him?"

She shook her head. "No. But when Araitea came in town last week he said that a man named Momoe had deserted the encampment."

"Damn," Jonas said softly. "When?"

"He didn't say. It was about six weeks ago that you were there, wasn't it?"

"About."

"I got the impression that the man deserted since then."

They were both silent, thinking of the implications of this possibility. Since Mr. Truelove's warning by the French, they had been more than ever aware of the seriousness of what they were doing. Court-martial — military execution — the words hammered in Marianna's mind. "Teaui should be in town in a few days," she said. "I'll find out then if Momoe was there when you were."

"Yes. Meanwhile, I'll have to assume that he was."

"What about Farenui?"

"That's what I'm wondering," he said. "You didn't notice any gendarmes hanging about here today, did you?"

"No."

"Good. That's what I wanted to know. Perhaps they didn't pick him up then. He's got a girl somewhere in town, but I don't know where she lives."

"You aren't going to look for him tonight?"

"No. I might blunder into a sentry."

"What will you do if the French accuse you?"

He shrugged. "Tell them I put in at Papenoo for repairs, and had no dealings with the camp. But Farenui's got to tell the same story."

In the dim lamplight she looked at Jonas thoughtfully, at the thick brown hair growing low on his forehead, and the bold nose above his incongruously tender mouth. Dispassionately, she was aware that he had been drinking — probably a glass or two of rum with Dr. Ferguson — but with the new sophistication born of her months in town, she knew that he was not drunk, and that it did not matter. With sudden intensity she felt the fact of his nearness; the little room had seemed to come alive with his presence. He can't be in danger, she thought desperately, he can't, he mustn't be —

"If only I'd told you earlier about Momoe deserting!" she said.

"It wouldn't have helped. I didn't know anything about him until an hour ago. Don't look so worried, Marianna!"

He got up and came over to her, holding out his hand to pull her to her feet. As she arose the dressing gown fell away from her throat, and he thought suddenly of the day he had seen her bathing in the valley pool. For a second he stared into her questioning eyes, dark and wide in the dim light, then he dropped her hands abruptly. "I must go," he said. "Will you look out and tell me if the coast is clear?"

As Marianna turned, there was the sound of heavy footsteps on the veranda. The door burst open and the bright beams of a lantern thrust into the room. Nari, one of the native policemen, was holding it, and in the shadows just behind him was a French gendarme, with a pistol in his hand.

206

"Qu'est-ce que vous faites ici, monsieur?" the gendarme said roughly. *"Vous connaissez le code martial!"*

Before Jonas could reply, Marianna said swiftly in Tahitian, "How dare you break in here like this?"

"You know the law," Nari said. "He's not allowed in another house after curfew."

"Put up your hands," the gendarme said to Jonas. "You're under arrest."

"What for?"

"For plotting against the French."

"Plotting with women?" Jonas asked sarcastically.

"Then why are you here?"

Marianna turned on him. "Blockhead, why do you suppose he's here? Why do your visit your *vahine* in the back street?"

"Marianna!"

"Go on, arrest him!" Marianna said. "Arrest him for something you do every night of your lives!"

The Frenchman and the native were gazing at her in astonishment. *"Aué!"* Nari breathed.

Slowly, the gendarme lowered his pistol, and a sly look of comprehension spread across his face.

"You swear he's your lover?"

"If I must," she said curtly.

"It's not true!" Jonas said.

Marianna was seized with a deep, unreasoning anger. Under the appearance of a caress she took his arm, and pinched it. "Be quiet!" she said in English. "Do you want to be arrested?"

"Don't be a fool," he said. "These two will tell the whole town of this!"

"They will in any case. For heaven's sake, do as I say!" She looked over at the two policemen, saw that they were watching them suspiciously, and linked her fingers in Jonas's, leaning against him possessively.

207

"He only wants to protect me," she said in Tahitian. "Now can't you be on your way and leave us alone?"

For a moment they hesitated, and then the gendarme said, "Very well. But I warn you, monsieur, if you leave this house before morning gunfire, your game will be finished!"

The last thing they saw as the two policemen went out was Nari's dark face, turned back to gaze again at Marianna in speechless amazement. The door closed behind them, shutting out the lantern light and leaving the room muffled in semidarkness.

Marianna dropped Jonas's hand and turned away, but he took her by the shoulders and pulled her about. "I'll be damned if I'll thank you for this," he said angrily. "D'you realize what you've done? Your name will be ruined in the town!"

"What difference does it make?" she asked impatiently.

He seized her shoulders more tightly, suddenly furious at the dilemma she had put him in, and at the awkward, impotent figure he had cut. "I was thinking of your happiness," he said, "and of how you destroyed it in a sentence."

Defiance reared up in her like a mounting wave. "You're very solicitous of my happiness on a sudden."

"By God, I am," he said. "I'm leaving."

She pulled away from his grasp and took a step backward. "Go ahead then, leave. Walk right into their arms. Betray yourself and Mr. Truelove and the men at Papenoo, and even me."

"There are all kinds of betrayal," he said.

"And you would choose the most preferable!"

"I don't choose to hide behind your skirts!"

"That's what you once told me you needed. The protection of a woman's skirts — a liaison with respectability."

"You'll hardly seem respectable to the community after those policemen start talking!"

"D'you think they believed me?"

"A Frenchman and a Tahitian? You little idiot, of course they did!"

"So much the better, then."

"Oh no it isn't. I'm going, Marianna."

The mounting wave broke, and all the old hurts and resentments he had ever inflicted on her boiled about her like a surf. "Apparently you prefer arrest and imprisonment to a night in my company!"

"I prefer it to your disgrace."

"How gallant! By all means, then, suit yourself."

Struck by the charge of bitterness in her tone, he looked at her searchingly, at her bright, defiant eyes, and at the little tremor on her soft lips. "Suit myself?" he said slowly. "Shall I?"

He moved toward her, his eyes fastened on hers. For a frozen and deliberate moment he stood before her, then his hands came out to touch her shoulders, slid down her immobile arms and locked behind her back. He felt her tense away from him, then, on a long sigh, she swayed into his embrace. Her lips were warm and tremulous, and his arms tightened, crushing the firm slenderness of her body against his own. After a few moments he drew away to look at her, raising one hand to touch her softly on the lips and cheek. "Marianna," he said wonderingly.

She said nothing, watching his face with the intent concentration of a child. When he began gently to pull the pins from her hair, she did not move, standing silently and obediently before him, her head slightly bowed, while the pins dropped to the floor and her pale, shining hair began to slide about her shoulders.

"I've wanted to do this for a long time," he said.

"Have you?" she said in a low voice.

It seemed to her that reality had utterly dropped away from them; they were like two creatures in a dream. From far off, locked in some remote and fabulous region of the senses, she watched him lift her hair in his hands and hold it against his face. She could still draw back, away from him, break the strange enchantment that held her bemused, and yet she did not. She could not have said at what moment volition deserted her entirely;

209

when he led her to the bed, when he bent over to blow out the feeble glimmer of the lamp, when he dropped down beside her and drew aside the ruffles of her dressing gown, laying his face against her breast . . . She only knew that sometime an urgency flooded over her that washed away all barrier of will, and there was no longer any alternative, no possible choice in the world except to be with him and follow where he led.

When she awoke the next morning it was like any other awakening, for Jonas had gone. After a moment memory returned to her, and she was instantly wide awake. She swung her feet to the floor and sat for an instant staring at the drawn shades on the windows, then she got up and raised them, letting a burst of sunshine into the room. Like someone in a daze, she dressed, brushed the wild tangles from her hair, pinned it up and went outside to the veranda.

Everything looked oddly unaltered, she thought childishly, just as if nothing had happened. Across the road a man was spearfishing, wading through the bright shallows, his eyes intent on the water. On the veranda of the Inn, Miatu was noisily setting the breakfast table, and along the path to the kitchen door a man was carrying some long nets of golden oranges hanging from a pole across his shoulders. Marianna leaned against a wooden pillar, screened by the jasmine vine, watching them idly. Three native girls strolled by along the road, laughing and chattering together; there were scarlet hibiscus blossoms thrust into the dark ripples of their hair. So this is what they had known, so often and so casually. . . .

Out on the *Moana* she could see Farenui drawing up water in a bucket and sloshing it against the deck; he was whistling as he worked. Then the French had not taken him after all; he had spent the night on shore with his girl. Farenui too . . . and now he was whistling. She stretched her arms above her head, smiling a little. Later on she would see Jonas, it did not matter when, and it would be as if they had never seen one another before, had never let stupid restraints and resentments come between them. All that was over, cut away by the sharp stroke of their passionate intimacy. She closed her eyes for a moment, a little giddily, suddenly overwhelmed by memory. Jonas had made her altogether his; not just because of the surrender of her will and body, but because of his unexpected tendernesses, his silent and compassionate understanding.

It was that wonderful quality in him, she thought, which made regret or guilt so utterly impossible; made anything unthinkable except this thankful acceptance of all that lay about her. Surely she had never before seen the bay so brilliant in the morning sun, nor the green mountains stretch so triumphantly against the sky. And it would always be like this, now that they knew they belonged together. Soon he would come to her, and they would make their plans; their lives would be united and the ugly waste of loneliness would be forever vanquished.

The sound of the breakfast bell cut across her thoughts. Breakfast to eat, school to teach . . . She'd surprise the children with a picnic this morning, she decided; take them to the little stream behind the town and show them how to sketch the flowers and ferns that crouched along the water's edge.

Shortly before noon Jonas rowed out to the schooner. After he had talked to Farenui and instructed him in the story they both would tell the French, there was not much to do, but he made a pretense of working about the deck, keeping a wary eye on the road. When he saw Marianna walking back from school he went around to the front of the cabin, settling down in the shade, his legs stretched out on the deck, his back against the bulwarks, out

211

of sight from anyone on shore. He would have to see her before long, there was no avoiding it, but he would choose his own time, when there were no prying eyes about.

He had brought a book with him, but after a time he laid it aside, staring out across the water to the far pinnacles of Moorea. By God, he'd got himself into a pretty predicament! After all the years of cherishing his freedom, courting it as some men courted an elusive woman, he had come perilously close to the point of throwing it away. In Tahiti, of all places, where love was to be had as easily as picking fruit from a tree, he must choose a missionary's daughter, a schoolmarm, girded in sanctity. A moment's curiosity, a moment's hunger, the old, insane impulse to use the resource of the body for the comfort that it could give and bring, and behold: a situation that lengthened itself out as far as the mind could see.

He leaned his head back, closing his eyes, remembering how it had happened, and his mouth slackened a little from the tight, contemptuous line in which it had been set. Marianna . . . Cool and clean-limbed, confiding herself to him without reserve. Afterward, holding her closely, he could feel her trembling, like a frightened animal in his arms, and he had felt a great tenderness for her, comforting her with the gentle stroke of his hands until her trembling stopped, and the slow swell of passion drew them together again. She had scarcely spoken at all, and when she did it was Tahitian that she used, the same phrases, totally physiological, bluntly tender, that he had heard from native girls, and in her low voice they had surprised and warmed him.

He opened his eyes again, frowning. Could he possibly be a little in love with her — with Marianna Moore? He had sensed that the narrow limits of her life enclosed an ardent and generous spirit, and he had pitied her bondage; he admired and respected her courage and her intelligence. And now there was another factor in his feeling toward her, no use to deny it. But love?

212

No! Love was a negation of liberty, another and more insidious form of servitude that he intended always to avoid.

Just as he intended never to marry. But suppose the relationship between them became generally known, what would the effect be on Marianna? There might be no other way to save her from disastrous disgrace except by marriage, and in that case he would have to go through with it. To think of it was like drowning, like suffocation in the bright, boundless air. He'd be no good for her, she was too stable, too conventional, too sensitive to link her life to one like his. He had left America to escape a similar situation, but by God he didn't want to leave Tahiti — not while this fight was going on and he could be of use. And by now he was too old, too rigidly fixed in some slow-growing tangle of ethics, to run away.

But perhaps it would not be necessary, after all. Perhaps no one would be the wiser, and they could go on as if nothing had happened. Marianna would never make any demands on him, he knew that, and there was no use to step precipitately into an entanglement that might be sensibly avoided. He had no reason to suppose that she wanted to marry him any more than he wanted to marry her. He would wait and see, he decided with an uneasy sense of relief, wait and see what happened. . . .

Faintly, he heard the sound of the Inn's luncheon bell above the soft lap of the water, and some time later he saw Marianna cross the lawn and go back into her cottage. He waited about ten minutes, then dropped into the dinghy and rowed ashore.

She came at once in answer to his knock, and when she had closed the door behind him she stood for a moment leaning against it, looking at him with shy inquiry. To hide his own uncertainty, he put his arms around her and pulled her close. She clung to him tightly. "Jonas," she murmured, "Jonas."

She drew away to look at him, her fingers resting on his shoulders. "You're all right? There's been no trouble?"

213

"None. But there might have been, if you weren't the foolish reckless creature that you are."

"What do you mean? What kind of trouble?"

"Nothing very definite. But Momoe's in town, working on Paraita's new house. Farenui saw him."

"Do you think he's told them about Papenoo?"

"I'm afraid so. The sentries must have been following me last night, Marianna. Otherwise, why did they come here? I was so sure none of the regular watchmen saw me."

Her eyes were dark with alarm. "If they know that you were in Papenoo, why haven't they arrested you?"

"They're probably waiting for more positive proof."

"Don't give it to them," she said passionately. "Promise me you'll be careful!"

"How can I come to any harm," he said, smiling, "with you to protect me?"

Her lips curved mischievously. "You still resent that, don't you, Jonas?"

"Furiously," he said.

A giddy happiness swirled up in her. She took his hand, and with complete naturalness drew him over to the edge of the bed, sitting down there beside him, his hand still clasped in hers.

"And what of you?" he asked.

With a little laugh, she said childishly, "I taught school today."

"Astonishing. And how was it?"

"Wonderful! The children were angelic, it has never been so wonderful!"

"Everything is wonderful? You're sure, Marianna?"

Her eyes met his, direct and luminous. "Quite sure," she said.

He had not known what her attitude would be, but of all the possibilities that had suggested themselves — shame, reproaches, embarrassment, restraint — it had never occurred to him that she would be like this. The radiance that illuminated her face,

214

the joyous warmth of her manner, surprised him and made him oddly uncomfortable.

"No regrets?"

"No." She looked away from him, and her voice was charged with wonder. "I know I should feel guilty and sinful, but somehow I just can't. It seems so right — as if we were already sanctified, even though it isn't — even though we're not yet — " Her voice faltered and she turned back to him just in time to see him avert his glance from hers.

He said nothing, and she saw that he intended no reply. The moment of silence stretched endlessly between them, and with a sickening sense of shock she realized its importance. Was it possible then that two people could be so close, and in another instant suffer this abrupt and terrifying cleavage? She had been so foolishly sure that nothing would ever separate them again! She must be imagining things, she thought desperately; a few seconds of silence could not possibly imply all she had read into them. Hesitantly, she said, "Should I — have regrets?"

"Of course not," he said. "Not unless you choose to have."

With artful casualness she drew her hand away from his, smoothing back a lock of hair. "I would never choose anything so unpleasant," she said carefully.

He saw that the dangerous moment had passed, but his evasion of it had left him curiously dissatisfied, perversely eager to make amends. Gently he turned her face toward his, drawing his fingers along the curve of her cheek. "You have the most eloquent eyes I've ever seen," he said softly. "Did you know that you were beautiful, Marianna?"

A wave of color flooded up into her face. "Don't," she said. "You don't have to — there are no sentries now."

"Must there always be sentries?"

She turned away, making a convulsive little gesture with her hands, but he drew her back again, kissing her eyelids and her

215

lips, so that he would not have to see the look of childlike pain and bewilderment that had crossed her face. How taut she was — and yet how readily the tautness flowed from her muscles as he held her against him. Suddenly disgusted with himself, he released her, but her eyes were still closed for a moment, and she did not see his frown. In Tahitian, she said, "Your lips are warm as the sea."

Before he could reply there was a light tap at the door, and Lily Nicholls stepped into the room just as he jumped to his feet. She stopped short, looking at them, amazed intelligence sweeping across her face. "I'm sorry," she said, "I had no idea — "

Marianna had already risen. "Come in, Lily."

Lily pushed shut the door behind her. "I may as well," she said, with her light, high laugh. "It's too late to retreat, isn't it?"

"There's no reason to retreat."

"Perhaps not. As a matter of fact, Marianna, I came over to give you a message for Jonas." Her glance, sharp and slyly mocking, swung between them. "I thought you'd know where to find him, but I didn't know he'd be quite so close."

"What was the message?"

"A word of warning, really. Captain d'Aubigny was a little — indiscreet — last night, and he indicated that you are being watched, Jonas. I've an idea they're planning to search your boat."

He whistled softly. "Why didn't you tell me before?"

"To tell the truth, I didn't remember it." She made a little face, drawing her hand across her forehead. "D'Aubigny wasn't the only one who took a bit too much wine. My memory didn't begin to function until about an hour ago."

"Lily, for God's sake, why do you spend your time with that Frenchman?"

She looked at Jonas mockingly. "So that I can do favors for you, of course. Why else?"

"I can't think of a better reason," he said sardonically.

"Can't you? There are some."

"It's quite a favor, at that," he said. "I'd better go along now, and have a look around the boat." He paused by the door, and made them a sweeping bow. "My deepest thanks. Where would I be without women?"

"In jail, where you belong," Lily said.

His laughter followed him out the door. Lily sank down into the chair. "I'm terribly sorry, Marianna. I supposed you were alone — I never should have burst in like that."

"It doesn't matter at all. I'm grateful for your warning."

Lily was watching her as if she had never seen her before. "Marianna."

"Yes?"

"Are you in love with Jonas?"

"Lily, what a — what a strange question."

"Are you?"

Marianna looked down at the tips of her fingers. "Yes," she said flatly.

Lily got up and went over to her, resting a hand on her shoulder. "You're too good for him," she said. "He's not worth it."

"Please, Lily — "

"Listen to me," she said urgently. "Take care. Don't let him hurt you."

"I won't." But in her heart she knew that he already had; without words, in a moment of terrible silence, he had shown her that she must not depend on him for anything. She felt Lily's touch on her shoulder, friendly, almost maternal, and suddenly she was swept by a sickening feeling of kinship with her.

♒

DURING THE THREE DAYS FOLLOWING LILY'S WARNING, JONAS DID not leave the schooner, sleeping on board and sending Farenui ashore to get supplies for his meals. He had grown so heartily

217

sick of this confinement that on the third afternoon it was almost a relief to see Monsieur Moerenhout, director of the police, accompanied by two gendarmes, row across the bay and climb aboard the *Moana*. The cat had pounced, at last.

For more than an hour the gendarmes, under the watchful direction of Monsieur Moerenhout, searched the boat, tumbling supplies from the lockers, pulling apart the bunks, prying boards loose from the deck and poking about in the bilge. It would take a week to get the *Moana* back in shape again, Jonas thought disgustedly. At last Moerenhout concluded the search and came up to Jonas, who stood leaning against the railing.

"Will you come below?" he said in French. "We can have a little talk."

Jonas followed him down to the disordered cabin. Moerenhout waved him to a seat on one of the bunks, with the air of one who was doing the honors in his own *salon*. "You speak such excellent French," he said amiably; "it is a pleasure to talk to a foreigner who has so ably mastered our tongue."

Jonas waited, saying nothing. In his early days in Tahiti he had found Monsieur Moerenhout a jovial and entertaining companion for a carouse, but for the last six or seven years, since Moerenhout had concentrated his efforts for self-aggrandizement toward inciting the French aggression, he had had virtually nothing to do with him. Moerenhout, more than any other single individual, was responsible for the plight Tahiti found herself in now. He was a small, dapper man, but tough and ambitious, an adventurer, incorrigibly cynical and passionately fond of intrigue. Although he was a Belgian, he cloaked his blatant opportunism under the guise of patriotism for France, just as he used his gift for friendship to bend people to his own purposes.

Moerenhout had pulled a cigar from his pocket — one of his own, Jonas saw — and lighted it behind his small, cupped hands.

218

"I regret," he said, "that we have had to make such a *bouleverse-ment* of your little ship."

"And to such small avail," Jonas said dryly.

"Perhaps." He patted a musket that lay beside him in the bunk. "This weapon, however. We shall be obliged to confiscate it, I'm afraid."

"But that's the only firearm that I own! You can't do that!"

"No? I think we can."

"I shall protest to the Governor."

"Just as you please. But I'm afraid it will do you no good. You see, Monsieur Burkham, we are not altogether unaware that you are unsympathetic to our cause. You are an American, and we have been lenient, but we cannot permit you to endanger French rule."

"With one musket? You flatter me."

Monsieur Moerenhout blew several precise smoke rings into the still air. "It's not just that." He smiled at Jonas, almost deprecatingly. "It's because we know you have been so markedly generous with the natives. In Matavai, for instance. In Raiatea, when you saw the Queen. In Papenoo, on the way back, when you dropped off all those supplies."

"I had to put in at Papenoo for repairs," Jonas said. "A squall caught the topmast and cracked it nearly in two."

"A formidable squall to put you so far off your course. No matter. As I said, we have been lenient." He delicately tapped off the ash of his cigar, and leaned back in the bunk. "For example, just three days ago you were observed to go fishing, outside the reef, with your native boatman. When you returned with your catch, the rowboat was considerably lighter in the water than when you went out. *Eh bien*. Whatever it was that you threw overboard will no longer make trouble for anyone." He held up his hand, as Jonas started to speak. "That's what we want, Monsieur Burkham. To avoid trouble. And because of that I

219

will tell you, as a friendly warning, that everything you bring aboard this schooner from now on will be most carefully examined. Particularly any goods from the stores of the estimable Monsieur Truelove."

"Are you trying to tell me that I won't be permitted to make any more trading voyages?"

"But no! All the voyages you wish — with passport, of course. Merely watch your goods for contraband, that is all!"

It was hot in the little cabin, but Monsieur Moerenhout showed no signs of wishing to be away. Across the ceiling reflections of the sun on the water outside the porthole rippled like a golden net. Jonas reached over to a box on the shelf beside him for a cigar, but the box was empty. He closed the lid with a little bang, and Moerenhout smilingly reached into his pocket.

"Have one," he said blandly, producing another of Jonas's cigars.

Jonas took it without thanks.

"It is a pity," Moerenhout said reflectively, "that your ideas are not more amenable to ours. With your knowledge of Tahitian and your fluent French, it would be a pleasant and profitable association. There are some interesting and cultivated French gentlemen here whose company you would enjoy."

"Even in a French colony I believe it is still permitted to choose one's own friends," Jonas said.

"Of course, of course." He smiled at Jonas ingratiatingly. "And you have such charming ones. Mademoiselle Moore, for example. One is always surprised at the warm depths that lie beneath such a cool and serene surface, is it not?"

"I see no reason to discuss Miss Moore."

"To the contrary, I wish particularly to discuss her. It is observed that she has so many visitors from the country. Perhaps it is not healthy for her to be so much with the natives. There is sickness in the camps, you know."

220

So they were watching Marianna, too! "The country people are her oldest friends," he said carefully.

"Just so. But perhaps you are in a position to give her my advice." There was a sly twinkle in the Belgian's eye; it was obvious that he was thoroughly enjoying himself. "Unbelievable how naive we Frenchmen can be. For a time we thought your association with Mademoiselle Moore was inimical to our cause. But the report from my policemen a few nights ago makes everything quite clear." He laughed. "At least we cannot be accused of being unromantic! You should have been arrested, monsieur, by any less sentimental race."

"I would prefer arrest," Jonas said wrathfully, "to these insinuations!"

"Gently, monsieur," Moerenhout said reproachfully. "I am doing you a kindness." He gave Jonas an impudent wink, and got to his feet, taking the musket with him. "As far as we are concerned, you may visit the lady whenever you please." Smilingly, he waved the gun to motion Jonas up the ladderway ahead of him. "For myself, I cannot think of a more delightful way to allay the suspicions of the police!"

MR. THOMSON APPEARED SO SILENTLY AT THE BACK OF THE CLASSroom that Marianna felt his presence there before she actually saw him. The children were droning through a catechism, which should please him, she thought, and since he always preferred his observation of the class to go unnoticed, she did not acknowledge his visit with even a nod. Usually he stayed only a few minutes, then slipped quietly away, but today he made no move to leave, even after the noon bell had sounded from the church next door and the children had darted out into the sunshine.

221

Marianna followed them down the aisle between the rows of benches, smiling a greeting to Mr. Thomson. The solemnity of his look ignored her smile as patently as he disregarded her outstretched hand. She let her hand fall to her side, regarding him in uncomfortable astonishment. Thomson was a man of about forty, with a narrow, nervous face and dark, thin hair; his brown eyes, depthless as pebbles, were today more impenetrable than ever.

"I wish to talk to you, Miss Moore," he said. "Please be so good as to step over to my office for a few minutes."

Puzzled and oddly alarmed, she went with him across the walk in front of the church and up the steps of the house that had once been the Pritchards'. As they approached it she glimpsed Mrs. Thomson hovering about the veranda; at the sight of them she disappeared, and was nowhere in view as they entered the house. Marianna sat down in the chair Mr. Thomson indicated, opposite the desk in his office, feeling a curious tightness creep into the muscles at the back of her neck.

Mr. Thomson was fiddling with some papers; he seemed all at once less purposeful, as if he had forgotten what he wished to say. At last he put the tips of his fingers together and cleared his throat. "As your pastor, it is my painful duty to repeat some gossip I have just heard concerning you, Miss Moore. Perhaps I am the last to hear it, but I want to be the first to give you a chance to deny it."

In the little silence that followed his words Marianna could feel the muffled, accelerated beat of her heart throbbing against her ears. She bent her head, concentratedly counting the number of floorboards spanned by the width of his desk. "Is it true, Miss Moore, that Jonas Burkham spent the night, alone with you, in your cottage?"

For a moment she could not speak.

"Come," he said, "is this true?"

She raised her head with a jerk and looked him directly in the eyes. "Yes," she said.

He drew in his breath sibilantly. "So! You admit it, then!"

She did not reply.

"Am I to understand that you indulged in carnal relations with this — wastrel?"

A wave of color washed across her pallor. "If you want to put it so."

"How else?" he said harshly. He leaned forward, striking the flat of his hand against the top of Mr. Pritchard's desk. "How long ago was this?"

"Two weeks ago."

His gaze had fastened on her face like a claw. "And how often since then has this — sin — been committed?"

Marianna half rose from her chair. Not once, not once, you prying busybody, not once again in these strange and dreamlike weeks, these curious days of waiting, of delight at an occasional tenderness, of bewildered surmise . . . In a high, strained voice, she said, "How can that concern you?"

"Your immortal soul is my concern! And the souls of the children who receive their teaching from you. Sit down, Miss Moore!"

His command had the effect of a blow at the backs of her knees, and she sank down into the chair again.

"You must marry this man," he said.

She stared at him. "I cannot."

"What! What are you saying?" He leaned toward her, lowering his voice. "Are you trying to tell me that the scoundrel forced you?"

"No, no, of course he didn't!"

He leaned back again, his brown eyes hard as stones. "It was your own sin, then. And yet you will not take the one step that might lead part way toward expiating it. Why not?"

How could she marry someone who did not want her, didn't

love her, who valued his freedom above any human relationship he had yet encountered? Many days ago she had found the answer to that question, in Jonas's evasiveness, and in her own upright pride. At least she would spare herself that final humiliation; she would never marry him.

Sharply, Mr. Thomson repeated, "Why not?"

"That is my own affair," she said.

"I don't think so." He looked at her shrewdly, speaking more slowly. "I can guess why. The blackguard has made no move to marry you — that kind never does! Well, let me tell you this, Miss Moore: I can make Tahiti so unpleasant for him if he refuses that he would have to leave the island. I'll handle this!"

"You mustn't do anything!"

"Oh, but I must! It's my duty. I can't see the daughter of one of my colleagues abandoned to a life of evil. I'll see that you are married within a week."

"You can't do anything!" she said. "Even if you force us to stand up together before you, I swear I'll never say the words that would make me his wife!"

"What sort of talk is this! Will you persist in crime?"

The anger that had been bubbling beneath her shamed confusion suddenly boiled to the surface. "Will you persist in talking this way of something you can't possibly understand?"

"Jezebel!" he said. "Repent! Repent before it's too late."

"Leave me alone," she cried.

"All right, woman! But understand this — you are never to enter my schoolroom again. Your teaching days are finished." They had both risen, and were staring at one another. "To think," he said, "that I had chosen you to guide my school for fallen women. You are no better than they yourself!"

She turned away blindly, and he came toward her around the desk. "Think of your father! What suffering his spirit must be enduring now!"

She started for the door. "Leave my father out of this!"

224

"I cannot forget whose daughter you are. Stay, and ask forgiveness. Open your sin to me, and I will pray with you."

"I don't want your prayers!" she said furiously. "And I don't want your pious curiosity!" She opened the door and banged it shut behind her, brushing past Mrs. Thomson who was loitering in the narrow hallway. Outside, the sunshine was like a giant, searching eye; she had a feeling that she was naked in it, exposed to any prying gaze. Her hands were trembling, and her face felt strangely cold, as if all the blood had drained from it and was pounding around her heart. She set her lips together, and hurried along the road.

This had been her world — a world of bigotry and cant, of meddlesome interference in other people's affairs — but it was hers no longer. The brutal impact of Thomson's words had left her shaken; now she was possessed of a fierce determination not to let an impinging reality destroy the delicate balance of a dream. His censure had brought into sharper focus the one thing that seemed of supreme importance to her — the depth and validity of her love for Jonas. To acknowledge regret would be to stigmatize herself as a loose, unstable creature who could fall from grace in order to satisfy a moment's bodily hunger. There was no retreat from the choice she had made; it was irrevocable as death.

She was walking so fast and so heedlessly that she almost bumped into Monsieur Moerenhout, who was approaching from the other direction. At her muttered apology he bowed, and held up a detaining hand. "You are anxious to get home, no? Eet is understandable."

She looked at him in vague surprise, and saw in his eyes a sly amusement, a salacious appraisal, that she had never seen in any man's eyes before. Here was another world, another judgment; his glance seemed to travel over her like a snail, leaving slime behind it. She turned away, her head high, and hurried down the road.

THE EVENING STAR, RISING ABOVE PAPEETE BAY ON THAT CHRIST-
mas Eve of the year 1844, was as hugely golden, as lone and
beckoning, as the star that once hung over Bethlehem must have
been. Marianna sat in the shadows on her veranda watching it,
watching the soft, scented pall of night drift upward from the
land and darken the lucency of the sky.

It was a week now since her dismissal by Mr. Thomson, a week
of idleness, of curious unreality. Instinctively as an animal, she
spent her time quietly, trying not to think very much, waiting for
the aimless hours to pass until the fresh wound of her interview
with Thomson might heal over and become only a scar on her
spirit. She had seen Jonas frequently during the week, but had
taken the utmost pains to conceal from him the fact of her dismissal. Her greatest dread was that in discovering it he would
make the gesture of "doing the right thing." For the moment
she could ask no more than a postponement of further hurt,
and there was nothing he could do from now on that would not
be painful to her. Nothing could change the obvious fact that he
had not wanted to marry her; and she had come to accept this
circumstance with some philosophy. Jonas was not to be blamed
because he was not in love with her.

She clung to the existing state of their relationship, wary of any
outside influence that might alter its fragile tenor. She recognized its fragility, but she was too inexperienced to recognize
how curious this tacit return to simple friendship was. Outwardly
it was as if that night they had spent together had never happened. Since the next afternoon, the afternoon when Lily Nicholls
had come to the cottage, neither of them had referred to it by
word or implication. But there was a subtle difference in them,

226

manifested on Jonas's part by an unwonted gentleness; and by Marianna in a warmth, a lack of reserve, an easy feeling of communication that she had never known with any human being before. She was, if not happy, at least so fully alive that each hour had its own significance; and the times that she spent with Jonas were transfigured with a special and unforgettable radiance. She knew that his kindnesses to her were inspired largely by a feeling of guilty responsibility, but her only concern was to conceal from him how much they meant to her. Long ago she had realized ruefully that for a man like Jonas to be loved by someone as fundamentally moral as she must be a burden, and she had no intention of letting it become irksome to him.

She saw him now, coming along the road with his long, characteristically impatient stride, as if he were bored with the mere act of walking, and as he turned in the pathway to her cottage she was suddenly aware of the scent of jasmine hanging in the air. It was impossible to keep the joyousness from her voice as she greeted him.

He sat down in the chair next to hers, stretching his legs out in front of him. "Have you been back long?"

"Back?"

"From church. Wasn't the carol singing this evening?"

Her fingers tightened against the arm of her chair. "Oh. Yes. I — didn't go."

"Didn't go?" he said in mild surprise. "I thought the children were to sing."

"So they were," she said, "but I thought they knew it well enough without me. I've been lazy all the day. What's the news from town?"

"Not much. The usual gossip, but nothing official."

Her fingers relaxed their grip on the chair arm; here was a safe topic. "No statement from the Admiral?"

Two days before, a French frigate, the *Virginie*, had sailed into port, with Admiral Hamelin aboard, and the town buzzed with rumors that he brought word that King Louis Philippe had repudiated the seizure of the island and would restore the protectorate.

"Not a word," Jonas said. "I don't think it matters, do you? Whether we're a protectorate or a French colony isn't going to make much difference to Pomare or her people. There they are, up in the mountains, and here are the French, and nothing happens. I can't see any end to it."

"It's a curious war," she said. "Like a stalemate." She leaned forward peering through the dusk. "Someone's coming — the Buelles, I think."

"Ah," he said, "prepare for further instruction in the tribulations of innkeeping."

"Sh-h." She got up to welcome them, standing at the top of the steps as they approached across the lawn, a lantern bobbing in Mr. Buelle's hand.

Mr. and Mrs. Buelle had come to Tahiti some fifteen years earlier, seeking a climate that might benefit what Mrs. Buelle referred to as "me 'usband's lung trouble." They were rather alike, both small and scrawny, with indeterminate features and faded, continually anxious eyes. Mrs. Buelle was the more positive character of the two, by virtue of the wiry energy she expended on running the Inn, and the soft-voiced, almost incessant complaints that were the chief feature of her conversation. It was difficult to imagine how they had ever had the audacity to leave their native England, which now, in their nostalgic references, took on the perfection of a Promised Land, but it was apparent that they were by now too settled and too timid ever to break away from the life they had made for themselves in Tahiti.

"Do come in," Marianna said. "I'm glad you brought a lantern; I've been too idle even to light my lamp."

The rays of their lantern struck against Jonas as they mounted the steps, and they stopped stock-still at the top.

228

"It's like they said, Ellen," Mr. Buelle said excitedly. " 'E's here! This must 'ave been going on a long time under our very noses!"

Marianna stepped back, her hand to her throat, and Jonas jumped to his feet. "What are you talking about, man?"

"Please, Jonas — "

Mrs. Buelle turned on Jonas, her voice sharp. "I'll tell you what he's talking about, you dirty renegade! The blame's all yours, I'll warrant! Sedoocing a Christian young woman like Miss Moore — "

"Watch your words!" Jonas said.

"That's right, Ellen," Mr. Buelle said. "Let's go about this calm and sensible like."

"The shock of it," Mrs. Buelle said plaintively, "me nerves are all of an edge. You tell her, Frank."

He turned to Marianna. "We were at chapel tonight, and the minister and his wife asked a word with us, after. They — "

"Jonas," Marianna said swiftly, "please go. This is my affair."

"I'm damned if I will," he said angrily, "let's hear these creatures out." He moved over beside her, taking her elbow in his hand. "Go on, Buelle."

"The minister said he had it from Miss Moore's own lips that you and she was committing mortal sin right under our own roof. To think of it! We tries to run a respectable place 'ere, though it's not always easy in this land, and Minister said 'e'd not consider us good church members if we let 'er stay 'ere longer."

"You're throwing Miss Moore out of your Inn. Is that it?"

"Well, sir, we 'ave to. We don't like it neither, she always seemed a fine young lady — "

"It's quite a coincidence," Jonas said acidly. "Eighteen hundred-odd years ago this very night some other people were turned away from an Inn — "

"Jonas!" Marianna cried.

"Oh, I'm not comparing you to the Virgin Mary," he said. "I

229

only wondered if lack of Christianity were one of the necessary qualities of a tavernkeeper."

"You 'ave the nerve, to talk about being a Christian!"

"Please," Marianna said. "No more of this. I'll go tonight. I couldn't stay here any longer."

"Not tonight, Miss Moore. We didn't hexpect that, what with the sentries and all — "

"You didn't expect her to go tonight, and yet you couldn't wait to come over here with your smug talk!" Jonas said. He went toward them menacingly, virtually pushing them toward the steps. "Merry Christmas," he said. "A merry, merry Christmas to you!"

They went down the steps rather hurriedly and crossed the lawn, without a backward look. Jonas turned to Marianna, putting his arm about her shoulders. "My dear, my dear, don't tremble so!"

She buried her face in her shaking hands. "It's so shameful," she said in a choked voice, "so horribly shameful! Jonas, I can't stay here, even tonight. I *must* get out of here!"

Gently, he pulled her over to a chair and made her sit down, drawing his own chair close to hers. "This is why you weren't teaching this week, isn't it? Not just a holiday, as you said."

She turned her head away, and he swore softly. "That devil Thomson! And who else, Marianna? Has the whole Christ-bitten crowd been taking pot shots at you?"

"It doesn't matter," she said faintly.

"Who else?" he persisted.

"Please, Jonas, what difference does it make?"

"A great deal!" he said. "Remember, this is my concern, too."

Her voice was suddenly tired and without defenses. "Mrs. Truelove wouldn't speak to me, when I saw her in the store the other day. And Mrs. Darling wrote me a note, from Punaavia."

"Stone-casting," he said bitterly. "How righteous! Why in God's name didn't you tell me?"

She looked down at her hands, and made no reply. After a moment, he said, "We must be married, Marianna. As soon as possible."

"No," she said into her hands. "No, I won't marry you."

"Don't be a little fool," he said angrily, "it's the only thing to do." He put his fingers under her chin and raised her face to his, altering his voice. "I won't beat you, y'know."

She turned her head away. "Please don't talk about it. I've got to think what I can do — where I can go. Tomorrow's Christmas — I can't very well look for a place to live on Christmas Day. If this were Matavai there'd be a dozen places to go, but here I know no one who — "

"How about my room at Dr. Ferguson's? And I can live on the schooner."

"No. Not there. I don't want the doctor mixed up in this."

They were silent, thinking. After a moment Marianna said, "I'd like to go away, far away, out into the wide, clean sea." It was like a cry of longing.

He straightened in his chair. "Marianna, how long will it take you to pack your things?"

"Not long. A couple of hours. There are only the books, and my clothes — most of the things are stored away."

"Good," he said. "You can do that tonight, and we'll leave at dawn."

She stared at him in amazement. "Leave?"

"Yes. In the schooner. We'll sail over to Moorea and stay there a few days until you can decide what to do. Moerenhout will arrange passports for me."

"You can't be serious!"

"Of course I am," he said impatiently. "It's the perfect solution. You can leave the things you don't need with Lily Nicholls, to keep until you get back."

"Jonas, you must be mad! Think how the town would talk!" She stopped abruptly, meeting his glance. Ruefully, she said, "But that's absurd, isn't it? The fat's already in the fire."

231

"And what's the difference if it burns a little brighter?"

"None. But it's still impossible, Jonas. I can't go with you."

"Why not, for God's sake?"

She looked at him directly. "I want it understood," she said steadily, "that you are in no sense responsible for me. There is no reason for you to do anything."

A hint of amusement crept into his voice. "All right," he said. "It's understood. Now let's discuss this thing intelligently." He leaned forward, taking her hands in his. "Look here, Marianna. You must get away for a while. As for me, I need it as much as you do. I want to remove myself from the temptation of breaking a few of the godly heads around town." He tightened his hold on her hands. "Ferguson's got a smoked ham and some salt beef I can take, and there's sugar and flour and salt aboard the schooner. We'll live like kings! With you aboard as mate we won't even need Farenui."

Her hands jerked a little in his clasp.

"You'll come, Marianna. Please say you'll come."

To get away from Papeete and the slyly prying eyes; to be in Moorea, beautiful Moorea, where she had gone to school as a child; to be with Jonas, day after day . . . It was a dizzying prospect, an irresistible one. Why fight any longer, she thought tiredly. There was no longer any battle she could win, either against her own conscience or against the already formulated verdict of the town. Her hands relaxed in Jonas's, and her fingers curled against his palms.

"I'd love to come," she said. "I'll start my packing now."

꧁꧂

THEY COOKED THEIR EVENING MEAL ON SHORE, AND THEN ROWED back to the schooner. Jonas pulled two mattresses on deck, and he and Marianna sat on these, their backs propped against the bulwarks. In this deep and nearly landlocked harbor, far from the sound of surf, stillness seemed to lie captive in the warm air; silently the mountains cupped in the last gold outpour of the setting sun. From this side of Moorea, Tahiti was not even visible. Less than twenty miles from Papeete, Marianna was thinking, and yet they might well be in another world.

Not a ripple disturbed the surface of the narrow bay; the green, crenelated peaks, closing around it like battlements against the sky, were mirrored darkly on the smooth water. The *Moana*, swinging to anchor far toward the end of the bay, was the only sign of human life; the few thatched huts along the shore were smothered from sight by huge trees. The place was uncannily, almost overpoweringly, beautiful. Even the quietness had an eerie quality to it, and the slow reach of shadows up the flanks of the mountains was a furtive thing, creeping forward to strangle the light.

Marianna felt herself shivering inwardly. All of her old life was as far away as Papeete seemed to be; there was nothing here that was real. It was a curious and frightening sensation; she found herself with a stranger in a strange place, as if she were locked in a dream.

The hiss of Jonas's cigar meeting the water broke the silence. He got up and stretched.

"I've had worse Christmas dinners," he said. "Chicken, roast breadfruit, fresh mangoes — who cares about plum pudding?"

She had forgotten that it was still Christmas Day. "No one," she said with an effort.

He looked down at her. "You're tired, aren't you? You didn't sleep last night."

She shook her head, and he turned, disappearing into the cabin. When he came back he was carrying pillows and two rolls of bedding. "You'll be more comfortable if you bunk on deck," he said. "I'll take my roll on shore and find shelter with one of the natives."

What was the stranger saying? She tried to concentrate on shaking off the unreality that held her, to re-enter the world of practicalities.

"The mosquitoes are bad here," she said. "You'll be devoured on shore." She had spoken without thinking that it must sound like an invitation to stay with her. Jonas, who had gone over to the binnacle, did not appear to have heard her.

She watched him silently as he lighted the lantern and hung it against the mast — the same lantern that she used to watch from her veranda, the lantern that had lighted Lily Nicholls's nocturnal visits to the schooner . . . He shook out the lucifer, threw it into the water, and turned back to her.

"That should keep the *tupapaus* away. You won't be afraid, will you?"

"My *tupapaus* are all inside," she said. Her voice broke a little on the words, and she leaned forward, resting her forehead against her knees.

Jonas looked at her searchingly, then he dropped down on the mattress behind her, pulling her close against his chest. In the silence she could feel the strong, steady beat of his heart against her back, and the secure rise and fall of his breathing. A comforting warmth spread slowly through her exhausted body. He was no longer a stranger, she thought, he was a refuge and a friend.

After a few moments he said softly, "Shall I stay here with you?"

Her reply was so faint that he had to repeat his question, leaning forward so that his ear was close to her lips. Even then he felt, rather than heard, her answer, fanned like a breath against his cheek. "Please stay," she whispered.

The sun, already high in the sky, was streaming goldenly across her face when she awakened next morning. The bay was brimming with light, the water shook and trembled with it, and the green hills above were laced here and there with the white rib-

234

bon of a waterfall. Marianna got up quietly and went down into the cabin to dress and comb her hair.

When she came up on deck again Jonas had already dressed and was pulling a bucket of water over the side of the ship. He put it down and came toward her, taking her elbows in his hands.

"You slept well?"

"Beautifully," she said.

He leaned forward and kissed her gravely on the forehead. For Marianna, from that moment on, the day became irradiated with a kind of magic, sparkling and intangible as motes glittering in a shaft of sunlight.

The days that followed were all suffused with it; even the most commonplace activities took on a special and unforgettable quality to her. Jonas had suggested that they live chiefly off the food they could forage from the land and sea, in order to make the stores they had brought with them last as long as possible. To do so became their main preoccupation, an absorbing game. Jonas had lived long enough in Tahiti to know some of the native ways of fishing and gathering food, and Marianna could teach him many more, half forgotten since her childhood.

They climbed the hills in search of oranges and *fei* and *mape* nuts, they fished the quiet bay from a borrowed outrigger canoe, they waded along the spiny reef in search of mollusks, with the white surf foaming about their ankles. Sometimes at night they speared prawns in the shallows of the river, the light from their torch wavering eerily around them.

One day, watching her prepare fish and yams and breadfruit for roasting in the stone-lined native oven she had shown him how to make, Jonas told her teasingly that she would make an admirable wife for a beachcomber like himself.

She made no reply, smoothing the leaf she was wrapping about a scarlet fish and skewering it with a sharp twig.

It was not the only time he had referred to their marriage, as if it were already a settled matter, and each time she let his allusion slide by in silence. What was there to say? In her own mind she had gone over and over the possibilities of such an exchange between them, and always they were the same. I will not marry you. Why not? Because you do not love me, and do not in your heart want marriage.

It was unthinkable; she would not place him or herself in any such uncomfortable position, she would never force from him the false and insincere protestations he would feel duty bound to make. Ordinarily, he did not ask an answer, but today he was more persistent.

"Did you hear me, Marianna? I paid you a compliment."

"Yes. I heard you."

"Then why don't you say something?"

"Thank you for the compliment," she said with mock primness.

"Is that all you can say? Don't you like the idea of being a beachcomber's wife?"

"It's a contradiction in terms," she said. "Beachcombers don't have wives."

"That's because they can't find wives like you. How many modern women know how to catch bonito on a barbless hook, d'you think?"

"All well-brought-up young ladies like myself," she said. She had placed the food in the oven, and was covering it with some plantain leaves. Jonas got up to help her, pulling flat stones into place across the top of the oven and sealing it with earth.

"There! Dinner will be served shortly."

Together they strolled down to the beach, kneeling on the white sand at the water's edge to wash their hands. The shadow of a palm tree beside them was imprinted with exquisite clarity

236

on the bright shallows. Marianna gestured toward it. "It seems a pity to disturb anything so lovely."

Jonas scattered the reflection with a scoop of water. "It'll come back." He took her wet hands and pulled her into the shade. "Rest a bit, while dinner's cooking."

They sat down on the sand, their backs against the hollow, silvery log of an old *purau* tree.

"Ah-h," he said, "this is better than my childhood dreams of a desert island. Did you ever read *Robinson Crusoe*, Marianna?"

"Years ago," she said. "It always seemed to me rather a desolate place to be stranded."

"I can see why. But to a New England child it was wonderfully exotic and lush."

"It's curious," she said, "if it were only climate that shaped our points of view, you should be the stern and puritanical one, not I."

"What did you say?"

She started to repeat herself, then glanced at him in sudden suspicion. "You heard me, Jonas!"

"Of course I did," he said blandly. "I only wanted to hear you speak. Can anyone be stern and puritanical, with a voice like that? It has all the tropics in it." He swung around so that he faced her, putting one arm across her body and bracing his hand against the sand at her other side. "Your voice makes me think of the scent of vanilla, Marianna. You should always speak Tahitian, never English."

His eyes, amused and mocking, were fastened on hers; his face very close to her own. She felt a flush spread upward from her throat to her cheeks. Sometimes, when the urge to express her feeling for him became more than she could resist, she would lapse almost unconsciously into Tahitian, letting the warm, half-humorous, earthy phrases cover the cry that echoed in her heart, I love you, I love you . . .

"Speak to me in Tahitian, Marianna."

237

"You are a crazy *popaa*," she said. "Witless as a sea urchin clinging to the reef."

"Beautiful!" he said. "Tell me more." His head bent closer to hers.

Still in Tahitian, she said a little breathlessly, "Enough flattery. Come and eat."

"In a moment," he said softly. His lips against her own were warm as the touch of sunlight on her skin.

Most of the time the prospect of the future scarcely troubled her. She drifted through the dazzling, sun-filled days, joyously content with Jonas's companionship, their shared activities, their idle conversations and their laughter. Behind it all was the deep, underlying memory of their nights together, and the ecstatic, illusory moments when his body silently asserted that he loved her, that they were one.

But there were times when she was engulfed by a wave of guilt, when all the rigid precepts of her childhood and upbringing came back to haunt her. She fought against these attacks of conscience, in the fatalistic knowledge that some day she would be able to do so no longer; and she concealed them from Jonas as carefully as she concealed the fact of her deep and abiding love for him.

One afternoon Jonas borrowed a musket from one of the natives and went up into the hills to hunt wild cocks. After he had gone she gathered together a bundle of laundry and paddled to the mouth of the little stream at the head of the bay, tied the canoe to a tree branch and walked upstream to a wide, deep pool farther in the woods. There was no one about. She undressed, wrapped a *pareu* about her body, as the native girls did, and squatted down on a stone at the edge of the stream with the bundle beside her.

Washing out the clothes and watching the white bubbles float lazily downstream as she rinsed them, she was idly contented. When she had finished, she hung the laundry to dry in the sunlight, and went back to the water's edge. For a moment she stood looking down at her reflection in the clear, dark mirror of the pool. During the days in Moorea her face and arms had taken on a rosy brown, and her hair was washed to pale gold by the sun. Jonas had teased her about her reversion to native life, calling her a blond Tahitian, an unregenerate savage. She knelt down on the grassy bank, staring gravely at her mirrored face. Once he had told her that her eyes were the color of the sea — as clear and as changeable in sunlight and shadow. Her eyes, her voice — he had created small vanities in her that had never been awakened before. Her voice, he had said, was like the scent of vanilla . . .

How strange, she thought, that I should be remembering things like this; and suddenly she was ashamed that she cherished them so. She got to her feet, still staring down at the water. The reflected figure, wrapped in a gay *pareu*, seemed to bear no resemblance to Miss Marianna Moore; it had a faintly raffish look. All at once she was washed by a sense of utter dismay. Where have I gone, she thought, what have I done with myself?

For the first time the fact of her relationship with Jonas, stripped of all the emotions and circumstances that had brought it about, appeared to her in the same outrageous nakedness it would show to Mr. Thomson or the Darlings. As if from an alien viewpoint, she saw the enormity of what she had done, the irremediable quality of her sin. She bowed her head in her hands, her father's sorrowing face suddenly vivid before her. The thought of him, above all others, was the one she most wanted to avoid. She had armed herself with defiance where everyone else was concerned, but there were no defenses against the fact that she was Nathaniel Moore's daughter.

239

Deliberately, she pushed aside the thought. At the back of her mind Mr. Thomson's voice said harshly, "Repent! Repent before it is too late!" Her hands dropped away from her face, trembling a little. It was already too late for repentance, and in her heart she knew that she could never have changed the course she had followed. She squared her shoulders, drew a long breath, and dived deeply into the pool. When she came to the surface she was shivering, and on her lips the salt taste of tears mingled with the cool, sweet water.

When they were together her happiness made such moments unimportant. The days fluttered by like birds across the sky; she could not waste them in regrets.

Jonas, save for infrequent lapses into moody silence, was in good spirits, meticulously courteous and considerate, lightheartedly affectionate. She had come to know his weaknesses by now, his impatience with boring duty or restraint, his essential selfishness, his hatred of routine, his quick grasp at any momentary delusion that might avert distasteful responsibility. Even though it closely affected her, her feeling for him was impervious to this knowledge, and her hunger for his love fed avidly on his occasional tendernesses.

They didn't spend all their time in the search for food; often they swam lazily in the shady river, or paddled around the coral heads in the bay, watching the jewel-colored fish suspended in the clear depths. Sometimes a gray squall of rain would loose itself from the hills and sweep across the bay, and they would take shelter in the hot little cabin, reading or talking. Jonas told her of his life in America and the New England village where he was born; about his mother, who had died when he was very young, and his father, whose stern, intolerant discipline had finally driven him so far from home. And he liked to hear her tell

240

of her childhood, of Tahiti in earlier days, and about her schooling with the other missionary children in the South Sea Academy at Papetoai, in the next bay along the coast, where the priggish and unimaginative routine contrasted so sharply with the wild freedom she enjoyed with her native playmates, away from school.

In the evenings they would pull their mattresses on deck and lie there watching the stars and talking. It was like a dream to her, this idle, unhurried conversation, and the slow growth of companionship between them. One night she said, "Tell me about snow."

"Snow! What do you want to know about it?"

"Everything. About how cold it is, and white, like the surf on the reef, and how it makes even the ugliest things look beautiful."

"It strikes me that you're pretty well informed already!"

"I know," she said. "When we were children, hearing about snow was our favorite story. But I'm sure there are lots of things I don't know about it."

"Do you know about making Jap wax?"

"Jap wax? What's that?"

"You take a large pan and pack it full of clean snow," he said authoritatively. "And then you heat up maple syrup until it's good and thick, and pour it here and there into the pan of snow. It solidifies into wonderful, sugary stuff."

"And you eat it?"

"Certainly!"

"Maple syrup. Is that rather like molasses?"

"Rather. No, by God, it's not," he said, outraged. "It's — Marianna, you've never seen a maple tree, have you?"

"No."

"Nor an oak tree, nor an elm? My God, woman, you're an ignorant savage! How can I talk intelligently to someone who doesn't even know that acorns grow on elms?"

241

"Look," she said suddenly. "Over there!"

A bright meteor had appeared above the mountains to the south. It seemed to hiss across the sky, its blazing tail extinguishing the nearby stars as it passed. Neither of them spoke for a moment.

"What an awesome thing!" Marianna said at last. "I see now why the natives think it's a bad omen."

"A bad omen?"

"They say a meteor is a portent of war."

"They may be right," he said somberly. "Haven't you been wondering how things stand at home?"

"Yes," she said. "Sometimes."

He rolled over on his side so that he faced her. "We've been here two weeks," he said. "The salt's almost gone, and so is the sugar." He reached out and touched her gently on the cheek. "It's been a fine holiday, Marianna. But we've got to think about going back."

The dream was ending, as she had known it must. "Yes," she said faintly.

He drew his fingers softly around the curve of her chin and throat. "After we're married we'll come back here again, whenever we get tired of people."

Her hands clenched at her sides. It had to be said, it had to be said . . . "We aren't going to be married. I've told you that."

He propped himself up on one elbow, looking down at her, and she could see the white flash of his teeth in the starlit darkness. "Marianna, sometimes you shock me profoundly," he said. "Here am I, hopelessly compromised by you, and you talk of casting me carelessly aside. Like a broken toy," he went on, his ironic voice warming to the theme, "like a teakettle with a hole in it!"

She tried hard to keep her voice as light as his, but there was a ring of desperation in it. "Nevertheless, we won't be married."

"Wait and see," he said. "Wait and see." He leaned forward, and as she started to reply, stopped her words with the warm, insistent pressure of his lips against hers.

242

The next day a small, weather-beaten copra schooner, belonging to one of the natives, came into the bay bringing news from Papeete. Admiral Hamelin had declared the restoration of the protectorate, by order of the King of France. The French steamship, which had been sent to Raiatea to bring back the Queen, returned with the report that she had fled to the mountain encampment on sighting the vessel, and would neither see nor make treaty with any French officer until they were prepared to surrender complete restoration of her rights. At this refusal, the first act of the protectorate had been to announce the formal deposition of Pomare, and the appointment of her former Prime Minister, Paraita, fat and corrupt, as Regent in her place. Other than this, there were no signs of any change in the government, and martial law was still in force.

"A wise meteor," Jonas said. "There's bound to be trouble before long." He would go to Raiatea as quickly as he could, he decided, to talk with the Queen and help strengthen the fortifications there.

Shortly after dawn the following morning they sailed for Papeete. There was barely enough wind to give them headway through the passage between the reefs, but once outside they had a slow, steady breeze behind them. Marianna sat in the stern, watching the wide, silent swing of the bay as they left it behind. She had known the greatest happiness of her life on that narrow blade of water; its memory would be a part of her as long as she lived. For as long as she could she watched it, until at last the mountains closed it completely away from her.

⁂

MARIANNA CARRIED A POT OF HOT COFFEE AND TWO CUPS INTO THE little parlor, set them down on one of the packing cases that littered the room, and lighted an oil lamp. It was nearly eight-thirty, and Jonas had said he would be back at seven. He had seemed so positive that he would return before curfew that she wondered uneasily if he had run into trouble with the sentries.

She sat down rather wearily and poured out a cup of coffee. Only the night before she had been lying on the deck of the *Moana* with Jonas, surrounded by the dark, magnificent quietude of the bay, still a part of that magical world private to them alone. Already it seemed in the distant past. Jonas had been with her nearly all of the day, helping her to move into the little house, but even then she had suffered an odd feeling of loss, as if they were being forced apart by the mundane realities of household matters, and by the prying eyes of the townspeople.

The house itself, which she had rented from a native woman, was as good a refuge as she could have found, she supposed. At least Jonas could visit her here, unnoticed and uncensured. It was a weather-beaten frame bungalow, sheltered by the trees that shaded the roadway back of town, a few blocks from the bay. There were two rooms and a lean-to kitchen at the rear. To Marianna, who had never before lived away from the sight of the sea, it seemed dark and cramped, but a small, dilapidated veranda, scarcely able to support the weight of the vines that covered it, clung to the front of the house, and from it one could see the green mountains rising behind the town, and a small stream slipping sedately between rock walls at the edge of the road.

She had finished her coffee when she heard Jonas. Before she could get up he had come in the door, slamming it savagely behind him. He stood looking down at her, his feet apart, the lamplight casting the bold shadow of his nose across his glowering face.

"God damn them," he said. "God damn their puny little souls!"

"Jonas, what is it? The sentries?"

He came over and sat down heavily beside her, and she could smell the ripe scent of rum that hung on his breath. "It wasn't the sentries," he said. "Nothing so harmless as that."

"Please tell me what's happened."

He picked up her hand, looked at it a moment, then held it against his cheek. "I thought I'd surprise you," he said. "I thought in my bland, complacent way that I'd have a prettily packaged little proposal to lay at your feet. Instead of that, I've brought a fine and stinging slap to lay across that soft mouth of yours."

She saw that he was somewhat drunk. "What are you talking about, Jonas?"

"I've been to see the Reverend Thomson," he said sardonically. "Your former employer, the man of God, the self-appointed arbiter of island morals. I told him that I wanted to marry you, and asked him when he could perform the ceremony."

She drew away from him, her eyes, wide and dark, fixed on his.

"Can you guess what he said, this man of Christ? Can you see how his narrow little soul rejoiced at this opportunity to rub my nose in the sand? He couldn't in conscience marry us, he said, not after our flagrant — Jesus, Marianna! You should have heard him! There's no one who can talk filth as disgustingly as a God-bitten bigot." He ran his fingers through his thick straight hair. "Briefly, his kindly proposition is this: if we live apart for a pure and sanctified year, and prove ourselves by sincere and humble repentance, then, and only then, will he condescend to speak the magic words that make us respectable again."

His voice, roughened with angry sarcasm, grated against her like raw coral.

He went on, "And what's more, he has already seen to it that all of his brothers in Christ will take the same tack. No one of them will marry us — not Simpson nor Darling nor Barff, not even old, half-blind Davies, out in Papara, who's too senile and feeble to have a mind of his own. He thinks he's got us on the run, but by God, we'll show him! We'll show him, won't we, Marianna?"

"You shouldn't have talked to him," she said with an effort. "It doesn't matter, anyway. I told you I wouldn't marry you."

245

"Oh, God," he said, "don't talk foolishness!" He pulled her half-averted face toward his, holding her strongly by the shoulders. "Look here, Marianna! I know you — I know you through and through. You love me, don't you — even if you won't say it."

Almost inaudibly, she said, "What if I do?"

His voice was still hard and angry. "Say it! Say the words!"

She drew a long breath, and flung back her head. "I love you," she said steadily.

His mouth softened, and so did his voice. "Sweet Marianna. My good little savage! You'll marry me, and you'll not regret it, not with more than a thousand tears." He was silent a moment. "The French might marry us. I hadn't thought of that."

"Oh, no! The priests wouldn't — we're heretics to them."

"Bruat might. A civil ceremony — he could do that."

"But I won't! It would be a — travesty. I won't do that!"

"Perhaps you're right. We'll manage, somehow. After the fighting is over we'll go away — to America perhaps, to California. There are other countries, thank God, and other pastors! We'll make our fortune, and raise a dozen brats. Christ, but I'm thirsty."

She slipped away from his grasp and got quickly to her feet. "The coffee's all made. It won't take a minute to heat it up."

"Not coffee! Sit down, Marianna." He pulled a bottle from his pocket. "A little rum, to wash away the taste of cant. Have some, it will be good for you."

She shook her head, and he tilted the bottle to his lips, then leaned forward and pulled her back beside him. She sat there stiffly, unwillingly. He looked at her with amused, drunken detachment. "Poor Marianna! Born to two worlds, and inheriting the worst of each. Berated by the godly, maltreated by the wicked, steering a lonely course from shoal to shoal — "

"Please," she said wretchedly, "please go home."

"Go home! You'd send me home in the darkness, too mentally

246

fogged to dodge the sentries, certain to be caught and rot out the rest of my days in jail? Do you want that, Marianna?"

"No," she said. "But there are two beds. I'll make the other one and you can sleep out here — "

"Sleep out here? Alone, under the aegis of the gentle Mr. Thomson? Is that what you want? To do as he required?"

"No. I don't know. I'm too tired to talk or think about it."

There was a note of such despair in her voice that it cut through his fuddled self-absorption. He pulled her closer, holding her head in the hollow of his shoulder. "Tonight's our betrothal, Marianna. Think of it tenderly, and remember, as I do, our marriage bed, cradled on the sea and lighted by the white glow of a thousand stars. Remember Moorea, Marianna. Don't pull away from me, even though I stink of rum."

His tenderness, rough and unpredictable as it was, was all she had left of tenderness in the world. She was aware, in the tired confusion of her thoughts, that he had failed her once again, and would always fail to give her the peace and loving kindness that she craved; but tonight, somehow in his drunken talk he had revealed that he needed her, too, more than he realized or would admit. She put her hand up to his cheek, suddenly sustained by that knowledge. "I'm here, Jonas, for as long as you want me. Mr. Thomson can't change that."

***

Captain d'Aubigny stood on the quarter-deck of the corvette *La Meurthe* watching the far, cloud-shrouded peaks of Tahiti slowly merge into the gray horizon. Soon he would no longer be able to see that strange and barbarous land that had been his home for more than a year, shortly it would be washed away completely behind the full wet-shining swell of the sea. *Adieu,* savage island, with all my heart, *adieu.*

Still, for the past few months, since the commencement of the affair with the English Lily, it had not been too bad a life. He stroked his fingers across his trim mustache, remembering her ardor, her passionate pleas that he take her with him to France. Poor little one! No wonder she was miserable, marooned in such a land with that worthless cuckold of a husband. Never, in all his life, had he seen a man wear his horns so lightly or indifferently! *Eh bien,* so much the better for d'Aubigny. Lily was a charming, volatile little thing; he had ended the interlude with genuine regret.

Far to the leeward a rain squall sieved darkly to the graying sea. Automatically he noted it, and that all was clear ahead. *La Meurthe* was racing along as if she were as anxious to reach France as he. Only a few more weeks and he would be home, he would have his leave, he would be in Paris, Paris, Paris. He stretched his arms above his head, smiling, and turned away from the railing. It had been a long and arduous day; now there was time to go down to his cabin and rest a bit before dinner.

The cabin was filling with shadows, and he turned to the door to call the cabin boy for a lamp when a slight movement behind the curtains of his berth caught his eye. He strode across the little room and pulled them aside, looking down at the bed in frozen amazement. *"Mon dieu!"* he breathed.

There was Lily, crouching on the bed, looking up at him pleadingly. Her face and arms had been darkened with a brown stain, a scarlet *pareu* was wrapped tightly around her small curved body, and there was a wreath of faded white flowers tipsily crowning her tangled hair.

" 'Ow did you get 'ere?"

She shrank back, pulling the *pareu* closer across her breast. "With the other women — to say good-by to the sailors. I hid —

248

behind that box. Nobody saw me when they searched the ship."

"*Evidemment!*" he said. "*Mon dieu!*"

She was staring at him fearfully. "What are you going to do with me?"

"That," he said coldly, "I ask of myself."

"Let me stay! Please let me stay!"

He sank down on a stool beside the bed and put his face between his hands. "You can't stay on the sheep."

"You're the captain," she said eagerly. "You can do what you like."

He lifted his head and gave her a baleful glare. "*La Meurthe* is not a pleasure sheep! Thees is the Navy."

"You can't take me back! You're too far out at sea."

"I could," he said. "*Merde,* what an embarrassment!" He was silent, staring down at his hands. If he took the woman back to Papeete, what a *brouhaha,* what a scandal! And he, d'Aubigny, would be the laughingstock of the island, the enemies of France would split their sides with mirth. Perhaps he could keep her aboard as far as Valparaiso — no one need know about it except the cabin boy. If the officers found out they would cover up for him; happily, they were all good types. But could the cabin boy be trusted? He looked at Lily sternly.

"What an affair! You will be my ruin, madame."

Her lips were trembling. "You said you loved me! You cried when we said farewell!"

He swept that aside with a gesture. "Conseeder what you 'ave done — what it might mean to my career!"

"I'm sorry, Henri. But I'll be so quiet — no one will know — "

"In Tahiti they will know! What of your 'usband?"

"Him!" she said scornfully. "What do I care for him?" She leaned toward him, her eyes dark in her tinted face, her words pouring forth passionately. "D'you know what he's like, that drunken, stupid beast? D'you know how he spends his days, now

249

that the plantations are gone? Stumbling from bar to bar, cadging drinks from whoever will pay for them, borrowing money from any sot who's fool enough to lend it. He doesn't think of me! He doesn't think of anything except who'll buy his next tot of rum. Why, for two months he hasn't paid the Buelles a farthing for our room and board!"

D'Aubigny was looking at her thoughtfully. "You 'ave no money, hein?"

"Nothing," she whispered. "Nothing."

"Suppose I take you as far as Valparaiso. What then?"

Tentatively, she reached out her hand, lightly stroking his arm, her eyes downcast. "I don't know. Someone would have to help me."

He pulled his arm away from her touch. "And 'oo will thees someone be? Henri d'Aubigny, is it not?"

"Please, Henri. I'll pay you back some day, I swear it."

She came closer to him, rubbing her face caressively against his hand. He looked down at her, his eyes shrewd. She could have money enough, this one, were she not so generous of her self . . . A little more kindly, he said, "Eh bien, there is nothing else to do. You can come to Valparaiso, and I will buy you passage in a sheep to England."

"Not England!" she said vehemently. "I won't go back to England! To France! To Paris, with you."

"After you get to Paris you are no longer of my responsible," he said coolly. "What will you do then?"

For a moment she hesitated, looking at him sidelong. "I'll be all right. I have — relatives there." Lily was a very poor liar.

"Reech ones, I 'ope."

She caught the flicker of his smile, and leaned forward from the bed, impetuously throwing her arms about his neck. A little package, wrapped in a handkerchief, thudded to the deck. D'Aubigny pulled away from her and stooped to pick it up,

250

weighing it thoughtfully in his hand. He handed it back to her with an ironic little bow. Two diamond rings and the brooch he had seen her wear. She would not do so badly after all, this little one.

"So you are not quite destitute, *chérie.*"

She didn't even blush. "Not quite. Thank you, Henri. But I haven't any clothes. What shall I do about that?"

He looked her over carefully. " 'Ere in thees cabin you will scarcely need them," he said blandly.

She gave him an absently playful little slap. "I remember your telling me," she said thoughtfully, "that when your great navigator — what was his name? — came to Tahiti years ago, there was a woman aboard ship, disguised in boy's clothes."

"Bougainville," he said. "Umm. Yes, I remember." Cautiously, he said, "Perhaps it is possible. The cabin boy is of your size, but, well, not so sweet a shape."

Far off in the ship a bell sounded, and he got up reluctantly. "It is of necessary that I go. I will send you something to eat more later." In the fading light he looked at her appraisingly. "You are a good sailor? *Bon.* Stay quietly here. And wash your face."

`He closed the door carefully behind him, and stood for a moment in the passageway, reminiscently patting his mustache. It would not be so boring after all, this passage to Valparaiso.

JONAS'S RETURN TO PAPEETE AFTER NEARLY FOUR WEEKS IN RAIATEA was soured at the outset by his required interview with the French Captain of the Port. He came away from Lieutenant Clon's office seething with suppressed resentment. In the future, he was told, only vessels flying the flag of France would be al-

251

bowed to trade in the Leeward Islands, just as in England the coasting trade was confined strictly to English vessels. In vain, Jonas had pointed out that Raiatea, Huahine, and the other Leeward Islands were independent kingdoms in no way subject to Tahiti, but his protests were useless.

He must know, Lieutenant Clon said suavely, since he had just come from there, that Raiatea and the other islands were now under the protection of France. Protection! Yes, he knew it — he had been aboard the *Moana* in Uturóa harbor on the morning that a small party of Frenchmen had stealthily slipped ashore from the steamship *Phaeton* — so early that everyone else was still asleep — planted the French protectorate flag on the jetty, and just as quietly had retired to the steamship again. Like everyone else around the bay, he was awakened to realization of what had happened by the pompous boom of the *Phaeton's* guns, saluting the flag they had planted on shore. Jonas, watching the events from the deck of the *Moana,* had had the joyous satisfaction of seeing the natives rush from their houses, tear down the flag, which one of the men wrapped around his loins like a *pareu,* and shout defiance at the Frenchmen aboard the steamer.

In somewhat the same manner they had hoisted a flag at Huahine, in the absence of Ariipaea, Pomare's doughty and fearless old aunt, who was Queen of the island. As soon as she heard of this action Ariipaea had returned and ordered the flag hauled down; at the island of Bora Bora the French, perhaps intimidated by these reactions, had made no attempt to land the flag on shore, but had merely hoisted and saluted it aboard the steamer as she lay in the harbor there. At none of the islands had they left a representative of France on shore.

What kind of protection was this? And how could they have the gall to tell him he might not trade there in the future? It was no more logical than if they had told him he might not go to Valparaiso or to New Bedford! The trading, God knows, was negligible, but his freedom of action was something no man could tamper with. The Queen needed someone like himself, some tenuous link with her sorely missed Tahiti, someone to goad her apathetic followers into brisker work on the valley fortifications, someone to bring her supplies. Poor woman! Since the French had seized all her possessions she hadn't the money to buy even a length of dress goods; it had taken all his tact to persuade her to accept the things that he and Truelove had sent her. When the land was her own again, she had insisted with pitiful dignity, she would repay them for everything.

Fuming, Jonas strode by the French military band that was performing its daily concert in front of the government buildings, surrounded by a motley crowd of natives who could not resist even Farani music, and cut through a shaded lane to the Broom road. Work on the French fortifications along the waterfront had not been furthered during his absence, he noticed; the half-completed gun emplacements and bastions seemed to symbolize the curious state of suspended hostilities that characterized the whole island. What an endless farce — and yet how tragic, with the flower of Tahiti still rotting out their lives in the incessant rain and mists of the valley encampments, living on roots and berries, sick and half hungry, but still patiently defiant, waiting, waiting, just as the Frenchmen waited for them to give in. By God, he wished someone would start a fight! This damned inaction was getting on his nerves.

Truelove's store was closed for the day, he saw, and though Truelove's house was only a few paces beyond, he decided to postpone seeing him until the morrow. No use to risk encountering old lady Truelove's disapproving sniffs and acid remarks on the subject of his behavior with Marianna. Even Truelove himself had been less openly friendly since their return from Moorea. . . . He'd go to his room at Dr. Ferguson's, he decided, to clean up and take a tot or two of rum to cool his temper.

253

It was nearly seven by the time he turned in Marianna's walk, and his attention was immediately caught by the new, neat little sign nailed against the rickety fence. He stepped closer to read it in the failing light. M. Moore — Dressmaking. So she was in want of money, then! He'd wondered about it before, and pondered what he could do, but he had thought that they would soon be married, and it would all take care of itself. He wasn't rich, God knows, but he had enough for the two of them to live on adequately. . . .

Since their marriage seemed indefinitely postponed he had simply shelved the question — more, he realized ruefully, from lack of courage than because he had forgotten it. He had simply not been able to devise a way in which he could tactfully offer to help her; not without running up against that stiff-necked pride of hers, that stubborn, immutable core of rectitude that was the basis of her character. In spite of her yielding sweetness, her candid and ardent dependence on him, he supposed that he was at heart a trifle afraid of her. He snapped his finger against the sign, smiling a little wryly to himself. With his remembrance of New England marriages, that seemed the right and proper way for a prospective husband to feel.

He was whistling softly as he mounted the veranda steps and rapped. She opened the door, leaning forward to see who was there, her soft hair haloed in the light of the lamp behind her.

"Jonas!" she said. "I — didn't expect you for another week, at least."

It was not the warmest welcome he had ever had. He stepped inside, shutting the door behind him, and put his hand under her chin, tilting her head back to scrutinize her sea-dark eyes and pale, unsmiling mouth.

"You sound disappointed," he said lightly. "Shall I go away again?"

254

She lowered her eyes. "Don't be absurd. Come in, and tell me about your trip." She led him across the room to the sofa and was about to take a chair opposite him when he reached out for her wrist and pulled her gently down beside him.

"Why must you be so distant?"

Again she wouldn't meet his eyes, unusual behavior for Marianna. "It's just that I'm still used to your being away."

"Adapt yourself quickly, then," he said. "I'm very close indeed." He leaned forward to kiss her, but she turned her head away, and his lips brushed clumsily against the smooth skin of her cheek. Puzzled, he released her, and leaned back, glancing about the room. The table by the window was piled high with bright lengths of cloth and varicolored spools of thread.

He gestured toward it. "I see you've gone into business."

"Yes."

So that was all she was going to say. "Is it going to be worth your while?" he asked tentatively.

A little sparkle lighted up the curiously lifeless expression in her eyes. "I've already had five commissions."

"Who are your customers?"

She shrugged. "The town belles, mostly. I don't inquire into their resources, but if I know French money will pay the bill, I charge them more. The *vahines* don't mind."

"Ill-gotten gains," he murmured.

"I work for it, at least," she said coolly.

"Don't work too hard."

"I won't. As a matter of fact, I had to refuse one order. Lieutenant Piccard's *vahine* wanted three dresses made up, but I — didn't have the time."

Lieutenant Piccard's *vahine* was Turia, Jonas's former mistress for so many years. He looked at Marianna in covert amazement. She would never be so tactless unless by intention, and her expression was so perfectly bland that he had to conquer a small im-

255

pulse to slap her. This, certainly, was no time to ask her if she needed money.

"Tell me about your trip," she said. "Was it rough? We've had strong winds and heavy rains."

"Pretty boisterous coming back," he said. He told her about Raiatea and about the sadly homesick Queen, half of his mind puzzling over the polite conventionality of her questions, the courteous but chilly attention that she gave his replies. At last, after a rather protracted pause, he said, "What's the news here?"

"Have you heard about Lily Nicholls?"

"Lord, yes. News of that dimension filters even to Raiatea." He caught her quick, sidelong glance, as if she would gauge the effect that Lily's departure might have on him. He laughed. "Lily's well out of it, I think."

"What will happen to her? D'you think that Frenchman will be kind to her?"

"Not indefinitely," he said. "But Lily'll be all right — happier than she's been in years. She'll live with a succession of rich milords, and retire comfortably to the Riviera when she's forty." His lazy voice warmed to the theme. "Then she'll marry her coachman, twenty years younger than she, who'll give her a good beating occasionally, and deceive her with the cook."

"It doesn't sound a very enviable future to me," she said frigidly.

Obviously, he had run afoul of one of the missionary prejudices, the ingrained conversational taboos that were still, although he had nearly forgotten it of late, part of Marianna's code. He changed the subject abruptly.

"Tell me about yourself. What's happened here?"

Things had been quiet, she told him. Two or three weeks earlier a United States brig, the *Perry,* had come into port, and on going to anchor saluted both the protectorate flag and the French flag with twenty-one guns. The *Perry's* commander had inquired jocosely if there were any further salutes to be made, but he had been meticulous in demanding a like number in return. When the French salvo fell short by one gun, he had sent an officer ashore to remonstrate, and the salute had had to be repeated from the beginning.

The polite animation of her tone told him that she had no intention of discussing anything more personal than such topics as this, and he became determined to find out what lay at the bottom of her reserve. Deliberately, he put his hand behind her back and began to stroke her hair, holding her arm close against his side with the other hand. "It's good to be home," he said tentatively.

No reply. From the tenseness of her muscles he could tell that she longed to break away, but with a malicious amusement he knew that she would find this hard to do without loss of dignity. Softly, his fingers continued their rhythmic stroking. Every now and then he slyly pulled a pin from the heavy knot of hair at the nape of her neck, and dropped it surreptitiously behind the cushions.

The silence between them was almost palpable. Suddenly Marianna said, "News from Raiatea travels to Tahiti, too."

Involuntarily, his hand faltered in its stroke of her hair, then hurriedly he resumed it again. "Does it? Important news?"

"Not very important," she said stiffly, "only that you had a *vahine* in Uturoa."

He whistled softly. "How very interesting!"

She pulled away from him and jumped to her feet, the loosened mass of her hair tumbling about her shoulders. "Interesting to your Maker, perhaps, if He still has any concern left for your worthless soul!"

"Don't trouble me with cant, Marianna," he said lazily. "I have a strong suspicion that you're jealous."

"Jealous! I'm not jealous of the sordid pastimes of a — beachcomber!"

He sat quite still, looking up at her, a faint smile lying like a shadow along his lips. How dark her eyes were, and how flushed her cheeks! With her hair falling about her face like that she looked like a handsome and passionately vengeful goddess.

"You should dress your hair more loosely after this, Marianna. It's very becoming to you that way."

"Be quiet!" she said venomously. "I'm not a *vahine,* to be bought for a night with cheap flattery."

By God, this was serious! He got up and came toward her. "It's not flattery, my dear. You're very beautiful, you know."

"Don't mock me!" she cried. "And don't touch me!"

He took her arms in his hands, holding her strongly. "Look here, Marianna! To the best of my recollection, I have no *vahines* in Uturoa."

"It's the only place you haven't, then! It seems to me every woman I meet was once your whore. No wonder you can't recollect them all!"

He had not known she was capable of such untrammeled anger. His fingers tightened their hold on her arms. "It's you who flatter *me,*" he said with asperity. "Don't talk such rot!"

"This is the end, Jonas," she said flatly. "You can leave now. I won't be another of your cast-offs."

"Be quiet," he said, "be quiet!" She tried to pull away from him, and he seized her strongly, kissing her savagely on the mouth. With his tongue he found the faint taste of salt between her lips, and when he let her go he saw that she was crying.

"Marianna," he said contritely, "darling Marianna!"

She stood quite still, brushing the tears from her cheeks with the tips of her fingers. "Please go away."

"I'll go if you like," he said, "but I'll be back. I love you, Marianna. I'll have to come back."

Slowly, she raised her wet lashes, gazing at him incredulously, and a faint light came into her eyes, like the gray shine of the

258

sea at dusk. For a moment she did not speak, then she moved her hands in a vague and helpless little gesture.

"Come back, then," she said. "I'll always want you to come back."

News of the death of Pomare's youngest child, the baby Victoria, reached Mr. Barff, the old missionary resident at Huahine, shortly after sundown one evening in June. The next morning at daybreak, he sailed for Raiatea. From Uturoa harbor it was seventeen miles by rowboat through the reef-studded lagoon to the foot of the valley of Vaiaao, on the north side of the island. He had had two stalwart natives to row him, but even so it was an arduous trip, and in the late afternoon, scrambling over the slippery path that led up to the Queen's encampment, Mr. Barff could reflect that he was no longer as young as he used to be.

As usual in that mountain fastness, it was raining; the huge drops fell in showers against his head and shoulders whenever a shudder of wind stirred the great tree branches above, and his trousers were soaked to the thighs from the wet clutch of the underbrush. Here and there the turgid river touched the path and then recoiled away again, arching its back to the patter of the rain.

Half an hour's climb above the sea his guides led him into a clearing where six or eight woven, coconut-thatched houses crouched along the grassy banks of the stream. One of the men hallooed softly, and several of the Queen's people materialized through the mist to show Mr. Barff to the largest house in the settlement. The little girl had died two nights before, they told him, and since then the Queen had refused to take anything to eat or drink. It was good that he had come.

Pomare Tane, dressed in seedy dungarees and smoking a cigar, was sitting in front of the house with some cronies; he greeted Mr. Barff rather sullenly, and jerked his thumb toward the doorway. The old missionary rapped against the doorpost and went inside. After a moment or two, while his eyes adjusted to the damp, shadowy dimness of the interior, he saw the Queen, dressed in wrinkled black silk, lying on a pile of matting in one corner. Two of her maids were with her, but at his approach she waved them away.

Mr. Barff, who had known Pomare since she was a small girl, squatted down on a cushion beside her and silently took her hand. He had expected sobs and lamentations at his appearance, but he saw now that the Queen was too exhausted for further expressions of grief; her cheeks were stained and channeled with the courses of her tears. Looking at her it was hard to believe that this was the same Pomare who only a few years before had horrified the missionaries with her gay and pagan revelries. A stranger might have thought her nearly as old as he was.

"I came as quickly as I could, Pomare, to bring you comfort from the Lord."

She looked at him bleakly. "My grief is too sore for comfort, Barffi."

"The Lord gives," Mr. Barff said gently, "and the Lord takes away."

Pomare turned aside her head. "She was so young, Barffi! So little, with great eyes, and a round dimple, here. When we tickled her she would laugh, and the dimple would jump out."

"She is safe with Jesus," Mr. Barff said. "You must think on that."

Her shoulders moved impatiently. "She would not have died if I had been in my own land, in Tahiti! It was the rains that killed her, the dampness in her lungs. She was the child of my sorrow," she went on bitterly; "when she was born, twelve moons ago, it was at the time I had had to fly from Tahiti, to escape the

260

Farani. My loins were sick with the long time on ship, and with the fear that griped them. What chance did I have to bring forth a strong and healthy babe?"

"The Lord's will was in it, Pomare. We cannot always see — "

"The Farani killed her!" she burst out. "The Farani killed her just as surely as if they had shot her with their dirty guns!"

"Vengeance is Mine, the Lord says. You must be resigned, Pomare."

She struggled up on one elbow, her distraught eyes fixed on him accusingly. "We called her Victoria, after your Queen. We thought the Queen might be pleased, and listen to our calls for help. But we have waited and waited, and no help has come. Now little Victoria is dead, and something in my heart has died also!"

"Be patient," he said. "Perhaps the ships will still be sent to help you." He looked away from the disbelief on her face, and his glance fell on a little stick with a shark's tooth set in the end of it that lay beside her mat. He started to pick it up, then hastily drew back his hand. One of the old, pagan scarifiers, with which the Tahitians, in any excess of grief, used to slash their foreheads till the blood ran! He looked back at Pomare and saw that her brow was marked with dark red scratches. He drew his finger across them gently.

"This is not good, Pomare."

"What *is* good?" she asked bitterly.

"The Lord is good. He will redeem us from our sins."

"I know the Lord Jesus is good," she said wearily. "But since my people have known of Him there has been nothing but sorrow and death in the land." She lay back again, her eyes fixed on the woven ceiling. "Your countrymen brought the Word, Barffi, but some of them brought sicknesses we had never known before, and rum, like my Tane drinks until he is made crazy with it. When we were troubled you made us promises, but where are those prom-

261

ises now? The *popaa* French have gobbled up the land like hungry pigs, and no one comes to stop them. And now my baby is gone, and I have nothing."

Stoutly, he said, "The Lord will help you, Pomare. Let us pray to Him." He bowed his head and began to pray aloud. Pomare lay quietly, her eyes closed, her lips not moving, but once, when he raised his head to glance at her, he saw that she had picked up the little scarifier and was twisting it restlessly between her brown fingers.

〰〰〰

H.M.S. *Daphne*, WITH MR. PRITCHARD ABOARD, BOUND FOR THE Navigators Islands, sailed silently, almost furtively, through the darkness off the northern coast of Tahiti. Mr. Pritchard, hunched in a blanket, sat on deck throughout the night staring at the black, unseen bulk of the mountains blotting out the lower stars. He could see nothing, nothing at all of this land he had been forced to leave more than a year before; even the far, murmurous reefs were dark, unlighted by the golden fire of any fisherman's torch.

Yet the island was all about him, close as a beloved woman asleep beside him in the marriage bed. The fragrance of the *hupé* fanned out across the sea, freighted with the scent of flowers and trees and ferns, with the sweet spice of vanilla, the clean smell of fresh water, and occasionally, almost shocking in its poignancy, the creamy, nostalgic perfume of the island gardenia. There was Tahiti, and here was he, gliding past it in the darkness, never again to set foot upon its green and troubled shores.

Dawn was breaking as the *Daphne* slid by Point Venus, at the northernmost part of the island, and as they sailed across the channel toward Moorea Mr. Pritchard had the melancholy satisfaction of seeing Tahiti's dark peaks stretch up to meet the morning sun. It was a relief when the shores of Moorea cut in between him and that view of a far and unattainable home. The *Daphne's* immediate destination was Papetoai Bay, in Moorea, where they would stop just long enough to fill the water casks and bring aboard fresh fruits, and the captain had warned him that he must stay out of sight in his cabin until they were again at sea. No one was to be allowed aboard ship except Mr. Simpson, the resident missionary, Mr. Pritchard's brother-in-law and long-time friend. Sleepless and haggard, Mr. Pritchard went below when the *Daphne* passed between the reefs and glided into the dulcet cleft of Papetoai Bay.

He heard the anchor drop, and the sound of canoes bumping against the side of the ship. Shortly afterward there was a rap at his cabin door. He pulled it open, his face alight. Alex Simpson! Gracious God, it was good to see someone from home again!

The two men embraced like brothers, speaking eagerly together. Simpson's wife and family were well; Eliza Pritchard and the children had all been fine when he bade them good-by in England . . .

"The captain tells me you're not stopping here," Simpson said. "Where are you bound, George?"

Some of the momentary light faded from Mr. Pritchard's eyes. "They're sending me to the Navigators Islands," he said with careful lack of emotion. "I'm to be consul there. Eliza and the younger children will join me after I've had a chance to get settled a bit."

He looked away from the expression of horrified amazement on Simpson's face. This was the reward his government had given him for all his impassioned work, his suffering at the hands of the French; a post in a remote and savage land where there was scarcely a British subject and where he would have no chance to do either good or harm. They hadn't dared to remove him

263

completely from government service, because of the feeling that had arisen in England for him and his championship of Tahiti, but he was being deprived of any chance to embarrass them again. They needn't have worried, he thought, there was no more trouble left in him. He had been taught a lesson in disillusionment that would last him the rest of his days.

Simpson had regained control of his expression and voice. "Of course you couldn't have stayed here, George. Foolish of me to ask. Those Frenchmen! They even use your name as an epithet. Anything annoying is *Preet-shard* —" He stopped, afraid that he had gone too far, but a little glow came into Mr. Pritchard's eyes.

"That so? I'm delighted to hear it. How do things stand now, Alex?"

He listened somberly while Simpson talked. The Queen an exile from her land, grieving for her lost child, the people still impotently penned in their mountain fortresses, the Leeward Islands blockaded to any ship except those that flew the French flag . . . Here was defeat, defeat because Britain had turned a cold shoulder to the pleas of an innocent people who were only trying to maintain what was rightfully theirs. What was Simpson saying about justice? Unwilling to saddle the Lord with an impossibility, Mr. Pritchard had ceased to pray for justice; his supplications now were for patience and resignation.

"The *Collingwood*, with Admiral Seymour aboard, is somewhere in these seas," Simpson was saying. "When she puts in — eighty-gun ship of the line — perhaps we'll have some action at last."

What a delusion, Mr. Pritchard thought, but he said nothing. Let these people cling to their hopes a little longer, if hope could sustain them. There was no way he could help them. God knows, he had tried; he had stood for right against palpable wrong, for weakness against oppression, for reason and logic against force, and he had garnered nothing but rebuke for it. The culmination of

264

his life and work had been reached in Tahiti; now he could spend his declining years in expiating his error of relying too strongly on the integrity of his own government.

Mr. Simpson, glancing at him covertly, all at once recognized the change that had puzzled him since his first glimpse of his brother-in-law. It wasn't that Pritchard was grayer, or that more lines were dug beside his mouth, it was that a meekness had settled over him, an absence of fighting spirit that was tragically irreconcilable in one who had been all fire before. He plunged into speech, in an effort to cheer him, if he could.

"Shortly after you left the island, George, your wife sent us a framed print of you which I hung on the wall in my study. You should have seen the natives' excitement! They flocked from miles around to see it, and some of them would sit down and look at it for hours." He chuckled, inconclusively. " 'Be quiet,' they'd say. 'Be quiet. Pritarde is behind there; he will soon come forth, and all will be well again!' "

To his dismay, Mr. Simpson saw that Pritchard had buried his face in his hands. When he spoke his words were so muffled that Simpson wasn't sure he had heard him aright. He could have been mistaken, but it sounded as if Pritchard had muttered, "I'll never come forth again."

D̲r. FERGUSON, VIRTUOUSLY CONSCIOUS OF THE FULL WEEK OF sobriety he had just achieved, left Mr. Thomson's door and turned his clumsy, ponderous steps in the direction of the back street where Marianna Moore lived. The puffy folds of flesh that encircled his small, shrewd eyes did not entirely conceal the look of satisfaction that glinted faintly in their weary and bloodshot depths. Bruce Ferguson, he thought complacently, still had enough of the old Scotch iron in his tongue to talk down a miserable, pious hymn-singer like the reverend Mr. Thomson. He came abreast of the Boar's Head grogshop, paused thirstily for a moment, then plodded purposefully on.

He found Marianna on her veranda, sewing ruffles along the hem of a billowing skirt. She piled her work on a table as he came up the steps, and pulled forward a chair for him.

"Uh-h," he said. "Good to sit down. Thought perhaps I might surprise a couple of charmin' ladies in dishabille in your front room."

Marianna laughed. "Is that why you came?"

"Not altogether." He pulled out a cigar, and behind the ritual of lighting it studied her carefully for a few moments. Amazing what love could do for a woman, he thought; Marianna had blossomed like a rose. It wasn't just that her hair was dressed more loosely and becomingly, or that her gown was cut in a way that even an old islander like himself could recognize as having style; it was a kind of softness that lay on lip and cheek, a luminosity that shone from the eyes. But his keen glance noted also that she was much too thin, and that there were faint signs of strain in her face and in the way she used her hands. Difficult to know how to handle these high-strung wenches, he thought; she'd not be so easy as Thomson. Playing for time, he said, "Passed Anthony Nicholls on the street just now, so drunk he could hardly navigate."

"Disgraceful," she said demurely. "Did you give him a temperance lecture?"

"Don't sass an old man," he said. "I came here to have a talk with you, and I want your respectful attention."

"It's all yours," she said. "I'm delighted and flattered. What is the talk about?"

"About you," he said gruffly.

"Oh." She leaned back in her chair, and a look of wariness came into her eyes. "That's rather a dull topic. There's nothing to say."

266

"There's plenty, if you'd only say it. See here, Marianna, I know I'm a meddlesome old man, but this situation can't go on much longer. It's too hard on you."

"I'm all right," she said. "You mustn't worry about me."

"All right!" he said. "Nathaniel Moore's daughter all right when the pious folk in town won't speak to her, when she's cut off from any church activity, when she's livin' in what she was brought up to believe was mortal sin!" He chewed viciously at the end of his cigar. "Don't evade me, girl!"

"I didn't mean to, Dr. Ferguson. Truly. I meant what I said. I'm quite happy."

"You don't fool me," he said. "I know too well that there's no happiness strong enough to stand by itself against the world, without the esteem of friend — and of self."

"But I have friends. I have you, and my Tahitian neighbors, and the girls who come here for their clothes. And sometimes Mr. Truelove will give me a wink when Mrs. Truelove isn't around."

He snorted disgustedly. "A fine lot we are! An old sot, a scaredy-cat storekeeper, and a bunch of light ladies."

"You're good friends," she said stubbornly.

"But how about yourself, Marianna? Is it easy to live with that rigid conscience of yours?"

She looked at him a moment, and then away, apparently studying the purple flowers of the bougainvillea vine that swayed down from the roof of the veranda. He waited, patiently, knowing what was going on in her mind. In the twenty-odd years that he had lived in the island he had never, drunk or sober, betrayed a confidence. He had lived with his fat and faithful Vahine, in a house littered with books — Greek and Latin — and with bottles — brandy and rum — and he had not betrayed his own story, either. No one knew it, and no one ever would. Drunk, he was a sodden pig; sober, he could practice good if somewhat irascible medicine, and his tolerant, weary wisdom had attracted more recitals of human woes than he cared to count. Marianna would talk to him, he thought; she must talk to someone, and there would be many things she could never discuss with Jonas. She looked back at him, and he saw the longing in her eyes.

"It's not easy, is it?" he said softly.

"It's easier than I thought," she said with sudden defiance. "I've lost the sense of sin."

"You mean you've lost your faith, girl?"

She shook her head. "Not that. My faith in God is just as clear and strong as ever. It's hard to explain — I can't talk any more in the old, evangelical language that used to come so glibly. I only know that it isn't the church I miss, because the church is made of people, and the people who made it great and good, like my father and Mr. Nott, aren't here any more." She looked at him despairingly. "I know I'm not right, and that I should feel wicked, and just the fact that I can't seems the most heinous lack of all."

He sighed. "You've not lost your sense of sin, my dear. Take it from an old Scotsman, people who were raised as you and I were will never lose that." He spread his hands. "It's like a fire, that burns in us all the time. I try to put mine out with liquor; you, perhaps, with tears, or just plain bull stubbornness."

She was looking down at her hands, which she had clasped to keep from trembling. The moment had come, he thought. "It would all be all right if you and Jonas were married, wouldn't it?"

"But we can't be! Not yet. You know the circumstances of that."

"I went to see Thomson just before I came here," he said slowly. "Had a talk with him. Rather an enjoyable talk — I like beatin' people over the head with home truths. At the end of it he agreed to marry you and Jonas whenever you wished."

She caught her breath. "Mr. Thomson — told you that?"

"He did, my dear. So you see, it can all be put right, as soon as you'd like."

"Does Jonas know this?"

"No. Not yet."

268

"You mustn't tell him!"

"Why not?"

"Because — because it's too soon. Promise me you won't tell him!"

"Too soon?" he asked ironically. "Some folk might consider it a little late."

"Please don't say that. You *must* try to understand."

"I understand nothing," he said a little irritably. "You want to marry Jonas, don't you?"

"Of course I do!"

"Well, then. What's the trouble? Doesn't he love you?"

"I think he does," she said slowly. "As much as he — can. But if he married me now he might feel pushed into it, and then, in spite of himself, I think he would always resent me." Her eyes were as eloquently pleading as the helpless little lift of her hands toward him. "I don't want our marriage to start under a handicap, Dr. Ferguson. He must arrange it himself. And now isn't the time for it."

"Why not?"

"Can't you see why? You must have noticed how restless he has been lately — how he chafes at this stalemate between the natives and the French, and at his own inactivity while other people are suffering. He's obsessed with the idea that he must help them, and he's being watched so closely that there's nothing he can do. And if he were made to think that he must marry me just now, I know he would feel like a man in prison!"

Gruffly, he said, "I have no use for people who would save the world and at the same time hurt the one soul who is closest to them."

"He doesn't mean to hurt me," she said defensively. "Jonas is good to me. But you mustn't force him. You mustn't tell him about Mr. Thomson. If we marry, it must be his own doing, or it won't be any good at all."

If we marry! He sat looking at her moodily. How this little missionary spinster had changed! Still, it wasn't altogether Jonas who had changed her; the island of her birth, with its lavish beauty, its subtle, insistent emphasis of all that was sensual and earthy, had ravished her long since. She was a Tahitian, Marianna was, and like the Tahitians she was being betrayed. Betrayed by promises that would never be kept, betrayed into patient waiting for something that would never come. He wanted to shout at her, as he frequently wanted to shout at the Tahitians when they talked about help from Britain, Don't trust people, don't trust anyone to help you if it inconveniences themselves!

"You love that worthless Yankee, don't you?" he asked suddenly.

She bowed her head.

"All right. Have it your own way. I'll promise you I won't tell him about Thomson. But I wish *you* would, Marianna. Will you?"

She raised her head, and her smile was warm and tender. "Some day, perhaps. Don't worry about me. But thank you for it, just the same."

He pushed himself to his feet, bade her good-by, and started down the walk. At the gate he turned homeward, then hesitated and faced back toward town again. There was nothing quite so thirst-inducing as to watch people refuse reasonable help and pursue their own determined course toward destruction. It would take a good many tots of rum to wash the taste of futility from his mouth.

***

Dᴜʀɪɴɢ ᴛʜᴇ ʟᴏɴɢ ʀɪᴅᴇ ᴏᴜᴛ ꜰʀᴏᴍ ᴘᴀᴘᴇᴇᴛᴇ ᴛᴏ ᴛʜᴇ ɴᴀᴛɪᴠᴇ ᴄᴀᴍᴘ at Papenoo, Lieutenant the Honorable Fred Walpole, of H.M.S. *Collingwood,* had plenty of time to chew over the distastefulness of the mission on which his admiral had dispatched him. The higher the sun rose in the faultless sky the lower his spirits dropped. His companions, the chaplain of the *Collingwood,* a native guide, and that Yankee chap, Burkham, who was to act as their interpreter, seemed quite as dispirited as he, and there was little conversation between them. Burkham, who could have told them much of interest about the country they passed through, never spoke except to point out, in a faintly accusatory tone, the ravages wrought by the French — the groves of girdled coconut and breadfruit trees, the ruined plantations, the abandoned houses. Dash it all, Lieutenant Walpole thought, he needn't be so uncivil; orders were orders in the Royal Navy, and as a mere lieutenant he was only a messenger boy for the powers-that-be.

It was a deuced unpleasant errand, though. Even in the few weeks he had been in Tahiti, he had been able to form some idea of what a blow to all Tahitian hopes today's official statement from the British government would be. The *Collingwood,* first eighty-gun ship of the line ever to appear in these waters, had been greeted by the natives like the coming of a Messiah. When, without so much as a by-your-leave to the French, she had sailed into Papeete Bay and serenely and imperiously dropped anchor just opposite the Protestant church, they had flocked down to the beaches by the hundreds, wildly excited, shouting and gesticulating, staring out avidly at her warlike broadside and triple battery. It wasn't until later that those on board realized that the natives were hopefully awaiting the *Collingwood's* signal for a concerted attack on the French, and that they supposed, in all their naive and insular innocence, that she had been sent out by Britain for just that purpose.

What a reception they had had! In all the ports the *Collingwood* had visited there had been nothing to touch it. At first it had been a joy just to walk along the roads and hear the greeting, *Ia ora na oe* (curious, it sounded like "Your honor, boy"), in

271

the soft eager voices of everyone they passed. But, as the weeks went by, Lieutenant Walpole had grown to feel as if their stay was merely an exercise in quenching the hopes of these trustful and confiding people.

His thoughts went back to the feast that Mr. Truelove had arranged for some of the *Collingwood's* officers shortly after their arrival, at the house of a native chief up in the Fautaua valley. They had bathed in the river, and watched the dances put on for their enjoyment; shy and pretty girls had anointed their hair with sandalwood-scented oil and hung wreaths of flowers about their necks; they had been regally feasted with roast pig and chickens, breadfruit and baked plantains. But even then a note of pathos had underlain the gaiety. He remembered how the bamboo houses had been hung with British ensigns, and how proudly the chief had shown them the ponchos, of their own design and manufacture, combining the English Union and the Tahitian colors, enscrolled with the words *Victoria e Pomare*. They had been made for the great day of jubilee, the natives said, when Britain and Tahiti would conquer the invaders and their Queen would be restored to them.

No amount of reasoning could persuade them that they must not count on help from England, and Lieutenant Walpole, helplessly accepting their hospitality, had felt uncommonly like a traitor. Odd, he thought, but here in this remote and tropical island an old-fashioned chivalry seemed to live again. It was apparent even in the natives' attitude toward their enemy. "If a Frenchman come unarmed," they said, "show him the road; if he thirst, give him your best; if he hunger, spread all your store; but if he come armed, kill or drive him back."

He jogged on, contemplating the bright stretches of water, the tropical panoply of foliage. No wonder they loved their land! Around a curve of beach they came upon a bold headland of black rock jutting out into the sea, and Burkham called to them

272

to dismount. Some natives who had been waiting nearby came forward, taking their horses to swim them around through the sea to the valley on the other side of the bluff. After a tortuous climb and descent on foot, the four men met their horses again and started up the valley to the encampment of Papenoo, several miles farther inland. Burkham, who seemed to know his way as well as the native guide, became more communicative as they approached their destination. The three great valleys of Tahiti, he told them — Punaavia, Fautaua, and Papenoo — each with its own fortified camp, all converged to the same virtually impregnable spot in the heart of the mountainous land. If the French successfully attacked any of the camps, the natives had only to retreat to an even more difficult position, farther to the rear, and as long as the supply of mountain plantains and fruits held out, they could hold their ground indefinitely. "The French might tire of this game eventually," Burkham said. "If the natives are given encouragement to remain steadfast in their present positions, the might win their battle by default."

Again here was that faint note of accusation in his voice. Lieutenant Walpole, feeling the stiff edges of his admiral's dispatch in the pocket of his coat, flushed uncomfortably. By God, he wished this day were over! He looked over at the chaplain, and saw that the padre's sober face was as unhappy as his own must be. There wasn't any glory in being a servant of the Crown today.

The ecstatic warmth of the welcome they received when at last they arrived at the little village just below the fortifications only increased his discomfort. Men and women of all ages surged around his horse, calling out greetings, their dark faces lifted to his in joyous welcome. On the outskirts of the crowd small children waved and turned cartwheels as if to show how glad they were to see these friends from Beretane. A tall, dignified man with a strikingly handsome face made his way toward them through the crowd, and raised his hand for silence. "Araitea,

273

chief man in the camp," Burkham said. The chief shook their hands warmly and gestured toward one of the houses.

"He would like you to come inside and give your message to the principal men in the camp before the public meeting is held," Burkham told them. "He asks God to bless you with all the good things of life."

The native guide stayed outside as Walpole and Burkham and the chaplain stepped into the cool dimness of the woven bamboo house. There were three rude chairs in the center of the room for the white men, and about ten men, most of them well advanced in years, squatted in a semicircle on the grass-strewn floor in front of them. After they had bathed their hands and faces in the bowls of water he brought to them, and refreshed themselves with drinking nuts, Araitea introduced them to the others. The chaplain said a brief prayer, and Walpole saw that the moment to read the Admiral's dispatch could no longer be postponed.

As he read it, waiting between sentences for Burkham to translate to them, he felt as if the words were like stones dropped into the still well of their expectant silence. "Pomare herself, by signing away her sovereignty, had established the French protectorate. . . . Since England now recognized that protectorate, they must not expect any assistance from the *Collingwood* nor any English ships that might come here. . . ." Their faces, at first so eager, became rigid with incredulity; in their eyes he saw the look of men who have been slapped across the mouth by a friend. ". . . Admiral Seymour advises you to submit to circumstances and live quietly under the protectorate. . . . England cannot interfere in this matter, but would ever regard Tahiti and Pomare with friendly interest . . ." In the back of the room someone gave a convulsive sob. Hurriedly, he read them Admiral Seymour's personal greetings and good wishes, and sat down.

The silence seemed interminable, but at last Araitea got heavily to his feet. "Is this the law of great lands?" he asked.

274

His deep ringing voice was charged with emotion. Pomare, he said, alone and frightened, torn with the pains of labor, had been compelled by force to sign away her rights. Yet even so, she and her people had submitted quietly to the protectorate until the French hauled down her flag, and insulted her and seized her lands by military strength. They could not ask the men of Tahiti to submit to such injustice!

Walpole sat staring down at the floor, unable to meet the eyes that were fixed on his face. In a low voice, he said to Burkham, "Please tell them that we are very grieved for them, but that we were sent only to deliver a message, not to argue, and we must obey our orders."

Araitea received his words with grave dignity, and signaled to the others that the meeting was over. One by one the men got to their feet and filed silently out, until the last one to go, an old man with white hair and a lined face, turned back at the door. His face was like a mask of agony, and there were tears streaming down his old cheeks. Sobbing, he tore off his shirt, threw it on the ground and stamped on it in a passion of grief. His voice was choked, but the bitter words came out in a torrent.

Helplessly, Walpole turned to Jonas Burkham. "What does he say?"

"He asks why you have behaved like this," Burkham said. His voice was all the more scornful because of its careful dispassion. "He says that it was because England promised help that they have fought unequal battles and lost their friends and relatives. He says it was because they waited for English help that they came here to the hills to live in privation and misery. He asks why you have let them hope if this is to be the end of it?"

"Tell him it isn't our doing!" Walpole cried. "Tell him our hearts are with them, but we have no voice in what our government decides!"

In Tahitian, the old man said, "If our mountains were gold and our ground silver, we would have help enough!" He rubbed the tears from his face with the back of his hand, and went out the door, his shoulders bent.

Burkham shrugged, not bothering to translate his words. "Perhaps we'd better join Araitea. They have a feast prepared for us."

"I can't eat their food," Walpole said. "I'd rather fight the French!"

The Yankee looked at him, his heavy eyebrows arching a little. "Who wouldn't?" he said.

But they did eat, although it was obvious that the painstaking decoration of their places had been designed to divert their attention from the meagerness of the mountain fare, and that the flowers with which the girls crowned their heads had been prepared in anticipation of a more welcome message. It was a lugubrious feast, but they responded as best they could to the gentle courtesy of those who surrounded them. Afterwards, at a public meeting for everyone in the camp, Walpole had to read the Admiral's message once again. This time, apparently at Araitea's orders, no one took exception to his words, although many of them wept openly as they listened. Prayers were said for the strangers who with sad hearts had brought them such sad news, and blessings were invoked on the Admiral and his nation. At the end of the meeting each of the principal chiefs arose and said a few sentences, and always the refrain was the same. They sent their respects to the English Admiral, but his message had not changed their determination. They would not submit to the protectorate; they were Pomare's to command, and would do as she willed. They had long ago pledged themselves as allies to England, and nothing would change that either. England might forsake them, Victoria's heart might grow cold to Pomare, but they could not forget so soon, and they still said England forever, England forever. . . .

It was those last words that kept ringing through Walpole's

head as the people came forward to shake his hand and give him their blessing. The sorrow that he saw in their faces was all the more poignant to him because of their gentle forbearance, their pitiful little pleas that he forgive them if they had expressed their feelings too warmly. "England forever, England forever!"

Abruptly, he turned to Burkham. "Let's get out of here! I can't stand it any longer."

"Nor I," Burkham said with sudden savagery. "Nor I."

THE RAIN WASHING AGAINST THE GLAZED WINDOW OF MR. THOMson's study was like a solid curtain of water, and the little light that penetrated it was gray as fog. For several minutes none of the four men there had spoken; the only sound in the room was the rapid *plink-plink-plink* of drops falling from the ceiling into a pan someone had placed in a corner beneath the leak.

Jonas glanced covertly at the others. Mr. Thomson's fingers were beating an absent tattoo against the top of his desk in perfect rhythm with the drops; Mr. Truelove, pulling a cigar from his pocket, glared at it a moment, then thrust it back; Mr. Barff, the old missionary from the island of Huahine, was tiredly rubbing his temples with a veined and knotted hand. The silence was too ponderous to be borne.

"It's an outrageous breach of faith," Jonas said. "Nothing but robbery, by God!"

It had been said before; and no one replied, no one even glanced at him. They were only too well acquainted with the facts. Nearly two months ago, just before Admiral Seymour left Tahiti, he had succeeded in prying from Governor Bruat an as-

277

surance that the Leeward Islands — Raiatea, Huahine, and the others — were not to be considered part of the French protectorate if they could be proved sovereignties independent of Tahiti. In the *Collingwood* the Admiral had gone from island to island, putting this question to the various chiefs, and had in every case received a vehement assertion that the islands were in no way subject to Queen Pomare. So much, at least, had the *Collingwood* accomplished, but shortly after she hoisted anchor for the last time and spread her sails for Mexico, Captain Bonnard, in the French frigate *Uranie,* had started for the same islands on an entirely different sort of mission.

At the tiny island of Maupiti, his first stop, he had demanded 120 Chilean dollars' indemnity from the natives for an alleged insult to the French flag. Miserably frightened, they had somehow managed to scrape together this amount, and Captain Bonnard proceeded to Bora Bora, where, perhaps in view of its larger size, he asked 300 dollars. And yesterday old Barff, arriving breathlessly from Huahine, brought word that Bonnard was now anchored there, and that he demanded 600 dollars from Ariipaea, Queen of the island, in addition to her promise that she restore to favor one of her chiefs whom she had dismissed because he had sold himself to the French. Ariipaea, relying on the assurances of Admiral Seymour that France had agreed to respect the independence of her land, refused to accede to Bonnard's demands, and had retreated, with her people, to an encampment at Maeva on the north part of the island. Enraged by this defiance, Captain Bonnard declared that if she did not yield within a certain time, he would destroy the principal village of Fare, opposite his anchorage, and then attack her encampment.

So matters had stood two days ago, when Barff left Huahine. Before his departure he had gone to Maeva to see Ariipaea, to advise her to pay the money under protest, and thus avoid a desperate and unequal battle. But the old Queen told him stoutly that she didn't have 600 dollars, and that she wouldn't pay it if she had. As for restoring Fatau, the rebel chief, she was Queen over her own people; if they turned traitor she would deal with them as she saw fit. The best that Barff could do was to wring from her a promise that she would do nothing rash in his absence, and he had at once set sail for Tahiti to raise the money needed.

That was the easiest part of his task. Mr. Truelove had pledged 400 dollars, Jonas another 100; Barff and Thomson 50 each. But this morning, as he prepared to sail back to Huahine, Mr. Barff was informed by the French authorities that Governor Bruat had not yet approved his passport, and that he would be indefinitely detained in Tahiti. His money belt, stuffed with notes, lay like a bloated snake across the top of Mr. Thomson's desk.

Jonas eyed it belligerently. There lay the price of peace, the ransom of brave lives, and there was no way in the world to get it to Ariipaea unless the other three men agreed to his proposal. And meanwhile the precious little time of truce was running out.

"You *must* let me go," he said with sudden vehemence, "it's the only way!"

Mr. Thomson's fingers missed a beat against the desk, and came to a sudden halt. He raised his head to glance at Jonas in cold appraisal. "Have you considered carefully what it would mean, Burkham?"

Oh God, if he hadn't he'd scarcely be here in Thomson's house today. "Certainly," he said.

"If you leave without passport ye'd sacrifice your neutrality, boy," Mr. Truelove said. "They'd never let you back in Tahiti again."

"I could stay in Huahine till things blow over. The war won't last forever."

"And who'd go with ye? You can't handle that schooner alone."

"My boatman, Farenui," Jonas said impatiently. "He's spoiling to do something for his people."

Mr. Barff, whose home had been in Huahine for nearly thirty

years, looked at him with gentle speculation. "Are you acquainted with the passage to Maeva?"

"I've been there once or twice before. I know it's difficult."

"It might be best to moor your boat at Faie and go along from there by foot."

"Yes. By keeping to the east side of the island, the French will never see me. I might even be able to get away again without their knowing I'd been there."

Barff pulled a sheet of paper toward him and started to sketch the route that Jonas would have to cover. As they discussed it in careful detail Jonas could sense that the other two men were gradually warming to this explicit projection of how the mission might be accomplished. Barff's matter-of-fact approach, his obvious sympathy for the plan, had done more to win them over than any of Jonas's vehement pleas.

At last Mr. Thomson said, "When would you leave?"

"Tonight. When it's dark enough to make sure I won't get caught."

"If the *maraamu* holds you'd fetch Huahine early tomorrow evening," Mr. Barff said. "There's Providence in the wind."

"Even so, it will be too late if Bonnard does as he threatened," Mr. Thomson said somberly. "The time limit's tomorrow."

Jonas pushed back his chair. "There's no time to waste, then. Is it settled, gentlemen? I'll have some arrangements to make."

They got to their feet. Mr. Truelove said, "How are your supplies, son? I'll send ye what I can without it seeming suspicious."

"There's enough for a day or two. I daren't put much aboard. Wish I had a gun, though."

"Stop by at the store," Mr. Truelove said. "I've one I can give ye. Perhaps you could manage it under your coat."

At the door to the veranda Mr. Thomson handed Jonas the money belt. As Truelove and Mr. Barff stepped outside, he put his hand detainingly on Jonas's arm. "Just a minute, Burkham."

Jonas pulled away from his touch. "I've much to do before nightfall."

"No doubt. But I must remind you of something you have apparently forgotten."

A gust of wind slammed the door shut, and they stood facing one another, alone in the narrow hallway. "What about Miss Moore?"

"What about her?" Jonas said curtly.

"When do you intend to marry her? Or don't you —"

Jonas took a step toward him. "You're a fine one to ask me that!"

"Why not? I have been deeply concerned."

"Look here, you pious windbag! Just a year ago in this very house you refused to marry us — or let any of your brothers in Christ do it either."

"Quite so," Mr. Thomson said coolly. "But I changed my mind, as you must know."

"What are you talking about?"

Mr. Thomson looked at him in genuine astonishment. "You mean you didn't know?"

"I don't know what you're talking about."

"I see." He paused, then said slowly, "About six months ago I had a talk with Dr. Ferguson. He convinced me that the best course of action was to sanction this — alliance. I told him I was prepared to do so at any time you wished me to. I believe you were away at that time, but I know he told Miss Moore what I had said to him. Why did she not tell you?"

Jonas was looking down at the money belt, his lips set, his eyebrows drawn together. "Doubtless she had her reasons. They're no concern of yours."

"But it *is* my concern, what will happen to her if you go off to Huahine and can't return. You're playing fast and loose with a human soul, Mr. Burkham! Have you no thought of her?"

Jonas gave him a look of angry contempt. "More than you have, my righteous friend! Somewhere, sometime, I'm bound to find a preacher with a more Christlike point of view than your own. Quite frankly, I wouldn't let you bury my dog!"

"Quite frankly, I wouldn't do it," Mr. Thomson said icily. But Jonas had wrenched open the door and was gone, head down, into the pouring rain, in the direction of the waterfront.

It was nearly eight o'clock when he dropped his soaking coat and hat on Marianna's veranda and knocked softly at the door. She came at once, putting out her hands to draw him inside. She was wearing a dress he had always liked — of faded, soft blue cotton that clung gently to the slender lines of her body — and her eyes were bright with a look of pleasure at seeing him.

"You're drenched!" she said. "You must be cold."

"I'm all right."

"I've some coffee on the fire. Sit down."

Before Jonas could protest she had gone, and he sat down on the sofa, stretching his legs out before him, his eyes fixed, unseeing, on the tips of his boots. All afternoon, while he worked aboard the schooner, the thought had kept reverting to him — that she had known, known all these months, that there was no longer any obstacle to their marriage, and yet she had said nothing. Facing it with sick shame now, he understood completely why she had not. She had supposed — and what else, from his behavior, could she think? — that he didn't want marriage, didn't want to tie himself to her by any bond more permanent than the one that existed between them now.

Christ, what a blind, selfish egoist he had been! Not since his first talk with Thomson a year ago had he taken any steps to further their marriage; blandly he had taken for granted that some day it would be possible for them, and in the meantime he

282

had scarcely mentioned it to her, letting the days slide heedlessly by, content to bring her his own problems and accept the warm comfort of her sympathy.

How little he had thought of her! But as he reflected on it now, the past year became illuminated with humiliating clarity. Of course a woman like Marianna could not easily accept the situation in which she had found herself! Every precept of her faith, every conception of right that had been drilled into her since childhood, would have warred against it. But she *had* accepted it, because she loved him, and because she loved him she had refused to make an irksome claim on him. By God, he'd make it up to her, somehow! — and yet just now there was no promise he could make her, no amends within the foreseeable future . . .

She came back into the room, carrying the coffeepot on a tray, and put it on a little table in front of him. "Be careful of the handle — it's hot."

He reached out his hand, pulling her down beside him on the sofa. For the first time since he had known her, he felt oddly uncomfortable with her. He leaned toward her, putting his hand on her cheek, gently turning her face toward his, studying for a moment the smooth brow, the full, curved lips, the clear and candid eyes that still could conceal from him those things she thought he might not care to know.

"You look so grave, Jonas," she said, smiling. "Is my hair awry?"

He smoothed back the pale, shining sweep of hair at her temples, and the wet sleeve of his jacket brushed against her cheek. "Now it's perfect."

"Even your jacket is wet!" she said. "The one I mended for you is here — let me get it for you."

"No, Marianna. I can't stay long. I — must get back to the schooner."

"The schooner! In this weather?"

He looked away from her. "I have to go to Huahine."

283

Her face reflected her bewilderment and her distress. "You're going to Huahine?"

"Yes. I must."

"You're taking Mr. Barff on the schooner," she said rapidly, as if she were trying to convince herself of the validity of her own words, "so he can give the money to Ariipaea."

"Barff isn't going back. The French wouldn't give him a passport. Just Farenui and I are going."

For a moment she was silent, then in a low tone she said, "They won't give one to you either."

"No. That's why we're going tonight. In an hour or so, when everyone's asleep."

"Tonight!"

"It's the perfect time," he said gently. "With the noise of the rain to cover us, and the full southeast trade to carry us over."

He saw her fingers twist suddenly together. "But Jonas, they'll never let you come back! You'll be openly their enemy if you go without permission."

"I have to go," he said. "It's the only thing to do — the only way we can get the money to Ariipaea and prevent a stupid, costly battle. You know how few arms they have — we can't let them die without a chance! Don't you see how important it is?"

"I see, of course," she said with an effort. "Of course you want to go."

There was an implication in her words that he shied from instinctively. To divert his own attention from it, he said, "Will you do something for me in the meantime? There are some supplies — medicines and bandages and poultices — that Dr. Ferguson got together for me to take out to the camp at Papenoo. Could you arrange to send them out? With Poriri, perhaps, if he comes to town?"

"Do you think they'll know how to use them?"

"Perhaps not," he said. "But there's going to be fighting soon. I know it. They'll need those things."

284

"I'll get them there for you," she said quietly.

He leaned forward, softly touching the thin blue material that covered her knees. "Perhaps when this affair blows over you could come and join me in Huahine."

She shook her head. "The French would never let me go there, you know that."

"They might," he said without conviction. He picked up her hand, pulling each finger gently through his own. "Marianna."

"Yes?"

"Why haven't you told me that Thomson said he'd marry us?"

Her fingers stiffened, and she pulled them away, leaning forward to touch the coffeepot. "You haven't had your coffee, Jonas! And now it's cold. Let me — "

"Stay here, Marianna! Why didn't you tell me?"

She leaned back reluctantly, not looking at him. "How did you know he said he would?"

"He told me so, today."

"Oh."

"Ah, darling," he said. "I know why you didn't tell me. God, what a stupid, callous fool I've been! I can never forgive myself for what this past year must have meant to you."

She looked at him then, smiling a little. "Why should you forgive yourself?"

"There's too much to forgive, I know that."

"Don't say it, Jonas! That isn't what I meant." She leaned forward, putting her hands over his. "Why should you forgive yourself for making me happy — making me really come alive? Can't you see how I have changed?"

"You haven't changed," he said. "You were always warm and honest and loving."

She bowed her head, tightening her hold on his hands. "When I remember my life before this year, it seems like a dream. And actually, I think I was living in a dream — not living, no, but moving about in one, quite apart from reality. Everything seems different to me now, Jonas — sharper and clearer and better. Even though I can see evil and unhappiness better, that's good, too. I'll never hide away from things again."

"You didn't hide," he said, "you were just sheltered. And when you're my wife, by God, I'll shelter you again!"

She laughed a little, and he leaned forward, kissing her with sudden passion. "When this is over it'll be like Moorea again, Marianna. We'll be together always — settle down in the country, where we belong, and raise a dozen children. Will you like that?"

In her eyes, naked and undisguised, he saw a look of poignant longing.

"Would I like paradise? Oh, Jonas, Jonas, you've already given me a glimpse of that!"

He kissed her again, gently and tenderly, holding her closely against his chest. When he drew away he said soberly, "I must go now, my dearest. Those are the hardest words I ever had to say."

Her hand came to her mouth, but she only nodded, silently. At the doorway he paused, taking her shoulders in his hands.

"It'll seem long until I see you again."

Barely whispering, she said, "I know."

His fingers tightened on her shoulders. "You're the only woman I've ever known who meant anything to me, Marianna. Why in God's name haven't I told you that before?"

A kind of radiance came into her face. "It's enough that you do now," she said simply.

"I'll be back," he said. "Wait for me, Marianna."

"Always," she said. "Take care, Jonas. Promise you'll take care."

"I will," he said. "Good-by, my darling."

He pulled her close to him in a fierce, brief embrace, opened the door and went out quickly into the rainy night. For a moment a gust of wind animated the little room, and then subsided as the door swung shut behind him.

286

He was too late, after all, to purchase peace for Ariipaea. When, leaving Farenui aboard the schooner, he went ashore the next afternoon at Huahine, the far-off boom of the frigate's guns across the island to the west told him that Captain Bonnard had not waited a moment beyond the time set to destroy the village at Fare. The rain-swept voyage, the moment of peril, sailing in black darkness through the pass in the reef at Papeete, when the frightening crash of breakers hard to starboard warned how close they had come to destruction, all that had been wasted. And yet the sweet taste of achievement still lingered in him; the trip across had been a joyous accomplishment, and perhaps it was still not too late to help Ariipaea if the encampment at Maeva were attacked.

He was in good time there and welcomed heartily. Another man — another gun! The encampment was alive with the expectancy of battle, exhilarated by the example of old Queen Ariipaea, who went about among her men, musket in hand, cartouche boxes buckled around her waist, exhorting them to courage. Shortly after dusk her scouts had come back from the hills above Fare with a report of the day's events. No one had been hurt; the village had been evacuated before the frigate's guns opened their heavy fire on the houses around the bay; but all was in ruins. French soldiers had come ashore after the firing, had plundered the houses, slaughtered all livestock, destroyed the food-bearing trees and plantations. The French steamer *Phaeton* had come over from Bora Bora to join the *Uranie* in the harbor, and it was certain that she would come around next day to make the attack on Maeva. One of Ariipaea's followers, pretending sympathy with her enemies, had found out that the rebel chief, Fatau, whose greed for rum and brandy led him to join the French, had informed Captain Bonnard that more than half of the natives of Maeva were ready to create a diversion in his favor when he attacked the encampment. Well, he would see — he would see!

287

Jonas, exhausted by the long voyage from Tahiti, slept well that night. The next morning, an hour or two after sunrise, watchers on the hills behind the encampment came running down to report that they had sighted the *Phaeton* rounding the northeast extremity of the island on her way to Maeva. In another hour they would meet their enemy in battle, and the heady excitement, the boastful impatience of the men, shook through the camp like a bursting wave.

The plan of action had already been settled upon. Maeva was almost perfectly adapted to defense. Had the French chosen to march overland through the hills from Fare they could easily have been ambushed and routed. From the sea the settlement was hardly more accessible. Hard behind it the mountains reared steeply to the sky, and before it lay the broad, still waters of Fauna Nui Lake — actually a lagoon, connected to the sea by a long, narrow channel extending two or three miles to the south, but so nearly landlocked that it could not be penetrated by any but the smallest boats. Directly in front of Maeva village was the mouth of the lake, about 500 feet wide, narrowing like a river into the shallow channel that twisted south, to the sea. Across the water, and enclosing it, like the curve of a great arm around channel and lake, was a stretch of low, heavily wooded land, at this place perhaps 300 yards wide, covered with dense verdure to the very edge of the sea beyond, and there protected by a barrier reef that would prevent the *Phaeton* coming in close enough to use her guns effectively.

It had been decided to meet the French there, on the low land, as they attempted to cross it. The natives were to scatter through the bush, lying hidden until the French advanced far enough into the thickets to be ambushed. It was a good plan, but if it failed it might well boomerang to the enemy's advantage, since the natives' only retreat to the encampment and the safety of the hills would be across the narrow, exposed lagoon. But there was

288

no thought in anyone's mind of failure, and Jonas, waiting with the others to be paddled across to the opposite shore, saw the futility of any attempt to warn them. He did not even consider it seriously; like the men around him he was alive with impatience for the battle to come.

The Queen's big canoe, with Ariipaea standing in the bow, edged into shore, and she motioned him aboard. Jonas squatted down in the narrow hull with the others who crowded in, looking forward at the Queen. What a doughty old Trojan she was! Her proudly molded face, once fiery with beauty, was netted with wrinkles, but her hair, twisted in a braided coronet around her head, was still dark and glossy; her carriage magnificently upright, and her waist, with the cartouche boxes buckled around it, still slender as a girl's. She turned her head, meeting his eye, and gave him a wicked and triumphant grin, from which a number of front teeth were missing. He smiled back, raising his hand in a salute. There was no doubt that she was leader of her people, in war as well as peace. . . .

The canoe grounded in shallow water and the men leaped out, pulling it onto shore. Ariipaea came up to Jonas. "Wait here, Tona," she said. "I have a special place for you — I'll show you shortly."

She disappeared with her men into the woods, and Jonas sat down on a fallen log near the water's edge. About a dozen canoes were plying back and forth, ferrying the men across the channel. He watched them, trying to estimate their total force. Not more than two hundred, at most, and many of them unarmed except for spears or clubs. It would be no picnic, this battle, and if it went awry it could turn into a slaughter.

He leaned back, locking his hands about his knees, raising his eyes to the mountains. In spite of the taut alertness that permeated every fiber of his body, with action so near at hand he felt a sense of peace more profound than any he had ever known

289

before. What a magnificent spot — how eminently worth fighting for! The rains had stopped the night before, and now the morning sun poured across the mountains and struck aquamarine brilliance from the smooth, shallow waters of the lake. Behind the settlement on the opposite shore the shapely cone of Moua Tapu — the Sacred Mountain — towered triumphantly to the sky. Here and there a small cascade fell like a white ribbon against the dark slopes of the hills. And everywhere there were trees, the glossy darkness of *tamanu* and *hotu* and breadfruit, the elegant crests of the coconut palms, the silvery gray fringe of casuarinas drooping gracefully above the water.

How Marianna would love it! Here was where she belonged; not in the crowded shabbiness of town, but here in this generous and beautiful country. He'd bring her back here some day, he decided, when the fighting was over. They'd raise some chickens and keep a few pigs; he'd have a garden, and they could go fishing, whenever they liked, in the teeming waters of the lake. There was a spot on the opposite shore, atop a small, rounded hill, shaded with great trees, watered by a small, bright stream in the ravine behind it. Perhaps Ariipaea would let them live there — he'd ask her about it, later on.

His eyes were still fixed on the small hill when Ariipaea came up behind him and tapped him on the shoulder. "Come along, Tona. There's not much time."

He followed where she led him through the trees. After the brilliance of the shore it seemed dark and gloomy in their shade, and the ground was marshy with the recent rains. For about 200 yards they twisted through the thick, labyrinthine woods, then came suddenly on what appeared to be an immense, massive wall of stone. Jonas let out a low whistle of surprise. He saw now that the structure was a long, rectangular platform, walled with huge, flat slabs of limestone, filled in with coral and other rubble, and supporting another, smaller platform atop it. Some of the upright stone slabs were at least ten feet high, and wider than his two arms would stretch. The whole place was dankly shadowed by enormous trees, and the thick trunks of vines writhed across it like sullen snakes.

Ariipaea was watching him curiously. "*Marae* Manunu," she said. "An old temple to our evil gods. My foolish people are afraid to come here." She gave him that wicked, gap-toothed grin, but he saw a twist of panic in it, like a child's bravado at a ghost story. "If a woman had come here in the old days, before we heard the Word, she would have been murdered on the spot."

"It's a good place for defense," Jonas said thoughtfully. "Strong as any fort."

"Yes. You stay here, and don't let the French get to it. There are men hiding all about you, through the woods. If you need them, call out and they will come. When they attack the French, you stay here to defend this place."

"How far away is the sea?"

"About a hundred paces, there." She pointed to a barely perceptible brightening beyond the heavy twists of foliage. "They'll come from there. We need you here, Tona. It's good to have a *popaa* who isn't afraid of ancient curses."

"It's only the ancient ones that don't bother me," he said.

Cackling, she turned away into the woods, her musket held lightly in her two hands. Over her shoulder she called back, "You won't have long to wait, Tona."

When she had gone, he loaded his musket, checked the cartridges in the box at his belt, and laid the musket carefully against the stones. One of the big slabs had fallen inward, and he scrambled up it onto the platform, his feet twisting among the smaller stones. Even atop the upper platform, perhaps fourteen feet above the ground, he could see nothing except the thick, interlacing branches of the trees. The shade was so heavy here that only an occasional small dapple of sunshine struck through it, winking in

291

the gloom like a little eye. His foot struck against a small, square cist of raised stone, and he pushed aside one of the flagstones laid across it. Inside were a few pieces of skulls and other bones, palely white against the gray stone. Involuntarily, he shivered. So this had been one of the *maraes* where human sacrifice had been offered! No wonder the people still dreaded to come here.

He climbed down again, went back to where he had left his musket, and leaned against one of the big gray slabs, feeling the damp, uncanny coolness of it penetrate through the stuff of his shirt. It still seemed to smell of death here, he thought, and he was shaken suddenly by a curious apprehension. He began to dread the time that must pass before he could be released by action.

From the woods about thirty feet to his right came a shrill moan, like a sea bird's cry, and other voices, around and beyond him, picked it up and carried it along like a signal, one to the other toward the sea. After a moment the voices came back the other way, this time repeating what the lookouts near the beach had told them. "The ship is coming — the ship is coming."

Jonas peered through the heavy shade, but he could see nothing, not even a trace of the men whose voices sounded so near to him. After a few minutes, a lookout spoke again, and the word was carried back along the hidden lines of men. "The ship is opposite — the ship is opposite."

There was no movement anywhere, and no sound except for the occasional calls back from the beach. In the intervals he could picture what was happening; and although the time, marked only by the rapid ticking of his heart, seemed hideously long as he waited, gradually the intervals between the messages grew shorter. The ship is slowing — the anchor has dropped. The boats are lowering from the sides — the men are getting aboard the boats — the boats are pulling for the shore. At last the voices, low and muted, swung the somber, freighted word back. "*Mamu, mamu.*" Be still, and let them come . . .

He raised the musket closer against his body, his fingers tightening around it. For many minutes there was no sound at all, and then, far to his left, toward the sea, he heard faintly the grating of boats beaching on the gravelly shore, and a Frenchman's voice, raised in command. Proceed into the bush — columns of four — deploy on the opposite shore . . . Good God, the crazy fools, they weren't even going to reconnoiter! They must be counting entirely on the help Fatau had promised them.

Shortly after that he caught the sound of men crashing heavily and clumsily through the underbrush, and occasionally the far, muffled grunt of a curse. The columns must be going through about a hundred yards or so to the south of him, he judged, and the first of them were now perhaps just opposite. When would Ariipaea's men attack? Interminably, the seconds thudded by; then, loudly, the sound of several shots, almost in unison, cracked through the waiting woods.

He leaned forward, trying to read from the confusion of shots and shouts and the heavy trample of running feet just what was taking place. All of the fighting was to the south of him, beyond his range of vision. God, how stupid to wait impotently here, but he could not leave this refuge unprotected for the French to take. A faint sound, much nearer than the distant noise of the fighting, caught his ear and he swung around toward it, peering intently through the green shadows.

Just beyond the coiled, upright roots of a *mape* tree about twenty yards to his left he caught a quick glimpse of red breeches, and then a white, frightened face peering between the leaves. The man stepped forward, and as he raised his musket, Jonas fired. Almost instantly, a shot came roaring back, and something hit him hard in the chest. He staggered back, and fell heavily to the damp ground.

For a few moments he lay where he had fallen, fighting to pull the wind back into his lungs. When he tried to get to his feet the ground whirled up to meet him, and he fell against it. Painfully, he turned over and crawled the few feet back to the wall of the *marae*, dragging his musket along with him.

Instinctively as an animal, he put his forehead against the cool limestone wall, and after a minute he was able to turn over and pull himself into a sitting position against the big slab. Tensely squinting, he looked around him, but the shadows seemed more gray than before, and the tree trunks wavered giddily. His thoughts seemed to have slowed abnormally, like the beating of his heart. That bastard — had a chance to fire — but I got him. No one in sight — no one in sight; and the sounds of shooting grew more distant as he listened.

Almost incredulously, he became aware of a warm, spreading dampness flowing down his ribs; the side of his shirt and his sleeve were bright with blood. The shot had struck him high in the chest, almost at the right shoulder. With his left hand he pulled his musket up close to his eyes, staring at it stupidly. Impotently, he let it fall again, and his head dropped back against the stone.

Dimly, he could hear the far-off sounds of battle; more closely and distractingly, the labored beating of his own heart. Fretfully, he became conscious of the coldness of the stone against which he leaned, and its contrast to the warm, slow spread of blood along his body.

The thought of Marianna came to him — actually an image, rather than a thought. He could see her there, in her faded blue dress, see the tenderness on her lips, feel her cool, compassionate hand on his forehead. Suddenly and urgently he felt a longing for her, felt it with the same violence with which, almost at once, the pain struck him. The image vanished, and for a long while there was nothing in the world but pain, tangible as an enemy, rocking him against the stones. He had no idea how long it lasted, but gradually it began to subside, and a dim clarity returned to his mind.

The shooting seemed to have stopped, he realized, and then he saw that Ariipaea with two of her men was coming toward him through the trees. She ran forward at the sight of him.

"You're hurt, Tona!"

He managed to nod his head. Ariipaea knelt down on the ground beside him, her fingers gentle on the buttons of his shirt. "*Aué!*" she cried, the old shrill cry of disbelief and lament echoing back from the stolid stones. "*Aué, aué*, your shoulder!"

"Not — bad," he managed to whisper. "French — what happened?"

"Finished!" she said. "Ran like dogs, with their tails between their legs!" Carefully, she tore his shirt, so that she could pull it away from the wound, talking rapidly as if to distract him from the pain that she must cause him. "We let them bury their dead and take their wounded back to the ship. Eighteen dead, and about fifty wounded! We only lost three, Tona, and now the ship is leaving. They won't come back to Maeva again!"

He listened to her carefully, letting the words, which seemed to come from a great distance, drop into his mind like pebbles into a still pool, sending their ripples to the far limits of his thoughts. Maeva was saved — saved for Ariipaea and her people, saved for him and Marianna. Perhaps, in a small way, he had helped to save it. He must ask her now if they could come here, so he could think on that while he was healing. He closed his eyes, suddenly aware that this had been the most truly complete and successful hour of his life.

***

FOR A MILE OR TWO ABOVE THE SEA THE TRAIL UP THE PAPENOO valley to the encampment followed closely along the gentle rise of the river, skirting away from the banks only when it must twist around one of the great trees that grew along the way. Except for

295

the muffled plodding of the horse's hoofs, the valley was as silent as the afternoon sun drifting through the leaves, quiet as the clear, black glitter of the river. Marianna, holding the reins loosely in her hands, let her horse choose its own ambling gait, its patient head bobbing up and down at each step. About thirty paces ahead of her Poriri, Teaui's son, rode bareback, leading a pack horse laden with the bundles of medicines and supplies Jonas had wanted her to send out to the encampment.

He turned his head, looking back at her. "We'll soon be there." She nodded. "Do they think — do they know I'm coming?"

"They prayed for it," he said. "I expect they'll rely on the Lord." He grinned suddenly. "And Poriri, who went to fetch you. Are you tired, Marianna?"

"I'm all right," she said.

He turned away and began to sing softly; the gentle notes, floating back to her, told her that Poriri was content to be going home, back to his wife and children, back to the encampment. It was good to hear him singing. She had been poor company for him, God knows, although she had tried, making a constant effort to inject some life into her voice and turn her smile into something more than a mere grimace of the lips. But to someone who had known her for as many years as Poriri had, the effort must have been only too obviously just that.

In her blind impulse to get away from town it had not occurred to her that the ride back into the country after nearly two years of being away might entail its own small shocks. The abandoned houses, the bleached limbs and leafless branches of the girdled trees, the glimpse of the deserted church and mission buildings at Matavai with a French blockhouse rising on the point beyond, the French sentries demanding her passport before she could continue on the road that led past her own old schoolhouse — all these things had been harder to see than to contemplate. It was difficult to imagine her father's gentle spirit revisiting the

296

vacant and desolate district; and her own recent past there seemed more ghostly than a dream.

Still, just to be in motion, to be going somewhere, however briefly, was a little better than the inexpressible leadenness of the hours in town. The eerie cry of an *itatae* wailed through the trees, and she saw its white wings flash above the river. An unformulated memory stirred within her, so vague that she could not define it . . . How long this time had she succeeded in keeping back the thought of Jonas? Five minutes? Seven, perhaps? Not even that, for it lay behind every thought, every action, as palpably as the sound of rain on a roof, pervading everything else. If only she knew what had happened to him, if only she could know! Wearily, her thoughts turned back over the familiar treadmill.

A month ago the steamer *Phaeton* had come back from Huahine, bringing the wounded French soldiers, and the foreign residents who had been evacuated from the ruined village of Fare. From the latter she had learned of the French rout at Maeva, but they knew nothing of Jonas, not even that he had been on the island. As a last, desperate resort, she had gone to Governor Bruat for information. Yes, he knew that Burkham had fought at Maeva; no, he had no idea what had happened to him. He had been kind, she thought drearily, telling her to come back a day later, after some inquiries could be made among his wounded men.

But his Gallic tact, and his sympathy, could not soften the blow he had to give her. One of the men had heard from another, who had since died, that a *popaa* had fired the shot that eventually killed him. He had fired in return, and he thought that the white man had been wounded, but he was not sure; there was no further information to be had. In any case, Burkham could not return to Tahiti, the Governor said with some sternness; he would be taken prisoner if he did.

There was no way out of the treadmill, no way at all. She could not go to Huahine; it was completely blockaded, and Captain

Bonnard, in the frigate *Uranie*, still lingered at Fare (against his Governor's orders) thirsting for a chance to take his revenge against the natives at Maeva. Huahine, a day's sail from Tahiti, was as remote as the most distant planet.

If only she could know! She could not live without him, could not live without hope, at least. And yet how hard it was to hold that hope, during the barren silence of the passing days. She had got so used to the expectancy of him that he had imposed upon the pattern of her life, the wonderful possibility, shining behind every hour, that he was on his way to her, that she would hear his steps on the veranda, his voice in greeting; the dumb, immutable expectancy that might never be realized again. . . .

Her horse stumbled against the root of a tree and she pulled up his head, suddenly aware that they were approaching a clearing. Poriri was waiting for her as she came forward into the slanting sunshine.

"We're here, Marianna." He gestured toward the thatched houses huddling in the shade of the trees along the river. "There's the village, and our gardens. Up above, where the valley narrows, you can see the fortifications."

Some children who had been playing by the riverbank came running toward them, and one of them, a boy of about seven, boosted a smaller girl up to the back of Poriri's horse. Poriri held the child closely, rubbing his cheek against hers.

"Behold the seed I planted! Does it grow?"

"Like the *purau* tree," she said. "I never should have known them!"

"Where is your mother?" he asked the children. "And your grandmother?" He tilted back his head, letting out a prolonged call, like a sea bird's cry. At once the little settlement seemed to quicken with life; men and women appeared in the doorways and from behind the houses, calling out greetings as they came toward them.

298

Marianna slid down from her horse, pulling the hat from her damp hair. Teaui was the first to reach her, folding her closely in a warm and comfortable embrace. "You're here, my little one, you're here!"

The others crowded about her, their soft voices raised in welcome; shaking her hand, rubbing their cool, brown cheeks against her own. Manu and Taua; Naria; Hina, Poriri's gentle-eyed wife; old Mama Ruau, more frail and wrinkled than ever . . .

Araitea, the chief, came forward through the group. "Welcome to Papenoo, good friend. All that we have is yours." He took her hand, looking at her closely. "We know that your man went away to fight for us, Marianna, and our bowels sorrow for you in this trouble."

There was a muted murmur of lament among the others, some of the women were crying. Involuntarily, Marianna sucked in her breath, her fingers tightening against the brim of her hat. Someone said, "We pray for him, Marianna."

The tears that she had refused to shed welled and knotted in her throat. She nodded dumbly, and Teaui took her arm, drawing her away. "No words now," she said. "Come to my house, Marianna, and refresh yourself. Just before sundown there's a prayer meeting. We'd be pleased if you'd come to it."

Here, up in the hills, with no formal guidance, no pastor to lead them, they still clung to the faith the missionaries had taught them. Only the ones who were younger than thirty had been born into that faith, but the older ones, who had so reluctantly renounced their savage gods, were perhaps more steadfast in it than any. Sitting with them in the wide, unwalled meetinghouse, Marianna thought what a joy it would have been to her father to see them now: unguided, finding their comfort in a time of trouble from the precepts he had given a lifetime to bring them. She closed her eyes, listening to the voices around her soar together in a hymn. It was good to be in church again. After more

299

than a year away from it, she realized more keenly than she ever had the simple solace, the solidarity of thus uniting in worship with her fellow men. The torment in her heart could find no resolution yet, but to the frenzied questions that cried out within her whenever she thought of Jonas, the singing voices seemed to answer: Wait and see.

She opened her eyes, glancing at the people around her. There was a look of spareness on their faces, as if they did not ever have quite enough to eat, and their clothes were pitiably worn and patched. But there was an exquisite neatness about them, an air of pride and discipline that was in sharp contrast to the sloppy disorderliness of town. And on their faces, worn though they might be, rested a kind of serenity that she had not seen in many months. Here, everyone was loyal to the same cause, and worked for it with the same will. No one need wonder, as they did in Papeete, if his friend might be, or could become, his enemy. . . .

Araitea was praying, and at the sound of her own name her attention jerked sharply back to his words. ". . . and for the good things she has brought us, the medicines and bandages to heal our sick and hurt, we thank Thee too. We pray, dear Jesus, that your servant Marianna will find it in her heart to stay here with us and teach us the wise healing that she knows; that she will stay and school our unruly children, who make mischief in the camp, and have not enough learning to scratch their own names in the ground along the riverbank. . . ."

Incredulously, she stared at the earnest mask of his face, the closed eyes, the shaft of sunlight lying across his dark, lined cheeks. They wanted her here — they wanted her to stay here, in Papenoo! She sat humbly through the rest of the meeting, turning the thought over and over in her mind, scarcely hearing a word of the other prayers and songs.

The sun had set as the meeting ended, and the swift darkness of the valley was rising between the hills. She was standing with

300

Teaui and Poriri outside the meetinghouse when Araitea came up and tentatively touched her sleeve.

"You heard my word, Marianna?"

"Yes," she said. "I am grateful that you want me here —"

"You will stay, then?" Teaui asked eagerly.

"Teaui, how can I? My passport is worthless after sundown tomorrow — I must get back to town."

Araitea looked at her gravely. "It is much to ask, Marianna. Too much, perhaps. But we need you here badly, to teach the children and help us with our sick. If you would stay, and take your chances with us, we'd protect you with our lives."

"But the French — they might make more trouble —"

"They can't make any more than they have," Araitea said.

Poriri said boastfully, "They won't come after you, Marianna. They don't dare! I can go back and get your clothes tomorrow, before they know you've gone."

"I'd like to stay," she said. "I don't want to go back to town. But have you thought, Araitea, that I'd be just one more stomach to feed, one more drain on your little supply of food?"

"Aué," Teaui said scornfully, "you've always eaten like a minnow, my child. Stay here, and live with your fat old Teaui."

"There is more in life than food, Marianna," Araitea said. "And it's the other things you can give us that we need."

For a few moments she was silent, hearing the soft voices and laughter from the shadows around her, watching the sparks of a bonfire in a distant dooryard kindle into flame as a child stirred it with a stick. How familiar it all seemed — and how far she had gone since she had last been a part of this simple, nostalgic life. Something had happened to her that all the years of careful propriety could never have brought about; now she understood these people, their virtues and their sins, just as they understood and condoned hers.

Someone was singing in a nearby house. Jonas, Jonas, her

301

heart cried out. Jonas had fought for these gallant and pitiful people, for a lost and hopeless cause; she, who loved him, could go on living and hoping because of them. For some reason that she did not immediately understand the pent-up tears rose to her eyes and slid silently down her face in the deepening twilight. I have come home, she thought, come home again at last.

A⟪T DAWN⟫ PORIRI WENT TO RELIEVE THE SENTRY ON LOOKOUT JUST below the fortifications of the Papenoo encampment. Far below, the sea was beginning to silver under the rising light, and behind him the black peak of Orohena, for once stripped of its veil of clouds, thrust nakedly into a pale blue sky. It would be good to have a sunny day to bake some of the dampness from his bones. Up here in the valley, his flesh felt mossy, like the green boulders beneath an *aoa* tree.

He stood on the lookout rock, sleepily thinking of nothing, letting his senses, tuned to the proper sound and smell and feel of the place, keep guard for him. Slowly and silently the light increased; the far black peaks began to slide with gold. Then, before a leaf stirred or stone rattled against stone, Poriri became aware that someone was coming up the trail along the river. Silently, he dropped down behind the rock, sighting along his musket toward the path below. Soon he could hear the voices of two men, speaking together in Tahitian, and some of the tension left his body. He raised his head as they emerged from the trees beyond him.

Aué! Marianna's *popaa!* With his boatman, Farenui! With an incautious shout, he leaped up and ran down to meet them, throwing his arms around Jonas.

"Tona! How did you come here?"

Wincing a little, Jonas drew away from his embrace, and his

302

left hand, which was carrying a musket, went up in an involuntary gesture of protection against his right shoulder.

"Sailed over from Huahine in Ariipaea's little boat," he said. "It's all right, Poriri, we landed last night, and no one saw us come. They won't find the boat, either — Farenui took care of that."

Poriri seized Farenui's hand. "It's good to see you, friend. Wait till your cousins in the camp hear that you are back!" He looked at Jonas, and for the first time noticed the arm hanging inertly at his right side, and the curious, incomplete look of his shoulder, sloping downward beneath the wrinkled folds of his shirt. "*Aué*, Tona, you've been hurt!"

Jonas grimaced. "It's all right now. *Aita peapea*." His brown hair was streaked with gray, and there were lines in his face that Poriri had never seen there before. "What's happened here, Poriri? Down below, there's not a house left standing, nor a breadfruit or palm tree that hasn't been destroyed."

"You haven't heard about the fighting? Here, and in Punaavia?" His face darkened. "They attack us, Tona, and drive us farther back into the hills, but they cannot beat us, with the mountains to protect us. In the end they go away, and take their revenge on our lands. They've lost many men, Tona," he said proudly, "far more than we have. And in Papeete the Farani shiver in fear of the men from Punaavia who come down and burn their houses and their forts."

"In town!" Jonas said. "What about — have you heard anything of Marianna?"

"Marianna!" Poriri said incredulously. "You don't know about Marianna?" At the look in Jonas's eyes he hurried through his words. "She's here, Tona! Right here in Papenoo."

"Here! In the camp?"

"*É!* She's been here — let me see — four or five moons, at least. She lives with my mother, up near the river."

"She's — all right?"

"She hasn't been sick, Tona, but her heart has grieved for you. I see it in her eyes, and hear it in her voice. Now that you are here, her voice will sing again."

Again Jonas made that involuntary gesture toward his right arm. Hurriedly, Poriri said, "We couldn't do without Marianna. She teaches our children and cares for our sick and wounded. There are many of them now."

For a moment Jonas stood staring down at the ground, then he raised his eyes to Poriri's. "I shouldn't have come here, Poriri. I can't fight for you any more."

"You have a gun," Poriri said. "Does it still speak?"

"Yes."

"Good. We have more men than guns. Many of our muskets are broken, and you can show us how to make them work again. We need you here. We need *popaa* wisdom to help us." He touched Jonas gently on the shoulder, a look of tenderness coming across his brown face. "Go up and find her, Tona. She needs you, too."

Farenui went off in the direction of the settlement in the clearing, but Jonas, following Poriri's directions, kept to the shadowed path along the river. Beyond the mango tree, Poriri had said, was Teaui's house — he would find Marianna there.

As he walked along he could feel his heart thudding against his ribs. In just a few minutes he would see her again, after all this interminable time. It was still impossible to believe; reality seemed to have become confusingly entangled in a dream. Oh, God, to see her again!

A stab of pain in his shoulder jolted him unpleasantly out of the dream. Since the long weeks of fever, pain had become such a part of every waking moment that sometimes he could even forget it, as one grows deaf to a constant noise — to the singing of cicadas or the eternal beat of surf. Then it would pounce again, as

304

it had now, bringing him sharply back to the realization that never completely left his mind.

I shouldn't have come here, he thought again; I shouldn't come back to her now. He had no business to be here — a half man, who could never use his arm again, a cripple who couldn't even cut his own meat . . .

The path curved to the right to follow a bend in the chattering river, and ahead of him he saw the mango tree, fixed in a shaft of early morning sun, its pale green fruit hanging from long stems at the end of every branch. In that cool, explicit light it looked like an enormous tree of jade. Beneath it a woman was standing, in a faded blue dress, bending over to braid the hair of a little girl who stood in front of her.

Marianna. With his left hand he lowered his musket to the ground, and stood there silently watching her. She was smiling at the little girl, he saw, but on her face was written a look of such sorrow that his heart seemed to stop for a moment. Did she look like that because of him?

He moved forward, and Marianna raised her head, staring at him. Suddenly her face became transfigured. He heard her say his name, and as she ran toward him he had time to think, almost in awe: That look was for me, too.

"Marianna," he said. With his left hand he reached out to touch her face, watching the incredulous shine of happiness in her eyes. She came close to him then, slipping her hand beneath his useless arm, holding him tightly around the waist. Already, without words, she seemed to have comprehended that hanging arm and the shattered indignity of his shoulder; and already it seemed to matter less.

"You've come back," she said. "You've come back to me, Jonas."

He put his face against the softness of her hair. "I've come back, my darling. I'll never leave again."

Epilogue

On the first day of the year of our lord 1847 the rain, which had been falling steadily for more than a week, poured relentlessly from a dark and sullen sky. Dr. Ferguson, a piece of tarpaulin draped like a toga around his shoulders, a broad straw hat protecting his old, bulldog face, stood by the fence gate in front of his house, chewing the butt end of a cigar and glaring ferociously down the road. Dr. Ferguson had taken a few fingers of rum to ward off the dampness from his lungs, but he was not yet drunk. Quite methodically, he was saving that for later, when his need would be more insistent than it was now.

A few minutes earlier one of Vahine's young nephews had run into the house to tell him that the people from the Papenoo encampment, coming to surrender their arms to the French Governor, had already reached the outskirts of the town. Dr. Ferguson, who had been unwise enough to witness, a couple of weeks earlier, the surrender of the people from the Fautaua and Punaavia camps, had no intention of watching this final capitulation. He knew just how it would be: how they would march to the Governor's palace, worn and bedraggled, and, with an intolerably pitiful air of submission, file by to lay down their rusty, battered muskets in a gradually mounting pile at the Governor's feet. Empty-handed, they would hear Bruat promise them amnesty, demand their allegiance, and direct them to return to their homes — or, at least, the place where their homes used to be. Then they would kneel down on the wet ground, bow their heads, and for the last time together like this unite in prayer . . . Oh, no, that spectacle was not for him; he couldn't stand it again.

His purpose in waiting now was to waylay Marianna Moore. How long had she been up there in that camp? Nearly a year, he figured; it must have been early in February last when she left town. By God, it would have been no picnic! In March the fighting had commenced in earnest, and during the battles that followed the natives had been pushed farther and farther back into the misty dampness of the mountains, constantly besieged, more and more dependent on the scanty foodstuffs that they could find growing wild in the hills. It hadn't been all beer and skittles for the French, either, he thought with some satisfaction; Bruat had lost more men than he would admit; his commander of the troops had been killed; the chief of staff had lost a leg.

The past year was one he did not care to remember. The bloody, hopeless battles, ending always in stalemate; the vengeful fury of the French, ravaging the lowlands, laying waste to miles of the fertile coast lands; the useless courage of the Tahitians, their ill-advised strategies, their dogged insistence to continue in a cause that was palpably impossible, had driven him to the bottle more than once. Two or three months ago 1500 additional French troops had been landed on the island, and the natives still had refused to surrender. They would probably be rotting up there in the mountains at this moment, he thought, if it hadn't been for the treacherous savage from the island of Rapa who had betrayed — for 200 dollars and a suit of clothes — a secret pathway up the cliffs to a position where the French could command the rear of the mountain fort, the heart of the island where the three valleys, Papenoo, Punaavia, and Fautaua joined together. That final encounter at least had been bloodless; when the natives saw that their last retreat was cut off they made

307

no resistance, but laid down their arms, saying, "Now the key is stolen, it is no use keeping the box locked."

Dr. Ferguson pulled the tarpaulin higher around his neck, and leaned across the gate, squinting down the road. Grayly, through the lashing rain, he could see a column of figures approaching, plodding along slowly on foot. Gnawing furiously at his cigar, he watched them as they passed. First came Araitea, the chief, carrying the protectorate flag, his unhatted head flung high into the rain; behind him walked his wife, with two women whom he recognized as the widows of other chiefs. Following them was a column of musketeers, walking two by two. Seventy of them, he counted; big, strapping fellows, but their muscles looked oddly unfleshed and their faces were gaunt. Behind them straggled a larger group of women and older men and children of all ages; some of the women were carrying babies in their arms, and all of them walked as if their legs would not carry them much farther. For a few moments he was afraid that Marianna was not among them, but at last he saw her, her head bent, walking slowly beside a man with a crippled arm. Christ Almighty, it was Jonas! His first attempt to call them broke in his throat, then he managed to roar out her name.

"Marianna!"

They saw him then, and came toward him, smiling at him through the rain. "Burrrkham! I thought you were dead — I thought you'd absconded!"

"You ought to know you can't get rid of a sinner as easily as that," Jonas said.

Dr. Ferguson put out his hands to Marianna and pulled her through the gate. She was as fleshless as a sea shell, he thought, but she looked all right; her skin had a gloss to it, and in spite of the faint lines that marked it, there was a look of serenity on her face.

"You're soaking wet," he said severely. "Come inside at once."

308

"I think we ought to stay with the others — "

"Nonsense. You *popaas* can make your peace with the Governor another day."

One of the women walking near the side of the road called out to them. "Go inside, my children."

"All right, Teaui. Come back here later."

Dr. Ferguson turned to Jonas, his shrewd eyes noting the downward slope of his shoulder, the dangling arm. Quickly he looked away. "Come inside," he said gruffly. "I want to get out of this beastly rain." He pushed them impatiently up the walk. "Even horses have better sense than to stay out in weather like this."

His woman, Vahine, was waiting on the veranda. There were tears on her face as she embraced Marianna and Jonas, and helped them off with their hats and coats, muttering "*Aué, aué!*" over and over to herself.

"Vahine," Dr. Ferguson said, "stop clucking like a chicken, and get out to the kitchen. Warm up the soup and make some hot food at once."

At Marianna's word of protest, Vahine gave her a wink. "Go in there," she said, "and keep the old man quiet till I get back."

Dr. Ferguson propelled them into his study and led them to his easiest chairs.

"Sit down, sit down. And take your wet shoes off. Marianna, do you hear me?"

"I'm used to them," she said. "They don't bother me."

"Woman," he bellowed, "do as I say!"

Obedient as a child, she bent over and pulled off her sopping shoes. When she raised her head he was standing in front of her, a largish glass of brandy in his shaky hand.

"Drink this," he said. "Doctor's orders."

She took the glass from him and he gave another one to Jonas, then sat down, pouring out one for himself. "Physician, heal thyself," he said. "Here's to your return. By God, I'm glad to see you both! Now tell me, Jonas. How did you get to Papenoo?"

"Sailed over, with Farenui, from Huahine."

"How long have you been there?"

"Since June, I think. About six months."

"You're gray as a timber wolf, boy!"

"So they tell me," Jonas said. He touched his thick, crisp hair. "I'll have to see a mirror sometime, to check on Marianna. *She* says it's becoming."

"What about that arm?"

Jonas shrugged his left shoulder. "It's healed, at least."

"I'll have a look at it, later."

"If you want to. There's nothing to be done."

Dr. Ferguson took a gulp of brandy, looking at Marianna across the top of his glass. "Marianna, take your medicine!"

Meekly she took a swallow, choking a little. "Thank you," she said. "It does warm you up."

"How long since you've been really warm? Or dry?"

"Weeks, I suppose. The rains have been torrential. When we left, the river was so swollen some of the fortifications were beginning to wash away."

"You should have come down long ago!"

"I suppose so," she said, "but no one thought of giving up while there was still the slightest chance."

"You and Jonas, I meant. You're not as hardy as these Tahitians."

"We couldn't. There was too much to do. You forgot your own hardships, up there."

"It must have been — pretty bad."

A look of pain swept across her face. "It was tragic. The sickness, the broken families, the struggle for food — you can't imagine it! But their bravery made it worth while, somehow."

"And now," Jonas said, "what's going to happen to them now?"

"The French have promised them forgiveness and amnesty. I think they'll treat them kindly."

"Now that they've got what they want," Jonas said bitterly. "Now that it's too late."

"They're going to reinstate Pomare as nominal Queen," Dr. Ferguson said. "She won't have any power, of course, but they'll treat her with respect. And they're going to pay her a yearly stipend, so she can live in comfort."

"Is she back from Raiatea?"

"Not yet. She's coming soon."

"How about Huahine and the other Leeward Islands?"

"They're still free."

"Thank God for that! We'll go to Huahine, then."

"What are your plans, exactly?"

"First off, we want to find Barff, and be married — "

"You're going to be married, eh?"

"Marianna insists on it," Jonas said.

There was something in his grin at her that made Dr. Ferguson suddenly happier than he had felt in months. He raised his glass to them. "My heartiest best wishes. What will you do in Huahine?"

A shadow fell across Jonas's face. "What can I do?"

Hastily, Marianna said, "He has his work, Dr. Ferguson. He'll write about the war, and how it happened, tell the world the truth — "

"As if the world cared," Jonas said. "What I can do is nothing. Put down some words, that's all, to tell what has already happened and never can be changed."

"Words of truth, boy, words of truth. There can never be enough of those." After a moment, he said gruffly, "You need some food, you two. That old Vahine of mine is slower than the hills."

As if to deny him, Vahine waddled into the room just then. "The soup is hot," she said. "Come and eat."

As they got to their feet they heard the first boom of a cannon, measured and solemn in salute, speak out from the direction of the harbor. Vahine stopped in the doorway, motionless, her broad, homely face immobile as a mask. Marianna went over to her, slipping her arm around her waist. Jonas was staring down at the floor, and his left hand strayed up to touch his injured shoulder. Six — seven — eight — Dr. Ferguson saw Jonas raise his head and glance over at Marianna and Vahine, the tight set of his lips softening a little. The doctor looked away, clumped over to the table, and poured himself a glassful of brandy. Relentlessly, the assured and ceremonial salutes to triumph boomed through the quiet room. Eighteen — nineteen — twenty — twenty-one . . .

Dr. Ferguson put down his empty glass. "Well, it's all over," he said. "Come and eat, my children."